WHITE CITY

Kevin Power is the author of *Bad Day in Blackrock*, which was filmed in 2012 as *What Richard Did*, directed by Lenny Abrahamson. He is the winner of the 2009 Rooney Prize for Irish Literature. His writing has appeared in the *New Yorker*, the *Dublin Review*, the *Stinging Fly* and many other places. Kevin lives in Dublin and teaches creative writing in the School of English, Trinity College Dublin.

Also by Kevin Power:

Bad Day in Blackrock

WHITE CITY

KEVIN POWER

SCRIBNER

LONDON NEW YORK SYDNEY TORONTO NEW DELHI

First published in Great Britain by Scribner,
an imprint of Simon & Schuster UK Ltd, 2021

SCRIBNER and design are registered trademarks of The Gale Group, Inc.,
used under licence by Simon & Schuster Inc.

1 3 5 7 9 10 8 6 4 2

Simon & Schuster UK Ltd
1st Floor
222 Gray's Inn Road
London WC1X 8HB

www.simonandschuster.co.uk
www.simonandschuster.com.au
www.simonandschuster.co.in

Simon & Schuster Australia, Sydney
Simon & Schuster India, New Delhi

A CIP catalogue record for this book
is available from the British Library

HB ISBN: 978-1-4711-3278-0
TPB ISBN: 978-1-84737-806-4
EBOOK ISBN: 978-1-84739-942-7

Typeset in Palatino by M Rules
Printed and bound by CPI Group (UK) Ltd, Croydon CR0 4YY

To Jo and Zoë,
with all my love.

And in memory of my father.

I here present you, courteous reader, with the record of a remarkable period of my life, and according to my application of it, I trust that it will prove, not merely an interesting record, but, in a considerable degree, instructive. In *that* hope it is, that I have drawn it up; and *that* must be my apology for breaking through those restraints of delicate reserve, which, for the most part, intercept the public exposure of our own errors and infirmities.

THOMAS DE QUINCEY,
Confessions of an English Opium-Eater

1

TRUE CONFESSIONS

Confession No. 1: I am a sick man, I am an angry man. I think my wit's diseased. Sometimes I think I understand those kids who shoot up schools, or those wild-eyed men in hot-wired vests who purge themselves in a blaze of gimcrack plastique and arcane political grievances. What do they die for, these men, these kids? They die for meaning, as far as I can tell. They blow themselves to bits in a desperate search for meaning.

Or, to put it another way: I am the bitter only son of a disgraced rich man and I have washed up here in rehab, at the end of every road, with zero money, zero prospects, zero hope. I have cheated and stolen and lied – lied to myself, most of all. I have consorted with fraudsters and war criminals. In an effort to beat my father at his own game, I failed: at love, at money, at life. I refused to grow for ten straight years. Does that last one count as a confession? Sure. Why not?

*

First things first. My name is Ben (I think I'll keep my surname off the record, at least for now) and I am a drug addict. Or so they tell me – and who am I to argue? Substance-free one week as of this morning, to the evident satisfaction of my sponsor, Dr Felix, who happens also to be the director of this clinic: the St Augustine Wellness Centre for Drug and Alcohol Rehabilitation, a detox tank and monitored care facility for the rich and the rich-by-proxy, for the gouged, the spent, the luckless, for the terminally upper-middle class. It's a fun-time place, the Centre. Check out the cheerless day room with its Lego sets and board games, the racks of pious pamphlets dense with self-chuffed shibboleths in ten-point type. Check out my fellow inmates, with their untenanted eyes – each of them a stove with the pilot light snuffed out. Dr Felix – who calls himself not my sponsor but my Partner in Recovery, capital letters very much *sic* – is Harvard-accredited and privately rich. Despite this he resembles a man who has laboured for decades at some shady and debilitating job: police informant, maybe, or unlicensed surgeon. His eyes are sunken, as though rimmed with kohl. His ears are pale and elongated, like the curved white interiors of mussel shells. He is unpredictably jovial. He is also unpredictably hostile – prone to outbursts of mean-spirited wit at my expense. Perhaps this is a therapeutic tactic. Every day at noon I report to his office. The wooden blinds are always drawn. In the grounds of the clinic the sun shines, the flowers bloom. I would rather shoot myself than go outside. I sit there in the partial darkness, clutching the flaps of my beltless

4

towelling robe, not speaking. Dr Felix regards me, calmly. Through the blinds behind him sunlight stutters, like strobe lighting at some celestial rave. I would rather shoot myself. I would rather.

'Here's what you need,' Dr Felix says. 'You need to start talking. If not to me, then to yourself. I look at you and my suicide alarm goes *pingpingpingping*. Even for a recovering addict, you look like shit.'

'You're the worst addiction counsellor I've ever met,' I say.

My relationship with Dr F is inherently asymmetrical. Like all outgunned armies, I have been reduced to committing cheap acts of terrorism, in the form of truculent remarks.

'I'm the only addiction counsellor you've ever met,' Dr Felix says. 'I'd call it a privilege, but it's no fun being somebody's only hope. Depression is contagious, you know. I'm risking my own mental health every time you pop in here for a chat.'

'Is that supposed to be a joke?' I say.

My robe is beltless, by the way, because I am thought to be a suicide risk.

On the desk between us is a bulky notebook, hardbound, and what looks like the sort of gold-rimmed pen that my father used to brandish during episodes of boardroom piracy. These items Dr Felix now nudges in my direction. 'We're going to try an experiment,' he says.

'Oh,' I say. 'Goodie.'

'You're going to write it all down,' Dr Felix says. 'In your own words.'

I make no move to pick up the notebook.

'It's not a suggestion,' Dr Felix says. 'It's an order. I'll be expecting regular updates on your progress.'

'I don't need a written list of reasons to hate myself,' I say. I tap my temple. 'They're all right here.'

'Don't start with your father,' Dr Felix says, ignoring this. He has removed his phone from his pocket and is frowning at the screen, as if it has just given him a terminal diagnosis. 'Start with something easier. Your girlfriend, maybe. Or your friends.'

'They were never my friends,' I say.

'Your girlfriend, then.'

My head shakes mutely of its own accord, as if to say: I can't go there. No, not yet.

'You used to write,' Dr Felix says. 'Or so you've told me. Now's your chance to put together something actually meaningful.'

This is not the first time that Dr Felix has made cruelly offhand remarks about the worthlessness of my writing – my writing, which did, at one point, give my life the illusion of purpose.

'So,' I say, 'it's not enough that I mortify myself verbally with you on a daily basis. You want me to commend my self-abasement to the ages, too.'

Dr Felix looks up from the screen of his phone. 'Your syntax and vocabulary are improving. A week ago all you could do was grunt and cry.'

'It was a simpler time.'

Dr Felix leans across the desk and pushes the notebook and pen into my lap. 'Writey-write,' he says. 'Chop-chop.' He dismisses me with a flourish of his wrist.

At the door I find myself loitering uncertainly. 'If I *do* write something,' I say, 'and I'm not saying I will. But if I do. Should I bring it to our next session, or—'

'Christ,' Dr Felix says, 'I'm not going to *read* it. There's enough bullshit in my life already.'

He has not looked up from his phone. With brisk thumbs he begins to type out a text.

And now for a quick personal message: Fuck you, Dr F. I bet you *are* going to read this. I bet you're reading it right now – I bet you've snuck into my cell at night while I'm asleep and you're flicking through these pages in search of psychological leverage, as if you needed any more than you already have. If so, I say again: Fuck you.

Yes, I'm writing. Yes, I'm writing in this notebook, as per instructions. But I'm doing it because I have literally nothing else to do, except stare in dazed horror at the ash heap that constitutes my life to date (or join my fellow junkies in their sad parade around the day room, which amounts, when you think about it, to more or less the same thing). Besides, it might be advantageous to have a complete written record of my mistakes – it will save me from having to dredge up all those suppurating memories afresh every time I happen to close my eyes or lie down in a darkened room.

There are no mirrors in St Augustine, because the inmates

can't be trusted not to break the glass and slash their wrists. We cannot see ourselves, as we weep and perspire, as we puke and totter and groan in the throes of detox. (As we pine for the only thing that made our lives worthwhile.) But writing is a mirror, whether you like it or not. In these pages I can see myself steadily and whole – the worst punishment I can think of. And so can you, Dr F, if you like.

Enter at your own risk, sucker.

Don't start with your father, the man says. But where the hell else would I start? It was my father's arrest that brought me here, although you could certainly say that I took the scenic route. I might, I suppose, start with The Lads, a phrase that I have always mentally capitalised without quite knowing why. Or I could start with Clio, who was – aside from being my girlfriend and my rescuer – my first enabler, in the sense that she enabled me to discover the solace and seduction of drugs (while remaining mysteriously immune to the lure of addiction herself: how did she *do* it?). Or I could start with BlueVista Marketing Solutions, where – according to the homiletic signage on the walls – THE BIGGEST ROOM IN THE WORLD IS THE ROOM TO IMPROVE. Or I could start with the Serbs – with Vuk and Nicolae and Ratko, with Maria, with Aleks the poet, with the crooked little skeletons and everything that followed. Or I could start with Nikki (Nikki!). Or I could start with the hideous afternoon on which I ran into my old school friend James Mullens in an expensive bistro in Ballsbridge, and the Serbian catastrophe was thereby entrained.

8

But no. I should start with the basics – of my life, of my decline. I should start with my father's arrest.

It happened on a Friday morning in October. I was twenty-seven years old. I still lived with my parents. I had, in fact, never really stopped living with my parents. My father was still in the first year of his retirement, and looked, as far as I was concerned, all set to subside into the usual blameless afterlife of putting greens and clubhouse chats about his prostate – into the reward that awaits all bankers once they gain what my father himself once called, non-ironically, 'the shores of settled prosperity'. My mother had also retired, in the sense that she no longer bothered to attend the wine-tasting courses or sewing groups or charity lunches that had served to while away her years as a housewife. Now she devoted herself full-time to tinkering with cocktail recipes at the well-stocked bar located in a repurposed broom cupboard just off our spacious entrance hallway. As for me: I was in the fourth year of a PhD programme in the English department of a well-known Dublin university.

In these four sentences I adumbrate an *Iliad* of error and illusion. Trust nothing, Dr F, from here on out.

I was woken at 7 a.m. by the sound of someone hammer-ing on our big front door. From my bedroom window I spied three cars parked in our lengthy driveway: cheap sedans of metallic blue. I had stayed up late, flirting via Google Chat with a girl I had met in a Hegel reading group. I had made serious plans to stay in bed till noon, or later. Now my day was out of whack. Groggily I padded downstairs, still in boxers and a T-shirt.

In the kitchen four enormous men were standing: two in dark pinstripe suits, two in vests of fluorescent yellow plastic. There was an aura about them of hurried shaves and tepid coffee – the aura, I suppose, of Irish officialdom, bearing bad news. *This is it*, I thought. *Somebody's dead.* It was a peculiarly exciting notion.

The kitchen was a crisis tableau. My mother leaned against the Belfast sink, her arms folded tightly across the blazer of her Hugo Boss executive business suit. My father also was in business mufti: in his case, a three-piece Louis Copeland, complete with watch chain and purple pocket square. It was as if they were already dressed for somebody's funeral. The room smelled of freshly brewed tea.

'Ah, Ben,' my father said, with a smile. 'Nothing to worry about. Just a formality. Wouldn't you say, lads?'

He turned his smile on the men in the pinstripe suits, who folded their hands in front of their crotches and shuffled as if they were forming a defensive wall on a soccer pitch.

My mother adopted an expression I knew well: as if she had been unexpectedly taxidermied at the precise instant that she had discovered a live rat in her gin and tonic. 'It had better be,' she said.

One of the yellow-vested Guards picked up a framed photograph from the sideboard and looked at it. It was a photograph of a greyhound.

'Shoot for the Stars,' my father said. 'That was the first

10

dog I ever won a hundred quid on. Nineteen seventy-seven. Used to spend my weekends at Shelbourne Park. I should head over there some night. Lots of free time. The curse of retirement.'

Beside the photograph on the sideboard was a model clipper ship on a wooden stand. It had been a retirement present from my father's colleagues at Atlas-Merritt, his bank. With a clublike finger the Guard probed its intricate rigging.

That clipper ship. My father used to spend hours fiddling with it – trimming the sails, lashing the gunwale (please insert the bullshit nautical phrase of your choosing). It was the closest thing he had to a hobby. He loved complex, miniature things. In a way, that ship synecdochised him more efficiently than even the electric golf trolley whose wheels he religiously cleaned every Monday evening, or the midnight-blue Landcruiser that marooned him in its interior acreage in a way that used to make me think of a tiny Jonah in the belly of a mechanical whale. He was a small, intricate thing himself, my father. The only thing he didn't have in common with the clipper ship was fragility.

One of the suited men – he was bald and had a gingery moustache that drooped at the sides – coughed and said, 'I'm afraid ...'

'Ah, yes.' My father was using his jolly-hockey-sticks, home-by-Christmas voice. He turned to address me. 'Just going to pop down the station with the lads here and sort a few things out. It's Bray you're taking me to, isn't it? Sure, the missus here can pick me up later on.'

The atmosphere of crisis seemed to be draining from the room. But I was slow to catch up. 'Who died?' I said.

My mother made a derisive noise. 'They're arresting your father.'

For quite a compelling moment I imagined my father in the dock for murder: the striped prisoner's jumpsuit, the look of fake contrition. But whom would he have killed?

The kitchen was cold: my mother was stingy with the central heating. I hugged my arms and tried to stand there in my boxers as if everyone else in the room was also wearing jammies.

'What for?' I said.

The man with the gingery moustache scratched his chin as if gratifying a muscular tic.

'I have to advise you,' he said to my father, 'that you may not be returning home this evening. You should budget for an overnight stay.'

'Ah,' my father said. He fiddled one-handed with his wedding ring – he had a habit of twisting it round his ring finger using his thumb and pinkie. 'Should I pack a bag, do you think?'

'We'll provide the necessaries.'

I seemed to have missed something. 'Hang on,' I said. 'What's the charge?'

The Gardaí seemed to defer to my father, as if he were in charge of things. My father whisked his hand vigorously in the air beside his head.

'A complete and total misunderstanding,' he said. 'Which

I'm going to help these gentlemen clear up at their earliest convenience.'

'Speaking of . . .' said the man with the gingery moustache.

'Right you are,' my father said.

In the driveway my father paused to give my mother a kiss. 'Won't be long,' he said, as if he were popping out for a quick nine holes before lunch.

The Guards led him to one of the blue sedans. One of them held the rear door open, like a chauffeur. Into the sedan's open boot a yellow-jacketed foot soldier was depositing bundles of files and bound documents – the contents, I assumed, of my father's study cupboards. The gravel turnabout was littered with yellowing crab apples. Past the gatepost I saw the black plastic of television cameras, glinting through the leaves of the dogwood hedge.

'This is a vendetta,' my mother said.

I scratched my head. 'That doesn't seem like a realistic assessment, Mum.'

'It's all lies,' she said. 'They're out to get him.'

'Who?' I said. 'Who's out to get him?'

My mother closed the door. I followed her into the dining room, where she removed her high heels, put them on the solid oak table, and massaged her bunions thoroughly. Beside the shoes was a vase of tulips. The blooms smelled like cold rubber gloves.

'I don't understand what just happened,' I said.

'Why don't we have a nice vodka and lime,' my mother said.

'It's not even eight o'clock,' I said.

'Some of us have been awake for hours,' my mother said.

It was only later that I realised what my mother's business-suit-and-high-heels combo meant. It meant the same thing as my father's watch-chain-and-pocket-square combo. My parents were dressed for business at 7 a.m. They had known the Guards were coming.

That was the beginning. The charges, it turned out, were plain enough. My father stood accused of stealing €600 million from the books of his own bank, Atlas-Merritt plc. The day after his arrest I spotted him on the front pages, as I bought my daily pack of Marlboro Lights in the Student Union shop. There he was, his image duplicated in rectangular ranks, like the results of a Google image search, or the tessellated squares of a Warhol silkscreen. In the paragraphs below were some technical details, about dark pools and hibernated loans, which I skimmed. My interest in the particulars of the case was, and would remain, minimal. Not because I didn't care, but because, in some fundamental way, I simply didn't believe that these details pertained to an actual event, to wit, my father's evolution from a man who had so little imagination that he owned seven ties of the same make and pattern into a criminal genius of historic proportions.

My father had returned from Bray Garda station that morning. His watch chain was no longer threaded through its appointed buttonhole. Shaking his head, he let the chain spool onto the sideboard.

'They made me take it off and give it to the desk sergeant,' he said. 'They asked for my shoelaces, too. I had to tell them, these are slip-ons.'

My mother had driven him home. Now she returned to the vodka and lime she had poured for breakfast and left half finished.

I noticed that the kitchen clock had stopped, at three minutes to midnight.

'So that's it,' I said. 'You cleared it up.'

'I told them,' my father said. 'I said, I understand. You've got to chase up every angle. The money is missing and people want to know what happened. They were extremely respectful, I have to say.'

'Okay,' I said.

'The main thing is for you not to worry,' my father said. 'This doesn't change anything substantial. You've nearly got the doctorate wrapped up, so there's nothing for you to be concerned about.'

The morning sunlight, pouring through the boundary beeches in the garden, was causing leaf-shaped shadows to shimmer on the hardwood floor.

'Right,' I said.

I did not, as it happened, nearly have my doctorate wrapped up. What I did have was a folder on my laptop labelled *PhD*, which contained three unfinished conference abstracts and two thousand words of a draft chapter that my supervisor, Prof. O'Farrelly, had described, during our most recent meeting, as 'skeletal'. The total computer memory occupied by the contents of this folder added up to 42 kilobytes. By contrast, the total computer memory occupied by the folder of downloaded pornography next door ran into the thousands of megabytes.

My thesis was supposed to be on *A Portrait of the Artist as a Young Man*, which I had read as an undergraduate and immediately adopted as a kind of lifestyle handbook. At one point, around 2013, I spent several hours online trying to source an ashplant walking stick so that I could more closely resemble Stephen Dedalus as I strode around campus writing epiphanies in a notebook and conducting Thomistic debates about the nature of aesthetics. Luckily I found no ashplant walking stick. I settled for trying to read Thomas Aquinas in cafés, and eventually for simply rereading the college chapters of *A Portrait* once a month or so. But it turned out that admiring Stephen Dedalus to the point of idolatry was not an adequate preparation for undertaking works of original scholarship about James Joyce. The size and scope of the extant critical literature on Joyce had long since defeated me. Now I regarded my old underlined Penguin Popular Classics copy of *A Portrait* as a kind of embarrassing ex-girlfriend to whom I was still attracted but with whom things had not really worked out. Every so often I had an idea that seemed to point the way forward for my ailing thesis: *What about the theme of confessionalism? Is that something?* These notes accumulated in the sparse pages of a dedicated notebook. Notebooks, notebooks. My life existed in notebooks long before Dr Felix challenged me to record the story of my disgrace. Something in that, perhaps. Or maybe not.

Until the morning of my father's arrest, and for several weeks after, none of this bothered me. I didn't really want to be an academic. I had other, grander plans. Instead of working on my thesis, I was working on a novel. When it was published, this novel would deliver me in a single stroke from any obligation to pursue a career (university lecturer) for which I could muster up no passion whatsoever. By enrolling for a PhD, four years previously, I had signalled to the world – i.e. to my father – that I was taking my professional prospects seriously and that I should be left to attend to my researches in peace. That I had attended to another dream entirely was all part of my plan – the plan, let me say, of a consummate fool.

My father, of course, had wanted me to study law, or to 'take articles', which seemed to mean 'become an accountant', though I was never 100 per cent clear on this. When I first told him, ten years ago, that I had been accepted to study for an English degree, he swallowed the news gradually, over the course of several hours, the way a snake swallows a small goat. Eventually my mother staged one of her sporadic interventions on my behalf. 'You can move into law with an English degree,' she pointed out, and that was that. My father began to enthuse about 'the great tradition of lawyers who write', and I was free to spend four years reading, which is, I now suspect (now that it is all too late), the only thing that I have ever actually wanted to do.

That English degree wasn't the first time that I had disappointed my father. He was an easy man to disappoint. Take the time he dragged me to a Schools rugby match. I was twelve years old. Picture us, clearing the turnstiles of the stadium in Donnybrook: my father short and stocky in his stylish pea coat, me in my shapeless jumper and precisely creased jeans (ironed not by my mother but by one of a succession of maids whom my parents described collectively as 'the women'). It was a Sunday afternoon clash between, oh, let's call them the Blackrock Old Barbarians (us) and the Belfield Visigoths (them). My father, of course, was a loyal Old Barbarian, still full of school spirit thirty years on. And I would be a disloyal Old Barbarian myself, starting that September. We were late. The players were already on the field. At the edge of the stand my father paused and looked around – possibly with a flat hand pressed nautically to his forehead, though my treacherous memory may be adding that in. Suddenly the ball came towards us in a lazy spiral. Seamlessly my father caught it, took a short, swift run, and hoofed it with the toe of his loafer – *WHAP!* It sailed between the posts of the near goal, twenty yards down the line. The crowd gave an admiring cheer. My father grinned and waved and reached out an unconscious hand to push me forward, as if to say, *My son, ladies and gentlemen! A veritable chip off the Old Barbarian block!* And to everyone who shook hands with him afterwards, he said, 'And Ben, of course, will be trying out for the Junior Squad himself this year.'

If any of these friends and well-wishers noticed the look of crucified boredom on my face, they were tactful enough not to mention it. When, two weeks later, I was not called up to play for the Old Barbarian Junior Cup Squad, my father said, 'Oh,' and never mentioned it again.

So you see, Dr F: I had no choice but to grow up and become someone else.

What does it mean to be the only son of wealthy parents? It means that you don't have to make your way in the world, because somebody else has already done that for you. I never left home because I never had to. For ten years – between my seventeenth and twenty-seventh birthdays – my father paid me an allowance: €1,500 a month, rising to €2,000, in line with inflation, when I began my PhD. The money was deposited directly into my bank account. My college fees were paid. (I didn't even need to sign the giro.) There was also, during these money-blizzard years, a steady sleet of coyly palmed banknotes, of bags full of new clothes left wordlessly on my bed, of bedroom decor overhauls and birthday gift certificates and costly orthodontic refits – and that's before you get to the lavish family holidays, in Biarritz, in Cannes, in Venice, in five-star condos on the Amalfi coast. I wanted for nothing – isn't that how kept wives traditionally put it, Dr F? After finals, my father sent me to San Diego for the summer. I didn't bother to get a job while I was there. I knew that if things got rough – if I ever actually did achieve the impossible and run out of money – I could simply call my dad. And I didn't bother to get a job when I got back, either: for a year, between the ages of twenty-two and twenty-three, I leaned and loafed at my ease, living off what I once described to an acquaintance as 'my private income'. It is surprisingly easy to lose a year – to spend twelve months doing absolutely nothing. Especially if your parents happen to be looking the other way.

'What we're talking about here,' Dr Felix said yesterday, when I told him the gist of the above paragraph, 'is privilege. You were and are a privileged person.'

'I *was* a privileged person,' I said. 'Not *am*. And hang on. I don't accept that. Privilege is a bullshit idea. Oh, you're privileged because your parents were rich. You try living with my parents and tell me you feel privileged.'

Dr Felix raised a wispy eyebrow.

When I thought about my father's job, as a child, I imagined him swimming through a magically permeable landslide of gold doubloons, like Scrooge McDuck, or beadily totting up enormous stacks of pennies at a dusty actuarial desk, like Bob Cratchit. That these images continued to strike me as realistic depictions of my father's career well into my twenties might say something about what it means to be a rich kid, with a rich kid's problems. Then again, it might say something more specific, about what it means to be me.

The established family narrative was that my father had fluked his way to the upper reaches of the upper-middle class through a combination of good luck and a stolidly bourgeois work ethic. 'I was in the right place at the right time,' he would say, whenever he was called upon to reveal the secret of his success. By the right place, he meant a boutique investment bank that had swollen during the boom until it counted 15 per cent of all fungible Irish real estate among its Assets Under Management. (This statistic courtesy of my father himself, who tended, at family mealtimes, to act as if he had just been called upon to deliver an off-the-cuff speech to industry leaders.) By the right time, he meant the boom itself. I have come to view this narrative with a degree of scepticism, for reasons that are perhaps less obvious than they might at first appear.

He was the second son of a Wicklow farming dynasty, which meant that he could still surprise you, on a family drive, with his knowledge of things like soil pH or drainage. His older brother, who had inherited the farm, died unmarried just before I hit my early teens. My father promptly sold the land to one of his developer friends, who turned it into an apartment complex.

'Land is the only asset you can really trust,' he told me, as we toured the site. The cowshed in which he had learned how to deliver a calf was now a concrete footer, six metres tall.

We lived in a mock Queen Anne house in a southside suburb that I should probably leave unnamed, in the interests of et cetera. The northeast corner featured a witchy turret, done in cod-Baroque style. The interiors, supervised by my mother during the Great Remodelling of 2004, were icily contemporary. Highlights of the Great Remodelling period included the morning the exterior wall was removed from the kitchen, and I found my mother staring out into the garden past piles of dusty bricks with her eyes narrowed like Captain Ahab on the deck of the *Pequod*, saying softly to herself, 'It *will* be worth it. It *will* be worth it.' And it *was* worth it, in a way:

21

when the Remodelling was over, we had underfloor heating, a smart fridge with built-in ice dispenser, and a fresh set of kitchen cabinets adorned with unnervingly vulval clamshell handles (to store the food that our maids would cook for us). And that's before we get to the Lounge, the Den, the Study and the TV Room, each like a room in a showhouse: the books and magazines arranged just so, the carpets deep-pile, the couches vast and square and immovable as standing stones.

'That's that,' my mother said, when the last of the builders had left. Then she went to the broom-cupboard bar and mixed an old-fashioned, minus the bitters, soda water, and the traditional orange-peel garnish. She never said a word about interior decorating ever again.

This was the house in which my dreamy childhood elapsed, and in which my dreamy adulthood began and eventually ended. From here every morning my father drove in his Landcruiser to Baggot Street, where he occupied a series of increasingly eyrie-like offices in the HQ of Atlas-Merritt. He became CFO, then CEO, then Chairman. He was famous for his probity, his reluctance to take risks. On the night of 29 September 2008, when the cabinet was meeting to avert the collapse of the banks, my father was at home in bed, reading a paperback thriller called (if I remember rightly) *See You in Hell, Darling*. When a journalist finally got in touch with him, the next morning, to ask what he thought of the state deposit guarantee, he said, 'A nod is as good as a wink to a blind man on a galloping horse.' He was briefly celebrated for the gnomic inscrutability of this remark.

'We were the only bank in the country that wasn't over-leveraged,' he would say, if he happened to be in a reminiscent mood. 'And we had a serious liquidity backstop. When they announced the guarantee, we were the only bank in Ireland that didn't need it.'

At his retirement party, in the hotel complex at Druids Glen, his grateful clients presented him with the clipper ship, and a jeroboam of champagne. My father accepted both items generously, waving away his lack of embarrassment. The band – a string quartet, hired for the evening – played 'For He's a Jolly Good Fellow'. The point of the clipper ship was that my father had been 'a steady hand on the tiller'.

'So that means you're sunk without me,' he said, causing the crowd to laugh indulgently.

Later that evening – I had gone outside to fidget with a cigarette – I saw my father standing on the terrace. He was alone. His hands were in the pockets of his suit. It was the sort of posture in which another man might have looked up at the country night sky (a black cloth, webbed with diamante-stud stars like a cheap Debs dress) and reflected on the progress of his life. But my father was staring straight ahead, into the darkness that covered the golf course. His expression was neutral – bereft of affect. His mouth was closed. He looked empty. Or, no: not empty. Blank. I turned away, convinced that I had seen something taboo, or perhaps – more disturbingly – that what I had seen was actually the absence of anything worth seeing, a nothing that had, for an instant, taken the shape of my father, for reasons of its own.

23

All of these things happened to me, and I had no idea what any of them meant until seven days ago, when I was driven to St Augustine, in the grip of the longest, harshest comedown of my life, and everything began, at long last, to make sense.

'Your father lost his brother,' Dr Felix said, as we were wrapping up today's curative exertions. 'What do you remember about that?'

'What does that matter?' I said.

'You think death doesn't matter?'

'Nobody made a big deal out of it.'

'Did your father cry?'

I laughed.

'How old were you?'

'I don't know. Eleven. Twelve.'

'And it wasn't a big deal.'

We had been trading barbs for two hours. I was desperate for some time alone in which to weep and curse and sob. Also for a cigarette or twelve. 'Don't you have other patients to badger?'

Dr Felix winked. 'Yeah. But none of them are as much fun as you.'

When I got back from my wasted summer in America, my father made one of his periodic attempts to instruct me in the facts of life. He sat me down at the dining room table and delivered his stump speech about wealth and responsibility. My task, he said, was to choose from among a range of opportunities that people from less privileged backgrounds would kill to get a sniff of. I could practise law – if I didn't fancy being a barrister, there was a good living to be made in conveyancing, which was a low-pressure gig if what I wanted was time to write. Or I could become a managerial consultant – he named some firms, mentioned the possibility of foreign travel. I could even – here my father's manner became artificially offhand – skip a few stages at Atlas-Merritt and learn the ropes of investment banking.

As he outlined these possibilities my father punched keys on the oversized electronic calculator that he used to do the household accounts, entering in the digital display a random seven-figure number that seemed to hint at the sort of astronomical salary I might take home if I set aside my creative ambitions and allowed him to 'pull some strings'.

My heart felt glutinous in my chest. For a moment I imagined myself occupying an eyrie-like office on Baggot Street, and foresaw, with a sense of panic and doom, the regularity with which my father would pop his head round the door to say, 'Just popping my head round the door!' Then, vaguely, I wondered what *conveyancing* meant.

'Actually,' I said, in a moment of terrible inspiration, 'I was thinking of doing another degree. You know, postgrad.'

'Smurfit,' my father said, nodding. 'An MBA.'

'I was thinking more literature,' I said.

My father looked at his calculator. After a moment, he pressed the button marked C. The long string of numbers disappeared.

A deal was struck. My father would fund a few years of

graduate study at my alma mater. 'Doing the PhD,' he said, as if to hear how it might sound over drinks in the bar of the K Club. As well as defraying my fees, he boosted my pocket money to €2,000 a month, retrieving the paternal calculator once again to explain how I might successfully save enough, over the course of three doctoral years, to cushion myself while I interviewed for teaching jobs later on.

This advice I scornfully ignored. As far as I was concerned, I had pulled off a major coup: I had managed to wangle another three years in the library, another three years of smoking and flirting outside the Arts Café, another three years of not working in an office or wearing a suit or pretending to know what a managerial consultant did.

I dreamed up a thesis proposal and pitched it to Professor Moira O'Farrelly, herself an eminent Joycean and one of the few members of the English department who was willing to overlook my 2:2 degree and my evident lack of practical sense and agree to sponsor my graduate studies. With her grey pebbledash cardigans and her owlish specs (and her bookshelves full of Derrida and Foucault), Prof. Farrelly seemed to me one of those institutional fossils whose grasp on reality has long since been eroded by time and by a basic sense of job security. Nonetheless she was a crucial ally in my covert war against my father's plans. For a year or so after my faith in my thesis collapsed, I continued to placate her with bibliographies and trumped-up notes for chapters. But my heart was elsewhere. I was working on a novel. And this novel was going to save my life.

*

'Why do you think your father tried to get you to follow in his footsteps?' Dr Felix asked this morning. He was clicking away fruitlessly at his computer screen, trying to install a Windows update.

'Why do I get the feeling you're not giving me your full attention?' I said.

'When you say something interesting, I'll let you know.' Dr Felix waved the pointer of his mouse around. 'Fifty-three per cent. It's been saying that for ten minutes.'

'He wanted me to be just like him,' I said.

'Who?'

'My father, for fuck's sake.'

'Just like your father,' Dr Felix mused. 'You mean busy? Respected? Financially secure?'

'I mean a mindless business drone.'

'Are you absolutely positive,' Dr Felix said, 'that your father wanted you to be just like him?'

'Don't parents always want their children to turn out just like them?'

'Most parents want their children to be happy,' Dr Felix said.

'That must be where my father went wrong,' I said.

My novel. Christ. Do we have to do this? I suppose we do. I had started it during my summer in America, scribbling excitedly in one of those marbled notebooks that American students use for school assignments. It was called *Decay: A Report*. It had no plot, as such. Instead I imagined a series of vignettes, each ending with a climactic moment in which one of my protagonists confronted the naked barbarism of life in the terminal years of the West. (There was going to be a shocking description of the murder of a homeless man that was, I now see, lifted wholesale from a similar bit in *American Psycho*, and another, even more shocking description of a house party that turned into an orgy, inspired by an actual occasion upon which I had attended a house party and two girls I knew from our school's collaborative Transition Year musical had kissed each other in the living room.) In practice, the manuscript devolved into several tenuously linked accounts of affairs with girls I had known in college, and thence into explicit descriptions of things I had done with these girls in bed. In fact, I may as well admit it now: the sexy bits were the only parts of *Decay: A Report* that I ever actually got around to writing out in full. The remainder of the text abided, for all my daydreaming, stubbornly in the realm of the conjectural. It's possible that the printed manuscript of *Decay: A Report* languishes still in my childhood bedroom, beneath a pile of semen-encrusted socks or a trove of sticky magazines, occupying – as it should – the lowest rung of the masturbatory ladder. Then again, it's possible that it was junked along with everything else when the house was put up for sale. I could, I suppose, ask my parents if they know what happened to it – if they took it with them, when they left.

But I won't be doing that, now, will I? For so many reasons: no. I won't be doing that.

*

Working on *Decay: A Report* in the Eng. Lit. section of the college library, I was, in my artless way, happy or something like it. Even now – here in the Hotel Anhedonia – I find I can summon up a sharp nostalgia for the smell of buckram bindings and photocopier ink, for the ghostly image of desks and stacks reflected in the wall-sized windows on a winter's night, for the vague erotic frisson of studying next to a pretty girl, with her specs and her pencil case and her textbooks on microbiology – and her golden forearm, just out of reach across the desk. What I thought I wanted was this: to be left alone in the college library with my books and my novel for the rest of my life. What I thought I wanted.

Moving on.

Perhaps, *pace* Dr Felix, I wasn't entirely self-deluded. In school, after all, I had been the class brain. 'Serious question,' Sean Sweeney once asked, turning to face me in assembly. 'Do you, like, read the dictionary?' (We'll be hearing a lot more about Sean Sweeney in these pages, so buckle up.)

Even a nerd less thin-skinned than I was might have felt the need to scan these words for mockery. But I didn't bother. In his way, Sweeney (that year's tight-head prop, whatever that is) was according me a certain respect. I was the smart one, and that was okay with him. The jocks found it perfectly acceptable for me to sit alone under one of our school's ancient beech trees at lunchtime, reading *Notes from Underground* or scribbling on a refill pad. In six years at Old Barbarian High, no one ever punched me or called me names, and before you try to suggest that I got off easy because I was my father's son, well, in rugby schools no one gives a shit about who your father is. That stuff only matters after college, by which time it has become the only thing that matters.

On the other hand, it was clear to everyone at Old Barbarian High that, of the two or three acceptable ways in which it is possible to be a heterosexual man, I had, with my books and my crusades against religious cant (and with the arch tone of voice in which I expressed my disdain for professional sports), chosen suboptimally. In Old Barbarian High there were men-men, book-men, and wimp-men. I was our year's best example of the book-man type. And while I had my place, everybody knew where that place was. And it was not the same place commanded by the men-men: by Sean Sweeney and his First Team friends, who occupied their time with protein powders and 6 a.m. drills, with mean-girl girl-friends and with the scrupulous maintenance of parentally purchased, climate-change-accelerating cars.

Sean Sweeney and his friends grew up, of course, to become The Lads – that granitic crew of jocks and jeerers, those slab-like avatars of heedless privilege, with their monster-truck shoulders and their buzz-cut designer dos. They grew up to become my business cronies, The Lads, they were my partners in the Serbian deal, and although almost every aspect of this sentence so far is a lie, I liked them – even loved them, in a way. In what way, Ben? Oh, let's say: in the way you love your family, i.e. until you start to think about it.

What was the difference between The Lads and me? Our

fathers were rich; we went to the same private school; we all tried to game a system that was itself a game. To that extent, we were alike. The difference is that The Lads were cool with things. They accepted the world into which they had been born. It never crossed their minds that things might have been ordered differently – that a kinder, or at least less vulgarly acquisitive, emphasis might have been chosen, back when the human species was first getting its shit together. The world they happened to live in – networked, brainless, awed by money, super-dense with artificial pleasures, rigged from above in their favour – was, for them, the only possible iteration of the human case. They were fine with it. It didn't bother them. And I never learned the knack of this – I never learned the knack of being at home in the given world.

Add this to the list of my confessions.

How am I doing so far, Dr F? I hope you're happy with the family stuff. I'd hoped to get through this whole account without mentioning my mother at all, actually – or perhaps by mentioning her only indirectly, like Perseus (is it?) looking at the Gorgon in his shield. If it's okay with you, I might skip over the real childhood stuff, or save it up for later. I have the strangest feeling that I'm running out of time.

Immediately after my father's arrest a kind of phoney-war period began: three or four weeks in which it seemed as if absolutely nothing had changed. There was my father, doing nothing (besides 'organising some files' in the air-conditioned shed at the bottom of the garden). There was my mother, doing nothing (besides drinking). And there was me, doing nothing (besides trekking into college and tinkering with the sexy bits of my largely unwritten novel). For whole days at a time, I saw no reason to be alarmed.

Every so often – and despite my best efforts – I caught a glimpse of some online news coverage: *Former Atlas CEO* [REDACTED], *widely admired for steering his bank through the aftermath of the 2008 financial crisis, now faces difficult questions about the fate of over €600 million in misappropriated funds . . .*

If I was able to dismiss this stuff from my mind, it was because I found it impossible to imagine my father doing something so ambitiously sly. If you had asked me, in those days, to sum up my father in a single word, that word would have been *guileless*. Oh, he might have been party to the odd *sub rosa* business deal – even then I wasn't stupid enough to assume that he could have become CEO of a major investment bank without occasionally engaging in some vaguely criminal mischief. But as far as I was concerned there was absolutely no way that he had the gumption, or the wherewithal, to become the most significant financial criminal in the history of the state.

Besides, I reasoned, if my father had spent ten years creaming profits to the tune of over half a billion euro, then why weren't we even richer than we were? Why did he keep telling me to get a job? Why hadn't he gotten the leaky gutter above the deck in the back garden fixed? Why had he installed a *deck,* for Christ's sake?

That the situation was worse than any of us was willing to admit was not a possibility that I seriously entertained until my father arrived at the door of my bedroom one evening in late October and said, 'I was thinking of heading down to the driving range in Greystones. Hit a few balls. Want to come with?'

In some families this is probably a perfectly normal thing for a father to say to his son. In our family, it was unprecedented. Out of morbid curiosity, I said yes.

We drove along the motorway as dusk obscured the eastern sky in sooty increments. To the left was the racecourse complex for which my father's bank had fast-tracked the finance, back in 2006. To the right were brand-new office blocks: the Atlas-Merritt logo (it was a stylised bodybuilder, holding up the armillary sphere of a hollow world) appeared on a hoarding as we sped past. I used to wonder if my father ever found it oppressive, driving around a city that was littered with his corporate spoor. But that just tells you how imperfectly I understood his world.

My father found a covered tee and set himself up with his driver and his bucket of hired balls. The fake fairway was enclosed by a huge green net, as if to keep out enormous mosquitoes. My father addressed the ball with his pro-coached waggle. *WHAP!* He sent a Titleist soaring out into the refrigerator light. The giant mosquito net trembled.

'Bastard,' he said. 'Sliced it.' He teed up another ball. 'I'm reminded of a joke.' *WHAP!* 'When you're getting ready to – you know. Make love. You help each other take your clothes off. But when you get dressed after, you do it alone. The moral of the story? Nobody helps you when you're fucked.'

'That's fucking offensive, Dad,' I said.

My father waggled and paused. 'How close would you say you are to finishing the doctorate?'

'Actually—' I began.

'Four years,' my father said. 'You must be nearly at the finish line.' *WHAP!* 'Get up, you hoor.'

'There's, uh, there's been a few delays.'

'The reason I ask,' my father said, 'is that we've hit a bit of a snag. Financially speaking.'

I said nothing.

My father switched his driver for a three wood. 'I suppose the main thing is that the house is in your mother's name. We were careful with that.'

'The house,' I said.

WHAP! 'The long and the short of it is this. CAB have frozen the bulk of my assets. I've spoken to Gerry Mason about it and he says he can get us sorted with some short-term finance, pay the bills and so on. And the key thing to remember is that you'll always have somewhere to live. The house isn't going anywhere.'

I vaguely recollected that CAB stood for Criminal Assets Bureau. 'So basically,' I said, with a hopeful tinge to my voice, 'this changes nothing. Right?'

My father looked out at the tall green nets. 'What it means,' he said, 'is that certain outgoings will have to be curtailed.'

I made an uncharacteristically sharp deductive leap. 'You can't pay my fees.'

'The money is there,' my father said. 'I just can't get at it. If I were you, I'd aim to get the thesis in some time in the next few weeks. Because after that, you're on your own.'

In some secret corner of my brain I felt a tug, and then a slump, as if some crucial beam or joist had finally given way to rust or metal fatigue. For a vertiginous moment, I contemplated the reality of my position. I had no income, no job prospects, no means of paying the €7,000 in fees that were due that month, no thesis to submit, no novel. I also had no savings. I had spent every penny of my allowance every month, in obedience to the well-known economic law which states that your expenditure will always grow to match your income, especially if you're an idiot. Most remarkably of all, I now had no father who could help me with any of these problems. At the back of my mind, for as long as I could remember, had been the reassuring thought that if becoming a writer somehow didn't work out, I could always give in and let my father get me a job at Atlas-Merritt. This, I now realised, had been the signature on the bottom line of my daydreaming. Now the chequebook had been torn up and all my debts were coming due.

'You're cutting me off,' I said.

My father took another swing. *WHAP!* 'It's going to be rough for a while. We'll have to tighten our belts. But your savings are safe. CAB can't come after those.'

'My savings,' I echoed.

'And the main thing to remember,' my father said, 'is that all this is temporary. There's no real evidence against me. I know you've heard us talk about the possibility of this going to trial.' Had I? 'But believe me when I say that won't happen. Certain people ...' He paused. 'Certain people would very much like to see me go down. But they won't be getting the satisfaction. I'm not a man who holds grudges. I fight fair. I know I taught you to do the same thing. So we're going to fight this. Above board. I suppose what I'm trying to say is don't worry. This will all get sorted. Okay?'

He grinned and teed up another ball.

Labouring over these pages, I experience incredible inner resistance, anxiety, heaviness of soul, as if—

Interrupted, just there, by my usual lunchtime chat with Dr Felix. One of the burly monoglot nurses – I think his name is Piotr – fetched me from my cell and escorted me to the main man's office. Today the Doc was garbed in tennis whites and had left a graphite racket propped against his desk. The whites did nothing to alleviate his sepulchral pallor. He moved his pen across some paperwork and sat back, giving me the once-over. IT WORKS IF YOU WORK IT, said a sign behind his head.

'Your mother's drinking,' he said.

'I hope you're not suggesting,' I said, adopting a tone of exquisite Oxonian condescension, 'that I took drugs simply because my mother was an alcoholic.'

'I'm not suggesting anything,' Dr Felix said. 'I'm saying it straight out. Your mother's alcoholism has given you severe psychological problems.'

'That's a bit neat, isn't it?' I said.

'This isn't a humanities seminar.'

'I told you,' I said. 'I took drugs because I like taking drugs.'

'We all like taking drugs,' Dr Felix said. He is fond of reminding me that he is himself a former user, though he has refused to disclose his drug of choice. (My bet is downers. According to a pamphlet I was given on the day I first arrived, Dr Felix was an emergency-room doctor for five years. Doctors always go for downers.) 'We like taking drugs because of our severe psychological problems.'

'My problem isn't psychological,' I said. 'My problem is that I'm an easy mark.'

'So we agree on something,' Dr Felix said. 'See you tomorrow.'

You know what? Fine. Fine fine fine. I'll write about my mother. Let's try to give the thing some epigrammatic snap, at least. My mother was a banker's wife who perfected the art of secret drinking at some point in the early 2000s, when I was eight or nine years old, and then, spurred by the restless ambition that drives all true professionals, moved on to non-secret drinking in the early 2010s, when I was in my early teens. As certain characters in fiction never appear without their signature accessory, my mother in my memory never appears without a tumbler or a snifter or a flute or a shot

37

glass or a punch cup in her hand. In a memoir I read when I was twenty-one, I encountered for the first time the phrase *high-functioning alcoholic*, and I thought, *Oh, so that's what she is.* It made perfect sense: the daytime cocktails, the glass of wine on the bedside table, the effortless ability to perform routine chores (driving, cooking, talking on the phone) while shitfaced.

It wasn't that my mother was cruel, or abusive, or distant. She wasn't. Her personality never changed. She drove me to the library and directed me to the children's section. She read stories to me at bedtime. She was a conscientious custodian of family lore: she would happily tell you about the time my father almost hit a deer while driving her to the hospital for a prenatal checkup, or the time I ate ashes from the grate as a toddler, or the time she stood in a playground for three straight hours because I had found a swing I loved and didn't want to stop. She just drank all the time – while all of these things were happening.

For years I assumed that this was simply what mothers did. I can't remember how old I was when it occurred to me that my mother wasn't like the mothers of my friends – those energetic housewives and career women, who despite the omnipresence of paid domestic help might nonetheless occasionally be glimpsed ironing a school shirt, or popping out to the garden to pluck socks like stiff grey fruit from the washing line. I didn't know quite what to make of the fact that my mother never did these things. I took my cue from my father, who never said a word about it.

By the time I graduated from college, I understood my mother's drinking as less a problem than a hobby – something to keep her busy, as the hours slowly passed. I did what kids do, when their parents are basically stable and predictable: I stopped worrying about it. I knew that my mother loved me – after all, she was the one who, when I recklessly announced one evening at the dinner table (aged, what – sixteen?) that I wanted to be a writer, said, 'You should do it. There's great freedom in it.' A remark, I now see, that contains a great deal of pathos, though I was too busy feeling vindicated to notice this at the time.

Clio – my darling Clio – used to maintain that everyone had a spirit animal, and that mine was a badger. 'Because you're so grumpy and so cute at the same time,' she explained. In this, as in so many other things, Clio was wrong. My spirit animal isn't a badger. My spirit animal is an ostrich.

The day after my father told me that he was no longer able to pay my fees, I went into college and knocked on the door of my supervisor, Prof. O'Farrelly. I had not seen her in six months. This was by mutual, if tacit, consent. Our relationship had deteriorated to the point at which I walked two kilometres out of my way every morning in order to avoid the Humanities building. Now she was my only hope.

Her office was plastered with conference posters and her desk was piled high with manuscripts and student essays. Behind her swivel chair were bookshelves containing complete sets of *James Joyce Quarterly* and *Irish University Review*.

Here was a vision of the life I might already have earned, if it had ever occurred to me that I needed to earn anything. On the wall beside her desk was a framed print that said: 'FOOD FIRST, THEN MORALS – Brecht'. The professor herself wore half-moon glasses that gave her face a permanent expression of ironic amusement.

Trying not to cough and splutter – or perhaps I was simply trying not to burst into tears – I explained that my family had run into some financial difficulties and that my fees for the year might be delayed.

Prof. O'Farrelly indicated, by elevating her nose a couple of millimetres, that she was well aware of my family's financial difficulties. I had, it seemed, contrived to forget that the details of my father's arrest had been national news for the last three weeks. Then she waited for me to make my pitch.

'I wondered,' I said, 'if there was maybe a scholarship I could apply for, to cover me for an extra year.'

'People who apply for scholarships,' Prof. O'Farrelly said, 'typically do so months in advance of the beginning of the academic year. The next round is in February.'

'I thought you might be able to pull some strings,' I said.

Prof. O'Farrelly said nothing.

'Like,' I said, hurrying to fill the silence, 'I don't know. With the scholarship committee.'

'Which particular scholarship committee did you have in mind?' Prof. O'Farrelly said. Her manner was bland.

'I also wondered,' I said, after a moment, 'if there was some way to stagger or defer my fees. Again, just for this one year.'

Prof. O'Farrelly folded her arms. 'There is an option to go off books. Typically this would be arranged for a student who's made substantial progress with their research and can be trusted to return for a final semester.'

'I've made substantial progress,' I said.

'Do you have a draft?'

'I can put together a draft.'

'By the end of the week?'

I was silent.

Prof. O'Farrelly's tone softened. 'How many semesters have you been here now, Ben?'

'Eight,' I said.

'And you think you need another year?'

When I got home, my father was sitting in the conservatory, using a rusty awl to dig dried mud from between the cleats of his golf shoes.

'I've dropped out of college,' I said.

My father let a lump of mud fall onto the pages of an old *Sunday Business Post* that he had spread at his feet. I could see the questions queuing up behind his eyes. But he said only, 'That's a pity,' and grimaced, before returning to his cleats.

It was a week later, I think, that I got home from town (I had been aimlessly dawdling around Stephen's Green, wondering if I should submit the extant pages of *Decay: A Report* to a literary agent) to find a ragged squad of protestors gathered at the front gate of our house. Two dozen people – many of them middle-aged men, some of them the sort of undergraduate socialists whom I had strenuously avoided during my own undergraduate years – waved signs that said things like PROSECUTE FINANCIAL CRIMINALS (the students) and WHERE'S MY PENSION? (the middle-aged men).

I wasn't remotely surprised to find my father standing in the middle of this group, holding a fat red Thermos and a sleeve of paper cups. He was listening with one hand pressed to his cheek while a young man with a shaved head made a complex point about the shadow banking system. But of course he was. This was how my father operated. He tended, during periods of crisis, to carry on like the hero of a film about British flying aces trapped behind enemy lines. *What ho, chaps! Pip-pip! See it through!* In fact, this basic impression of my father remained so vivid in my mind that it survived several weeks of accumulating evidence that he was no longer, as he himself might have put it, 100 per cent tickety-boo.

'Don't use the house phone,' he said one evening as I passed his study door.

'What are you talking about?' I said.

'The landline,' he said. 'Incoming calls only, and don't say anything that might be used against us later.'

'Are you saying,' I said slowly, 'that you think the house phone is bugged?'

'We can't be too careful,' my father said, before closing the study door in my face.

A few days later, he asked me if I knew anything about keylogging software. 'They can use it to find out your passwords,' he said, scratching the chin he no longer bothered to shave.

He made a series of late-night trips to the recycling bins, carrying big pappardelle nests of shredded paper. He cleaned out the shed at the end of the garden and lit our ancient barbecue, on whose grill he proceeded to immolate stack after stack of documents, turning the blackened pages with a two-pronged fork and waving the smoke away from his eyes.

He locked himself in his study for extended sessions on a gym-scale rowing machine (also liberated from the garden shed). Every evening for hours at a time the noise of this machine came grinding up through the ceiling into my bedroom, like the labourings of a troubled conscience.

He also became monomaniacal on the subject of financial prudence – insisting, for example, on doing all the grocery shopping himself. (Formerly, of course, this had been my mother's job, which meant, in practice, that a superabundance of luxury goods was delivered to our door every Monday by a private shopping service. In one haul, once upon a time, I had chanced upon fourteen jars of Fortnum & Mason cognac butter. My mother had presumably meant to order fourteen bottles of cognac, and clicked the wrong link on the online form.) Once CAB had frozen his assets, my father abruptly became a sad little fixture of the matriarchal weekday morning streets of Sandymount and Blackrock, trotting along with his red twine bag and his hand-scrawled list of staples. 'Eighty cents for a bag of red onions!' he said. 'You can't do better than that.'

In his downtime he took to muttering darkly about the Minister for Finance and the National Asset Management Agency – 'The number of people who stayed out of NAMA because of me' was one phrase I managed to overhear – while he puffed away on a stale Romeo y Julieta out on the backyard deck. He waved his arms and ranted as the cigar smoke cast its frail grey scarves against the shedding beeches.

One morning I found a tattered spiral notebook open on the dining-room table. The words FINANCIAL REGULATOR had been circled in red. Beside them was a small stick-figure, pointing a gun at its own temple.

It must also have been around this time that I chanced upon an envelope on the hall carpet, addressed to 'The [REDACTED] Family'. As a member of said family, I opened it. I found a green-inked letter with no salutation or signature. Some phrases from this letter still chime against my inner ear: *Prickface retarded cunt with your smug idiotic grin*, went one of them. I was also struck by *Hope your kid rots from every disease going*. Not knowing what else to do with this letter, I left it on the desk in my father's study. I wonder if he ever got around to reading it. Or, no: delete that. Because of course he did. He got around to reading it all.

A night or two after this my mother cornered me in our food-crammed utility room (which she insisted on calling 'the pantry'), where I had gone to find some pickles for a sandwich. She was carrying a large rattan basket full of my father's Charvet shirts (his collection ranged from white with blue pinstripe to blue with white pinstripe: all the colours of

44

the corporate rainbow). Under my sceptical gaze she set the basket on the tiled floor and began to stuff shirts into the washing machine.

'Having a midnight snack?' she said, as she frowned at the box of laundry capsules with its childproof lid.

'It's nine p.m.,' I said.

'You always got hungry after dinner.'

'Do you, uh,' I said uncertainly, 'do you want a hand with that?'

'I wanted to make sure you're doing okay,' my mother said. She had succeeded in wrenching open the box of laundry capsules. Now she yanked open the white plastic drawer of the washing machine and popped a capsule inside.

'I think you just put that in with the clothes,' I said.

'I'm sure it's fine,' my mother said. She pressed the button labelled START and the machine made a sound like the humming of overhead electrical wires. 'Really what I wanted to ask you was how you think your father's doing.'

'How he's doing?' I said. I made a point of browsing among the jars of preserves stacked on bespoke shelves above the sink. 'He's losing his mind. Other than that, I'd say, pretty normal.'

'He isn't used to being unpopular,' my mother said. 'I worry about how it's affecting him.'

The washing machine made a gargling sound and suddenly emitted a panicked whine.

I had located a jar of pickles. 'He said it himself,' I said. 'This will all blow over.'

My mother was regarding me with unwonted keenness. 'If he asks you to do anything,' she said, 'anything at all, just tell him you'll do it and then come to me. All right?'

I had the queasy feeling that I was being enlisted in some sort of intra-family black op or covert strike. 'What,' I said, 'like bury a body?'

'Just anything at all,' my mother said. She looked at the washing machine. 'How long do you think it takes? Three hours? I'll come back in three hours.'

'That should do it,' I said.

So you see, Dr F: as a family, we were completely unprepared to cope with a crisis of this magnitude – a crisis that demanded the sort of *esprit de corps* we hadn't been able to muster even when things were going well. Instead of rallying, we each pursued a separate strategy of avoidance: my mother with her drinks cabinets, my father with his evidentiary barbecues, and me, with my last best hope for rescue: my friends, such as they were. And it was through my friends that I hooked up with Clio – right at the point when I should have been doing almost anything else.

One more relevant biographical datum, actually, before we move on. When I was thirteen years old my parents commissioned portraits of themselves in oils and stuck them up in what my mother called the drawing room. They had engaged a fashionable painter whose name was Graham. He had a satanic goatee and long, slender fingers – 'Artist's hands,' my mother noted approvingly.

For weeks on end my parents sat in state while this smocked goon mixed and smeared with brush and thumb-gripped palette. My father's portrait depicted him emerging from baronial gloom in a lemon-yellow argyle vest, like the results of a matter-transportation accident involving a conquistador and a traffic warden. My mother, in her portrait, posed with a stoat on her lap – a small, white-bellied mouse-like creature with anthracite eyes whose hard gleam echoed, I hesitate to suggest deliberately, the hard gleam of her own black eyes above. The stoat, I should probably explain, was added in during post-production.

They stared down from the drawing-room wall, these portraits, throughout my adolescence, discomfiting anyone who looked at them – discomfiting me especially, so that finally I preferred to avoid the drawing room altogether. My parents were never sure how they felt about these portraits. When Graham was finally finished they threw an unveiling party for their friends and spent the whole time saying how much better a portrait was than a photograph, how much more profoundly it revealed the human essence of the sitter, and how the whole business had been fifteen grand well spent.

But after a while they, too, preferred to avoid the drawing room, and the portraits accumulated a layer of furry grey dust that dimmed their colours, until at last they looked like pictures of dead people, hanging on the wall of a house in which they had perhaps once lived.

I adduce the portraits now as evidence for the possibility

that vanity and self-delusion have been double-helixed into my DNA from the get-go.

Not that that's much of an excuse.

By my friends, I mean my literary-academic friends – a loose assortment of junior scholars, zine editors, slam poets, bloggers, graphic designers, publishing interns and student journalists who were, I used to think, the people through whom culture truly lived. We went to book launches and flirted with each other. Occasionally one of us published something (though I never did: nothing, not even a short story), or had a gallery show, or wrote a style piece for the *Irish Times*. We complained loudly and often about how Dublin was being taken over by vulture funds that had rendered the city unaffordable for artists. We lived on allowances from our parents, or in apartments in boomtime residential units bought for us as graduation presents. Although none of us had, in artistic or financial terms, quite succeeded, none of us had ever come remotely close to failing, either. It had never occurred to us that the padded floor on which we stood was in fact sharply hinged, and beneath it lurked the blunt, bruising teeth of the real, unfunded world. (There was one more thing we had in common, though it probably goes without saying: we had all gone to private schools.)

In the aftermath of my father's arrest I spent as much time with these people as I could. For a while I staved off my fear of the future by describing the high points of my father's emotional collapse for the amusement of whoever might be listening. But even as I stood in some wine bar or beer garden and recreated my father's mincing movements with the two-pronged fork as he torched his papers on the grill, I knew that I was trying to cover my rage and fright with the thinnest and most moth-eaten of blankets.

One of these friends – let's call him Alan – had recently set up a small press. He published neglected Irish classics and snarky political pamphlets, which he called broadsides. Alan was the sort of person who read Charles Bukowski and travelled everywhere on a foldable scooter and made his own coffee using the bespoke French press that he kept in a vintage leather satchel that never left his shoulder. I had known him since college, when he had edited the campus tabloid. One night I had a long-delayed brainwave. I could ask Alan for a job at his press. I could become a commissioning editor, or a proofreader. These seemed like the sort of prestigious, low-maintenance jobs that I could easily handle.

Alan, I knew, could usually be found at book launches, taking advantage of the free wine. There was, as it happened, a launch scheduled for the very next evening. There it was, in my Google calendar. My salvation was at hand.

I was also quite keen to escape the atmosphere at home. For several days my parents had been conducting some kind of silent argument, making obscure points by opening and closing doors at irregular intervals. The whole house felt gilded in a fine frost of anxiety. Eschewing the customary taxi, I took a bus into town. There was just over a hundred quid left in my bank account. I was hoarding it carefully.

49

The book being launched was an anthology of slam poetry. As I shouldered my way through the throng I heard a female voice say through a microphone: 'Did love do this to me, or was it Twitter?' I took up a position by the drinks table and scanned the room for Alan. The location was a pop-up store called Mask & Mantle, which seemed to sell remodelled typewriters, or possibly just framed pictures of remodelled typewriters.

Standing behind the drinks table was a girl in a black cocktail dress. 'Hey,' I said. 'Could I get a glass of red, please.'

The girl glanced at me – she was listening to the woman on the stage. 'You can get whatever you want,' she said.

'That's my kind of policy,' I said. I helped myself to two glasses of red wine. 'Sorry. Do you know where I can find Alan McArdle?'

'I don't really know that many people here,' she said, and folded her arms.

It was around now, I think, that I noticed that she was beautiful. And no matter what happened later, I always found her beautiful: my Clio. Actually, let me revise this milquetoast remark: I entered a state of sexual red alert every time I found myself in Clio's company. Please imagine here a paragraph describing the sort of stricken lustfulness that I am too depressed right now to contemplate, let alone to recreate in prose.

'Aren't you one of the organisers?' I said.

'Not the last time I checked.'

'So why,' I said, 'are you serving drinks?'

She pivoted to face me. I felt the sudden lovely pressure of her attention. She was half-smiling in a vaguely hostile way. Her arms were now even more tightly folded. 'Did you just see a woman standing near the wine table and assume she was serving drinks?'

I blushed.

'I saw someone,' I said, 'who looks like they're in charge of the situation. So naturally I deferred.'

'Oh,' she said. 'You deferred.'

'I always defer to powerful people,' I said.

'I'm Clio,' she said. Her smile had lost its hostile edge. 'It's short for Clionadh.'

'Ben,' I said. 'It's short for Benjamin.'

Another reading was in progress. A woman who wore a bowler hat and held, but did not play, a blue ukulele, was reciting what seemed to be a confessional monologue about her first period. To this performance Clio listened with her palms crossed at her chest. Her empty wine glass was held against her shoulder. 'Women are powerful castrating witches,' the girl in the bowler hat may or may not have said.

I whispered in Clio's ear. 'I don't get the witches thing.'

'Witches were burned at the stake just for being women,' Clio said. 'There's this whole movement to reclaim being a witch. Like, calling yourself a witch is a way of saying you're not ashamed of being a woman.' At the podium, the woman in the bowler hat was now playing a ukulele solo. 'I was just in a play she wrote,' Clio said. 'She's this incredible wordsmith.'

I spied an opening. 'You hang out with those writing and publishing guys, right?' I said.

But the ukulele player was stepping offstage, to tepid applause.

Clio said, 'Can I serve you more wine?'

'I should do the serving,' I said.

But as I snagged two glasses, I ran out of clever things to say. For a hideously prolonged moment we stood side by side, conscious only of our own inability to sustain the kind of effervescent banter that buoyed aloft even the most pro forma of flirtations.

'Maybe we should buy the book,' Clio said at last. She was staring at someone on the other side of the room.

'You said you were in a play,' I said, suddenly inspired. 'I wish I'd seen it.'

She touched her hair. 'No, you don't,' she said. 'It wasn't what I'd call my finest hour.'

'If you have half the charisma on stage that you have in real life, I *know* you were amazing,' I said, accidentally inaugurating a dynamic in which I became the loyal custodian of Clio's fragile professional self-belief.

Clio looked down and smiled. 'You didn't have to say that.'

'I never have to say anything,' I said, 'unless I mean it.'

'Who are you looking for?' Clio said.

'I need to see a man about a job,' I said.

'Jobs are boring,' Clio said. 'You should come to the afterparty.'

'I don't think I'm invited.'

'I'm inviting you.'

'Well in that case,' I said, 'I defer.'

She smiled. So did I. We were smiling together.

We shared a cab back to the party. Like a cur, I let Clio pay the fare. On the way we talked about art, of course. 'Come on,' I said, with cocked head and rakish smile. 'You don't really think that woman is an incredible wordsmith.'

Clio bit her lip and scrunched up her face in a way that meant, *If I'm being reluctantly honest?* 'Her play wasn't about witches or her period. I swear.'

'You're a good friend,' I said.

'Loyalty is important.'

'What role do you most want to play?' I said. 'Dream role. Go.'

'Hamlet,' Clio said at once.

I risked it: 'You're too beautiful to play Hamlet.'

'That's a very minimising thing to say,' Clio said, after a moment.

Another misstep. 'All I meant,' I said, 'is that Hamlet's a loser. It would be a big leap for you, to imagine what it's like to be a loser.'

Clio smiled. 'Next left,' she said to the taxi driver.

In a sense, that party – which took place in the sort of bean-bag-strewn post-college digs that I would later come to recognise as a classic session gaff – represented the shadow-line between the old life and the new. Nothing would be the same after that. I had hoped to find Alan and his foldable scooter in attendance. But by the time we arrived I was so drunk that using my vague literary connections to find a publishing job no longer seemed like a particularly urgent task. Instead I talked to Clio in the hallway. Between us was the idea that we would sleep together (obviously). But there was also something else. We were good for each other's confidence, or so it seemed. She recited her audition speech. I listened in grave, admiring silence. I told her about *Decay: A Report*. She said it was the kind of book she would buy the minute it came out. I promised to send her some pages. Around us – several hours had now passed – the party seemed to have undergone a qualitative change. The lights had gone out and the music now looped endlessly: a bass-heavy *whompf-whompf-whompf* that pulsed through the walls like a foetal heartbeat. I had the strange sense that in rooms just out of sight people were engaged in violent and obscure activities. In the submarine murk I glimpsed the flushed faces of strangers with fever-clouded eyes as they lurched past, giggling. Over Clio's shoulder I seemed to see a girl slump against the wall. She had a child's pink pacifier in her mouth. I realised what was happening an instant before Clio produced two small misshapen blue pills and said, 'So are we going to do this, or what?'

I reached for the pill, and paused. I felt a premonitory shiver, as if I knew in some banal but thrilling way that I had met my fate. I'm overselling this. Blame my drug-nostalgia. I blinked and swallowed the pill.

In the months that followed – the months during which, under Clio's tutelage, I discovered drugworld – many things became clear to me. The social scene into which I had wandered, in the early years of my so-called maturity, seemed, in those months, as I went from taking ecstasy at parties to taking everything everywhere, to make sense at last. It was as if I had been watching a 3D film without 3D glasses and had suddenly put them on. Everything gained a new depth of field, and the behaviour of my contemporaries, formerly so mysterious to me, disclosed, in a series of convulsive, joy-filled weekends, its secret engine. That terrible clumping music they all listened to? You were supposed to take drugs before you listened to it. The issue-based ahistorical leftism that constituted our politics? It was the politics of the session: *Why can't everyone just, like, empathise with each other, man?* The heaving dancefloors doused in obliterative light and noise? The dismal music festivals, with their septic urinal troughs and their mud-caked beer tents? Drugs, drugs, all drugs. Our generational culture, like some fairy-tale secret kingdom, existed on the other side of a magic pill. How had I never noticed this before? Why had it taken Clio, this beautiful stranger, to show me the truth about the world in which I lived?

Once I had swallowed the pill it took half an hour before anything interesting happened. Then I ran for the upstairs bathroom and joyfully vomited. Now the floor was covered in vomit and piss. Was that my doing? Oh dear. With quivering hands I made sure to lock myself in. Then I made sure three or four more times. I seemed to have forfeited the use of my thumbs.

Everything was taking a very long time and then hurrying up, like rush-hour traffic. I appeared to be kneeling on a stained towel, and I was inspecting my surroundings closely. To look at the world (currently represented by various blue-tinged ridges of calcified toothpaste-drool adorning a stained sink) was like watching television underwater, in an earthquake.

I had already been in the bathroom for more than an hour, which was very bad form, I thought. Clio would be missing me. But I was unfit for human consumption, as matters stood. I had taken drugs and I was out of commission.

I had hauled myself semi-upright. I was leaning on my thighs. My palms were getting sore. I had stayed braced for too long in the same position. There were small red patches of rug burn on the skin of my hands.

For an intriguing spell I developed the capacity to regard myself as a neutral observer might. I thought: *This is pretty sordid, isn't it?*

I thought about my father's arrest. I thought about the fact that I had no money and no future. These were interesting trifles: worth considering. The main thing now was to pull myself together. The party was almost over. I had been in the bathroom for hours and I had missed the whole thing.

'Ben?'

It was a woman's voice. Someone was knocking gently on the door.

'Yeah,' I said. I sounded surprisingly good. On the basis of my voice alone, I would have described myself as a capable citizen, in full possession of his faculties.

'Are you okay in there?'

It was Clio's voice. Incredible sound.

All at once I knew that it was possible to a) stand up straight and b) talk to another human being. I unlocked the bathroom door.

'How long have I been in here?' I said.

'I don't know,' Clio said. 'Like, five minutes?'

'My jaws,' I said.

'You need some chewing gum.'

I did: I did need some chewing gum. Clio produced a dusty packet of Doublemint from her handbag. She was so well prepared. She was practically a Boy Scout.

'You're a Boy Scout,' I said, grinning and chewing.

'I know,' Clio said, as if she understood exactly what I was talking about. She took my hand. 'Come in here,' she said. She led me into a darkened bedroom. We sat on the bed, holding hands.

'I think my life is falling apart,' I said.

'What happened?' Clio said.

'My father was arrested,' I said. 'Your hand feels amazing.'

'Yours too. Is he guilty?'

'I don't think so,' I said.

'You'll be okay,' Clio said.

'How do you know?' I said.

'Because you're going to be a writer,' Clio said.

We were kissing. Clio's mouth, or possibly my mouth,

57

tasted of Doublemint gum. Time passed: by which I mean drug-time, which passes in gulps and stops and ravishing *longueurs*, which eats up the hours but fattens the minutes until they burst their seams and it feels as if you will never grow old or die because you have so many minutes left before anything has to change. I became aware, sequentially, of the music downstairs, the furniture around us, the warmth of Clio's hip beneath her dress.

'Why didn't you kiss me sooner?' Clio said, when the kiss ended.

'You're so hot,' I said. 'I was intimidated.'

Clio knelt beside the bed. 'I want to show you,' she said, 'why you shouldn't have been intimidated.' She unbuckled my belt, not without some logistical difficulties. Then she put my cock in her mouth – my cock, which was, for some reason, as small and shrivelled as a little boy's.

'Sorry,' I said after a few minutes. 'I don't know what's wrong.'

'It's the yokes, you muppet,' Clio said. 'No one can get hard on yokes.' She was smiling. 'Don't worry. We'll do it again.'

'So this is normal?' I said.

Clio smiled and frowned at the same time. 'Wow,' she said. 'Have you actually never done yokes before?'

'It's my first time,' I said.

'My God,' Clio said. 'You're such a sap.'

My body had broken out in gooseflesh. I grinned and grinned, as if everything in my life had just worked out for the best.

Sap, n., Hiberno-English slang. A gauche person; one ungifted with social nous. Also: a dupe or mark. The butt of the joke. That one person at the party who just doesn't get it and never will.

Early this morning Dr Felix appeared at the door of my cell in his long white coat and said, 'We've mentioned integrating with the other clients.' They don't refer to us as *patients* or *inmates*, here at St Augustine. They refer to us as *clients*, as if we were all engaged in some kind of mutually beneficial business transaction. Of course, Dr F has, for once, a point. I have not been integrating – I have not been discharging whatever social obligations accrue to the involuntarily confined. But neither has anybody else. There are good reasons for this. How would you like it, Dr F, if you locked eyes with every loser in the place and saw reflected there, with perfect clarity, the precise dimensions of your own regret?

To Dr Felix I said, 'I'm not all that keen on the other clients.'

Dr Felix sat on the edge of my bed, the way my father used to when I was a child. 'They're going through the same thing you are.'

'No,' I said. 'They're not.'

'You're crying a lot at night,' Dr Felix said.

'That doesn't sound like me.'

'And you haven't left this room in forty-eight hours.'

'It's so comfortable here.' I lifted my head from the pillow. I was, as usual, in the foetal position, and my muscles felt like old elastic bands. 'When can I get the fuck out of here, anyway? Isn't my time almost up?'

'We might do something about your energy,' Dr Felix said. He began scribbling on a prescription pad. He wrote more than seemed strictly necessary, as if he were using the pad to draft a sonnet. 'Take this to the dispensary,' he said, and tore the top sheet off with a flourish.

'You're giving me drugs?' I said.

'Cold turkey is bullshit. But don't expect anything fancy.' Dr Felix stood. 'I'm glad you're writing. It's a positive sign. But try to keep the language as neutral as possible. Stick to the facts.' He tapped the doorframe with his pen and left.

A positive sign. I lay back on my bunk and looked at the pine-laminate furniture of my cell: at the desk, the single spavined chair, the hooded lamp with its film of faded dust. Dr F's prescription lay on my bedside locker. Through the open window a smell of warm garbage seeped, like the odour of my own rank soul.

How's that for neutral language.

The morning after the party, I awoke in Clio's bed. She lived in a third-floor apartment in a Georgian building on Baggot Street – disconcertingly close, I was later to note, to the head-quarters of my father's former bank. Clio's apartment wasn't bad. Her hospital-consultant parents were, she told me later that day, paying her rent while she established herself as an actor. I should perhaps have regarded this as a warning sign. Clio was, after all, no more economically self-sufficient than

I was. But I had more immediate priorities. Besides, when I awoke to the migraine light of my first-ever comedown – oh, *why* was my body so *heavy* and *sore*? – it was to find that Clio and I were now flatmates. This, at any rate, was the understanding we seemed to have arrived at during the night. My first thought on waking was of my father. I seemed to see him standing before a room of uniformed Guards with a bemused frown on his face and his hands open before him, as if to say: *I throw myself on the mercy of the court.* My second thought, which followed with terrifying speed, was that I had no future. What had I *done* with my life? Summoning the courage to open my eyes, I found Clio sitting up in bed beside me, drinking from a carton of orange juice and thumbing through a document on her phone. 'You're an incredible writer,' she said. 'This is *so* good.' I had, it seemed, emailed her the manuscript of *Decay: A Report* in the small hours of the morning. 'I love the way you write about sex,' Clio said. 'I seriously think you should send this somewhere.'

'I'm going to be sick,' I said, lurching upright.

'Look at you,' Clio said. 'Your pupils are like saucers. You're still rolling.' She dug around in her handbag and produced a small white pill. 'Here.'

Aha, I thought: so there was a pill for this bit too. I swallowed the little ingot with some orange juice.

Clio propped her head on a manicured hand. Her arms were pale and freckled. With a kind of abstract interest, I noted that she was naked except for a silver bangle on her left wrist. Her makeup was immaculate, which meant (I later realised) that she had gotten up early to redo it. 'That'll bring you down a bit,' she said.

'What is it?' I croaked.

'Xanax,' Clio said. 'I have a prescription.'

I lay back. Beneath my head was a stuffed toy rhinoceros, which I had soaked with slobber in the night.

'You're the solution to all my problems,' I said.

Three hours later we fucked for the first time. As soon as I came, I said, 'I love you,' and Clio began to weep softly in gratitude, pressing her damp face against my shoulder. I would describe this as the worst thing I have ever done if I hadn't managed to trump it, a thousand times over, in the course of the fucked-up year that followed.

Commenting on my oral recitation of the above scene yesterday evening (I had popped in for a visit on the way back from the dispensary), Dr Felix nodded like a Zen master and said, 'It was you who had thrown yourself on the mercy of the court.'

'What the fuck are you talking about?' I said.

'Have you ever heard the phrase *nolo contendere*? Do with me what you will? That's what you were saying to Clio. You still didn't want to take responsibility for your actions. So you handed yourself over to her.'

'What would you have had me do?'

'You could have found a job.'

'It was at the top of my list, I swear.'

'It's a mistake to think other people can save us. Especially if we don't bother trying to save ourselves.'

'She seemed to like me,' I said. 'She seemed to want to help me.'

'Was she wrong to like you?'

'Evidently,' I said.

'Did you hurt Clio?'

A prickly sensation arose among the hairs on the back of my neck. 'If we're talking in aggregate terms,' I said, 'I'd say she hurt me more than I hurt her.'

'Still not taking responsibility,' Dr Felix said. He shook his head and picked up the *Irish Times* crossword.

It was late the next day before I felt able to trek home and pick up my clothes and laptop. The house was in disarray. Even the dual portraits had been removed from the drawing room and now reposed, like stills from a high-toned horror film, beside the HD TV in the living room. The door of my father's study was open. He was using the rowing machine: puffing and straining as he tugged on the rubber handles, watching the yards rack up on the little LCD screen in front of his face.

'What the fuck is happening?' I said. 'Are you moving out?'

My father kept rowing. 'Civil forfeiture,' he said. His shoulders tensed, relaxed. 'CAB. Storage.'

'You mean the repo men are coming?' I said.

'Proceeds of crime,' my father said. 'Hasn't happened yet. Take no chances.'

I couldn't imagine what the Criminal Assets Bureau would want with a painting of my mother holding a stoat. Or, for that matter, what they would do with the cabinet full of

Waterford Crystal that my father had won over the years at golf. I was forced to conclude that my parents had lost their minds. It gave me a surprising sense of freedom to believe this, as if it had been true all along and I had simply been unable to see it until now.

Halfway up the stairs my mother was piling a Louis Vuitton suitcase with choice examples of menopausal bling. 'They come after everything,' she said. She held aloft a fox-fur coat. 'You'd never get away with wearing that nowadays.'

'I'm here to get my stuff,' I said.

My mother looked at me. Her face made a sympathetic moue. This moue was, in itself, alarming. I had never seen anything like it before.

'I'm so sorry you have to do this,' she said, taking a sip from the glass of Grey Goose in her left hand. With her right hand she was folding a cashmere shawl. 'I've put some boxes in your room already.'

'I'm not putting my stuff in storage,' I said. 'I'm moving out. I've met someone and we're moving in together.'

For a moment my mother failed to move, as when an online video arrests itself in order to load.

'A girl,' she said at length.

'Yes, Mum,' I said. 'A girl.'

'That's lovely,' my mother said. Again she essayed the sympathetic moue, but now something seemed to have gone wrong: the moue curdled at its edges, and her eyes assumed, as if out of habit, their customary hardness.

*

In my room I threw some clothes and books into a backpack. I would like to say that I paused to acknowledge the poignancy of the moment – that I studied fondly the framed prints of classic book covers on the wall (Christmas presents from my parents), the ranked spines of my collected paperbacks (all that literary theory, which I had not read, and all those novels, which I had). But I did not. I went through my drawers for loose change. Then I fell asleep. I regained consciousness three hours later to find that the house was dark and still. I shouldered my backpack and went downstairs. My footsteps echoed strangely, as if I were trespassing in a museum at night. Of my father there was no sign. On the divan in the drawing room my mother was sleeping, making soft glottal sounds as she snored and still clutching, impressively I thought, a tumbler of gin in her left hand. The curtains were open. I closed them. I set the tumbler on the floor. In a cardboard box by the window I located a fleece blanket, which I draped across my mother's sleeping form. For a few moments I lingered. But she did not wake up.

My few possessions made no impact on the threadbare order of Clio's digs. In a way this was the point: I was a free man, unencumbered by the flotsam of the past. Unencumbered also by a job, a plan, a way to stave off my fear of the void. No, not quite free, or not entirely. I was now Clio's boyfriend. Who was Clio? She was an actor. Her life, like an obedient puppy, was going just the way she wanted it to. This did not, of course, make her immune to crises of confidence, or to the crises of authenticity that plague all actors from time to time. Am I fake? Am I fooling myself? In certain moods – I thought of them as her acting moods – her smallest gestures were delivered as if between quotation marks. A good-humoured chuckle became 'a good-humoured chuckle'. A shrug became 'a shrug'. But these moods passed quickly. She was broad-hipped and small-chested. On holidays, she wore the top and bottom halves of two different bikinis. (She had sent me some sexy beach snaps to use as iPhone wallpaper.) She smoked menthol cigarettes and read books called *Monologues for Women* or *The Excellent Audition Guide*. In her bedroom was a white Ikea bookcase packed tight with paperback playscripts: Tony Kushner, Sarah Kane, Caryl Churchill. She also read gossip magazines called things like *Tittle* or *Tattle* or *Hot* or *Pink*, whose pages she turned with sceptical speed, saying, 'I have no idea who these people are. I used to know all the celebrities. Now everyone's famous from their YouTube channel.' Casting the magazines aside, she would gossip instead about the Dublin theatre scene: about who was about to get MeTooed, or about who had shown up drunk to an audition. Every evening she made overnight oats in a repurposed jam jar, and every morning she used a stopwatch to ensure that she brushed her teeth for the regulation two minutes. She spoke about her parents as if she genuinely liked them – as if she genuinely enjoyed their company. What a thought! On one of our first evenings together in her flat, she tried to persuade me to join her and her father for a drink in the bar of the Conrad Hotel. He had just finished delivering a keynote, and 'he's super-curious to meet you'. I weaselled my way out of this, and would continue to weasel my way out of meeting Clio's parents for several months. When I asked her about her Xanax prescription – 'Don't they give that for anxiety?' I said, noticing, belatedly, this particular red flag – Clio said, 'Oh, I just get it so I can sleep on planes.' There were startling gaps in her general knowledge. On the other hand, she knew a lot of poetry by heart. One morning, when I was trying to convince her to give me a blow job, I said, 'Had we but world enough and time, this coyness, lady, were no crime.' 'We could sit down,' Clio said at once, 'and think which way to walk, and pass our long love's day. But we don't have a long love's day, do we? I have rehearsals, and you have to get a job.' I wanted her. I needed her. She was the one who could explain the world to me, or at least guide me in my quest to take more drugs. There was also her body, in which my interest never waned, no matter how grim things got later on (and they did get very grim). Who was it who said, *Hitch your wagon to a star*? I hitched my wagon to Clio. To her, I must have looked like a solid bet. I had the right parents. I had gone to the right school. I talked a convincing game about my art. It wasn't Clio's fault that my wagon turned out to be full of shit.

'What do you want out of life?' Clio asked me, more than once, during our first few weeks together. The words had not yet taken on the accents of frustration or despair that they would accrue as the months rolled by. She was genuinely curious. 'I want to be a writer,' was my usual response – to be followed by a well-rehearsed aria about 'plunging my characters deep into the tank of the contemporary, and watching them flail'. But even then, lurking visibly beneath the surface of my waking mind like a fat white koi in a shallow pond, was the suspicion that the truth was otherwise: that what I actually wanted was to be taken care of; that what I actually wanted was to be lovingly divested of all responsibility for the management of my own life; that what I actually wanted, if you got right down to it, was to be left alone to do nothing at all.

I once asked Clio: 'Same question to you. What do you want out of life?'

'I want to self-actualise,' she said.

Although I tried very hard not to, I found myself thinking about this for a very long time.

Being intelligent in one way only – the literary – was and always has been my fatal flaw. Writing this down, I see that, like most confessions, it is actually a sort of boast. But even a vitiated man finds himself clinging to the last gruesome scraps of his self-worth. And in the name of my new regime of the spirit – repudiating former laxities – let me add that I wasn't even that much cop as a literary man. In my mock exams – practice for the Leaving Cert – I scored a B in English. In maths, biology, history and French, I flat-out failed. My points totted up to 240. It was the lowest score that year. Expectations had been high. No Old Barbarian had ever scored less than 500 points in the Leaving Cert proper, barring a couple of exceptional cases having to do with drug overdoses or severe head injury. It wasn't stupidity so much as laziness that had caused me to tank so many papers (though what is laziness except a version of stupidity?). My father, having scanned the school letter that announced my results, shook his head and left the room, as if to say, *I give up on you entirely.* My mother held up my English B as proof that I could ace the real thing, if I tried. She drove me into town and bought me a new leather jacket, and, in Hodges Figgis, a complete set of Proust, unopened to this day.

'Is it just that you can't concentrate?' she said, as we motored home along Rock Road.

'Don't *worry*, Mum,' I said. 'It's just the mocks. Nobody bothers with the mocks.'

We never said another word on the subject. I put the new leather jacket in my wardrobe and ignored it. Wearing it would have felt like wearing my failure. Or, no: not my failure. My parents' failure. Though why this should be so I cannot say.

In my actual Leaving Cert I scraped sufficient points to get into my second-choice university. When the offer arrived, my mother nodded for a while and then seemed to be at a loss. Eventually she stuck out her hand and said, 'Put 'er there, son.'

I shook my mother's hand, feeling – as far as I could tell – not much at all, and wondering what, indeed, I was supposed to be feeling, at such a crucial life juncture.

To mark the occasion, my father bought me a Gucci

briefcase. It was the same as the one he took to Atlas-Merritt every day.

The long-postponed moment of crisis finally arrived one morning in the middle of November. Clio was in rehearsals for a new play. I had a lot of time on my hands. I ventured out of the apartment in search of cigarettes. Hitting up an ATM on Leeson Street, I found that I had at last run out of money. Contemptuously, the ATM blew a raspberry – it stuck out its tongue, in the form of my deadbeat card. And that was that. I had nothing. I was definitively without resources. Having paid no taxes, ever, I didn't even qualify for social welfare. For several minutes I hyperventilated. The experience was – how to phrase it? As if the material substance of the world had abruptly disclosed a nauseating fault, down there in its moist inner workings. But let's not get too metaphysical. I was panicking. I went back to Clio's apartment and curled up on the couch, hugging my knees, like the sad man on the cover of a book about depression. I must have stayed there for five or six hours, unmoving. When I swallowed, I tasted a ferrous tang. It seemed to me that I had wandered haplessly across some secret threshold – crossed the wrong frontier, carrying the wrong passport. Instead of the country of privilege, I had ended up in the country of failure. Instead of the country of pride, I had ended up in the country of shame. Instead of the country of art, I had ended up in the country of life. And who, I asked myself with a hot snort of derision, ever wanted to end up *there*?

When Clio got home, she stood over me with her hands on her hips and said, 'My poor badger. Please don't stress. We'll find you a job. You'll be fine.'

For an instant, I allowed myself to believe her. But the streets outside were dark, and the darkness was pressing heavily on the glass of the grimy windows, and it was getting very cold.

What I was doing, that November, in the weeks before I ran out of money, was falling in love: not with Clio, but with drugs. With that first blue pill, a door had sprung open in my mind. Suddenly I was moving with corrupt ease through a world of tremulous light and mumblecore chats on bean bags, of rollovers and comedowns, of an unprecedented ability to be honest about my feelings while talking to people I had only just met. There was always another club night. There was always another session. This, it turned out, was how Clio and her friends lived. Very quickly, it became how I lived, too. What was I? I was an ostrich, and I had found the biggest pile of sand in the world. It was simple: pop a pill and gaze upon the fallen world redeemed. There were drugs for every occasion – all those wonderful substances, each one offering to interpose between your ailing heart and the world its soothing chemical buffer. 'WHY DON'T WE DO THIS ALL THE TIME,' I yelled at Clio, as we zoned out in the techno gloaming of yet another all-night rager. And I meant it. Given the choice, I would never have come down at all. I should not have been surprised when the ATM spat out my card. I knew where the last of my money had gone. I had bankrupted myself buying drugs. A pattern was establishing itself. I might have seen it coming. But I didn't.

For the sake of my own self-respect, or what's left of it, I'm going to fast-forward through the events of the next few months, pausing only to draw your attention to a handful of pertinent highlights, as follows:

1) The first time I tried pure speed, and stayed awake for sixty-two hours, explaining the vision behind *Decay: A Report* to an audience of Clio's actor friends and promising, when everyone told me that it sounded amazing, to turn it into a play for the Dublin Fringe Festival.

2) The first time I exceeded the recommended dose of benzodiazepines, swallowing Clio's entire stock of Xanax while she was out at rehearsals because I had nothing better to do and lapsing into an eleven-hour coma, from which I awoke with one of those headaches that seems to portend a major neurological catastrophe.

3) The conversation during which Clio extracted from me a promise to find a job. 'My savings can cover us for a couple of months,' she said, having put on a pair of black-framed glasses for the apparent purpose of seeming more business-like, 'but after that we really need to have more than just my income.' I was struck by two aspects of this statement, to wit: did *everybody* know that you had to have savings? Why had no one ever explained this to me? And I wondered to what, specifically, Clio was referring when she mentioned

her 'income'. Her profit-share plays did not show profits. Did she mean the fact that her parents paid her rent? It took me several months to twig: she was claiming the dole. Her acting career – which was, if we're being strictly accurate, more a project of the imagination than a set of verifiable facts on the ground – was being funded by the taxpayer. This didn't really bother me. After all, I had never paid a cent of tax in my life.

4) Clio's various attempts to help me find a job, during which she sat up in bed, her face blue in the screen light of her high-spec MacBook, pointing at drop-down menus headed SECTOR. These headings (PROCUREMENT? DATA ANALYTICS?) meant nothing to me. 'What about hospitality?' Clio said. 'You're good with people.' I refrained from suggesting that *good with people* had only very recently become clickable on the drop-down menu of my personality, and that even then it had only happened because I was frequently high on speed or pills. The problem wasn't limited, in any case, to my personality. My CV listed my 2:2 BA degree and nothing else. 'You have to stay positive,' Clio said. 'I am positive,' I said, swallowing bile.

5) The time I caught a glimpse, more or less by accident, of the recent Google searches on Clio's iPhone. These included 'in a relationship with a narcissist what do' and 'are seahorses real horses'.

6) The first time I met the man who would become my primary drug dealer, Barry 'Baz' Hynes, a former Schools rugby player (an Old Ostrogoth or Vandal) with permanent five-o'clock shadow and the kind of serrated voice

that would have stood him in good stead as a fruit-seller or cigarette-hawker on Moore Street. Baz's ostensible day job was 'nightclub event promoter', but no one who calls himself a nightclub event promoter is not also – is in fact usually primarily – a drug dealer. Baz dealt pills and weed and coke from the pockets of a capacious army-surplus camo jacket that he never took off, even in the basements of crammed clubs or in the saunas that tended to ornament the houses of the parents of his clients. Often the grams of coke he sold came wrapped in glossy pages torn from *Hello!* magazine. I asked Baz, once, if this was intended as some kind of joke or ironic comment on the omnipresent hegemony of consumer-capitalist culture. 'Nah, man,' he growled. 'The old dear just reads *Hello!* magazine. Tonnes of them around the gaff. You know what I mean?' Baz wanted to be an actor (this was how he knew Clio). The first time I met him, at 5 a.m. in the kitchen of someone's house in Ballybough, he recited the 'Tomorrow and tomorrow and tomorrow' speech from *Macbeth* while sipping steadily on a gun-sized vape machine. Once I had sussed that Baz was always holding, I keyed his number into my phone. I must have texted him at least once a day for the next nine months. Christ, what a dispiriting thought.

7) My first real fight with Clio, which was, predictably enough, about money. 'I'm paying for everything,' she pointed out one afternoon, after I had once again failed to spend the day looking for a job. 'I'm paying rent for two people. I'm paying the bills. I'm paying for all the drinks. I'm paying for all the food. And you're just luxuriating in your

own misery.' 'I'm looking for a job,' I said, gesturing vaguely at my laptop. 'No, you're not,' Clio said. 'All you do is sit around all day saying you have a headache.' 'Well, I do have a headache because I'm really stressed.' 'Oh, you're the only one who's stressed. You're the only one who's stressed about this. You're bringing this whole atmosphere of self-indulgent misery into my life and you haven't stopped for *one second* to think about how it's affecting me.' 'Look, I *don't* think I'm the only one who's stressed about this whole situation but I'm in a really difficult position right now and I thought you understood that.' 'You're the ONLY one who's in a difficult position. The ONLY one. That's your whole fucking life. You have *no* idea how stressed it makes me, *waiting* for you to get up off your *arse* and actually DO something with your life.' 'I HAVE NO QUALIFICATIONS,' I said. 'I don't even qualify for the dole because I've never paid any fucking taxes!' 'So you get an entry-level job like a normal fucking person!' Clio said. 'You accept that you're not fucking special! You accept that you were unlucky and you fucking go from there! You're just sponging off me and that's *super* unfair!' (I got out of this argument, incidentally, by bursting into tears. 'Oh, my badger,' Clio said, her face crumpling. 'Come here. I'm sorry.' Et cetera.)

8) The weekly phone calls from my father, which did have the merit of being largely devoid of actual semantic content, but which nonetheless encouraged me to spiral, when they were over, into further paroxysms of rage and self-disgust. 'We, ah, it's strange, being in the house ... Well, you know

what I'm trying to … No news on the legal front, I'm happy to say. No news is good news.' And so on.

9) Various low points, including my first coke nosebleed, my first bad trip (during which I seemed to have become my own unhappy ghost, there in the corner of the club), and my first real visitation from The Fear, in the depths of which I seemed to sense again that nauseating fault in the fabric of reality – the fault that I had last encountered, or sensed, on the afternoon when the ATM spat out my card – and I found myself marooned afresh in a world of vanished purpose, vanished vigour, vanished love. Oh, it was heavy going, taking all those drugs. It really took it out of me. But I held my course. I did. I saw it through. After all, I was committed. I wasn't going to be discouraged by anything so petty as a bout of crippling ontological despair.

10) Various efforts to deflect my parents' curiosity about Clio.

11) Corollary efforts to prevent Clio and my parents from ever actually meeting, not because I was embarrassed by my parents (although I was), or because I was embarrassed by Clio (although I was), but because I was selfishly unwilling to sit through an encounter in which I was constrained not to blurt out the truth ('Clio, this is my mother, an alcoholic, and this is my father, an increasingly mad old man; Mum and Dad, this is Clio, an unemployed actress who takes a lot of drugs').

12) The eventual failure of these efforts, when my father invited Clio and me to Christmas dinner and Clio persuaded me, out of what I now dimly perceive to be actual kindness, to

accept, and we showed up at my parents' house for a meal that took place in an atmosphere of etiolated dread not unlike that of the later verse plays of T. S. Eliot. 'We're in a much stronger position,' my father said, as he tackled a withered turkey that seemed visibly to deflate as he pierced it with a carving knife. 'Some new information on the way. Level the playing field.' He was talking about his legal troubles, although I had explicitly asked him not to. His habitual positivity had taken on a hysterical edge. He reminded me of one of those sadly enterprising homeless people who scrawl uplifting quotes on bits of salvaged cardboard. At the other end of the table my mother held aloft a brandy balloon full of Château Lafite (plainly, the contents of her wine rack had escaped the Great Purge) and squinted at Clio the way a teacher might squint at one of her less intellectually gifted students. Clio seemed oblivious. 'I've heard of, like, these legal cases where the whole thing dragged on for years and then the person was totally acquitted,' she said. My father gave a genial nod. 'We all have our demons to slay,' he said. 'What's that story about the monster, and you have to turn to confront it before it stops chasing you?' *Me:* 'That's not a story, Dad. That's something you just made up.' *Clio:* 'No, I know that one. That's, like, Greek, or something.' *My mother:* 'You must, of course, be intimately familiar with the Greek myths, Clionadh, as a working actress.' *Clio:* 'Oh yeah. Like you end up knowing the plays really well. Like I played Medea in college. And it's *such* an amazing part. It says so much about, like, families and how they relate to each other.' *My mother:* 'Mmm.' 'Your mother hates me,' Clio observed, accurately, as we waited for a cab. 'Don't take it personally,' I said. 'She hates everybody.' (You may be wondering how I paid for Clio's Christmas present. The answer is, I didn't. I wrote her a cute little story about a hippo who gets stuck up a tree and can't get down. He gave plaintive voice to my malaise, that hippo.) 'Has it ever occurred to you,' Clio said, 'that your parents are going through exactly the same thing you're going through right now?' 'No,' I said flatly. 'It hasn't.'

13) Somehow, in the midst of all this, Clio continued to encourage me to write. She also continued to praise in non-specific terms the feeble scraps I did produce – the adventures of the tragic little hippo, for example, or the page of stilted monologue I wrote for her to perform at auditions. Of course, Clio was an actor, which meant that she was constitutionally incapable of distinguishing good writing from bad. But I clung to the frail thread of her regard as if my life depended on it. Which, in a sense too profound to contemplate, it did.

14) Finally, the crux. It was late January. Clio had chipped away at her savings to the point at which my joblessness became impossible to ignore. 'I'm going to ask my parents for a loan,' she said. 'But you obviously can't do that for reasons that are totally not your fault, but still. So you're going to have to get a job. We can't live on one person's dole.' I had made no progress in finding work. That very evening, Clio took this task upon herself, and accomplished in a day what I had failed to do in three months. 'Amber's boyfriend knows this marketing company,' she announced. 'You don't need any experience, they give you all the training you need, and he

says they're hiring.' 'I'll take a look,' I said, hoping to ward off further conversation on this topic. 'You don't need to,' Clio said. 'I already sent them your CV. They're going to call you in the morning.' 'That's amazing,' I said, and my smile felt like rigor mortis even as it wormed its way across my face.

The company for which I interviewed over the phone the next day was called BlueVista Marketing Solutions. A cursory Google search informed me that they provided 'a range of outbound customer experience services', including 'Content Marketing Practice', 'Demand Generation', and 'Targeted B2B Messaging'. Since I had no idea what any of these terms meant, I imagined that my interview would go poorly. But I was wrong. 'You've a good, educated voice,' said the woman who asked me a short series of suspiciously generic Yes/No questions ('I prefer to work as part of a team, Yes or No'). This, along with the fact that I was compelled by circumstances to work for minimum wage, was apparently enough. I was hired. For the first time in my life, I was a salaried employee. I was twenty-seven years old.

'I'm so proud of you,' Clio said. 'I bet you blew them away.'

(DR FELIX: So, in a sense, Clio did exactly what you wanted her to do. She gave you somewhere to live. She found you a job.

ME: Hooray for Clio.

DR FELIX: We often hate the people who've seen us at our weakest moments.

ME: You should be a psychotherapist.)

*

BlueVista's call centre was located in a rented suite of third-floor offices off Capel Street, above a Chinese acupuncturist and below a defunct German export firm. You swiped your badge at a nondescript front door and rattled upwards in a coffin-sized lift. The whole operation was avowedly low-overhead, stopgap, make-and-do. The entranceway was permanently jinxed by the smell of human piss. My co-workers were students working part-time, or – if they were on the full-time roster – drop-outs and dead-enders who had wandered into developmental cul-de-sacs and seemed unclear about what exactly had gone wrong with their lives. Sitting beside me, on that first day and for a hundred days thereafter, was Pete, a bug-eyed headcase in his late forties who had spent twenty years working as a roadie for a band I had never heard of, until a stand-mount speaker had fallen from the stage one morning and broken his spine. Periodically he rose from his desk and straightened, causing his bones to crunch like gravel in a sock.

My job at BlueVista involved wearing a pair of sponge-covered headphones and using dialling software on my PC to call a list of corporate numbers. In this fashion I made four hundred calls a day. When people answered, I read from a prepared script: *Hello, sir or madam, how are you today? My name is Ben and I'm calling from BlueVista Marketing Solutions in Dublin, Ireland, and I'd like to talk to you today about rack servers/ growing your sales funnel/driving intelligence with next-generation networks/turnkey storage solutions.* We were supposed to say *today* a lot: this 'created urgency'. We were also supposed to ask questions to which the answer was yes. 'Get them to say yes three times,' said our Team Leader, Richie Gibbons, 'and you're halfway there.' If the conversation went well, I opened up a spreadsheet and ticked a box. These ticks (or 'leads') were then sold to BlueVista's clients, who presumably used them to initiate some kind of equally vacuous hard sell. What BlueVista did was called B2B (for 'Business-to-Business') Lead Generation. Hearing Richie Gibbons describe this process on my first day, I concluded that B2B Lead Generation was as close to meaningless as any human activity could get without being describable as a persistent vegetative state. But I had no choice: I was broke, and I wanted to avoid another fight with Clio, and it was, I had heard, easier to get a job if you had a job already (although it seemed to me that working for a company like BlueVista meant that I would only ever be hired by more companies like BlueVista, which felt like a fate worse than homelessness or death). Hoping to generate enough leads to meet my daily targets, I dutifully clicked and dialled. After my first week, I sank into a trance of inanition, nine to five. I flopped, slack-limbed, in my broken swivel chair. Every five minutes, Pete stood up and cracked the bones of his poorly knitted spine.

In the mornings, before we slouched to our desks and fitted our headsets, Richie Gibbons gave us a pep-talk. He had once played Gaelic for Tipperary, and as he delivered his morning speeches, he tended to pass a miniature leather football from hand to hand, throwing it up in the air to emphasise a point.

'This is Champion's League stuff, guys, hokay? We need

81

to drive the numbers on this. We need to smile and dial. The smile is as important as the lead, hokay? It's important for us that you're happy. Miserable bastards don't get leads. Now. Shake it handy, and if you can't shake it handy, shake it hard.'

What kind of boss was Richie? Whenever he left the room, people murmured the word *dickhead* under their breath. He sat at his Team Leader's desk with his feet propped up on the laminate and his hands entwined behind his head, looking up at the ceiling like a man suffering himself to be apologetically fellated. He made his own phone calls, which we overheard. 'Here, tell Peter Fitzgerald to fuck someone at IBM so we can get that account, hokay? And tell him – listen, tell him, I don't care if it's a man or a woman, hah?'

On my second day Richie put his hand on my shoulder and said, 'No phones at the desk, yeah? I'm going to have to write you up for that. Fair warning.'

I had been reading a text from Clio that said UR MY BADGER XXX. I put my phone in my pocket and found that I was cringing and blushing simultaneously: cringing as I had in school whenever a teacher dressed me down, and blushing at how much I hated myself for what I had done to my life, or for what had been done to my life: I drew no distinctions, in those bitter days, between the two, which was, I now reflect, a kind of wisdom, in its way.

Every day I spent at BlueVista left behind a residue of humiliation and disgust that stained my evenings like the rings of grime in a dirty bathtub. For a while, even Clio's most candidly depraved sexual propositions failed to rouse me. When I got my first month's paycheque (€1,267.86 net), I bought forty Xanax from Barry Hynes. Popping them at work – one an hour – seemed to help. I slurred my script into my headset: 'An' can I ask about your current data replication environment?'

My former life began to seem impossibly remote. Six months previously I had been loitering around the college library, dreaming of a career as a writer. Now I was marooned in the BlueVista call centre, which, with its moribund ferns and grime-fogged windows, seemed to represent a twilit world of radically lowered expectations. I wondered: *What the fuck am I doing here?* Wasn't I supposed to have leap-frogged over all this entry-level servitude? Wasn't I supposed, by now, to have alighted with gymnastic grace on the fluffy pillows of ferocious solvency? Wasn't that the whole point of people like me? But here I was. Through a concatenation of circumstances that I didn't fully understand, I had been banished to one of capitalism's dingy boiler rooms, where I stoked profits for people I would never meet. Things had gone wrong. It was easy to blame my father. So I did. If he had never been arrested – I told myself – I would never have been forced to take such a dehumanising job. I could have continued to fly first-class through life, aimed at a luxury resort, with acres of legroom, a fully reclining seat, and all the cocktails I could quaff.

Still, there were always drugs, for what they were worth (and they were worth quite a lot, I found). In short order I developed a Xanax tolerance that meant I was unable to fall asleep at night. Lying there in the darkness of Clio's bedroom, I seemed to hear the ticking of an invisible clock: *Tickticktick-tickticktickticktick* ... It seemed loudest in the early hours, when I was most awake.

It's coming, I would whisper to myself as Clio slept obliviously beside me. *It's coming.*

What was coming? More bad news. The summer was already well advanced – it was the beginning of June – when my father called and invited me to a family lunch. He named a stodgily upmarket bistro in Ballsbridge. I was noncommittal. Passing a newsagent's on my way to work that week, I had seen an *Irish Independent* with my father's picture above the fold, captioned with the word CROOK! 'And please extend the invitation to Clionadh,' he said, before coughing, speaking briefly to someone else on the other end, and hanging up.

That was also the morning on which I found several empty jars of baby food in the recycling bin under the sink. Apple and parsnip, potato and broccoli.

Bewildered, I asked Clio: 'Are you eating this?'

'It gives you all the nutrients you need,' Clio said. She was breezy. 'And it's, like, minimal calories.'

'You're eating baby food,' I said.

'They prescribe it for people with IBS,' Clio said.

'Do you have IBS?' I said.

'I have a dicky tummy sometimes,' Clio said.

I wondered, for a while, what to do with this information. In the end I did nothing. ('Did Clio drink a lot of milky coffee?' Dr Felix asked, when I told him about the baby food. 'What the fuck are you talking about?' I said. 'There's a theory,' said Dr Felix, 'that the popularity of milky coffee – you know, places like Starbucks – is because it reminds people of infancy. You know, mother's milk. Maybe Clio was looking for comfort, with the baby food.' 'Why would she have been looking for comfort?' I said. 'Well,' Dr Felix said, 'let's think about that for a minute, shall we?')

Privately I disinvited Clio from lunch with my parents. But before I could say this out loud, she told me that she would insist on coming along. 'It might be weird for you,' she said. 'I'll be there for moral support.'

'Maybe we shouldn't go,' I said.

'You can't run away,' Clio said. 'Nothing bad will happen. Especially if I'm there.'

I studied Clio's face – the dreamy brown eyes, the nose that wrinkled cutely whenever she was puzzled or sad. She was so beautiful. And if the smooth surface of our love was stippled from time to time with argumentative bumps and other negligible irruptions, didn't that just make it texturally all the sweeter? (No, is the answer to this question. It did not.)

'Okay,' I said. 'Just let me do the talking.'

'Of course, honey badger,' Clio said, and kissed me lightly on the cheek.

On the appointed day, I ordered a taxi to Ballsbridge. For actual moral support – despite her best intentions, Clio could have no idea of what we were dealing with here – I tucked a tinfoil scrunchy full of downers into the pocket of my jeans. (I almost wrote: Downers were my drug of choice, whenever a crisis impended. But who am I kidding? *Drugs* were my drug of choice, whenever *anything* impended.) I was taking no chances. I was planning to leave before dessert was served.

As it happened, that was the very afternoon on which I ran into my old school friend James Mullens, and my adventure with The Lads began.

The bistro my father had chosen had been his favourite dinner joint, back when he was the kind of customer whom waiters automatically seated in their spiffiest nook. Now, of course, he was the Typhoid Banker. It was the table by the jacks for us, assuming they didn't actually seat us in a toilet stall. Why did he *do* it? Why did he keep opening himself up to public view like this? Other men in his position, naming no names, have typically hauled their arses Stateside and paid a brute-squad of lawyers to contest the extradition. Why did my father insist on hanging around?

When we arrived, shortly after 1 p.m., my mother was already halfway through her first bottle of Pinot Noir. She leered briefly at Clio and then made a little show of squinting short-sightedly at her menu. My father, on the other hand, rose and greeted us as if he were the maître d'.

'I always have the lamb, whenever I come here,' he said, pulling out a chair for Clio. 'Though I must say, today I'm tempted by the guinea fowl. They do it in a beetroot *jus*. Absolutely delicious.'

He pronounced the word *jus* as if he were a Frenchman saying *juice* in English: *zhoose*. His hair and skin were greyer than I remembered. It was as if he had walked through a cloud of chalk.

I said, 'We can't stay long.'

We kitted ourselves out with napkins, glasses of water. We were, I noted with satisfaction, ringed by a *cordon sanitaire* of empty tables.

Clio was perusing the drinks menu. 'I'm totally having a Bellini,' she said. 'Do you think they have those raspberry Bellinis?' The ominous mood of the gathering had eluded her: lucky for some.

My mother seemed to be attempting to swallow her own upper lip. Beside her, my father was smiling down at his hands. Abruptly he coughed, patted the tablecloth, and said, 'How's the hard-working man?'

I looked around and said, 'Do you mean me? Oh, I'm fabulous. Absolutely tickety-boo.'

Even I was surprised by how bitter I sounded.

I saw the cancelling flicker in my father's eyes as he decided to ignore my tone. 'I have to say I admire you,' he said, avoiding my gaze. 'Some of the most successful men I ever met started out where you are now. Down there in the trenches. Learning the ropes.'

Not for the first time I wondered why I had told my father about BlueVista. When Stalin got sick of Gorky, he set him up in a plush dacha and had a special edition of *Pravda* delivered every morning that contained only the news that

Stalin wanted Gorky to hear. This is what we should all do with our parents.

My mother had a stultified look on her face. 'I'd think you'd be keen to get out of there,' she said.

I took perhaps too much pleasure in saying: 'I haven't got a huge number of options, Mum.'

'Always options,' my father muttered.

I sneered briefly in my father's direction. 'I'm selling my time for money,' I said. 'Like a normal person. I go in, I switch off my brain, I go home.'

'There's a difference between selling yourself,' my mother said from behind her bucket of wine, 'and selling yourself short.'

There was a pause, during which everyone tried to work out what this meant.

'Maybe I'll have a mimosa,' Clio piped up.

'What your mother is saying,' my father said, and stopped.

My mother picked up the conversational baton. 'You haven't asked us for help,' she said.

I felt my brow crease. 'Why the hell would I ask you for help?'

'We're not pariahs,' my mother said. 'We still have connections.'

I looked at the moat of empty tables that surrounded us. 'Is that so?'

'Oh my God,' Clio said. 'I just realised. I shouldn't be ordering expensive drinks. I'm so sorry.'

As far as I was concerned, it was already nuclear-option

time. I excused myself and, ignoring Clio's beseeching glare, bolted for the gents'. Bathrooms in restaurants – don't you find? – exist largely for people who just need a minute. Who just need a minute away from whoever they're with, out there. I liberated two slabs of Xanax from my tinfoil scrunchie and swallowed them with a handful of tap water. After a moment or two, my heartbeat returned to its normal sluggish tempo. I felt a stoic's resolve. Whatever came next, I felt, I could handle it. No big deal. My face in the bathroom mirror looked strangely concave. I was lantern-jawed, pale of brow. I necked another Xanax, just to be on the safe side.

Back at the table my father was ordering champagne. 'Do you have the Laurent Perrier?' he said to the waitress. 'The 2002?'

'I love champagne,' Clio said, inanely. As I resumed my seat she favoured me with a single raised eyebrow, the import of which was unmistakably some version of *Look what you've reduced me to.*

My father proceeded to engage the waitress in a discussion of the farm-to-fork model of sustainability. My mother, pointedly silent, clutched her empty wine glass by the stem. Already my shoulders were slumping: the Xanax was kicking in.

'Champagne,' I said, when the waitress had left. 'We must be celebrating.'

'Living well,' my father said, 'is the best revenge.' He exchanged an inscrutable look with my mother and cleared his throat. 'Actually, this may be the last chance we get to celebrate for a while.'

I thought: *Here it comes.*

'I think it's important,' my father said, 'to look on the bright side. This is a chance to get a fair hearing. It's a chance to state our case clearly and unequivocally before an impartial court. In that sense, it's good news.'

'You haven't,' I said, 'actually told us what the news is yet.'

My mother folded her arms. 'Your father's case is going to trial,' she said.

Clio put a hot palm on my knee.

My father raised his chin. 'This is a positive development,' he said. 'I wouldn't want anyone to think that this alters our position in any way. To all intents and purposes, we're still in exactly the same spot we were in before we heard this news.'

'Well,' I said, 'that's all right, then.'

Our champagne arrived. My mother took the bottle from the waitress and filled both her wine glass and her champagne flute before handing it back.

My father was twisting his wedding ring around his finger. 'Unfortunately,' he said, 'we do have it on good authority that this next bit is going to be heavy weather, in publicity terms.' He lined up his knife and fork on the tablecloth. 'What we'd like to do is limit your exposure,' he said, 'and combine that with, ah, with maximising your opportunities.'

I gave a wise nod. 'I have no idea what you're talking about.'

'How would you like to spend some time in America?' my father said.

The Xanax was pacifying my facial muscles, meaning that I tried to raise an eyebrow and mostly failed.

Beneath the table, Clio's hand was still on my knee. 'We've talked about spending some time abroad,' she said, apparently under the impression that what my father required was encouragement. 'We've never taken a holiday together. Not even a city break.'

My father was looking at me. His eyes – it was one of those quasi-medical conditions – were vaguely egg-shaped and seemed to bulge from their sockets. Without his glasses, his vision was so bad that he had once walked the wrong dog home from the park.

'We have a few bob left in your mother's name,' he said. 'And we've been looking at houses in – where is it?' A glance at my mother, who said nothing. 'Connecticut. A friend of mine, Jim Haines, works for a bank over there. They're always looking for graduates.'

'You're looking at houses,' I said, stupidly. 'In America.'

Clio had abruptly withdrawn her hand from my knee.

'Not for me,' my father said. 'For your mother. And maybe for you. We're talking about an opportunity to start again. Put all of this behind you. And when the trial is sorted, I'll come over.'

'You just want me out of the way,' I said.

I turned to Clio, in search of the promised moral support. But then, involuntarily, I said, 'Oh shit.' Since I had last looked at her, Clio had managed to cover her face with tears. Her lower lip quivered. She jumped to her feet and marched off in the direction of the bathroom, dropping her napkin into a potted plant along the way.

'What the hell,' I said.

My mother sipped champagne. 'She should be on the stage,' she said.

'She is on the stage,' my father said.

My parents laughed in unison: a truly disconcerting sound.

Wearily, I stood up. 'Two minutes,' I said, and followed Clio into the vestibule.

The vampire squid (*Vampyroteuthis infernalis*) turns itself inside out when threatened, to frighten predators. This was a favourite tactic of Clio's, too, especially when she was in one of her acting moods (which tended to coincide, I now perceive, with periods of tension, anxiety, dread, et cetera). Before the door of the ladies' I prevaricated. Clio, I knew, would expect me to play along: to storm in manfully, proffering tissues. But I didn't feel particularly manful, right at that minute. A few yards away, near the cloakroom, a stranger stood, intent on the screen of his phone. He was posed like a model in a Remus Uomo ad – one hand hooked into the slacks pocket of his dark-blue suit, one knee casually bent. A heartbeat later, I recognised him and quailed. Yellow alert! His name was James Mullens, and he was, in all the world, the person I least wanted to run into just then. Taking the hint, I heaved through the twinned oak doors of the ladies' and blinked in the tiled glare. Clio was standing by the sinks, poking at her mascara with a wadded paper towel. Mentally

auditioning various possible approaches – tenderly solicitous? empathetically outraged? – I took the lazy man's course
and settled on crudely bewildered.

'What the fuck just happened?' I said.

Clio met my eyes in the mirror and began, once
again, to weep.

'Come on,' I said. 'Help me out here.'

'You know what just happened,' Clio said.

'I really don't.'

'You didn't even pick up on it,' Clio said. 'They're taking
you *away*. That's the whole point of this lunch. They want
you to go to America and they don't give two *fucks* about
how I feel.'

'How you feel,' I echoed. But I was no longer listening.
Belatedly, it had dawned on me that my father had recently
spoken the following words: *We have a few bob left in your
mother's name.*

In fact, they had enough money to buy a house in America.

There had been no need to cut me off.

They weren't broke.

They never had been.

'Those miserable fucking bastards,' I said.

'They *are* bastards,' Clio said, with a mollified sniffle. 'I
love you. And I think you love me. And they obviously don't
care about that at all.'

'Yeah,' I said. The world tilted beneath me. 'I just have
to . . .' I began. Then I went reeling out into the vestibule . . .

*

... and ran straight into James Mullens. 'Benjamino,' he said, gripping my hand so tightly that my fingers audibly crunched. 'What's the story, man? Long time no see.' He pumped my arm like he wanted my vote. I bared my teeth and my upper lip adhered tenaciously to my Xanax-parched gum. In order to get it unstuck, I was compelled to make a series of wild gurning movements with my mouth as I said, 'James. Hey. How's it going?' My voice was a senile semi-quaver.

'You're looking well,' James Mullens said, appraising me from head to toe as if I were a girl he was sizing up in a club.

Mullens was looking – no denying it – fairly well himself. His bespoke suit seemed to absorb the ambient light. He was clearly one-per-centing it: riding high. Versus me, who belonged, if I belonged anywhere, to the other one per cent – the one on the bottom end.

I scraped together the residue of my *savoir-dire* and said, 'Look, I'm kind of in the middle of—'

But at the same time Mullens spoke: 'How's tricks?'

'Yeah,' I said, after a moment. 'Tricks are ... Yeah.' I wondered how acceptable it would be if I simply walked away and did not look back. What degree of social obligation pertained here? Once upon a time Mullens had been one of our alma mater's foremost creatine-pumped behemoths – I can see him now, trundling down the rucked pitch, wide as a wheelie bin, whamming aside the brick-shithouse fly halves of that week's opposing squad. James 'The Man-Mountain' Mullens, distinguished Old Barbarian, Captain of the Senior Cup Team during my Leaving Cert year: an old school pal, if you prefer, which I did not. We had not been friends in school. I owed him nothing. What business did he have, turning up like this, at the peak or nadir of my troubles?

'Glad to hear it,' Mullens said. He ran his fingers through his hair and favoured me with a look that suggested collusion, complicity, connivance. 'What are you working at, these days?'

At any moment I expected Clio to emerge from the ladies', all set to make the situation worse, or at least exponentially more embarrassing. Without thinking about it, I said, 'Place called BlueVista. It's, uh, marketing.'

'Oh yeah?' Mullens said. 'I heard you were doing a PhD. I was, like, yeah, obviously, smartest guy in our year, of course he's doing the doctorate.'

'I had to put that on ice for a while,' I said.

'Oh, right,' Mullens said. I saw the deduction cross his face: *His father was arrested, he couldn't pay his fees.* 'BlueVista,' he said. 'Is that, like, corporate?'

I tried to nod without nodding. 'I've really got to—'

'Cos I know that world a bit,' Mullens said, 'and the name doesn't ring a bell. I must look them up.'

Mullens, I vaguely remembered hearing, had one of those banking or broking jobs that involve keeping an eye on sums of money as they move, or are moved, around the world, in the process putting on weight, like American tourists. When he said *I know that world a bit*, he was being modest about his success in a way that I recognised from listening to my father talk to his friends.

95

'Yeah,' I said. 'Do that.'

My agitation must have been palpable. Mullens gave me a sidelong look. 'Everything okay, man?' he said, frowning.

'Yeah, grand,' I said automatically. 'Just, you know. Family lunch, or whatever.'

'Ah, here,' Mullens said. 'Fucking 'mare. Am I right? I have lunch with the old man once a month. It's fucking excruciating.'

At that moment the doors of the ladies' swung open and disgorged Clio, who strode up to me, put her hands on her hips and said, 'I don't know if I can stay.'

I caught myself making a warding-off gesture. 'James Mullens,' I said. 'This is my girlfriend, Clio.'

Mullens extended a manicured hand. I watched Clio change gears like a juggernaut on a dual carriageway. 'It's short for Clionadh,' she said, proffering a limp wrist.

'*Enchantée,*' Mullens said. But he was still looking at me, with – I was shocked to discover – something like sympathy. 'I gather you're having a stressful lunch,' he said. 'But here. If you ever fancy a pint, give me a bell, yeah? There's a project you might be able to help me with.' He cocked his head to one side. 'Could be a real opportunity.'

He produced a business card made of an inflexible substance that resembled – but surely could not possibly be – ivory. JAMES MULLENS – BROKER – STANDISH, CURRAN, it said, in minuscule embossed print. 'We'll see what we see.' He winked Masonically. 'And give my best to your old pair, yeah?'

At this point, my memory plays a mean-spirited trick on me: I seem to see Mullens stepping directly into a low-slung red convertible and speeding out of the restaurant with his arm around a blonde girl in the passenger seat. But that can't possibly have happened. Can it?

Glumly, I pocketed his card. Beside me, Clio was standing with her arms folded. Her smile had disappeared. 'I'm serious,' she said. 'I don't think I can actually stay here.'

'No one's asking you to stay,' I said.

Through the dense fronds of a potted palm, I could see my parents, sitting at our table. They were not speaking.

'No one's asking anyone to stay,' I said.

Rehab update. My new prescription pills, whatever they are, have done nothing to help me sleep. I still stay conscious all night long, introspecting in the dark like a brain in a jar. Ugh. Twice a week I haul myself to group and audit my fellow twelve-steppers as they warble and weep about their car-crash lives. Given the choice, I'd rather join the burnt-out cases in the day room, the ones who yammer and screech about their extraterrestrial hook-ups or their homemade tinfoil hats. They, at least, want nothing from me. They, at least, don't care whether I live or die. Ah, God. No more today.

Looking back over the last few pages, I find I want to assert that it wasn't shame that caused me to flinch when James Mullens shook my hand – though certainly I was ashamed: of my parents, my job, my girlfriend, my life. No, it was more like outrage at the workings of fate. Mullens's father was a property developer – in other words, he was also, basically, a banker, like my dad: a mover of money, a shaper of the built world. But Mullens's father remained unarrested, and Mullens had not staked his life on the dream of becoming an artist, and here he was, in his €4,000 suit, checking his heirloom wristwatch as he glided past on his way to make more money. Because of the cruel whimsicality of fate, Mullens's life was a standing reproach to mine. That's what I would have told you, if you had asked me back then. But I should have known better. There is no such thing as fate. There are only people, and the decisions that they make behind your back.

I made it clear to my parents that I regarded their plan – to fly me to America, set me up in a house with my mother, and find me a job in an American bank – as a risible imposition on my time and goodwill. 'Maybe at some point in the future,' my father said, digesting this. His smile (never, to me, particularly convincing qua smile) was now unignorably a grimace of pain.

There was at least one advantage to saying no: Clio took my refusal to go to America as proof of my love for her. 'We're building a life together,' she told me, snuggling close.

I had my doubts about this. But I had practical reasons for staying with Clio. My BlueVista salary would not be enough to pay rent on a place of my own. And my only friends were now Clio's friends. There were also the drugs:

then and always my primary reason for sticking it out with Clio. A Greek philosopher – Aristotle? Plato? – tells us that the soul is a winged chariot drawn by two horses. One of these horses is noble, and is drawn to what is beautiful and true. The other horse is mainly in it for whatever the ancient Greek equivalent of the session was. You can guess which horse was in charge of my chariot that summer. I hoovered up as many drugs as I could borrow or buy. I doubled down on double-dropping. I smoked and rolled and sniffed. If at any point it looked as if I were in danger of sobering up or coming down, well, there was always Barry Hynes, with his coat of many pockets, and there was always Clio, who was perennially ready to hit up the clubs and raves, and who usually had friends who were holding. If I had stopped to think about it, I might have noticed that Clio consistently single-dropped when I double-dropped; that she always took a half when I took a whole; that she made a point of beginning to drink herself down as soon as she came up; and that she never seemed to feel as bad as I did the next day, when all the joy-producing neurotransmitters receded and we were left alone in the apartment with our poor, bare, forked, inhuman selves. But I did not stop to think. Which was, of course, the point. My whole life was about not stopping to think: not for a single second, if I could manage it – and I tried.

In the weeks after that appalling lunch, I found myself brooding obsessively over my encounter with James Mullens. Unwisely, I googled him, and read about his First from Trinity Law, his MBA from Smurfit, his spells at various brokerage houses, his rapid ascension through various junior executive positions. I also googled 'Standish Curran salaries' and almost wept at the figures thus disclosed: it was like reading a list of telephone numbers. I was haunted by the possibility that the difference between Mullens and me was that Mullens knew something I didn't, and that what he knew was both the precise tonnage of reality and where to put the lever if you wanted it to move. The seamless upward curve of his career mirrored so perfectly the seamless downward curve of mine that it was almost beautiful. We had started life from the same point. But our paths had cruelly diverged. I resolved many times never to see him again: to avoid the bars and bistros he frequented, to cross the street if I saw him coming. Then I would start obsessing about him all over again. (Dr Felix calls this 'ruminative thinking', and cautions me against it. But what the fuck other kind of thinking is there?)

Towards dawn every morning, as I lay awake with an army of importunate chemicals marching across the gaps between my neurons, I listened to the ticking clock, getting faster, getting louder.

Ticktickticktickticktickticktick . . .

Every St Augustine inmate who is neither certifiably catatonic nor demonstrably insane is sooner or later assigned an hour of 'occupational therapy'. Mine involved washing dishes in the cafeteria kitchen. Only dishes: there is no cutlery (no knives, no forks, no spoons: no suicides at the dinner table).

Marigold gloves. Big sink. Foamy suds. Rinse plate. Stack. Repeat. The process had, for me at least, a certain novelty value. I would have enjoyed it more if I had been left alone. But Dr Felix kept me company. He did no rinsing or stacking. Instead he propped himself against the door of a stainless-steel fridge and looked at his phone. I rinsed, stacked.

'So as well as treating us for addiction, you're also exploiting our labour,' I said.

'Tell me about your uncle,' Dr Felix said. 'The one who died.'

'This again.'

'Gratify my curiosity.'

'I didn't really know him.'

'Tell me what you remember.'

'Frank. Big guy. Hair growing out of his ears. Wore wellies the whole time.'

'A farmer.'

'My parents thought it was *déclassé* to come from farmers.'

'I doubt your parents thought that. But you clearly did.' Dr Felix scratched the tip of his nose. 'Did he look like your father?'

'I suppose.'

'Families come out of families,' Dr Felix said. 'They bring the other families with them. Did your father love your uncle?'

'How the fuck should I know?' *Families come out of families.* What kind of platitudinous inanity was this?

'You know.'

'Yes,' I said. 'I suppose he did.'

'What did he die of? Your uncle.'

'Cancer.'

'What kind?'

'I don't know. Pancreas, I think.'

'That's a bad death.'

'Okay.'

'Your father saw it. He saw his brother die.'

'He never talked about it.'

'Did you ever ask him?'

I snorted: as if that was the sort of thing that families did.

Dr Felix stood with his back pressed against the stainless-steel fridge door and looked up at the yellow rectangles of fluorescent lighting. 'People change, when they go through something like that.'

'It's a theory,' I said.

'Theories are all we have,' Dr Felix said. 'With the right one, you can move the world.'

'I'll take your word for it,' I said.

Three days after our lunch in the bistro my father texted me to say: TRIAL DATE SET FOR 2ND OCT SRY TO BER BAD NEWS X (he was an inveterate all-caps texter). I did not reply. Nor did I reply when he sent a follow-up message: OTHRWISE ALL GOOD. I had decided to cut off all communications. The only reason I didn't change my phone number is that I couldn't afford a new SIM card.

*

In mid-June I scored some Zimovane from Barry Hynes, which temporarily cured my insomnia. Things were not what you would call good. But they were, broadly speaking, stable. And stability was all I wanted out of life, having so bravely (I told myself) learned to live without hope.

It was early in July when I went with Clio to a rave in the abandoned premises of a big-box hardware outlet on the Naas Road. You could hear the music, like the pounding of jackboots, from three streets away. Inside, we hastily dropped and danced, as if we were trying to get some unpleasant business over and done with. Along the warehouse walls lay DIY materials: long beige planks of medium-density fibreboard, stacked white tins of mould-proof paint. In one corner a whole display kitchen stood, chrome fixtures and eggshell-blue cabinets beaming through the skewed light like a flashback in a ghost story.

After an hour, I lost track of Clio and went in search of water. I found myself standing in the display kitchen, where someone had piled bottles of water by the sink. 'SINK,' I said to a man I didn't know. 'WATER.'

'MAKES SENSE,' he said, giving me the thumbs up.

An excellent interaction: I congratulated myself. The pills made the water taste like battery acid. But I was feeling chipper: no complaints. The world made sense. It made sense because it no longer had me in it.

On the warehouse walls above me were plasma-screen TVs. On their ranked screens, women in bikinis stood under waterfalls and ran their fingers through their hair. It may have been a music video or it may simply have been generalised aspirational pornography. It was difficult to tell.

'Benjamino!' a voice said. 'Hey, man! What's the craic?'

I turned to see the man who shouldn't have been there, and greeted him as if we were old friends.

'I HAVEN'T BEEN ON A PROPER MAD ONE IN AGES,' James Mullens yelled.

'YEAH, ME NEITHER,' I yelled back, although of course I had been on a proper mad one the previous weekend, and the weekend before that, and all the other weekends before that.

We were still in the display kitchen. Mullens had propped his fly-half bulk against the countertop. He was wearing jeans and a logoless white T-shirt. But a basic aura of corporate formality lingered. The effect was oddly like that of running into your school principal on his day off.

'WHAT ARE THE CHANCES OF RUNNING INTO YOU AGAIN?' he said, putting a warm hand on my shoulder.

'I KNOW,' I said.

'I WAS, LIKE, THERE'S NO WAY THAT'S BEN,' Mullens said.

'YEAH,' I said.

As high conversations go, this was actually pretty lucid: practically Wildean, in fact, by the standards of my usual Saturday-evening chats.

'IT WAS AMAZING, RUNNING INTO YOU THE

OTHER DAY,' Mullens said. 'I HOPE I WASN'T RUDE OR ANYTHING.'

'YOU'RE NEVER RUDE,' I said.

The problem with being high on MDMA – as I am scarcely the first to observe – is that it tends to make you say the first nice thing that comes into your head. The other problem with being high on MDMA is that it tends to make you *believe* the first nice thing that comes into your head, which is perhaps more of a problem than it might at first appear.

'THANKS, MAN,' Mullens said. He shook his head fondly. 'THAT'S A REALLY NICE THING TO SAY.'

There followed some guff about how we had always admired each other but had always been too shy to say it out loud.

Mullens tilted his head back appraisingly. 'How are you doing, like, actually?' he said. (I think I'll forgo the ALL-CAPS SHOUTING, henceforth, for my own convenience. You can safely assume that everything we say is being screamed at maximum volume.)

'I'm not too great, if I'm honest,' I said.

And just like that, my buzz went sour: as if my heart had turned some secret interior corner and led me into a mono-chrome alley of panic and dread. Hearing the words I had just spoken, I experienced a *grand mal* seizure of regret. I think I actually reached my arms out hungrily, as if to claw back the past ten seconds of my life.

But it was too late. Mullens was nodding. 'I looked into that crowd you're working for,' he said. 'BlueVista. Bit of a Mickey Mouse operation, no?'

I was shivering. 'Yeah,' I said, helplessly. 'I couldn't find anything better.'

'I don't mean to pry,' Mullens said. 'Like, tell me to fuck off or whatever.'

'You're not prying,' I said. I could smell his aftershave. His sculpted muscles, packed tightly in his tight T-shirt, made me think of the word *beefcake*. This was disturbing. *You're just high,* I thought. *You almost certainly don't want James Mullens to actually fuck you.* The bolus of chewing gum in my mouth was irritating my gag reflex. My eyes were rolling backwards in my skull. I had the presence of mind to say, 'I'm in no fit state for this conversation.'

But I must have mumbled, because Mullens said, 'WHO?'

I shook my head.

Mullens carried on. 'I look at you,' he said, 'and I see a guy who should be doing something better with his life.'

The two pills I had taken earlier that evening were now definitively wearing off. What I needed was to take two more. But, in a foolish and highly uncharacteristic gesture of trust, I had left my stash with Clio. Desperately, I scanned the warehouse, trying to peer between the stuttering flares of dancefloor light. Every girl I saw looked just like Clio: the black hair cut in a fringe, the minuscule glittery dress.

'That card I gave you,' Mullens was saying. 'It's out of date. I'm not with Standish anymore.' He dug around in the pocket of his jeans and handed me another business card. I was too high to read what it said. 'Me and a few of the lads,' he said. 'We're setting up a right.'

'A right?' I said. I blinked in an effort to dispel my creeping double vision. 'A right to what?'

'No, REIT, R-E-I-T,' Mullens said. 'Real Estate Investment Trust. We're looking for good people. There's a project. I can't say much about it. But it might be worth thinking about.'

My stomach lurched. With a sense of mild fatalism, I now accepted that I was going to be sick.

'Okay,' I said, waving Mullens away. 'I'll give you a bell.'

'I don't want you to think of this as me doing you a favour,' Mullens said. 'We need smart people. And, like I say, smartest guy in our year.'

'Yep,' I said. 'Great.' I swallowed bile.

'Don't take too long to think about it, okay?' Mullens said. 'The timeline is fairly short on this. I'd need to hear from you by the end of the week.'

'Roger that,' I said.

'Keep it,' Mullens said, indicating the business card, which was apparently still in my hand.

With some difficulty (my pockets seemed to have sewn themselves shut, and my hands had somehow transformed themselves into fingerless flippers), I pocketed the card. When I looked up, James Mullens had vanished.

'Do you ever get bored, doing this every weekend?' Clio said, later that evening – or perhaps it was early the next morning. We were lying on the floor of a blacked-out basement flat, staring up at the ceiling and caressing one another with fond, compulsive gestures. I had no idea who owned the flat, or where in the city it might be located. The people around us were strangers, but they had become our friends in the way that people become your friends when you take ecstasy with them: that is, as if for the sake of argument.

'Bored?' I said. I thought about this for a minute. Then I said, 'I don't understand the question.'

The next afternoon, when I found Mullens's new business card in my pocket – this one seemed to have been forged or moulded from some space-age material: titanium, iridium – I threw it in the recycling bin in what I still very much thought of as Clio's kitchen. If I was going to escape from BlueVista (and somewhere in the back of my mind I knew that if I didn't escape from BlueVista, and from the life that I had stumbled into more generally since my father had announced his bank-ruptcy, I would be finished, as a functioning human being, in another couple of years), it wasn't going to be with his help.

It was, I now reflect, perfectly in character for James Mullens to offer me a job with his incomprehensible new company. This was the sort of thing he did. Back in Fifth Year he had gone to some trouble to befriend a boy named Richard Maguire. Richard had suffered from a syndrome of some kind that manifested as a sequence of compulsive jerks – every five or six seconds, as we sat in class, Richard would wince and blink and then abruptly duck his head, before snapping it upright again with a cough or snarl. *AaaGHM!*

was the sound he made. Imitations of Richard's tic became hard social currency among what passed for our school's elite. 'Here, Richard – *AaaGHM!*' 'Yeah, *AaaGHM!* Ha, you all right there, Richard?'

James Mullens put a stop to this. He stood up in front of the class one morning before our teacher arrived and sent Richard out of the room. Then he said, 'My cousin has ME. She can't walk down the street by herself. She can barely get out of bed. What do you think she needs, lads? Do you think she needs the piss ripped out of her? Or do you think she needs a bit of a helping hand, now and then?'

His point was taken. No one ever imitated Richard Maguire again.

Now Mullens was going out of his way to help me. He knew all about my father's arrest, and about CAB's seizure of our family's assets, and about my failure to complete my PhD. He knew all about BlueVista (I pictured him scanning their website with a look of scornful pity on his face). I was in trouble: everybody knew it. And since helping me now fell within the scope of Mullens's powers, he was bound by the Old Barbarian code to offer me a job.

And since I was equally bound by the tattered remnants of my own ethical code, which went something like *Stay away from the philistines,* I said no. Oh, sure: I hadn't read a book in months. Oh, sure: the idea that I might one day be a writer now surfaced only during the most caustic of my nocturnal bouts of self-recrimination. But I had my dignity, in a way.

Mullens had asked me to call him before the end of the

week. Pointedly, I did not. I went to work at BlueVista and I drank cheap red wine with Clio and I helped her prepare for her latest audition and I made no effort to retrieve Mullens's card from the recycling bin.

As far as I was concerned, Mullens's proposal was exactly the sort of offer that my father had been making since I was old enough to work: of a job that looked like a sinecure but was really a trap; a job that you couldn't leave because you had been hired as a favour and were now permanently indebted to your boss, or to your boss's boss, or to your boss's boss's boss; a job that immured you for thirty years in an airless world of slapped backs and hail-fellow chit-chat with men who still talked about the class trips they had taken in their teens.

I'd need to hear from you by the end of the week, Mullens had said. The week ended. I did nothing.

And that was that.

On Monday morning I arrived at the BlueVista offices to find an email from Richie Gibbons, my Team Leader, in my inbox. COACHING SESSION 09.30, it said. 'How's she cuttin'?' Richie said when I reported to his desk. 'Feeling good about the new campaign?'

Since any given campaign was indistinguishable from any other, it was more or less impossible to tell when a new one had begun. I gave the standard answer: 'Yeah, looks good.'

'I'm looking at your numbers,' Richie said. He retouched his gelled quiff with a tentative pinkie. 'I'm sure you're looking at them yourself.'

I was not. 'Holding steady, I thought,' I said.

'What were you yesterday, six? Seven?'

'It's a tough campaign,' I hazarded (this was a strategy that had worked in the past).

Through a gap in the partitions, I saw two of the part-timers wheeling themselves to the water cooler in their castored chairs. It was like watching an all-paraplegic remake of *Night of the Living Dead*.

'Is it the campaign,' Richie said, 'or is it the attitude?'

'It's the campaign,' I said.

Richie sat up. 'Look,' he said. 'This is a metrics game. That's the business we're in. And I look at the numbers and they tell me you're below target for three weeks running. Your own commission tells the story. You could be pulling down big bucks on this campaign.'

Big bucks? My commission had never risen above €70 per month, and was in fact capped at €130. I said, 'Well. I mean, come on. The targets are just made up anyway, aren't they?'

'See, this is the attitude, hokay?' Richie said. He was avoiding my gaze. He was also blushing, as if he found our conversation embarrassing. But he was not embarrassed: he was angry. 'It's attitude that drives the numbers, up or down. Yeah? You're out there on the floor and you've a face on you like a miserable cunt. And when I say miserable cunts don't get leads, what do I want to see? Do I want to see a room full of miserable cunts?'

This question struck me as essentially rhetorical, so I said nothing.

'Do you know what staff churn is like in a place like this?' Richie said. 'There's twenty lads queuing up to take your job.'

'Really?' I said, genuinely surprised.

Richie reclined once again. 'I'm going to future-forward on this, hokay?' he said. 'And what we want to see is that this time next month, we're gonna be hitting every one of those targets. Otherwise, we're looking at disciplinary action. Hokay?'

'. . . Hokay,' I said.

'Hokay,' Richie said, looking satisfied.

At lunchtime (I was on Capel Street, solacing myself with a cigarette), my phone rang: WITHHELD NUMBER. Like a moron, I pressed ACCEPT.

'I don't know if you got my texts,' my father said.

'You didn't send me any texts,' I said, sighing a cloud of cigarette smoke into the petrol-tainted foliage of an ornamental urban shrub. On my way to work that morning I had passed the usual newspaper kiosk and seen, on the front page of the *Irish Times*, the headline JUDGE TO RULE ON ATLAS TAPES.

'No, leave it over there,' my father said. He appeared to be talking to someone else on the other end. 'No, in the corner. Ben? Are you there?'

I said, 'Is there an actual point to this call?'

'I just wanted to let you know that we're sending your mother over to – where is it? – Connecticut for a week or two, you know, for house-hunting purposes.'

'That's fascinating, Dad.'

'The option is there, I'm saying, for you to go along.'

'Bye, Dad.'

'We're not talking luxury hotels here,' my father said. 'Motels. Cheap motels. Just while she looks around. We could set up some meetings for you. Give you a sense of your options.'

I looked up. Across the street, James Mullens was leaning against a parked car – not a red convertible after all, but rather a voluminous black Mercedes: the sort of car that looked as if it worked part-time as a nightclub bouncer.

My father was still talking. I ended the call and stood there, strangely immobilised, as James Mullens sauntered towards me.

'You tore up my business card,' he said, from behind his aviator shades.

My heart revolved. 'How the fuck did you know that?'

'It's what I would have done,' Mullens said. He coughed into the crook of his arm. Across the street was a dental clinic whose scrolling digital readout promised ROOT CANAL – VINEERS – EXTRACTIONS – LOWEST PRICE. 'I wanted to say sorry. I was mashed off my tits the other night. I'm pretty sure I came across as a condescending prick.'

The urge came over me to say: *You could never be a condescending prick!* How odd, I thought, that I should feel like saying this, even though I was no longer high.

I said, 'I don't think either of us was at our best.'

Mullens laughed. 'No. But still.' He stood with his hands in his pockets, still looking away. 'I don't want to be a white knight, or whatever. I said I don't want you to think of this as a favour. But that's bullshit. It's totally a favour. But listen. Favours are how it works. And you don't do favours for people you think are dickheads. You get me?'

I looked up, at the section of sky closed off by the grimy roofline. Clouds hovered, white and frilly. It was like looking at the window of a bridal boutique. With palsied hands I brought a fresh cigarette to my mouth and lit it. 'Favours are how it works,' I said.

'Setting up this whole REIT thing,' Mullens said. 'I needed a shitload of capital. Where do you think I got it from? You think I saved it up?'

I said nothing.

'This is a serious offer,' Mullens said. 'It's a real job and good money. But I want to be completely on the level with you. What we're doing isn't, by shall we say certain standards, one hundred per cent kosher.'

'And what standards are those?' I said.

'It's not illegal,' Mullens said. 'I've no interest in that. Let's say we're exploiting a loophole. I don't know, some people might have ethical issues with it. But I wouldn't be doing it if it was proper shady.'

'Wouldn't you?' I said. I was doing my best to sound hard-boiled. My shaking hands were probably undermining the effect somewhat.

'You know me,' Mullens said. He took off his shades and squinted at me. 'I'm taking a risk here, is what I'm saying. I'd like to be working with people I trust.'

'On the evidence of my family,' I said, 'you'd be pretty stupid to trust me.' Now where had *that* come from?

'You're not your dad,' Mullens said, with some vehemence. 'I wouldn't ever think anything like that. And neither would the other lads.'

'These other lads,' I said. 'Who are we talking, here?'

Mullens shrugged. 'Sean Sweeney. Bobby Hayes. You'd know them.'

I would know them: they were the Old Barbarian Senior Cup team from my Leaving Cert year. I had spent my whole life avoiding them.

'The best of the best,' I said.

'You probably think they're all thick as shit,' Mullens said. 'And compared to you they probably are. But they're not fucking around when it comes to making money.' He put his shades back on: a nice effect, I thought. 'And neither am I.'

'So you're doing me a favour,' I said.

'I'm doing you a favour,' Mullens said. 'I'm telling you I've got a can't-lose opportunity here, a bit hush-hush, not spreading it around. And you can be in on it. Just come for a drink with me. We'll talk details.'

I checked the time on my phone. My lunch hour was almost over. Upstairs, Richie Gibbons was waiting for me, with another new campaign.

'The Radisson,' Mullens said. 'Half seven. No hard sell.'

He handed me another business card. It glinted blackly in the fume-laden sunlight.

*

Early this morning – it was 3 a.m. – Piotr the Ukrainian security guard foiled my attempt to crack the keypad code on the day-room fire door. I hadn't gotten far. I had, in fact, managed only to ascertain that the code was not 1-2-3-4 when Piotr loomed up behind me, silent as a ninja, and shook his head, making a *tut-tut* noise and pointing towards my cell. It wasn't that I was trying to escape – well, all right, I may have been planning to flag a cab to town and buy some pills from the tenement housewives who sell their prescription downers on the boardwalk by the river, but I fully intended to come straight back to St Augustine the minute I had scored. This argument cut no ice with Piotr. He clamped my left wrist in one spadelike paw and dialled up Dr Felix on his pager. The good doctor – does he sleep in his office? What the hell was he doing here at 3 a.m.? – walked me back to my cell. As usual, he wanted to chat. Dialogue only – I can't be bothered with the usual stage business. Not tonight. (Strangely, the Doc made no allusion to my efforts with the keypad, as if it didn't matter. As if it was the sort of thing that happened all the time.)

DR FELIX: You wanted to be a writer.

ME: Why do you keep asking me that?

DR FELIX: I'm not asking anything. I'm stating. That was your ambition.

ME: It was a daydream.

DR FELIX: What's the difference?

ME: I was fucking deluded. Okay?

DR FELIX: And yet, when an opportunity came your way, you thought: *Hey! I might use this to become a writer after all!*

ME: No. I wanted to be rich. I thought I *might* write a book. As a hobby.

DR FELIX: Come on.

ME: This is my stop.

(We had arrived at the door of my cell.)

DR FELIX: Why did you want to write?

ME: What do you want me to say? I wanted a nice life. Fame. Money. Not having to do anything.

DR FELIX: Some jobs are instrumental. You do them so you can pay for what you really want to do. Have kids. That sort of thing. But some jobs are the point. You do them so you can put something in the world. What do you want to put in the world?

ME: You're nicer at night.

DR FELIX: I asked you a question.

ME: I don't want to put anything in the world. What I want to do is take myself out of the world. One way or another.

DR FELIX: You're out of the world right now. Call it a period of seclusion. But sooner or later you'll have to go back.

ME: We'll see.

Stalemate, I think. For now.

No hard sell. When I arrived in the dining room of the Radisson at 7.30 that evening, I found Mullens dressed in gym gear: a sleeveless nylon top, skin-tight cycling shorts and a pair of box-fresh running shoes.

'I missed my workout this morning,' he said. 'You don't mind if I get in a quick one, do you? You're welcome to join.'

I thought of the two Xanax I had swallowed on the bus. 'I'll just wait in the bar,' I said.

Mullens frowned. 'You've no kit,' he said. 'Here, I'll tell you what. You can borrow my spare.'

'I really don't—'

'The gym here is pretty solid,' Mullens said. He was already striding through reception. 'What do you do, bench-press? Row?'

Seeing no alternative, I trotted after him. 'I, eh, I row a bit,' I said.

'You want to balance a workout,' Mullens called over his shoulder. I followed him down some stairs and along a series of corridors. 'I try to do two hours a day. Don't always have the time. Like today I had a meeting with these VC guys at seven a.m. and then just emails back and forth all day.'

I wondered what VC stood for, apart from Viet Cong. We arrived at a glass wall, through which the hotel gym was broadcasting its motion frieze of tame gay porn. Mullens thrust a sports bag into my arms. 'Spare kit.'

'I should really just wait in the bar,' I said.

Mullens said, 'Sure, hop on the rowing machine. I'll only be half an hour.'

In the locker room (it was, as I had feared, a humid orchid-arium of dangling testicles), I changed into Mullens's spare tracksuit bottoms and some sort of nylon T-shirt and then joined him on the gym floor, which, with its pumping dance tunes and defining air of diligent solipsism, eerily resembled a rave, except that nobody seemed to be having any fun.

Mullens strapped or wedged himself into a machine shaped like an iron maiden and began moving parts of it with his arms and legs.

'Some of the lads are into four or five hours every day,' he said, in a level voice. 'I used to be mad into it back in school but the whole career thing kind of takes over, you know?'

The rowing machine was a few feet away. I eyed it, thinking of my father, tugging along in his tattered old Fred Perry golf shirt. If he could manage it – I reasoned – so could I. Gamely, I tackled the machine. After a few minutes Mullens disengaged himself from his iron maiden and gently showed me how to strap my feet into the stirrups.

'It's a different model to the one I normally use,' I explained, hotly.

'They're actually fairly standard,' Mullens said. 'Here.' He pressed some buttons on the LCD screen. 'That's your metres, that's your time, that's your split.'

'Of course,' I said.

Mullens departed for the far end of the gym, where he began lifting silver barbells steadily, frowning at himself in the floor-to-ceiling mirror. I began pulling on the handle of the rowing machine. The machine kicked up a busy whirr beneath me. I kept pulling. There seemed to be something wrong with the machine. There also seemed to be something wrong with my stomach, and also with my arms and with my legs. I pulled on the handle again, and then I pulled some more. I felt I had a pretty good rhythm going, for a while. Then the situation deteriorated. I was pulling not just against the machine but against the inertia of my Xanax-softened limbs. The blood had drained from my head and I was feeling a strong urge to take a nap. All at once the contents of my stomach presented themselves at the back of my throat. I panic-swallowed and stopped rowing. I looked at the screen. It said that I had rowed thirty-two metres. The elapsed time said 1.17. My skin had broken out in a fever sweat. I took several deep breaths to calm myself down and then vomited profusely all over the floor of the gym.

Fifteen minutes later, my humiliation was more or less complete: Mullens had finished his workout, showered, and changed into a €6,000 suit while I – no, hang on. This account is already an exercise in self-abasement. Let's just skip over the part where I was forced to point out my pile of vomit to the gym trainer and stand there, mumbling apologies, while she mopped it up. Let's also skip over the part where I shamefacedly explained to Mullens why I had been obliged to curtail my workout and, while we're at it, let's breeze past Mullens's suggestion that he call his GP ('Seriously, it's not something you should just ignore'). Let's just take all that as read, shall we, and go straight to the part where Mullens puts down his Martini and says:

'Serbia.'

We were upstairs, in the residents' bar. The decor was pseudo-*moderne*: globular lighting and wingback chairs in on-trend teal. My hands were shaking, conspicuously. Mullens's hands, equally conspicuously, were not.

I said, 'Serbia,' just to stall for time.

Mullens handed me his phone. The screen displayed a revolving computer graphic: a three-dimensional blueprint that evolved into something that looked like a palatial hotel.

'An eighteen-hole golf course,' Mullens said. 'Designed by a pro. A driving range. Serviced apartments. A luxury day spa. A crèche. A Michelin-starred restaurant. An artificial beach. You can buy or you can visit. Doesn't look too bad, does it?'

'You're building this,' I said.

'I'm not building shit,' Mullens said. 'I'm getting some other suckers to build it. This is the pilot project. You know what a REIT is.'

I said nothing.

Mullens propped his right ankle on his left knee. 'We're talking 2013. You have all these financial institutions looking to deleverage. So the REIT comes in and snaps up the asset for half nothing. Fair enough. But the side effect is, it opens up the market for a whole new range of property ventures. You get me?'

I sipped my cocktail: a rum and Coke. Mullens's words seemed to be coming to me as if from a great distance – as if they were broadcasts from Alpha Centauri picked up by an orbital satellite and relayed, with considerable degradation of signal, to a poorly tuned radio in my head. I had no idea what *deleverage* meant.

'Let me tell you a story,' Mullens said. 'There's a bunch of businessmen. Honest guys. They're living in a country that's still getting over a war. Cities are still bombed out of it. The state is applying for EU membership but it's not official yet. Our lads are looking to make some money. They want to attract investment, but they've got a problem. Their country was on the wrong side of the war. They're the bad guys, according to everyone. The countries next door – we're talking Croatia, we're talking Romania, we're even talking *Bosnia* – they're tourist hotspots now. People from Western countries are lying on the beaches, they're buying shit in the shops. And these lads in Serbia, they're looking around, going, *How do we get in on this?*'

Without appearing to have ordered two more drinks, Mullens had ordered two more drinks. Playing along, I made a vague effort to recall some details about the Balkan Wars, which had ended – my recollection was hazy – during my last year of primary school.

'What I'm saying is, these lads are *desperate*,' Mullens said. 'Their government is doing fuck-all to help them. They're in a situation where, if someone from a rich country comes along and says, *Let's do a deal*, they're not in a position to say no. Are you with me so far?'

'Sure,' I said.

On the table between us was a folder of black cardboard. This Mullens now held aloft.

'Here's where it gets, uh, a bit dicey,' he said. 'We've found a loophole in the double-taxation convention between Ireland

122

and Serbia. I'd explain it to you, but to be honest, I'm not a hundred per cent sure I understand it myself. What I do know is what it means. It means we have to put down less than five per cent of the initial capital.'

In an effort to halt the flow of Mullens's spiel, I said: 'The initial capital on what, exactly?'

'The golf resort,' Mullens said, shaking his head as if to ward off a mosquito. I felt, rather than saw, his muscles exert themselves in an effort of self-control. 'We had the lads at Healy-Dunlop draw up the plans. It's based on the K Club.'

'And you want to build this golf resort,' I said, 'in Serbia.'

As I may have said before, nothing gets past old Ben.

'It costs fuck-all to draw up the plans,' Mullens said. 'The real work is finding the site, getting the permits, tendering the contracts. But we won't be doing any of that. We'll just be coming in, waving our money around, and going home. The way it's going to look, we're throwing in a sixty per cent stake. This is how we convince the Serbs to get on board. The way it's actually happening, we're throwing in five per cent. They're going to be left looking for government tax breaks to offset the difference. They're tied up in applications to two governments. Meanwhile we've sold off plans to a few lads we know. They're holding the bag and we're out of there. Boom. Gone.'

This made no sense to me. But I remembered that money, like God, needed only faith to work. In any case, I grasped the gist.

'You're defrauding them,' I said.

Mullens pursed his lips. 'Not defrauding. Taking advantage of a loophole.' He uncrossed his legs and leaned forward suddenly. 'We've checked these guys out. They don't know what they're doing. They can't believe we're willing to get into bed with them. They're lying awake at night dreaming of living in a country where rich people spend money on trips to five-star resorts. We dangle that dream in front of their faces.' He sipped his Martini. 'Imagine where Ireland was thirty years ago. That's where these guys are now. And we're like fucking Americans, coming in, flashing the cash. We're not breaking the law. We're just working for our own advantage.'

'I'm struggling,' I said, 'to see what my job would be. Theoretically.'

'Theoretically.' Mullens smiled. 'Let's say we call you a Development Consultant. We go over there. We wear some fancy suits. We talk up a storm. We get them to sign. Maybe we visit the site. What I need from you is to talk a good game. Maybe even write the ad copy. The lads I'm working with, they're smart guys but they're not – what's the word? – rhetoricians. You know what I mean? I need someone who can bamboozle these fuckers with some fancy lingo. That's your job. Get them to sign. As soon as they do, we're in the black. And I mean majorly in the black.'

'How majorly?' I said.

'Current calculations?' Mullens said. He paused for effect. 'Seven figures. High seven figures. Each.'

I coughed.

Mullens was still leaning forward. 'I'm putting myself out

there,' he said. 'Telling you this. This is within-four-walls stuff. Maybe six people know the details. You're number seven. It's a lucky number.'

'What's the, uh,' I said, scrabbling to sound businesslike, 'the timeline? When do they sign?'

'We go over there in two months,' Mullens said. 'End of September. They wine us and dine us. We get names on contracts. We come home. And all of a sudden we're a lot better off. All you need to do is come on board as Development Officer, or whatever the fuck. We can do that tonight.' He scooped up his phone and stood. 'I've to make a quick call. You can take a few minutes to think about it.' He stopped. 'I'll say one more thing. I left a good job for this. I'm in the wind. Do you seriously think I'd have taken a risk like that if there was even the *tiniest* fucking chance of this going tits-up?'

He waggled his phone beside his ear and walked off towards the lobby.

'No hard sell,' I said aloud.

I'd like to say that at this point I finished my drink and left, and that James Mullens returned from his undoubtedly strategic phone call to find nothing but an empty seat and a lingering sense of outraged propriety. But I wouldn't be writing these words if that were so. Instead I propped one ankle on the opposite knee, as if to imagine how it might feel to be James Mullens, pitching shady deals in an upscale hotel bar. As soon as Mullens had said *Seven figures*, my imagination had lit up with a vision of the future. It was a multiform vision – it conjured many places. It was, in fact, a vision of possibility itself. I saw myself in a beach hut on a tropical shore, freed from financial anxiety, enjoying another mai tai sunset. Or ensconced in a log cabin on some misty peak, writing (like a twenty-first-century Thoreau) about the fruits of the day's mellow introspections. It occurred to me that this was how I had always wanted to live: alone, in dreamy pastoral seclusion. I might write a novel. I might not. The point was not to become a writer. (Take that, Dr F!) The point was to escape from the narrow range of possible lives that had been offered to me by my family, my education, my country of birth. This, I saw in a flash of insight, was what *becoming a writer* had meant to me all along.

And now I was being offered a much less arduous path to the promised land, a path that did not involve years of painful graft and disappointment, a path that involved no grim negotiations with my own fragile ego, or with the fragile egos of my parents, or of my friends. All I had to do was hang out with some old school pals for three months, act like a businessman, take advantage of the poor suckers that Mullens had targeted with his scam, and then I would be rich enough to remake my life for ever. I could sublime, like dry ice, and drift into a higher sphere of being. Art, it turned out, was a blind alley. Only from atop the mountain of achieved wealth could the world's eye adequately be met.

For a glorious moment I envisioned it: waving goodbye to Clio, placing myself beyond the reach of my father and his hideously public disgrace. It was, I thought, typical: in the person of James Mullens – a man I had always regarded as a pompous dickhead, a man who embodied precisely the world I wanted so desperately to leave – fate was offering me the greatest opportunity I had ever been given.

All of which is an elaborate way of saying that as I sat there in the residents' bar of the Radisson, chewing on an ice cube that still tasted of rum and Coke, I decided to say yes to Mullens's offer: with a single proviso, a single *sine qua non*, details to be clarified before I signed a single sheet of paper.

By the time Mullens returned – and here he comes, steering his way among the bar's herded leather couches, followed by a blonde woman in a little black dress – I was a man with a plan.

'This is Nikki,' Mullens said, placing a hand on the woman's lower back in such a way as to establish, for my benefit, that she was his girlfriend.

Nikki smiled and shook my hand, somehow conveying through these unemphatic gestures a perceptiveness of such depth and scope that I looked away in shame. How long had it been since I had found myself in the presence of an intelligent human being? (How do we know intelligence when we see it? It's in the eyes, isn't it? It's all in the eyes.) Suddenly I wanted to hide my bloodshot peepers and my sweat-slicked brow and my limp hair and my lazy-man's stubble, and offer Nikki a frank and open smile – it was the least she deserved. But my face had long since been closed for emotional business. All I could manage was a feeble leer.

'I hope you don't mind me crashing,' Nikki said. 'I was at a conference in UCD and James said he'd be here.'

'Not at all,' I said, looking at Mullens. He had ambushed me: with Nikki there, how could I say no? But I was ready for him.

'Nikki's a radiologist,' Mullens said, in the same offhand way that he might tell you he drove two Porsches, or holidayed in Davos.

Interestingly, I saw Nikki wince at Mullens's possessive tone. She looked at me and said, 'I gather you're getting the sales pitch.'

I tried to think of something witty to say. Even then, after a few seconds' acquaintance, I sensed that it was important, always, to say the best possible thing to Nikki, to come up with my best material. That was the effect she had.

'Something like that,' I managed, shifting in my seat.

'Every so often I catch him trying to do the sales pitch on me,' Nikki said. 'Tell them a story. Get them to say yes three times. There's something kind of sad about it, isn't there?'

Something passed between them. Don't ask me what. I was never what you might call a cunning registrar of interpersonal nuance.

Mullens adopted a sheepish expression. 'When you love your job, you sometimes take it home.'

'I don't want to interrupt you guys,' Nikki said. 'I'll go to the bar. What can I get you?'

Mullens put a hand on her thigh and said, 'Stay. We're basically done. Aren't we?'

I kept my gaze steady. 'Basically,' I said. 'But I want assurances.'

Mullens made an open-handed gesture.

'I want a signed statement,' I said, 'that says what you told me here tonight. A memorandum of understanding. As soon as these guys sign their end of the deal, we get a payout. I want some paperwork.'

'You know that's not a guarantee,' Mullens said.

'I don't want a guarantee,' I said. 'I want a promise in writing that the second they sign, I get paid. And I want it notarised, or whatever.'

Mullens was trying not to smile. 'That's it?' he said.

'We haven't talked salary,' I said.

Now Mullens was frankly smiling. 'No,' he said. 'We haven't, have we? All right.' From the recesses of his suit he produced a small square of paper and what appeared to be a sterling-silver fountain pen. 'I'll make it easy.' He scribbled briefly on the piece of paper and made a crude aeroplane. This he darted across the table into my lap. 'Open it.'

I looked at Nikki. Her mouth was creased, perhaps in amusement, perhaps in disapproval. I wanted to tell her: *I know this is bullshit! I'm not like him! I read books!* But of course I could not. I would, I told myself, have to live with Nikki's disapproval for the duration of Mullens's scam. I had lived with worse.

With trembling fingers I unscrambled the paper plane. Written inside, in clear blue script, was '€200,000'.

'Per annum,' Mullens said. 'Just so we're clear. Might be able to swing you a signing bonus, too.'

I cleared my throat – like my father, I grow hoarse when strong emotion impends – and raised my glass.

'Favours are how it works,' I said.

Mullens grinned. 'Favours are how it works.'

My new pills – if I may return, briefly, to the dismal present – have kicked in at last. Side effects include cyclical nausea (worse in the mornings), cottonmouth, and spastic limbs. Fun times. Dr Felix has been encouraging me to walk in the grounds, to top up my vitamin D. Here, every morning, my fellow junkies parade in circles around a decommissioned ornamental fountain, like stale planets orbiting a dying sun. Meanwhile, in the sky above, distant aeroplanes go about their silent work of exporting people to other countries, where they will have a better time.

'You're trying to poison me,' I said to Dr Felix this morning, as we strolled past the tennis courts.

'Every drug has side effects,' he said.

We kicked aside some leaves and turned left, into the main drive.

After a moment I said, 'I want to know something.'

Dr Felix was silent.

'Why did I want James Mullens to like me?' I said. 'Why did I keep trying to impress him? Using the fucking rowing machine. I humiliated myself.'

'Why do you want me to like you?' Dr Felix said.

'I don't give a shit if you like me or not,' I said.

'Wrong,' Dr Felix said. 'Tell me about your father.'

'I've told you about my father,' I said. 'There isn't anything more to tell.'

'Wrong again,' Dr Felix said. 'But keep talking. I'm enjoying your refusal to face the facts.'

'Eventually,' I said, 'you're going to have to actually help me.'

'We'll see,' Dr Felix said.

Looking back over these pages, I seem to glimpse a series of vanished selves – each of them an enigma, each of them apparently a mortal enemy of mine, bent on my destruction. Perhaps if I keep going I will eventually find the reason why I've spent my whole life trying to fuck myself up. But I'm not optimistic. After Dr Felix left me this afternoon, I came up with the perfect retort to his nonsense: *You don't know anything about me. You just pretend you do. Rehab is a hoax, and you're the fucking con-artist-in-chief.* Since he's been secretly reading this notebook at night anyway, I trust he will take my point. No: I'm not optimistic. What is there to look forward to, except more self-abasement? For me there is no looking forward, period. All I have is the past, that ambush predator, lying in wait with its patient claws. No more future, not for me. My heart is a closing door.

Well. Let's get it over with, shall we?

2

CROOKED LITTLE SKELETONS

Serbia

Coming in over Belgrade, my plane was struck by lightning. I know this sounds like bullshit, but it's true. Later there was footage on the news: *voilà*, the pearl-handled Boeing, banked for a descent, the grey clouds teetering in a morbid sky, and then *BAM!* – a jagged tongue of white-pink voltage licks the tip of the fuselage and the plane turns puce, like someone on a very bad trip. Inside the cabin, we were braced and belted for an emergency landing. The engine made a sound like a pair of shoes turning over in a washing machine. I asked a passing stewardess – she was German, and pinch-faced, like Ilse Koch – for another gin and tonic but was informed, quite rudely I thought, that beverage service had now been discontinued. The recirculated air took on a petroleum reek. Beyond the plastic porthole with its fringe of stratospheric ice the grey clouds loomed and roiled. Over the PA system the pilot hummed some reassuring lies. The lights went out. This was it. We weren't going to make it. I would never buy that cabin in the woods, with its king-sized bed, its cellar stocked with Californian wines. My plan was going to fail and – adding injury to insult – I was going to die in a plane crash. I viewed these developments with equanimity. I had taken six precautionary Valium before takeoff.

We bumped down in a field forty miles outside Belgrade. The plane deployed its inflatable slides. We were, briefly, children again: *Wheeeeeee!* I tumbled earthwards and rocked to my feet to find myself surrounded by army men with flat-top hair-dos and frowns of cold command, like extras in a film about defecting to the West. Gesturing with their Kalashnikovs, they herded us into canvas-backed trucks and sat beside us unsmilingly as we were driven to the terminal at Tesla. One of them dashed a cigarette from my hand when I tried to light it, and screamed at me in a language that was presumably Serbian. 'Jesus,' I said. 'Chill.' Through the canvas flaps I glanced back at our plane. It was tilted forward alarmingly. The front landing gear had buried itself in the earth of the tilled field.

'Is normal,' said the moustachioed middle-aged man sitting next to me. 'Happen when there is storm.'

'Yeah, cool,' I said.

Double-bagged and taped to my shaved inner thigh was a pharmacopoeia of powders and pills – benzos, uppers, sleepers, codeine, coke, weed – which had managed to pass

unmolested through the security systems of two major air-
ports. Things, I felt, were looking up.

The first tremor of doubt assailed me when I cleared Arrivals.
With my venture capitalist's eye I took in the shabby terminal buildings, the fields of ashen grass, the empty shipping
containers stacked like broken Lego bricks at the edge of the
airport drop zone. The wheel arches of each idling taxi had
been eaten through by rust. I looked around for traces of
high-fructose capitalism, for the neon heraldry of the market
state. But the general vibe, hereabouts, bespoke an ongoing
and tragic mismanagement of the means of production.
Off in the distance a huge white mist was swallowing the
countryside, field by field. I looked back into the underlit
Arrivals hall. Through the gloom a lurid green NO EXIT
sign blinked steadily off and on, like bad news glimpsed in
a dream. This was it? I thought. This was the new frontier
of development opportunity? Then I remembered: we were
taking these suckers for a ride. Mullens's plan – and therefore my plan – relied quite heavily on the desperation of our
Serbian partners. And if I lived here – I told myself – I would
certainly be desperate.

I took out my phone, which in its secretive way had
located a carrier called something like GLOBSKI KAPITAL,
and texted Mullens: IM AT AIRPORT WHERE R U? Fifteen
minutes later, he still had not replied. Passing Serbs were
beginning to look at me in a way that suggested I was being
sized up for a mugging. I dialled Sean Sweeney's number

and got the Out of Service message. Vaguely, I remembered an email that Mullens had sent me, containing the address of our hotel. For ten minutes – I was sobering up horribly – I scrolled through my inbox in search of it. At last – bingo! HOTEL KARLOVSKY, followed by an incomprehensible address. Injecting some entrepreneurial brio into my stride, I went up to the nearest taxi driver, who seemed to be chewing on a mouthful of brown grass. 'I need to go here,' I said, in a loud clear voice.

Without looking at my phone, the taxi driver said, *'Nema problema,'* and grabbed my suitcase. 'Four hundred dinar.'

'I don't know how much that is,' I said.

'Is good rate,' the taxi driver said. He wore a greasy cloth cap and had the hopeful, corrupt look of an immigrant who might eventually make it as a bent cop in the big city.

I pointed at the next driver along. 'Will he do cheaper?' I said.

You had to negotiate: this was what Mullens had taught me.

The second driver looked at me and spat into the gutter.

'Four hundred dinar,' the first driver said. 'You stay Hotel Karlovsky. I take.' He also spat. The brown grass was, it appeared, some form of popular local chewing tobacco.

'What's your name?' I asked. Asking people's names was Step One in a rapport-building technique that I had learned from James Mullens. Step Two: Share a Problem. Step Three: Make a Joke.

The driver mumbled something that sounded like the word *Stradivarius* spoken through a mouthful of mushy peas.

I shrugged. 'I'm going to call you Boris,' I said, opening the rear door. 'Hope that's cool.'

The logo on the fender of Boris's crumpled car said YUGA.

We had been trundling along the motorway for fifteen minutes when the Yuga mounted a grass verge and puttered to a stop. Boris unlatched his seatbelt and peered at me via the rear-view mirror. 'Friend of mine,' he said. 'Also taxi driver. Leave his phone in my car. Now he drive back to airport this way. This way.' He waved vaguely at the opposite lane, where no traffic could be seen. 'I meet him to give him phone. Five minutes. You wait.' He pointed to the ancient analogue meter. The dial turned over, rhythmically. 'No charge, no charge.'

'Ah, here,' I said.

But Boris had already slammed the Yuga's flimsy door and trotted across to the highway's median strip. Here he stood with his hands in his pockets, rocking on his heels, the way my father does when he is trying to dissimulate impatience.

I looked around. The motorway was deserted. Clearly, I was about to be raped and killed. What was the best course of action here? Get out and run? I fished a pinner from my packet of smokes and hesitated. It wasn't that there was a problem with smoking in the cab per se. As we had veered out of the airport onto some kind of ersatz off-ramp I had asked Boris, 'Cool if I smoke?' 'Smoke, smoke,' he said, waving a hand, changing lanes aggressively. 'Is sick country. Everyone smoke.' It was more the legal question: was this the sort of country that handed down life sentences for possession? I

139

cursed myself for having done no research. Then I said, 'Fuck it,' and lit the pinner. After all, I reasoned, I had just survived an emergency landing. Plus I was about to be murdered by my taxi driver. It was time to cut myself some slack.

Over on the median strip, Boris was now talking into a cellphone and looking directly at me. Then a rust-spangled Soviet-era car – the Yuga's pitiful twin – rattled to a stop beside the motorway divider. Boris passed something through the window. It was a small black object that looked very much like a cellphone.

For a moment Boris and the driver of the car seemed to look across at me and laugh uproariously. Then Boris jogged back across the pitted tarmac.

'No charge for delay,' he said. 'You stay Hotel Karlovsky. With Irish.'

'With Irish,' I said. 'Yeah. Exactly. With Irish.' Then, a moment later, I said, 'Wait. How the fuck do you know that?'

Soon we began to pass buildings: huge cinder-block rookeries that loomed darkly out of the white mist like dormant volcanoes; grim little roadside shacks guarded by malnourished dogs. Gesturing with a cigarette (I had offered him one of my Marlboros, which he had accepted in a spirit of awed gratitude), Boris indicated two identical behemoths of pumice-coloured stone and said, 'You see towers?'

'I do see towers,' I said. The weed had calmed me down and Boris and I were now getting on famously.

'Was built as expression of Communist power,' Boris said.

'During time of Tito. All around, people have nothing. No food, no clothes, no electricity. But the Communists, they build this for themselves, so everyone can see where real power is.'

'Shit one,' I said.

Boris coughed and spat. 'Now is owned by Genex Corporation,' he said. 'So everyone still know where real power is.'

'Aha,' I said. I peered through the gradually dispersing fog. 'What are those, eh, burn marks on the side there?'

'NATO cocksuckers,' Boris said. 'They do this. Bombs, rockets. Now, I drive you to Belgrade, it take hour and a half. Before, like that.' He snapped his fingers damply. 'Before, three bridges in Belgrade. Now, only one. Blown up. Boom.'

'That's a pain in the tits,' I said.

'Is shit,' Boris said, nodding vehemently. 'Is shit. NATO cocksuckers.'

Bridgeless Belgrade presented as a cluster of precast concrete slabs and weathered onion domes tottering ominously above the confluence of two churning rivers. Clearing the outskirts, we passed what looked like a tenement building, urine-coloured. In front of it was a disused parade-ground scattered with rusted flagpoles and clumps of blackened crabgrass. 'Seat of Yugoslav government,' Boris said, keeping up his tour-guide patter.

'No more Yugoslavia,' I said dreamily (the weed was doing a number on my conversational skills).

141

'Is administrative offices now,' Boris said.

'Christ,' I said. 'You mean people *work* there?'

'My wife work there,' said Boris proudly. 'Also my girl-friend. Is nice place.'

Boris was now nosing the Yuga through steep narrow streets: past statues of tyrants on horseback, past long rows of shuttered dry-cleaners, past defunct municipal parks. Beyond a vacant lot I caught a glimpse of a shattered bridge, three great marooned stanchions of yellow stone broaching the whitecapped river.

'Hotel Karlovsky,' Boris said. The car lurched to a halt.

We were parked in the middle of a large city square, beside what appeared to be an abandoned detergent factory. (There was a sign that showed a washing machine surrounded by soapy bubbles.) This, it gradually dawned on me, was the hotel. Why, look – Boris was already tugging my suitcase up its chipped steps, pausing at intervals to expectorate dark gobs of emphysemic phlegm. Worriedly, I dialled Mullens's number. The cunt wasn't answering. Across the square I could see a café with clouded windows, like a dirty fish tank. The mist had cleared but now the sun seemed to be setting in the wrong corner of the sky. The desolate square was doused in gloomy rust-red light and there was a pervasive smell, unmistakably, of boiling cabbage.

'You've gotta spend money to make money,' I said, and climbed out of the cab. The handle of the Yuga's frail door came off in my fist.

*

The first thing I saw in the lobby was the brass rail of a hooped luggage rack that looked like it had been doing time there since the days of the Austro-Hungarian Empire (or whatever the relevant vanished empire was, around these parts). The second thing I saw was a gaunt youth in a ratty oversized waistcoat, standing behind a cheap plywood desk.

'You have passport,' he said in a sepulchral undertone as I approached.

'Eh, I do have passport, yeah,' I said. I looked around. There was no one else in the lobby.

'I take,' the youth said without moving.

'I don't fucking think so, pal,' I said. My mood was see-sawing unpredictably and seemed to have dipped towards a phase of outraged hauteur.

'Is okay,' Boris called from across the lobby, where he was cramming my suitcase into a small iron-barred cage that may or may not have been a lift. 'Is safe. You get back.'

Warily I presented my passport. The youth put it in his waistcoat pocket and went back to not moving.

'Uh,' I said.

'You get key,' Boris called.

'I mean, that's the usual procedure,' I said, eyeing the gaunt youth sternly. At length, he produced a key and began laboriously filling in the columns of an elephantine ledger. 'Could you hurry it up there, please,' I said. I had become aware of a burgeoning crisis. My stomach was beginning to cramp. It was the weed. Or the booze. Or the Valium. Whatever it was,

143

I required a toilet, pronto. I began to shift my weight from foot to foot.

Finally, the youth handed over my key. There followed a horrifying interlude in the lift (it *was* a lift!) as Boris – who apparently double-jobbed it as a concierge – repeatedly jammed the button with his nicotined thumb and I tried valiantly not to shit myself, while the gaunt youth regarded us impassively across the lobby from behind his desk. At last the lift shrieked and juddered into life and we began to climb ponderously upwards through the stale floors.

'Is good hotel,' Boris commented, with an appreciative wag of his chin.

At the door of my room I shoved a hundred-dinar note into his hand and bolted for the bathroom, where I noisily excreted a dozen fluid ounces of what felt like warm chilli soup.

Following a prolonged clean-up that eventually necessitated more than a dozen wads of doughy grey toilet paper, I crawled out into the room itself. It was not a five-star room. It was possible, in fact, that the Hotel Karlovsky was operating in negative-star territory, ratings-wise. The carpet, elaborately furred with dust bunnies, was the colour of powdered red brick. The flyblown window overlooked a car park in which no cars were parked. What the fuck were we doing here? Was this the best that Belgrade had to offer? Weren't we supposed to be flashing our affluence, to impress our co-investors? Something had gone wrong. I had flown to the wrong country. Or I had flown to the right country and The Lads had stood me up, for sinister reasons of their own.

To ease my shakes I reclined on the unleavened mattress and consulted my phone. There were seven ALL CAPS messages from Clio, which I deleted unread. We were going through a bit of a rough patch: more on which anon. There was also – at last! – a WhatsApp message from Sean Sweeney.

U TRYIN 2 RING ME? it said.

YES, I typed back, WHERE THE FUCK ARE YOU?

Sweeney: GUD FLIGHT?

Me: I'M HERE WHERE ARE U

Sweeney: U AT D HOTEL???

Me: YES FFS

Sweeney: NICE ROOM YEAH

Me: SRSLY WHERE THE FUCK R YOU CUNTS?

Thirty seconds later a message came in from a different number, that of James Mullens. It said WERE STAYING AT THE HYATT YOU DOUCHE HAHAHAHAHAHAA!

'Oh, you fucking cunts,' I said aloud.

Dublin

I hope you won't mind, Dr F, if I bounce around in time a bit. I can barely keep this stuff straight in my head, let alone set it down in an orderly fashion on the page. The deck of my memory has been shuffled and it would require a lengthy game of Patience to put everything back the way it was.

And Patience is something I no longer have the patience for. Or the time.

Oh yes. I was a man with a plan. Better than that, I was a man with money. My life had been remodelled – set right-side up, at last. The morning after our conversation at the Radisson, James Mullens couriered me a cheque for €25,000. *Signing bonus – part one!* said a note. *Part two payable on signing of contracts. Will arrange. Meanwhile, celebrate! J.* It wasn't until much later that it occurred to me to wonder how exactly it was that Mullens knew my home address. But by then, of course, I had bigger problems. A gold-foil logo in the corner of the cheque said *Echo REIT LLC.* This, I gathered, was the name of the company for which I would be working for three months (and not a second longer, if I could possibly help it).

It was a work day. I was due to report to BlueVista at 9 a.m. I waited until noon before getting a taxi to Capel Street. I brought the cheque with me. When I sat down at Richie Gibbons's desk, he thrust himself upright in his chair and waggled his elbows like a bantam cock. He had been preparing a speech. 'Nice of you to join us,' it began.

'Yeah, yeah,' I said. I summoned the ancient tonalities of Old Barbarian condescension. 'Listen to me for a second. I want to tell you something. Everyone in this office thinks you're a dickhead. Me very much included.' I showed him the cheque. 'I don't know if you've ever heard the term "Fuck You money". You can consider this my notice. I won't be in tomorrow.'

It wouldn't be 100 per cent true to say that my fellow phone jockeys burst into applause as I strode towards the door. In fact, it wouldn't even be 1 per cent true. But they didn't need to. I didn't need applause. I didn't even need to see the expression on Richie's face as I left. Because I had something better. I was already gone.

Of course, the sensible thing to do would have been: put the money in a secret bank account, tell Clio nothing, and wait to see how Mullens's shady Serbian deal actually played out. This would have been the sensible thing to do. Instead I ducked into various shops and alleyways on my way home, bought a magnum of Krug *grande cuvée* (€350), a new suit (€950) and an eightball of cocaine from Barry Hynes (€400, possibly overpriced) and, when I arrived back at the apartment, told Clio that I had found a new job and that our money problems had been definitively solved. I did not – to my credit – mention the quasi-illegal nature of Mullens's deal. Nor did I suggest that I intended to use my seven-figure windfall to abandon her and go to live in the High Sierras, presuming that the High Sierras were a place that actually existed and in which people could safely live. But the problem was that I had already been keeping secrets from Clio. I had not told her about my appointment with James Mullens to begin with (I had cited 'a quick pint with Baz Hynes' as the reason for my absence the previous evening), and now I had upended my life without giving her advance notice. She was, I supposed, justifiably upset.

'Who is this guy, anyway?' she said. 'I've never even heard of him before. Now he's supposedly your best pal.'

'We were friends in school,' I said. 'Well, no. Not friends. We were in the same year.'

'And he shows up and offers you a job.'

'It's what he does,' I said.

'He just goes around offering people jobs.'

'Not people,' I said. 'Just people who went to my school.' I had returned home in a state of elated clarity. Once it had become clear that Clio had no interest in joining me in this state, I had lapsed into truculence. 'This is a phenomenal opportunity,' I said, casting around for ways in which to frame the good news. 'We don't have to stay here. We can move into a better place.'

'A better place?'

'I mean a bigger place.'

'So, what?' she said. 'You're going to be a property developer. Like your dad.'

'My dad's a banker,' I said.

'Like you know the difference,' Clio said.

'This is good news,' I said, following her into the living room. 'You know? I just increased my income by a factor of ten. I'll be able to cover the rent for a while. You've been covering it all year.'

'Here's what couples do,' Clio said. 'They talk to each other before they get new jobs.'

'Okay, then,' I said. 'What would you have told me to do? If I'd asked you?'

148

'I can't answer that question,' Clio said. 'Because you didn't tell me. You lied to me instead.'

She waited. The invitation was there: at this point, I could apologise. But I did not. I wanted Clio to *see*.

'This is more money than I've ever made in my life,' I said. 'I do this for a few months. I save up. Then I do something else. Because I'm *free* to do something else. Because I have *money*.'

'I'm not a child,' Clio said. 'You don't have to talk to me in short sentences.'

Anticipating the wrong objection to what I was saying, I had already made a slight course correction. '*We're* free to do something else,' I went on. 'Because *we* have money.' I raised my arms and let them fall despairingly. 'We're a couple. When one of us has money, we both have money. That's what love means.'

'Since when did you care so much about money?'

'Money is *all* I care about!' I said. Hearing how this sounded, I supplied a gloss: 'If money means being free. If money means being able to do things, *together*, that we can't do now.'

'This isn't the person you were supposed to be,' Clio said.

My truculence now devolved into surliness. 'And who the fuck is the person I'm supposed to be?' I said. 'Entry-level wage slave? College drop-out? What?'

Clio's severe expression had softened. She crossed her arms. 'When I met you nine months ago,' she said, 'you were kind of an asshole but you were also basically a decent person. I don't

149

go out with people who are just assholes. I tried that and I got hurt. Now you're turning into an asshole and nothing else. And the worst thing is, you're doing it behind my back.'

'I'm sorry,' I said. 'Please don't go.'

'I can't go through this again,' Clio said. 'Someone lying to me. Making me paranoid. Gaslighting me. It makes me feel so *worthless*.'

'I'm not keeping anything from you,' I said. 'Look. I can prove it.' I took my phone out of my pocket and offered it to her. I couldn't think of a gesture that required more trust in another person: *Here's my phone. Read my messages. Check my browser history. I am an open screen.*

'I don't want you to prove it to me,' Clio said. 'I want to be able to trust you without thinking about it.'

'You can,' I said.

Clio said nothing.

I pocketed my phone. 'I need you to be on board with this,' I said. 'It's what I want to do. I need you to support me.'

More silence.

And then I was suddenly inspired. Not for nothing had I spent three years writing and rewriting forty pages of a novel. 'Who am I?' I said, assuming a rhetor's confident stance – I may have jabbed a finger at the ceiling, as if to say, *Point one!* 'I'm a man who was walking along the street and suddenly, one day, oh shit. I fell in a hole. I wasn't paying attention. But I'm paying attention now. And you don't fall back *out* of a hole, do you? You have to *climb* out. This is me, climbing out. And I need your help.'

Clio's arms were still folded. But there were tears in her eyes, and my arms were open to greet her when she crossed the room for a hug.

Speaking of my father: by the time I received my signing bonus from Mullens I had not heard from the old man in over two weeks. During that time the newspaper headlines about his case had taken on an increasingly hysterical timbre: OSLO LINK IN [REDACTED] PROBE; JAIL THIS MAN; [REDACTED]'S FLOUTING OF LAW INDICTS A WHOLE BUSINESS CULTURE, that sort of thing. Glancing at the papers, I had felt no urge to contact him. If he did indeed have 'a few bob in your mother's name', then he was clearly well cushioned against even the harshest headlines. But things had changed. Now that I was rich – and about to become even richer – I felt a cruel urge to pay him a visit. I wanted to check in at home, before I checked out for ever.

The garage door was open. In its shade my father was kneeling on an inflatable bath pillow, dabbing at the paintwork of his Landcruiser with a small stiff brush.

'One of those discount supermarkets,' he said, indicating a deep groove in the driver's-side door. 'I was coming out of the car park and I scraped it on a pillar.'

'They're designed for smaller cars,' I said. 'You know, the sort of cars that poor people drive.'

'I was distracted,' my father said. 'Lucky it wasn't worse, I suppose.' He hauled himself upright. Since I had last seen him he appeared to have aged several decades. He stood with one hand pressed medicinally to his lower back, like a pregnant woman. 'It's good to see you.'

'Just checking in,' I said. 'I have some good news, actually. I've got a new job. Six-figure salary.'

My father fumbled for a paint-stained cloth and began to clean his hands. 'So you're leaving that other place,' he said. 'That's good. They weren't using you to your best potential.'

'That's one way of putting it,' I said. 'Just wanted to let you know I probably won't be contactable for a while. Heading away for a bit.'

'International,' my father said.

'Something like that.'

'You can't go wrong with a land deal,' my father said.

For a horrible instant I entertained the suspicion that he knew all about James Mullens's offer, that he knew about the Serbian scam, that the whole thing had, in fact, been his doing, and I had walked into another one of his silk-lined traps without first doing my due diligence. But then he said, 'If you've a few bob spare, I mean. Great security in land. This house was the best investment we ever made.'

I kicked at an empty paint can. 'Where's Mum?' I said.

'Over in Connecticut,' my father said. 'Looking at houses.'

I found it difficult to picture my mother successfully navigating the US property market. But then, I found it difficult to picture my mother doing anything, except mixing cocktails and drinking them.

'How's it all going, then,' I said. 'The trial.'

My father looked surprised. 'Oh, you know,' he said. 'I've

put together a great team. It's been difficult, you know. The press. The other day I had a lad with a camera here. Down at the end of the driveway from six a.m. I brought him a cup of tea and he asked me if I regretted ruining so many lives. I said, it's my life that's ruined. My own family . . .' He stopped. 'And how are you?'

'Rich,' I said.

My father nodded. 'Hang on to it,' he said. 'Rough times ahead. But money's a great comfort.'

'It is,' I said. 'It is a great comfort.'

I turned to go.

'I heard a joke the other day,' my father said. 'Three ladies of a certain age are having lunch at the golf club. A man gets lost on his way back from the shower and he wanders through the bar, stark naked. A towel over his head, you know, drying his hair. The first lady says, "Well, it isn't my Gerald." The second lady says, "Well, it's certainly not my Frank." And the third lady peers over her glasses and says, "He isn't even a member."'

'See you later, Dad,' I said.

This morning Dr Felix took me out to the tennis court. From here, if you stand on tiptoe by the laurel hedge, you can see the main clinic building, front-elevation view. Originally a Big House, in the nineteenth-century landed-gentry sense of the term, it was, in the 1950s, transformed into a TB clinic. Then TB was cured and people began to come here with new-model diseases, located largely in the mind.

The Doc flapped a hand at the tennis court and said, 'Do you want to hit a few balls?'

I torched a cigarette and said, 'Isn't that what we're already doing?'

'Ah, yes,' Dr Felix said. 'Very good. Very good.' He fiddled with the frayed net, which twanged along its length. 'You didn't ask Clio about her exes. The ones who cheated on her.'

I sat down on the faded red clay. 'How do you know they cheated on her?'

'She said they lied to her. What else do men lie about?'

'You have a very reductive view of men.'

'Hearing about a partner's past relationships is a way of learning to empathise with them. Finding out who they are. How they feel about their life.'

'I get it,' I said. 'I didn't empathise with Clio.'

'But you didn't want her to leave you.'

'She was very hot.'

'You can do better than that.'

'What do you want me to say? That I was scared shitless? That Clio was the only person in my life I thought I could trust? That she was the only person who was nice to me, not because she had some weird agenda, but because she actually thought I might be worthwhile?'

'That's a start.'

I threw the butt of my smoke at the net. It bounced, landed, smouldered. Dr Felix stepped forward and snuffed it out with his wingtip.

'Are you sure you don't want to play?' he said.

'I was wrong to trust her, though,' I said. 'Wasn't I?'

Dr Felix stood with his hands in his pockets, gazing up at the roof of the main clinic. 'Let's not get ahead of ourselves.'

Echo REIT – the concern for which I now worked – operated out of a Georgian building on Harcourt Street. The office had very recently been redecorated. There were still small piles of sawdust in the corners. The colour scheme was charcoal grey. The boardroom carpets were charcoal grey. The boardroom table was charcoal grey. The boardroom chairs were charcoal grey. My office contained a charcoal-grey desk and a brand-new MacBook, also charcoal grey. From the office next door – it belonged to another Old Barbarian, Sean Sweeney, who was, Mullens informed me, the Chief Financial Officer – I could hear a pinball machine throwing its tantrum of electrified jollity. Across the street was a construction site – every street in Dublin had its construction site just then: hoardings, scaffolding, plastic sheets, green safety netting, acoustic baffles (diamond-patterned, like a dirty old quilt), cranes, skips, fencing, and a fine white Pompeiian dust settling on the cars and parking meters. Even in the vacuum-sealed hush of the Echo REIT offices you could hear the sounds of drilling and hammering, of building and tearing down. I had been abruptly elevated to the world of money-men: the world of men who made such things happen. It was, of course, my father's world. But I would not be staying long.

At 11 a.m. on my debut morning at Echo REIT, Mullens brought me into the boardroom and laid out six or seven densely printed documents at one end of the charcoal-grey table. At the other end, a shaven-headed man in circular specs who bore an unnerving resemblance to a young Bertolt Brecht poked at a laptop and did not acknowledge us.

Mullens offered me his sterling-silver pen. 'We've had the lads at Sliney and Nihill do up the contracts and so on,' he said. 'They're my dad's guys. Just a formality. We'll get your bank details too.'

'The first thing I sign,' I said, holding up a hand, 'is the memorandum of understanding. I want it in writing, what's going to happen.'

Mullens smiled. 'You don't trust me.'

'I do trust you,' I said. 'I just want a clear timeline on this. You said two months.'

'Our flights are booked,' Mullens said. 'Two months' time, we've been to Belgrade, we've got our signatures. It's in the bag.'

'That's what I want in writing,' I said. 'The payout happens the second we sign the deal.'

'Not the exact second,' Mullens said. 'You're looking at a few days for the transfer to go through.'

'I'm aware of that,' I said.

Mullens produced a single sheet of ivory-bond paper. 'Okay. So this is where Mr Macken comes in. Alan?'

Bertolt Brecht looked up from his screen. 'Morning,' he said.

Mullens flourished the sheet of paper. 'Alan's our independent witness. He's with Carrigan Stuart. You ever see those signs that say, "Commissioners for Oaths"? That's what

Alan does. We sign this in his presence, he notarises it. Bang. We're done.'

I took the sheet of paper from Mullens's hand and scrutinised the blocks of print that it contained. In orotund legalese, it said just what I wanted it to: payment contingent on signing, signing to take place no more than one hundred (100) days from date of first employment at Echo REIT, also contingent on fulfilment of required duties by Benjamin [REDACTED], here undersigned, et cetera. Belatedly, it occurred to me that I should have hired my own lawyer to draw up the memo. But Mullens's version seemed kosher – to the extent that I was competent to judge these matters. And it was, by now, too late.

'You first,' I said.

Mullens signed two copies. I signed. Alan signed. Alan stamped.

'Alan's going to hang on to our copy,' Mullens said. 'And now, the real deal.'

He gestured at the documents lined up on the lacquered table. The cover sheets bore the insignia of Echo REIT LLC, or (the next one along) the logo of Healy-Dunlop, Architects, or (in several cases) the plumed crest of Sliney & Nihill, Corporate Solicitors.

'This is your employment contract,' Mullens said. 'This is your liability waiver, this is an application for credit facilities, this is your basic nondisclosure agreement, blah blah blah. You're welcome to read them, but they're all standard boilerplate.'

'What's this one?' I said. I had found a cover sheet that said

'Trade Exchange Holdings LLC', above an address: 34 Jens Bjelkes gate, Oslo.

'Oslo,' I said. 'Someone was talking about Oslo recently.'

'Probably one of the lads,' Mullens said. 'We set up a dummy LLC in Norway. Friendlier tax laws. Again, totally standard practice. This just adds your name to the list of partners.'

I toyed with Mullens's pen and was, all at once, assailed by doubts. The massed documentation in front of me must have totalled two or three hundred pages. It would take me hours to read it all, and I would have no way of determining which if any of these papers concealed a nasty surprise. But it was – I reassured myself – a moot point. As soon as I got my seven-figure payoff, I would be free to violate any contract Mullens cared to enforce. I would be on a plane to Goa before he even managed to raise Bertolt Brecht on the phone.

I signed and initialled all seven contracts.

'Boomtown,' James Mullens said. He clicked open his briefcase and handed me a small white envelope. 'The other half of your signing bonus. Listen. I'm really glad you're on board. We're gonna do some amazing work here. And you're gonna be a huge part of that.'

'I already signed,' I said. 'You can stop selling.'

Mullens laughed. 'Fair enough. All right. I've got to drop these off.' He indicated the contracts on the table. 'You go chill out for the rest of the day. There's nothing doing around here anyway. Go and have a drink. Do whatever. I'll see you tomorrow at some point.' He gathered up the contracts – they made a thick pile, like the manuscript of a novel – and slotted them into his briefcase. He paused at the door. 'Here,' he said, and winked. 'Welcome to the world of getting away with it.'

And he was gone.

At the other end of the table, Alan stood, clutching his briefcase in front of his crotch. 'Have a good one,' he said, looking at the floor.

Okay, I thought. So far, so good.

Serbia

'They tried to put us up in this shithole,' Sean Sweeney said from behind his mirrored shades. He took in the lobby of the Hotel Karlovsky and lowered the volume of his voice until it was merely obnoxiously loud. 'And we were, like, eh, obviously we'll be at a better hotel? I mean, it's not like we don't have the fucking money. And they were, like, all pissed off, like' – he adopted a gruff sub-Soviet accent – "This is four-star hotel." And *we* were, like, Yeah. You people have no fucking notion of what a four-star hotel is. Well, obviously we didn't say it out loud. But we got on the blower to the Hyatt and guess how much a room is there.'

'I don't know,' I said.

My stomach was churning and my whole head appeared to have broken out in gooseflesh. It was the drugs, I thought.

Or it was the trauma of that emergency landing. I wondered if it might be advisable to lie down for a quick nap, perhaps on the lobby floor.

Sweeney guffawed and said, 'The guy on the phone is, like, five thousand dinar. And Mullens fires that into the old currency converter and it's *forty quid a night*. You can get a bottle of Heino for *fifty fucking cents* here. We're millionaires in this country, Ben. Actual millionaires.'

Waiting for Sweeney to arrive in the limo, I had taken two Solpadol, theorising that the codeine would help to bung me up, in case of further diarrhoea. But the pills were mingling strangely with the other drugs in my system and it seemed likely that I would now simply pass out. I tried to adopt a philosophical view. Abusing prescription painkillers, after all, is not an exact science.

'My plane got hit by lightning,' I said, in a dreamy voice.

Sweeney frowned. 'Sorry about sending you here, man. The lads thought it would be gas. Here. Tell Igor over there to get your luggage. The limo's outside.' From behind the front desk, the gaunt youth was glaring at us with fevered eyes. 'Here, Igor,' Sweeney called. 'We're checking the fuck out, yeah? Let's get this man's luggage, chop fucking chop.'

'I think my taxi driver ripped me off,' I said, feeling, for some reason, the impulse to unburden myself of all my woes. 'He charged me four hundred dinar.'

'Dude,' Sweeney said. 'That's, like, two-fifty. And do you know what the amazing thing is? He *was* ripping you off. By his standards, that's ripping you off. And we're all there, like, eh, sorry? I pay forty quid for a taxi from Ballsbridge to Dame Street every Friday night, pal. Do your worst.'

There was another Igor at the Hyatt, loitering in the purple-draped lobby, waiting to take my bag. The Hyatt was unmistakably five-star – the lobby was lined with mirrors and marble and felt oddly pressurised, like a hyperbaric chamber – and the Hyatt Igor was correspondingly hand-somer, or at least less noticeably resentful. 'We call all the concierges Igor,' Sweeney said, as we whooshed upwards in the gilded lift. 'It's, like, give them a tenner and you can call them whatever the fuck you like.' Inside his Armani suit Sweeney was pumped up with muscle and he was chewing gum moronically. 'We shelled out for the penthouse, obvs,' he said, clicking his fingers and nodding his head. 'I mean, we are still basically slumming it, in the sense of, there aren't enough towels and you wouldn't be mad keen on letting the maids in when you're not around, but ...' He went on, outlin-ing the benefits of staying at a proper hotel. The lift opened into a marble vestibule lined with oak-panelled doors. Igor darted ahead of us and began fumbling with a jailkeeper-sized bundle of keys.

'They don't even have, like, those key cards?' Sweeney said, not remotely *sotto voce*. 'They use actual keys. But we tip them so much they actually just run ahead and open all the doors for us. I haven't even *seen* my room key. It's like we're fucking ... Prince Rainier of Monaco, or someone.'

Igor had located the correct key and opened the door. Now

he was standing aside with a shy smile. Sweeney palmed him a banknote as we passed.

'*Hvala*,' Igor said. It sounded like a hacking cough.

'Koala to you, my good man,' Sweeney said. To Igor's departing back he then said, 'You pick up the lingo fairly quickly, like.'

Ape-neck Sweeney. Formerly – during his, or our, golden years – the meanest Schools prop in Leinster, with his permanently cauliflowered ears, his large, rudimentary arms and shoulders. More recently a consultant for the Tenex Advisory Group (his father sat on the board), squiring deals in Abu Dhabi, Frankfurt, Washington DC. In school he had been a famous dunce, chortlingly indulged by our rugby-mad teachers – 'an ornament to the school', our headmaster called him during his graduation address. Sweeney's dismal Leaving Cert was overlooked by UCD's sports scholarship committee, who wanted him for the First Team squad. But a torn ligament put him out of commission straight away. He limped – in both senses – through a business degree and was hired by his father's firm right off the block. After which he disappeared into the ether of international finance capital and I lost track of him, more or less. Now, a few years later, Sweeney and I were business partners: co-directors of a real estate investment trust, whatever that meant. On my second day at the office (I was dutifully scrolling my way through sheaves of PDFs about urban renewal incentives, double-taxation agreements and rezoning regulations, in order to give my sales patter a veneer of plausibility), Sweeney appeared in my doorway, filling it with his gym-rat bulk.

'What the fuck are you doing?' he said. 'We're not paying you to work, you tit. It's the fucking cocktail hour.'

The charcoal-grey clock on the wall of my office said 11.15 a.m.

'I'll let you in on a little secret,' Sweeney said half an hour later, as we chugged White Russians in the smoking garden of a bar in Blackrock. 'This job is a complete piece of piss.'

And he was right: it was. All through that first week I kept wondering: *Where are the grown-ups? Who's keeping an eye on all this?* But there were no grown-ups. Or – and consider this, Dr F, if you will – we *were* the grown-ups. The keys to the kingdom were ours.

Now there's a thought.

In the penthouse suite of the Belgrade Hyatt – where I dumped my suitcase on a velour chaise longue – The Lads were, very clearly, at the tail-end of the previous night's debauch. In the middle of the room was a mirrored coffee table scattered with credit cards and lightly floured with coke, like the illustration on the cover of a nihilistic 80s novel. On a four-poster bed the mountainous figure of Paul Tynan lay as if biered, his hands crossed at his heart. Over by the window, James Mullens, wearing only his boxers, was studiously ironing a pink shirt. I picked my way through the empty Cristal bottles and shook his hand. His presence, I found, was strangely reassuring. 'You made it,' he said. 'How was the flight?'

'We got struck by lightning,' I said.

'Shit buzz,' Mullens said.

From an adjoining room or antechamber Bobby Hayes – Echo REIT's Director of Communications, or so it said on his business card – emerged, noisily hacking up what sounded like a double shot's worth of phlegm. His lower half was wrapped in a small white towel. Unbidden, I recalled a phrase from my postgraduate seminars: *homosocial spaces.* Where men were manly together and everything was incredibly, overtly gay, but you weren't allowed to point that out. 'The fucking cavalry,' Bobby said, when he saw me. 'We were about to run out of Daz.'

'No more Daz for a while,' James Mullens said. 'We have to meet Vuk and his lads now.'

'Fuck?' I said, frowning.

'He hasn't got a clue,' Bobby Hayes said.

'We'll fill you in,' Mullens said. He was buttoning the collar of his shirt. 'I need everyone to get their shit together.'

'My shit is together,' Bobby Hayes said.

There was a rime of coke around the edges of his nostrils.

Excusing myself, I gained the bathroom, where I peeled the sellotaped baggie from my damp inner thigh and triaged the contents. Sleepers, benzos, speed and codeine I kept to myself. Coke, weed and pills were designated For General Use. The crucial thing was not to reveal to The Lads that I had brought a stock of downers, or they would gobble up the lot and I would be left with nothing. My iPhone rumbled in my pocket, filling up with messages from Clio. The little black slab seemed to grow very slightly heavier with each SMS it received. I ignored it. As far as Clio knew, I was still in the air. (I had been deliberately vague about my flight times.) I gave myself a once-over in the gilded mirror. My pupils were huge, my hair greasy. The first wave of the codeine had peaked and that lovely intestinal glow was tapering off. The path of all drugs follows the tragic curve: up and then down, down, down. The task at hand was the preservation of my emotional wherewithal. We were about to meet our Serbian partners – though the word *partners*, whenever James Mullens had cause to utter it, came freighted with its own little backpack of irony: none of The Lads, in fact, could bring themselves to say it without a half-suppressed chortle or a pair of waggled air quotes. We were taking these guys for a ride. What was called for was a display of professionalism and polish: a surgical strike, as Mullens had put it in his most recent boardroom pep talk.

Someone was hammering on the bathroom door. 'Are we partying here or what,' came Bobby Hayes's voice.

I had never been Bobby's biggest fan. Back in school, he had been the sort of peeved *Untermensch* who would punch you for reading a book. But we had been doing some male bonding of late. It turned out we had a shared interest: getting off our tits.

'Let's do this,' I told my reflection, which leered greenly back at me, like a waterlogged corpse.

*

Promptly at six, suited and tied, we descended to the lobby, where our investment partners (ho ho ho) had gathered to greet us – more specifically to greet me, since I was the last of the Echo REIT posse to arrive in Belgrade. There had already been, I gathered, some desultory schmoozing – first contact had been established with our Serbian counterparts – but now it was time to get the real stuff rolling. As we stood crammed together in the lift, Bobby Hayes was monologuing nonstop about 'the colour temperature spectrum'. I felt good. I felt pimped up, chock-full of my own tactical brilliance. Investment partners? Piece of piss. From somewhere behind me Mark Foley – our Brains Trust, with his receding hairline, his large pale brow, his 2:1 BESS degree from Trinners – said in his high nasal voice, 'We really have to make a good impression on these guys, yeah? They're staking their pensions on this. If they think we're taking the piss, they'll bolt.' Mark had spent four years watching micro-trades trickle across the screen of a Bloomberg terminal. It had left him with a scholarly stoop that made him look like an Anglepoise lamp.

There was a brief moment of silence. Then Sean Sweeney said, 'I need to take a fucking shit.'

Up in the penthouse, a few minutes before, James Mullens had given me the low-down on our co-investors. 'The main lad's name is Vuk,' he said. 'He said it means *wolf*. And this guy's seen some serious shit, all right? He was telling us this story the other night about how when he was a kid, the

Communists or whoever came to his village and cut down all the trees.'

'Why?' I said.

Mullens shook his head. 'Just to be cunts. Like, these guys have had hard fucking lives, you know?'

'And he's a builder?' I said.

Mullens made a meaninglessly expansive gesture. 'They're all builders. They run businesses out of this place called Republika Srpska. Vuk says he was a doctor, like a GP? Before the, before the war or whatever they had over here . . .' Mullens's expression turned briefly abstract. 'But now he's head honcho at some place called Free Serbia Progress Construction – their English isn't exactly A-1 but that's what Google Translate came up with when I stuck it in. And the other lad, Nicolae, his crowd supposedly built the town hall for their second-largest city.'

'And Vuk's company,' I said, 'is the one sourcing the, eh, the supplies and so on? The materials.'

I became aware that my vocabulary, so richly furnished with names for the constituent ingredients of pharmaceuticals, was rather poorer when it came to designating the kinds of things that might be needed to build a luxury golfing resort. Concrete? Nails? Wood?

'They have the government contacts,' Mullens said. 'Like, we've met the Mayor of Belgrade and some lads from the local parliament. There was a reception last night. They were basically fawning over us. I'd say this is in the bag.'

In the bag. Tucked into the breast pocket of my suit was my copy of the Memorandum of Understanding. For almost three months now I had kept it with me at all times, consulting it at regular intervals and envisioning the future concealed behind its recondite clauses. I saw myself rising at dawn to swim in my own private lake. I saw myself keeping a journal of my woodsman's day. I saw myself living in splendid isolation, pure in body and mind, unworn by the cares of the life into which I had been cast by the malign capriciousness of biology or fate. I had conjured this vision many times. By now it had accrued a verisimilitude that made my heart leap up with desire: I was *so close*! I was actually here, in Belgrade! The money was circling overhead, the notes stretched out in a fluttering line like planes queuing up above an airport. We were about to meet our 'partners'. We were T-minus one week, and counting.

'I'm not going to relax until we've got their names on the contract,' I said.

Mullens nodded. 'That's why I hired you,' he said. 'Head for business. Are we ready?'

We were ready. In fact, I was baroquely confident. (I was on cocaine.) When the lift doors opened I saw, standing in the middle of the lobby, a group of men gathered in a dark-suited conspiratorial knot. With a purposeful sniff – breathe the glacial air! – I strode forth. Everyone shook hands, slapped backs. We were all friends here. 'Keep it together,' Mullens hissed in my ear – suggesting, perhaps, a mild disparity between the impression I thought I was making and the impression I was actually making. After a moment I found myself thrust forward until I was violating the personal space of a short, middle-aged man in a long black coat. 'This is Vuk,' someone said.

The man in the long black coat regarded me with dark, expressive eyes. He clasped my hand with priestly solicitude and drew closer, seeming to grow in stature until he commanded my entire field of vision. The black eyes peered out at me from under ferocious bushy brows, the long unkempt hairs there wheedling like antennae, as if every part of his face's equipment were hungrily scanning for information. Above the brows you might – if you were in the mood – mark the strangely lobed white forehead with its intercessionary widow's peak, which might – again, if you fancied it – rather unnervingly remind you of something like the heraldic crest of a house of famed impalers.

'Vuk Mladic,' James Mullens said, arriving at my side. 'The main man.'

The dark eyes took my measure calmly.

'Nice to meet you,' I said.

'*Dober dan*,' Vuk said. 'You are welcome to Belgrade.'

'Cheers,' I said, nodding perhaps a shade too rapidly.

'You know what this means, Belgrade,' Vuk said.

'I actually, eh,' I said.

'Belgrade is from *Beo Grad*,' Vuk said. 'The White City. As Dublin means, *Dubh Linn*, the Black Pool. This you have heard of, in your books?'

He was still clasping my hand between his own. His skin

felt strangely smooth and lumpy, as if calloused by scar tissue.

'Uh,' I said. 'Rings a bell, all right.'

James Mullens was twitching at the pockets of his slacks with restless fingers.

'The synchronicity of this I like,' Vuk went on, smiling. His teeth – a little row of tombstones – made me think of the words *Soviet dentistry*. 'The black and the white. The *yin* and the *yang*. There is a poetry to it, no? A balance?' The smile became wistful, dreamy. Behind the eyes, memories were crowding. 'I wrote poetry once. When I was very young. But young men write poetry, do they not?'

'Eh, depends which young men,' I said, essaying what seemed like an acceptable *bon mot*.

'Ha,' Vuk said, without laughing. 'You, perhaps, are a poet yourself?'

At this point Mullens could no longer restrain himself. He stepped in and said, 'Ben here is one of our Development Officers. He's basically in charge of strategy and marketing.'

'Yes, I see,' Vuk said. He had not looked away from me once. 'Your strategy and marketing,' he said. 'I ask about it.'

'Well,' I said. I scrambled to recall some of the promotional 'content' I had cobbled together for our portfolio. 'It's basically, you know, the tag-line is Luxury Affordability in the Wilds of Beauty, you know, so the strategy will obviously have to, eh, be basically in line with that, and I mean going forward, we'll have a few meetings to discuss, you know, content. We were actually just talking about which side of the colour-temperature spectrum we're going to emphasise in the lobby, which is—'

'We should introduce you to the rest of the lads,' Mullens said, putting a stern hand on my shoulder.

'Yes,' Vuk said, still smiling, still looking at me, still clasping my hand. 'The man from the Black City. We meet now the men from the White City.' He released my hand and raised his arm expansively. 'I introduce my associates,' he said, in a booming voice.

I turned to confront a surly wall of Slavic rock – five or six enormous, interchangeable men in leather jackets, all with the same gunmetal haircut and the same mistrustful frown. I groped my way through a series of handshakes, catching no names.

'So these guys are basically the consortium,' Mullens murmured. His hand was on my lower back, as if he were escorting me round a Debs. 'Like, they've bought in? But we don't actually deal with them as such. Vuk's gang are the *actual* partners.'

'Grand, yeah,' I said. My high was curdling into the jitters. Somewhere nearby I seemed to hear the sound of dead leaves skirmishing in a dead-end street. This, of course, is the problem with cocaine: once the first big bump has waned, you become terrified of everything and all you really want to do is snort more cocaine, and then snort more cocaine, ad infinitum. It's an incredibly stupid drug and I've been saying so for years.

Luckily, I appeared to be running out of hands to shake.

The mountain range of Serbs parted at last to disclose the two men who were, Mullens whispered, 'Vuk's actual lads.' The shortest of the two stuck out his paw.

'Ratko,' Vuk said, bowing regally at my side.

I recoiled, but Mullens shoved me forward. From somewhere in the back of my throat I produced a strangulated 'Hey.' Reluctantly, I shook Ratko's hand. He had the slicked-back hair and grifter's 'tache of a pool-hall dandy and he was regarding me with coroner's eyes: pale, affectless, cruel. The face was pinched, and tapered to a craggy point, as if it had recently been sliced and suctioned by some powerful machine. He wore a black leather jacket and army-surplus boots, also black. He was, by some considerable distance, the most terrifying person I had ever met.

With a flourish, Vuk said, 'Also there is Nicolae.'

Nicolae was twice as tall as Ratko, and twice as wide. His dyed hair was the blue-tinged black of crow's feathers. His moustache was tightly bristled, like a worn little nail brush. His left eye was covered by a patch – a black triangle of cheap plastic twanged in place with elastic bands. The sight of this patch did nothing to cure my jitters. I decided to tell myself that I simply hadn't spotted the patch – I erased it from my short-term memory. Like most things, I thought, it didn't bear thinking about.

'Nicolae also is poet,' Vuk said.

Nicolae cracked a cold smile, as if Vuk had casually referred to his proficiency with the jailhouse shiv.

'Yep,' I said. 'Yep yep yep.' I was staring helplessly at

Nicolae's eyepatch. *Christ on a bike,* I was thinking, *I don't know about this at all!* Who the fuck were these fuckers, anyway? They looked like thugs or criminals. They looked like they would have no serious quarrel with the concept of beating your wife. If Mullens was planning to defraud these guys, I hoped he hadn't given them his home address. Oh, bad! Oh, very bad!

Mullens appeared to be beaming a frantic telepathic message my way.

'Yep,' I said again. 'It's, eh ... It's fantastic to be here.'

Vuk led a brief round of applause. 'Here we are always told about Ireland,' he said, chewing on his tombstone teeth. 'The economic miracle. The recovery. The Irish example is for us a noble thing to hear of. And to work with Irish ...' He made a dismissive gesture.

'Hear, hear,' Sean Sweeney called, from where he stood leaning against a marble pillar.

It was, more than anything, the frank boredom conveyed by Sweeney's pose – he stood there like a man waiting for an afternoon train – that calmed my jitters. The Lads, Sweeney's pose suggested, were in control of things. They had done their due diligence. There had been background checks, discreet enquiries made. Everyone's credentials had come up solid: *nema problema.* The Serbs may look like butchers or bruisers (or, in Vuk's case, like aristocratic vampires fallen on hard times), but they were the ones at a disadvantage here. They were the saps. They were the marks. We were the money. We were the nous and the know-how.

My meet-and-greet ordeal was almost over. 'Ultimately of all, you meet translator,' Vuk said. He pointed at a man in his late thirties who was loitering nearby. I had assumed him to be a hotel cleaner or bucket boy. He was dressed in military-green khakis and an olive-drab shirt that was at least three sizes too big for him. 'Aleksandr,' Vuk said. Avoiding eye contact, Aleksandr concentrated on rolling a cigarette between two freakishly large thumbs. I was wondering whether it might not have made more sense to introduce the translator first when Aleks spoke up. 'I am translating here for English to Serbian and for Serbian to English,' he mumbled. 'Questions you need, to me you ask.'

'Their English is amazing here,' Sweeney said in a fruity tone. The Lads were sniggering openly. I tried to control my darting drug-eyes.

Vuk raised a long white finger and said, 'We are planning to show you dinner this evening, yes? Then is club called Pravda, is very exclusive Belgrade club. But before this, we have dinner. Cars are waiting.'

'They're planning to show us dinner,' Sean Sweeney said.

'Cars are waiting,' James Mullens said, glaring at The Lads. As we walked towards the revolving door Nicolae put his huge hand on my shoulder and left it there, saying nothing. I began to hiccup with fright.

In the limo, James Mullens took a moment to remonstrate with his giggling troops. 'Can we all just try not to talk total bollocks for the rest of the evening, yeah?' he said. 'This won't work if we look like amateurs. I don't know how many times I have to say it.'

The car was cruising through dusk-infused and strangely empty streets, bearing us towards – what? Through the tinted windows, unpeopled Belgrade swam past in sepia, like a photograph in a history book. The Serbs had taken their own cars and were up ahead, storming also through the barren evening city.

'For Vuk's sake, lads,' Paul Tynan said.

Mullens tutted and slumped back into the limo's jump seat, brooding.

'Lads,' Sweeney said, holding up a hand. 'Lads? Have you seen the limo?'

We looked around approvingly at the limo's interior: the black leather seats, the wet bar, the flatscreen TV.

'It's a good limo, yeah,' said Tynan, sniffing. (Had he done a cheeky bump?)

My hiccups had finally abated. Through the sunroof I could see the sky above the city. The clouds were a massed and thunderous grey, edged with the last of the light.

Dublin

In order to keep things looking – as he put it – 'properly legit', Mullens organised a launch party for Echo REIT's debut development deal, which he was calling Echo Lake. For the launch, I expected bottles of mid-priced wine in a rented hotel conference room. But Mullens hired the ballroom of the Shelbourne and sent press releases to every newspaper and business website in Ireland. The cocktail menu was bespoke. The *hors d'oeuvres* were artisanal. There was a Nigerian girl at coat-check to take your Russian sable stole, and a videographer soliciting congratulatory verbiage from the circulating guests. There was even a red carpet and, in the foyer, a pyramid of champagne glasses, in front of which Clio immediately snapped an Instagrammable self-portrait. 'This is so swish,' she said, as I swept her down the steps and into the ballroom proper. I had hoped to dissuade her from attending. In the aftermath of our fight about my new job, it seemed to me that the fewer bits of actual evidence of that job's existence that Clio encountered the better. But Mullens had couriered two pasteboard invitations to her apartment, and she had immediately gone online to order a suitable dress. I had done the logical thing and brought along insurance: safe in the pocket of my brand-new tux was a pouch of powdered Ritalin. As it happened I had inhaled a toot or three before the cab arrived and as we skirted the dancefloor my nostrils burned sweetly and my vision was sharp and clear.

'This was money well spent,' James Mullens said when we found him by the stage. 'I'm getting plenty of pics. Bit of video. We're going to send them on to the Serbian guys. It's going to be, like, check out our operation.'

'You're not fucking around,' I said admiringly.

'If you don't have a disruptive product,' Mullens said, 'you go classic.'

'This is *so* nice,' Clio said. She was patting her updo and half-curtseying. I had noticed it before: whenever she was around James Mullens, she became a ditz. I didn't blame her. Mullens had the same effect on me.

'I meant to talk to you, actually,' Mullens said, frowning at Clio. 'The director of the Gate is here. You should have a chat.'

'Are you serious?' Clio said.

'Yeah, come on,' Mullens said. 'I'll introduce you.'

Clio raised her eyebrows at me and allowed James Mullens to take her hand. Over her shoulder Mullens winked, as if to say: *Thank me later.* Watching Clio pass through the crowd, I felt yet another twinge of something that I had been feeling, off and on, since our fight over my decision to take the Echo REIT job. It wasn't guilt, exactly. It was more like an isotope of guilt: differently weighted, at the atomic level. I was lying to Clio, after all. When the payout came through, I was planning to leave her. But it wasn't personal. It wasn't Clio I wanted to leave. It was everything.

Set free, I bumped my way through the multitude of noisily mingling bigwigs, in search of a drink. People nodded in my direction, or shook my hand. In a sense I was surrounded by people I knew: bankers, developers, business journalists, editors, restaurateurs, heirs. These were my father's people: gene-pool money. They had roots in the system. Their beer-keg paunches (the men) and their Botoxed foreheads (the men and the women) spoke of beta blockers, unencumbered assets. They had lurked at the edges of my awareness for most of my conscious life, these people. But in another sense, I knew nothing about any of them, having chosen, many years before, not to take them or their lives seriously. Now I was among them: passing for one of their drab ilk. I felt like a spy behind the Iron Curtain. I was here on secret business, my true purposes known only to myself.

There was a long queue for the bar. I found myself standing beside a waist-high table on which stood an architect's model made of white plastic and green baize. There was a castellated hotel, and some villas, scattered like dice. This was Echo Lake: the Serbian golf resort that would save my life.

'I don't think everyone's going to fit,' said someone at my shoulder. It was Nikki. She wore a figure-hugging dress of some forest-green fabric. The effect of the dress was to make her hips and breasts completely unignorable. Studiously, I ignored them. I directed my male gaze elsewhere: at the rococo scrollwork above the bar, at the bottles of booze in their apothecary colours.

'Uh,' I said, in lieu of a wittier response.

'Though the finished product will presumably be bigger,' Nikki said, coming to my rescue.

'Presumably,' I said. My mouth was dry, my joints ached. The speed was advancing on my constitution unstoppably, like an argumentative idiot. The words *I want to lick your pussy* presented themselves in the lobby of my consciousness. It took me a moment to work out that this was not the thing that I should say next.

'James said you were working on a PhD,' Nikki said, fixing me with her peculiarly undesigning gaze. 'In English.'

'Yeah,' I said. 'But, you know … It didn't work out.'

'Why not?' Nikki said.

'Wow,' I said, reeling. 'That's kind of a hostile question.'

'That's kind of an evasive answer,' Nikki said.

We seemed, in some strange, well-mannered way, to be fighting. How had *that* happened? Like the pilot of a stricken oil tanker, I began laboriously to spin the wheel of our conversational ship and steer it away from the rocks, not my best-engineered metaphor but I'll come back and fix it later, if I can be bothered. 'How did you meet James?' I said. But as I spoke, my most recent toot of Ritalin seized my jaws and clamped them shut, so that I sounded, to my own speed-enhanced ears, like a man trying to make cocktail-party chit-chat while straining to pass an unusually large bowel movement. At the same instant I noticed that the forest-green fabric of Nikki's dress had begun to shimmer or fold internally, like a neon advertisement reflected in an oily puddle. Hallucinations, now. How splendid. The suspicion began to dawn on me that it might have been a tactical error to snort all that Ritalin *before* the party, when the wiser course might have been to snort it *after*.

Nikki put a hand on my wrist. 'Are you okay?' Frowning, she grasped me tighter, in a vaguely diagnostic sort of way. 'You feel kind of feverish.'

'Hot in here,' I managed.

'Do you suffer from social anxiety too?' Nikki said.

179

'Something like that,' I said.

'Here, take this. You need it more than I do.'

She handed me her glass of champagne. Gratefully, I chugged the lot.

'Thanks,' I gasped, returning the empty glass.

'We met at the Trinity Ball,' Nikki said. 'To answer your question. But it turned out we knew all the same people. Which is what always happens in Dublin, isn't it?'

It was working: the champagne was chasing the worst of my speed high away. The material of Nikki's dress was no longer wobbling of its own accord. I began to return to my normal state (i.e. queasy and confused, but basically lucid). I said, 'I don't know. You and I have never met before.'

'But we have James in common,' Nikki said.

'I'm sorry you have social anxiety.'

'That's what therapy is for,' Nikki said.

'I didn't finish my PhD because I wanted to be a writer instead,' I said.

'But here you are,' Nikki said, 'building golf hotels in the Balkans.'

'You gotta spend money to make money,' I said, vaguely aware that, in the context of our conversation, this made no sense.

Nikki pursed her lips. 'It can take a long time,' she said, 'to get the balance of meaning in your life right. Do you know what I mean?'

'Sure,' I said.

'I'm probably talking rubbish,' Nikki said, her gaze un-wavering. 'I'm just always curious about what people choose to do with their lives.'

'I don't intend,' I said, 'to devote my life to building golf hotels.'

'No?' Nikki said, with a slight movement of her chin that said, *You have a funny way of showing it.* 'Because James really does. He knows himself, he knows what he wants to do. I think it's what makes him so attractive.'

'I guess,' I said. I felt – for reasons I didn't quite grasp – slightly offended.

'Certainty is attractive,' Nikki said. 'Or maybe the projection of certainty.'

'Did you always know,' I said, 'that you wanted to be a radiologist?'

'Really I'm an academic,' Nikki said. 'I do research. And yes, I always knew I wanted to do research.'

'You must have been a fun kid at parties,' I said.

'You knew James at school,' Nikki said. 'What was he like?' She had ignored my faintly hostile sally and was regarding me curiously.

'He, uh,' I said. 'We all thought he was going to play for Ireland.'

'Then he had you all fooled,' Nikki said.

Before I could ask her what she meant by this, we were interrupted by a loud, rasping voice saying: 'These cocktails are fucking phenom.' It was Sean Sweeney, striding towards us with that butch walk of his – the walk of a runway model with an untreated testicular infection. 'Look at you,' he said to Nikki. He kissed her smartly on both cheeks. 'Three hours to get ready. It was worth it. You look amazing.'

Without seeming to squirm away, Nikki squirmed away. 'Sean,' she said, in a peculiarly flat tone.

Sweeney was sipping from a small fishbowl filled with blue liquid and chunks of pineapple. 'Have you seen the state of Tyno?' he said. 'I told him, you're too fucking short for a three-button suit. He looks like a fucking lowland gorilla. Here, Mullens is looking for you.'

'What for?' I said.

Sweeney shrugged. 'I'd get myself a drink first, if I were you. I can see how tense you are from across the fucking room.' He nodded at Nikki and moved on.

'I hate these things,' Nikki said.

'Yeah,' I said.

She pointed to the architect's model. 'Hey. See the little people? Little fake people, to show the scale? There's a name for them. They're called *render ghosts*. I learned that today. Isn't that cool?'

'Yeah,' I said. 'That's cool.'

Render ghosts. Nikki wasn't quite accurate in her usage of this term (I looked it up the following day). *Render ghosts* refers not to the faceless figurines who populate architect's models but to their digital cousins – to those computer-generated homunculi who promenade through the shadowless non-space of real estate investment videos, emptily shopping, golfing, drinking tea. Nowadays, of course, I know exactly how it feels to be a render ghost. Devoid of love and purpose, I am a ghost in the world's rendering, casting no shadow in the pale and even light. Back then, of course, I felt solid all the way through. Which is the illusion?

I found Mullens on the dancefloor. 'Can I grab you for a quick download?' he said. My speed high had now entered the teeth-grinding stage. On the other hand, I had successfully equipped myself with a drink: a tumbler of Macallan, neat, which I had decided would be my drink until the deal was done and I could stop pretending to be a business dickhead. Calmly, I followed Mullens into an antechamber of the ballroom, where he handed me his fountain pen and pointed me towards a valuable-looking escritoire on which a wodge of printed documents reposed.

'We've hit a snag,' Mullens said. He ran his fingers through his hair and looked, as a model might, off to the left: out of frame. 'I'll spare you the finer details. Basically nine a.m. tomorrow's the deadline for some of the tax-break stuff. But the lads in Belgrade haven't got the paperwork through. We can get our own end through but I need signatures from everyone so I can courier it over to the Department of Foreign Affairs tonight.'

'Why didn't they get their paperwork through?' I said. 'Are they backing out?'

'Some hold-up,' Mullens said. 'They said their local bureaucracy is giving them shit. I'd say they're dealing with some pretty creaky red tape. Red as in post-fucking Soviet.'

183

'But if we get our end in,' I said, 'that'll be enough?'

'I've a lad at the Department who's helping me out on this,' Mullens said. 'He should be able to get us an extension. But he says we need to get signed documents to him tonight.'

The speed and the heat of the crowd had soaked me in sweat. The pen was slipping though my fingers.

'So what am I signing?' I said.

'You're signing as an officer of Echo REIT, saying you're undertaking the application in good faith,' Mullens said. He, too, seemed to be perspiring.

'Should I read these?' I said.

'I don't mean to pressure you,' Mullens said. 'But I've got to get signatures from the other lads before nine.'

I scribbled my signature along some dotted lines (the final document, I noticed, bore the green harp logo of the Department of Foreign Affairs and Trade). 'Okay,' I said. 'Can I get copies of these?'

'Yeah, yeah,' Mullens said. 'I'll email you a scan.'

I put my hand on his arm. 'This is definitely going to go through, yeah?'

He smiled. 'I forget you're new to this shit. Relax. Happens all the time. Nikki always slags me for getting so stressed. But I'm a stickler.' I remembered what Nikki had said about him: *He knows himself, he knows what he wants to do.* 'Speeches in ten,' he said. 'Game face on.'

To still my ragged heart, I popped outside for a quick cigarette or four. I was unnerved. For the first time I was seriously entertaining the possibility that Mullens's plan, and therefore my plan, was vulnerable to misfortune or incompetence – to a bolt of lightning from the clear blue sky. The idea that I would spend three months hanging out with The Lads only to end up in Dublin, working for Echo REIT, with no prospect of a payout to liberate me from my family and my life, was too grim to contemplate. I solaced myself with the thought that I would, at least, still be drawing my salary: my first paycheque had arrived earlier that week, and my bank balance hit me like a dab of MDMA every time I thought about it. But I didn't want to be reasonably well-off in Dublin. I wanted to be very rich in another place entirely. This was the only way I saw to save myself – from Clio, to whom I was now lying on a daily or even hourly basis; from my parents' betrayals; from the way I felt nauseated and angry and stupid all the time.

Fear at the prospect of exchanging a seven-figure windfall for a six-figure salary may strike you, Dr F, as quite the First World problem. But a trap is a trap, no matter how beautifully appointed. Why do we look at the rich with envy and super-stitious awe? Because secretly we know what they've done. Like gods, they have mastered the trick of escaping from the prison of the self.

From the steps of the Shelbourne I looked across into the gloom of Stephen's Green. A pale, discouraging rain was visible in the downcast glow of the streetlamps. I lit a smoke. The force of the speed was ebbing. Tactical errors be damned: I would need a top-up soon. Across the street a man in a brown trenchcoat seemed to be standing, half hidden by some willow branches that spilled past the railings of the park. He seemed to be staring straight at me. I felt a sudden squeeze of panic – as if someone had crept up behind me and pressed a razor blade to the base of my skull. *Calm blue ocean,* I thought, *calm blue ocean.* It was just The Fear, advancing as the speed declined. When I looked again, the man was gone. *No big deal,* I thought. Definitely time for a top-up. The answer, of course, was more drugs. The answer, in those days, was always more drugs.

Back in the ballroom, the speeches had commenced. At the podium, peering through his bifocals at a small stack of index cards, stood James Mullens's father, Martin. Martin Mullens was a short, barrel-chested man who had a habit of rocking back and forth on his heels in a way that tended, for some reason, to make me think of the word *hooves.* He was also one of Ireland's richest property developers. He had built the X Hotel and the Y Convention Centre. He had built the A Private Clinic and the B Residential Complex. He owned twenty racehorses and the stables in which they lived. His black bow tie was askew. '... an oasis of luxury in the heart of Old Europe ...' he was saying, a warm handshake in his voice, as the crowd attended carefully.

I shouldered my way through the press of tuxed and sequined bodies. I was looking, half unconsciously, for Nikki.

'... but I did have one question.' Martin Mullens paused, and looked over his bifocals at the crowd. 'I accosted James and I said: "James. If the development is called Echo Lake, tell me one thing ... Where's the fucking lake?"'

Everyone laughed generously.

'The name needs work,' Martin Mullens said, causing the tide of laugher to crest again, before it decayed into sighs of fondness, little flutters of calm goodwill.

'On a personal note,' Martin said, 'I'd just like to say how marvellous it is to see the boys we raised turning into such fine young men. Fine young men.'

Applause. From the rostrum behind Martin Mullens, Sean Sweeney called, 'Speeeeeeech!' A classic Sweeney witticism, this. Martin Mullens uttered a noise that made it seem as though the words *HA HA HA!* had been printed on one of his index cards. Ranged around him like an honour guard stood The Lads and their dads – James Mullens, loyally attending; Paul Tynan and his dad; Sean Sweeney and his dad; Mark Foley and his dad; Bobby Hayes and his dad. They were all smirking, like the perpetrators of some successful practical joke. The Lads were, of course, taller and wider than The Dads. But everyone was demonstrably of the same model and make. It was like looking at the results of a successful experiment in corporate eugenics.

James Mullens, spotting me in the crowd, jerked his chin in the direction of the rostrum – *Get up here!* But I shook my head and looked away. I suddenly wanted, very badly, to be elsewhere. Because how might it feel, I thought, if I were standing up there solo? – the only grown-up company executive without a grown-up father standing proudly by his side?

Serbia

'I'd say a fair few heifers died to make this place happen,' Sean Sweeney said, adopting what he clearly believed was a confidential tone.

Down at the other end of the long table Vuk raised his head sharply and seemed to sight along his nose, as if at a moving target in the near distance.

James Mullens winced.

We – that is, The Lads (me, Mullens, Sweeney, Bobby Hayes, Mark Foley, Paul Tynan) and the Serbs (Vuk, Nicolae, Ratko, Aleksandr) – were presently the only customers in what Vuk had described to us as 'the steakhouse of finest Belgrade'. And Sweeney was correct: the vault-like interior of the restaurant was indeed oppressively bovine in theme. The walls were draped with the splayed hides of Herefords – footless and headless, like the victims of a sacrificial rite. The tablecloths were made of leather. The chairs were covered in leather. The placemats were made of leather. The menu offered a dozen cuts of beef—

'But no burgers,' Bobby Hayes said, pantomiming incredulity. 'What kind of fucking steakhouse doesn't serve burgers?'

In order to downplay how much it was costing me to sit in a restaurant among other human beings, doing and saying normal restaurant things, I was trying to speak and move as little as possible. I felt I was doing okay, so far. As long as no one important tried to converse with me, there was very little that could really go wrong. To my right sat Aleksandr, the translator. He was drinking a pint of Guinness – getting into the spirit of things, I thought. He was also methodically rolling cigarettes and lining them up next to his soup plate. 'Is good to get them prepared,' he said, with a diffident dip of his large, turnip-shaped head.

I thought about the various harmless things that a normal person might say at such a moment and came up with, 'Uh . . . are real smokes expensive here?'

Aleksandr's head wagged sadly. 'A pack of real smoke is two hundred dinar,' he said.

On my left-hand side, Paul Tynan was tapping at his iPhone. 'Benjamino!' he said in a gleeful stage whisper. 'That's like one fifty. *One fifty!*'

Aleksandr was unperturbed. 'Average salary in Serbia is not so much as in other European countries. We make, what you say, monkey nuts. Economy is severed from euro, so balance is difficult in our favour.'

In my peripheral vision, black-jacketed waiters were flitting. This was not good news. I was going to have to eat something. I was going to have to eat a *steak*. With trembling hands – oh *why* were my hands always shaking? – I lit a Marlboro, theorising that if I could simply smoke my way through dinner, then no one would notice if I didn't actually eat. Forgetfully, I then lit another cigarette. I had three going now. This kept happening. It wasn't chain-smoking. It was more like relay smoking. One smoke took over when the other got tired. My section of the table had its own little weather system of nicotined fumes.

A waiter placed a bowl of brown liquid on the table in front of me. It resembled to an uncomfortable degree the diarrhoeic gruel that I had deposited in the toilet at the Hotel Karlovsky.

'You are smoking much, in Ireland,' Aleksandr said.

'Not really,' I said, feeling vaguely insulted. I pointed to the bowl of brown liquid. 'What, eh … What is this?'

'Beef goulash,' Aleksandr said. 'Is national delicacy.'

Paul Tynan nudged my elbow. 'Seriously,' he said, 'there has not been one single fucking meal here where someone hasn't gone, "Is national delicacy", about some random fucking food that they have fucking *everywhere else on earth*. We turned it into a drinking game: every time somebody says "Is national delicacy", take a drink.'

And indeed, all around the long table, The Lads were discreetly sipping at their bottles of beer.

I pushed my plate of goulash away. Beside me, Aleksandr was consuming spoonfuls at a rapid clip, his face very close to the bowl. 'You are finding much help from family,' he said.

'Excuse me?' I said.

'In dealings of business,' Aleksandr said. 'Is much help from family. Especially from fathers. This I hear yesterday evening in town hall.'

'Ah,' I said. 'Uh, yeah. Some of the lads … their fathers …' This seemed to be all I could manage, in the way of verbal discourse. I had broken out in a frigid sweat. I was breathing through my mouth and I sat hunched forward over my cigarette, waiting for another spasm of nausea to pass.

'And your father,' Aleksandr said. 'He also is helping.'

'No,' I said. 'Not exactly. He's, uh … He might be going to jail.'

Aleksandr chewed on a mouthful of goulash. 'Your father is criminal,' he said.

'No,' I said. 'Well, maybe. I don't actually know. There's been an issue with the trial.'

'So is not in business,' Aleksandr said.

'No,' I said. 'Not anymore.'

'This I am sorry to hear,' Aleksandr said after a moment. 'It must be toughening for your family to go through this.'

'Toughening,' I said, 'is not the word.'

Aleksandr was looking at me with frank sympathy – the same look that Nikki had given me when she had heard about my father's legal troubles. (Have we gotten to that bit yet? No? Does it matter?) Considering this, I waved a dismissive hand. I had no need of sympathy. I was one week away from never having to think about my father ever again. My nausea was gradually abating. Up at Vuk's end of the table, Nicolae and Ratko were contentedly shovelling goulash into their faces. The thought occurred to me: *They're killers.* Oh, my. I was full of interior babble. That coke was some strong stuff, clearly. Well, I thought, if you do have to deal with some fucked-up shit, you might as well do it while you're coked off your gourd.

'Your father's crime,' Aleksandr said. 'It is what?'

'It's …' I said.

But now something was happening, up at the other end of the table. Vuk was dabbing at his downturned mouth with a napkin and climbing to his feet. From the Serbs, a patter of applause. '*Hvala*,' Vuk said, levelling a conciliatory hand. The pale head hovered above the dark shirt, above the winged collar of the cape-like coat. 'You are most kind.' Sean Sweeney tapped his knife against his bottle of Heineken for silence. Paul Tynan slid his iPhone under his napkin and then stared down at it with manic fixity. 'It is falling to me esteemed honour,' Vuk said, 'to welcome Irish guests. I hope a few words to strike your ear.'

'Strike away,' Sean Sweeney said.

Vuk held up his wine glass, which was empty. 'There is old joke about national character of Serbia,' he said. 'We are *inat*.'

Nicolae and Ratko chuckled darkly. I leaned in to Aleksandr and said, 'What does that mean?'

Aleksandr gave a tight shake of his head and did not look up. He was making cigarettes again, the pyramid of rollies by his plate growing exponentially.

'*Inat*,' Vuk said, smiling. 'Stubborn. Contrary. We will fight! We will not do what you say! We will do what *we* say! If we see that land by rights is ours, we will take. We may ask politely, or we may ask not so politely. But we take! Yes, yes. Some say this is defect of Serbian character. But without *inat*, what? NATO' – Vuk permitted himself a low cough that might have been a laugh – 'NATO, she does not like *inat*. Does not think Serbs should be proud of what they do. And now, thanks to NATO, there exists much peaceful between Serbia and her neighbours.'

I was finding it difficult to gauge the precise tone of this speech. Vuk seemed to be speaking mainly to his retinue. The Lads also looked a bit bamboozled. Paul Tynan was now frankly texting, and Sean Sweeney was looking around for a waiter.

'Peaceful, yes,' Vuk went on. 'But peaceful does not bring investment of itself. It does not bring exports to Serbia. In capitalist dream, other countries of Europe see past NATO and tensions. They bring investments.'

A waiter had arrived. Ignoring Sweeney's clicked fingers, he began filling everyone's wine glass with a clear yellowish liquid.

'But things now change, at last,' Vuk said. His eyes twinkled greasily, like little spheres of wet coal. 'From Ireland, great European country, with great European economy – investment comes! And from Serbia, there exists now much love for the Irish.'

'Hear, hear,' James Mullens said, in a hearty House-of-Commons voice.

'On occasion of arrival of Irish investors,' Vuk said, 'I wish to erect a toast.'

At this, Sweeney and Hayeser collapsed into giggles. Nicolae, who had picked up his glass, now set it down, and with hypnotic slowness turned his eye-patched stare in their direction. Immediately the laughter snuffed itself out.

James Mullens was thin-lipped. 'A toast,' he said.

Vuk let a brief silence fall. Then he said, '*Da*, a toast. For best wishes and good cooperation. For the Echoing Lake. For *inat*!'

Everyone swooped their glasses through the air and drank.

'*Fuck* me,' Bobby Hayes said. 'What the fuck is this?'

'*Rakija*,' Aleksandr said morosely. 'Brandy of plum. Is national drink.'

Some of The Lads, caught out by the *d* of *drink*, had raised their beers.

'That counts,' Bobby Hayes said.

'That totally counts,' Paul Tynan said.

But now something truly untoward was taking place: Sean Sweeney was lumbering to his feet and tapping his bottle again for silence. 'Eh, sorry there, lads,' he said. He slipped the fingers of his left hand under his belt. 'I'm just going to erect a bit of an oul' toast there myself, as I think is only appropriate.' At the far end of the table, Mullens gave a corpse-like grin. *It's our fathers,* I thought. *We inherited the compulsion to make speeches from our fathers.* 'It gives me great pleasure,' Sweeney said, 'to raise a glass to Vuk and the rest of the lads here in Belgrade. I know you lads here had a fairly hard time of it before the Wall fell, yeah? But we're here to tell you, you're basically in the First World now. And can I just say, this restaurant is a great spot but, you know, bring on the Serbian hookers, you know what I mean, lads? Ah, yeah! Cheers!' Sweeney quaffed the last of his *rakija* and resumed his seat in a silence so total that I could hear a dropped glass smash behind the padded swing doors of the kitchen, two hundred feet away.

*

Beyond the restaurant's windows, night had fallen. There seemed to be no streetlights in this particular quarter of Belgrade. In my parlous state – with my coke high now unignorably waning – I seemed to see the unrelieved darkness as the very stuff of mortality itself: the darkness that waits beyond the light. I set about finishing my three extant cigarettes, so that I could get on with lighting another one.

On my plate was a marbled slab of blue meat, fist-sized, and a single cold tapeworm of what appeared to be pasta. Turning to my right, I said, 'So, eh, Aleksandr, how long have you been a translator?' It had occurred to me, belatedly, that as someone who worked for Vuk, Aleksandr might be able to offer some useful information about our Serbian partners, to wit: were these guys on the level? And if so, why were they so frightening? Mullens had assured me that Vuk and his gang were desperate – that they were mugs, grubbing for foreign cash. But they were not, to my mind, acting like desperate men, or like men who wanted to get paid. Instead, they seemed to be laughing at us.

'I am not translator,' Aleksandr said. 'You please to call me Aleks. You see I drink Guinness. My friends call me Aleks Guinness.'

'Ha,' I said. I frowned. 'I thought Vuk said—'

'I work half-time as translator,' Aleks said. 'Of necessary. In actuality I am poet.'

Aha, I thought. *No wonder the guy dresses like he hasn't got any money.* 'Published?' I said politely.

'I publish small book,' Aleks said. 'Small book of size

called chapbook in English. But is not big audience for poetry in Serbia. So I work as translator for men of business. Pay is not so good, but when I am not working, I am writing.'

At the back of my mind a small and sneering voice said: *Hey, even this loser is a published writer. What have you ever published, you prick?* But I suppressed the thought: becoming a writer was no longer, for me, the point.

'What about Vuk,' I said. 'Have you worked for him before?'

'Not before,' Aleks said. 'I am stranger here, like you.'

'So you don't know much about his business,' I said.

Aleks looked away. 'Serbia is small country,' he said. 'I know of Vuk before many years.'

'So he's, like, well known,' I said. 'As a builder.'

'Builder,' Aleks said. He was caressing a rollie between finger and thumb. 'No. Not as builder. Has had many parts of life. Now he is builder. He is very happy to have Irish men of business at work with him.'

'You're working for him,' I hazarded, 'so you obviously trust him.'

Aleks said nothing. Then he said, 'You are not eating your steak.'

I made a vague attempt to cover my plate with my hand. 'I'm not hungry,' I said.

Dublin

Jumping backwards, for just a moment, as my memory swerves and refocuses, and it is the night of the Echo Lake launch in the Shelbourne ballroom, and Clio and I are slow-dancing in the middle of the darkened floor (all the adults have left, and it is just us kids), and I am crushing Clio's body close to mine, and I am developing one of those mysteriously powerful drunken hard-ons that sometimes arrive unheralded, like the grace of God, and I whisper 'I love you,' in Clio's ear, and Clio whispers back something that sounds like, 'You haven't got a hope,' and it strikes me, in a flash of terrible lucidity, that Clio knows exactly what is going on, and that she has always known, and that she always will.

How goes it here in rehab, by the by? Well, after four days on my new pills, my baseline mood has exhibited no perceptible uptick. My baseline mood, Dr F, remains unalterably saturnine. When I went to see the good doctor today, he indicated this notebook – whose pages are now overrun with my scribblings – and said, 'Is it helping?'

'I'm trying to find a stronger word than mortifying,' I said. My head was in my hands. 'How did I not see?'

'You didn't want to see,' Dr F said. 'But you want to see now, I think.'

'You're not giving me a choice,' I said.

'There's always a choice,' Dr Felix said.

197

'What's the point of doing this, anyway?' I said. 'Am I supposed to wallow in my own stupidity for so long that I never do anything stupid ever again?'

'The point is to develop self-knowledge,' Dr Felix said.

'So why,' I said, 'don't you just send me to India for a year so I can do transcendental meditation, or some shit? Why make me comb through my mistakes like some sort of . . .' I gave up: I was too exhausted and demoralised to invent an appropriate simile.

Dr Felix tilted his head. 'Self-knowledge isn't some sort of wellness-promoting buzzword,' he said. 'Real self-knowledge is cultivated at enormous cost. It often forces you to confront truths that you'd rather ignore. Most people won't do that. That's why most people have no idea who they are.'

'You mean,' I said, 'they're happy.'

Dr Felix paused. 'People think they can grow through taking adventure holidays, or getting a new job, or having children, or writing a book, or sleeping with strangers. But that's just change. There's only one way to grow. You work out who you are. Without illusion. You try to see yourself without hope and without despair.'

'Why do I have to grow at all?' I said. My tone was sullen. 'What's so great about growing?'

Dr Felix was moving his fingers through a cone of sunlit dust. 'You grow or you die,' he said.

Serbia

The doors of the restaurant swung open. At once Vuk raised his arms to heaven like an old-time revival preacher and said, very loudly, '*Mačka!*' He stood up to greet the young woman who had just entered, enfolding her in his long black coat in such a way that, for a moment, it looked as if she had been swallowed by a large bat. When she emerged, I saw that she was roughly my age, i.e. twenty-seven or thereabouts. I felt a premonitory shiver: as if I had just heard a knock on the door at four o'clock in the morning and spotted revolving blue lights through my bedroom window. I had the distinct impression that things were getting out of hand. But Mullens was sawing aggressively at the stringy remnants of his steak as if nothing was amiss. Presumably, this was what we were all supposed to be doing.

In an undertone, Aleksandr said, '*Mačka* is term of endearment. It means pussycat.'

'So her name is Pussycat?' Bobby Hayes said.

Sean Sweeney made an inane face. 'Eh, we met her yesterday, Hayeser? Her name is, like, Maria, or something?'

'Maria,' Aleksandr said, nodding gloomily. 'Is nephew of Vuk.'

'Nephew is right,' Sean Sweeney said, chuckling.

Aleksandr blushed. 'Niece,' he said. 'My English is mixed, sometimes.'

Vuk's niece. The young woman thus introduced wore an oversized yellow jumper whose collar hung loose off her

199

bare left shoulder. Also a pair of skintight jeans, ripped at the knees. On her head was a baseball cap that bore the logo of the New York Yankees. She surveyed The Lads with an indifference that bordered, I thought, on contempt – as if she had seen our type before and was wise to all our bullshit moves. She did not smile. She scared the hell out of me, just as Vuk and Nicolae and Ratko did. What was she doing here? Was she in on the deal? Would I have to schmooze her, too? Guided by Vuk, the young woman walked to the head of the table. As she passed Nicolae, she put her hand fleetingly on his shoulder. There was something else: she walked with a faint limp.

'To investors of Ireland,' Vuk said, 'I present Maria.'

The Lads mumbled a suite of *How're you doin'*s.

'In particular,' Vuk went on, 'I introduce newest arrived.' With a curled hand he beckoned towards something at the back of the restaurant. I looked around, expecting another pockmarked Serb to emerge from the upholstered gloom. Then I realised what was actually happening: Vuk was beckoning to me. I looked around for support. But The Lads were directing their attention elsewhere – all except for Bobby Hayes, who regarded me steadily with a beatific grin on his face.

'Me?' I said.

'Come,' Vuk said.

I stumbled to my feet and made my way to the head of the table. The Lads were now watching, riveted. Still not smiling, the young women presented her hand to be kissed.

Her nails were long and painted crimson. I grasped her hand and pressed my lips to her skin, feeling the tingle or pressure of unwanted intimacy. Discreetly, I wiped my fingers on the backside of my suit pants.

Vuk had joined his own hands together and was moving them up and down like a priest at a wedding. 'She is very beautiful,' he said, as if inviting agreement. In my peripheral vision I saw Sean Sweeney stuffing his napkin into his mouth.

The expression on Maria's face was sourly expectant.

'Lovely,' was what I eventually came up with.

'Another leprechaun, I hope you are not,' Maria said.

'I, uh,' I said.

'Too many Irish leprechaun men I have met this week,' Maria said. 'Short men with no balls. I hear before that there are real men in Ireland, but I start to doubt if this is true.'

There seemed to be nothing I could safely say in response to this. Confronted with rudeness on such an epic scale, the civilised mind is, I've found, largely without recourse. I thought about saying, *Well, fuck you, too!* But Vuk stepped in. 'Leprechauns,' he said, cackling indulgently. His arm rose from the folds of his coat and settled paternally just above my elbow. 'Is good Irish joke,' he said, giving me a meaningful glare.

'Aha, ha,' I said, looking at Maria and then back at Vuk, who was now smiling in horrible approval.

'Maria is scholar,' he said. 'Is studying for philosophy.'

'How lovely,' I said.

Maria's nostrils flared. 'I do master's,' she said. 'Everyone in Serbia have master's. I find this is not so for Irish lepre-chaun men.'

I felt the keen prompting edge of Vuk's gaze. 'What did you, uh, do the master's in?' I asked.

'I do master's in Schopenhauer,' Maria said. She was look-ing at the table, at the ceiling, at the floor, and tapping her right foot arrhythmically, like a student actor who has been told to play *bored*.

'Not a huge fan of women, Schopenhauer,' I observed.

The room's ambient emotional temperature dropped below zero.

'You will talk much to Maria,' Vuk said, clapping his hands once and smiling. 'When we arrive at club. You will get to know each other perhaps, and a friendship will be born.'

Maria looked up at the leather-lined ceiling and folded her arms.

'Christ,' Sweeney said, reclining in the limo's moneyed hush, 'the fucking *state* of her.'

'I'm fairly sure she used to be a man,' Bobby Hayes said, thoughtfully. 'And fairly recently, like.'

We were rolling past wan streetlights that flickered on and off like glitches in the system of the world. As the limo bounced along the cobbled streets The Lads were snorting and numbing their gums and I felt, as I always did at this stage of a night on coke, that I had borrowed my teeth from someone else – an elderly relative, perhaps, who had spent a lifetime eating raw cane sugar and never brushing.

'Here,' I said, remembering suddenly. 'What about the contracts? Are we keeping an eye on that?'

'Bit of a delay,' James Mullens said. *Sniff!* 'I was talking to Vuk about it. Basically their solicitor is out of town. He says tomorrow at the latest.'

'Okay,' I said, 'so we're not worried about this, then.'

'Jesus, man,' Mullens said. 'We're not worried about *anything.*' *Sniff!*

I looked out of the window. The city was throwing its waste light skywards, staining the combed-over clouds a bilious green. In my pocket, my phone buzzed. I checked the screen: DAD CALLING. My finger hovered over ANSWER. But in the end, I waited until the call rang out.

My first thought, as we passed through a pair of red velvet drapes and moved along a tunnel lined with smoked grey mirrors, was *This is more fucking like it!* My coke-astonished heart began to pump with happy purpose. Here at last, I thought, was a semblance of the techno-consumerist burnish that I had been looking for since I first arrived in Belgrade, all those hours ago. Things were looking up.

But when we entered the club's main cavity, it was deserted. We were the only customers. Some dismal Europop beats pounded emptily across the dancefloor. By the entrance to a roped-off enclosure – a little cubby ringed with stained banquettes – Nicolae and Ratko stood with their hands clasped tightly in front of their crotches. We passed between them, not speaking. In one corner of the cubby Aleksandr sat with his triangular head bowed, listening to Vuk, who as he spoke concealed his mouth with one large white clawlike hand. Aleksandr kept nodding and looking away, nodding and looking away, as if (I couldn't help thinking) he just didn't like what he was being forced to listen to. At the other end of the table Maria sat, her pinched, unhappy face illuminated from below by the cracked yellow light of an ancient Nokia. I perceived at once that she was the sort of girl who would make a point of demonstrating how alone she felt in night-clubs. Meanwhile The Lads were circling bullishly in the small enclosure. They were all rubbing at their nostrils with thumbs and forefingers, trying to hold in the usual melting mixture of cocaine crystals and snot. A gloomy busboy took our orders for drinks.

'Macallan,' I said, 'on the rocks, with a twist.'

Aleks, who had escaped from his conversation with Vuk, was now sitting beside me. He lit a spliff-shaped rollie and nipped a fleck of tobacco from the tip of his tongue. 'You are loyal to Scotch whisky and not to Irish,' he said.

'Eh,' I said. 'I'm not sure what Macallan is, to be honest.'

'You are very young for businessman,' Aleks said.

'I suppose,' I said.

'In Serbia,' Aleks said, 'is very difficult to succeed in business for many people of younger generation. Because of extreme negative conditions of economy, yes, but also because so much of money and resources is controlled by older gen-eration. Still are businessmen who were successful in days of Yugoslavia the businessmen of the present time.'

'Yeah,' I said. My right foot was jiggling fiercely of its own accord.

'Older generation have monopoly on decisions of banks,' Aleks said. 'Often they propose what seem good work to younger generation, but is merely ruse. Young people end up investing and owing all their money.'

'Shit buzz,' I said.

Now Aleks was leaning in, his big oddly shaped head close to my shoulder. 'Nicolae is not from Serbia,' he whispered. 'Is former employee of Securitate in Romania. Came to Serbia after fall of Ceaușescu regime.'

'What is that,' I said, 'like, Group Four? Private security?'

'*Hola*, lads.' This was Sean Sweeney, bopping over, red-faced, his crotch low-slung in a burlesque of a boogie. 'Not too many birds in this fine establishment. Here, Ratko, or whatever. What's the story with the birds, yeah?'

Ratko, in expressionless conference with Nicolae over by the velvet rope, slowly swivelled his rodentine eyes in Sweeney's direction, a dull smile on his lips. Sweeney seemed to shrivel, his limbs retracting like the touched eyes of snails.

'Tomorrow,' Ratko said, in a voice like a saw catching on a rusty nail, 'we bring you to animal sanctuary. Plenty of birds.'

Ratko and Nicolae laughed without moving their mouths. The effect was maximally disconcerting, like seeing someone run with their arms held straight at their sides. My Macallan arrived, with no rocks, no twist.

'Christ,' I said, and knocked it back in one.

*

And now, it seemed, Maria was standing in front of me, still wearing her Yankees cap and leaning noticeably on her left leg, as if favouring it. 'You buy me drink,' she said. It was an instruction, devoid of humour or flirtatiousness. She did not expect me to say no. The words *DO NOT BUY THIS GIRL A DRINK* scrolled across my mind in fizzing red neon. 'I think the bar's over there,' I tried to say. But somehow we were already standing by the chrome-trimmed counter. Oh boy, was I high.

'I will have sex on beach,' Maria said, tossing her head. 'You know what this is, leprechaun man? Sex on Beach?'

'One Sex on the Beach, please,' I said to the Igor who lurked behind the bar. 'And a whiskey. Not Macallan.'

From some hidden corner of the club a smoke machine was distributing carbon dioxide. It now settled as a dense fog at waist height. I thought of blasted heaths and then I thought of *Lear*: *All dark and comfortless*. I recognised this mood. My mind was sliding on the black ice of too much coke.

Maria was staring at me. 'So short,' she said, looking me up and down. 'If I put on my heels, I could eat out of your head.'

'Why would you want to, would be the question there,' I said.

'You order shot also,' Maria said. 'Two shots. Doubles. Of *rakija*.'

The Igor behind the bar had made no move to mix our drinks. I waved a 500-dinar note and said, 'You heard the lady.'

Our shots of *rakija* arrived. Maria drained them both. 'You think one shot was for you,' she said. 'But were both for me.'

'Ah, you fooled me,' I said.

'I am crazy bitch,' Maria said. 'My friends say I am crazy bitch. Maria, you are crazy bitch, they say.'

'They've got your number,' I said.

The Igor behind the bar reappeared, bearing a tall glass forested with paper umbrellas and jagged slices of fruit. 'Sex on Beach,' he said in a robotic voice. Maria sought with her mouth the end of an elaborately curled pink straw and began fellating it, all the while maintaining pointed eye contact.

'You have Sex on Beach in Ireland?' she said.

'Let me ask you something,' I said, deploying a subject-changing tactic I had seen my father use on salesmen. 'If you're doing a master's in philosophy, why are you hanging out with your uncle's business partners? This isn't' (here I indicated the darkened nightclub, the perspiring Lads, the swirling dry ice) 'a particularly philosophical way to spend your time.'

'I am not here for philosophy,' Maria said with a scornful toss of her head. 'I am here to meet husband. I will marry a man who will take care of me. Only rich man can take real care of his wife.'

'. . . I guess the news is slow to get here, huh,' I said.

'What news?' Maria said. 'What is news? You tell me.'

Things, I felt, were going poorly. To distract myself, I fiddled with a cigarette. For some reason I couldn't seem to get it properly lit. Then, with horror, I saw that I was trying to smoke the taped-up fifty-dinar note that we had been using to snort coke in the limo. I crammed it into my pocket. Maria seemed not to have noticed.

In the bathroom I swallowed two Xanax and leaned against a cubicle door while I waited for the sweat to dry on my armpits and chest. I could hear a low *thumpity-thump* that was probably a concussive bass track playing in the club next door but might also have been the pulsing infrasound of my own anxiety as it gathered force under the auspices of the coke and of Maria's frankly hostile flirting. I switched on my phone to check the time. It was 12.46 a.m. The phone shivered and gave up its cargo of queued messages. Two missed calls from my father, and a sequence of WhatsApps from Clio. The next-to-last of these said FINE FUK U I CAN FIND SUM1 ELSE. The last one said I'M SRY BADGER I LOB U. Since this conversation seemed to be getting on okay without me, I ignored it. The problem was that Clio had been in a state of high tension ever since she had landed a starring role in a Fringe play about, I gathered, the refugee crisis. Distracted by my secret plan – and spending quite a bit of time with The Lads – I had failed to devote sufficient time to shoring up her professional confidence. Our relationship – fractious at the best of times – was now characterised by snippy text exchanges followed by passionate make-up sex and very few actual conversations. I accepted my share of the blame for this. After all, I was now simply killing time with Clio until I could begin my new life in California, or Acapulco, or Belize. From my perspective, our relationship was the

208

walking dead. There was still the problem of my guilt. But what was Xanax for, if not the alleviation of unwanted and probably unnecessary guilt?

You asked me this morning, Dr F, why I didn't simply do the honest thing and break up with Clio. I believe I've already told you the answer: I was afraid. For almost a year Clio had represented the only safe port in my storm-tossed life, and the idea of leaving her before I was rich enough to immediately flee the country and escape the fallout made my heart clench with dread. In other words, I needed her. I was too much of a coward to do without her. I say it again: Clio's crime was that she liked me. She may have been the only person who ever did.

My heart rate slowed. The Xanax was doing its job. I hauled myself out of the cubicle and washed my face in a putrid-smelling sink. Then I stared at myself in a stainless-steel mirror. Cognitively, I think it would be fair to say, I was at something of a low ebb. I splashed some more foul water on my face. The light in the bathroom was the colour of sour milk. But it was okay – some remnants of the coke were still hustling through my system, bigging up my self-regard. I could handle this shit. It was no big deal. I would stride back out there and make some further small-bore conversation with Maria or whoever and before I knew it the night would be over and I could go back to my hotel room and safely black out.

Suddenly a face swam into focus in the mirror beside me. 'Mother Vukker,' Bobby Hayes said. 'Hear about the afterparty?'

'The what?' I said.

'Strip club, mother Vukker.' Hayeser located a urinal, tugged open his fly, and unleashed a powerful surge of urine, accompanied by a baritone gasp of relief. 'Fucking get it *wet*, yo,' he said, in parodic Americanese.

My head began to ache. 'How long,' I said, 'is this night going to last?'

'Party till dawn, bro,' Bobby Hayes said. He was wearing a pair of Wayfarer shades and rocking his head back and forth like Stevie Wonder. The stream of his piss wavered and overspilled the porcelain edges of the urinal.

'Oh,' I said. 'Yay.'

Bobby Hayes. His father had scraped a fortune in gravel from the hills of the border counties back in the late 1980s. The father had now retired, to while away the summers of his senescence floating in the amniotic shallows of a variety of tax-sheltered Mediterranean coves. An older brother had been put in charge of the gravel concern, leaving Bobby to his own entrepreneurial devices – a source, I gathered, of some bitterness. In school Bobby had been famous for two things: being an unreconstructed mucker from Bogtown, and wearing a pair of blue suede loafers all year round. The loafers, I suppose, might have hinted at a thwarted dandyism of some kind – a half-awakened longing for the finer things in life. But from the feet up, Bobby was all thug. He was in continual motion, forever jiggling a knee or flexing a fist, belching, cackling, throwing shadow hooks, throwing proper punches. I had never seen him sit still for more than thirty seconds. Plus he had one of those large, spherical, boiled-ham heads and a broad pink face that flushed easily. You had the sense that at any moment he might hotly overflow with some private, embarrassing passion – or that he might virulently lose his temper on the flimsiest of pretexts. For the last five years Bobby had worked as a 'strategist', whatever that was, for something called the Tycho Group, which seemed to be a multinational investment consortium of some kind (it was peculiarly difficult to google). In his grown-up incarnation, he was, according to James Mullens, 'a real business mind'. And who was I to disagree?

Now, as a tall, sallow-faced woman in white stockings and suspenders flossed between her legs with his Christian Lacroix tie, Bobby made a sneering O-face and said, 'This is more fucking *like it!*' The tendons in his neck stood out like a ship's rigging. As she danced, the woman looked down at him with zero-affect eyes. '*TAKE* it off!' Hayeser said, whooping. The woman bent and thumped her ass against his crotch.

I was perched in an octagonal alcove, looking out: at the velvet curtains, the steel poles doubled in the mirrored walls. Around me, the low red light was like an embolism. I was not alone. I had assumed (I had hoped) that Maria would not be accompanying us to the strip club. But here she was, occupying the stool next to mine, feasting on another umbrella-and-foliage cocktail. So far, she had said nothing. But it was only a matter of time.

Vuk, too, had accompanied us to the club. He had hung around for twenty minutes, bleakly surveying The Lads and the girls with his blank bituminous eyes. Then, waving a pale hand, he had departed, leaving Nicolae and Ratko behind as his viceregents or proxies. They now sat, these two, at a small tin table, holding shot glasses full of *rakija* but not drinking. Although no one had said so out loud, it seemed that our night was fated to continue for as long as they remained to oversee it. Not that The Lads were keen to leave: they had convened in the bathroom in wily pairs and now they were ready to party till dawn. Even so, we felt uneasy. No one was keen to talk to Nicolae or even look at him directly. Almost as soon as we had arrived in the club, he had peeled back his eyepatch (it now clung to his ear like a black bandage) and The Lads had collectively suppressed a groan of terror and disgust. Where Nicolae's right eye should have been there was instead a meatball-sized lump of scar tissue, obscenely hairless, and fringed with tiny burns, as from a cigarette. Ratko, too, with his pocked and suctioned face, discouraged scrutiny. Who were these fuckers, anyway? Before leaving the nightclub bathroom I had typed the word *Securitate* into my phone's search engine, and then immediately deleted it, reasoning that I had more pressing troubles. Thinking strategically, I made a point of changing my phone's wallpaper to a glamour shot of Clio (beach, bikini, duck-billed lips). My plan was to angle the screen in such a way that this photograph became unignorably visible to Maria as she continued to chat me up. So far, this plan did not appear to be working.

Edging her bum closer to where I sat, tossing her hair like a model in a shampoo ad, Maria now said, 'You really have no purpose in life, do you?'

In desperation I said, 'I have a girlfriend.'

Maria seemed to take this as an explanation for the absence of a stripper on my lap. 'These girls?' she said, surveying with disdain the dancers as they grooved, stony-faced, in the nether light. 'Pah! I know why you no want dance from these girls. These girls are Bosnian. All Bosnian women must work as whores. This is because Bosnian men are stupid and lazy. They are known for this all over Europe. So their wives, their daughters, they must make money lying on their backs. What could be easier? Pah!'

'It doesn't look that easy to me,' I said.

'I am self-sufficient,' Maria said. 'I am not like stripper who must dance and fuck her way to husband. You see arm?' She was pointing to a spot high up on her left arm, tugging down the loose collar of her jumper and indicating a mark that might have been an unusually large inoculation scar, and at the same time revealing – I assumed this was, as Marxists say, no accident – a hefty scoop of her breast. 'Was first bullet,' she said. 'Age eleven. And I am fine. I not even need to go to hospital. My father remove bullet and I recover. Is no deal.'

'No deal,' I echoed, looking helplessly across the room to where Paul Tynan was motorboating a bored-looking woman in a studded red G-string.

'I have only one thing in common with these girls,' Maria said. Her face contracted in what might have been a sexy wink but could just as easily have been a stroke or a *petit mal* seizure.

'What's that?' I said, dutifully returning the ball.

'I also am hairless,' Maria said, pointing south. 'Like nine-year-old.'

'Jesus Christ,' I said.

Quite apart from anything else, I was now dangerously close to that stage of a night on drugs past which all sensory input begins to decay into mere stochastic noise. Beyond this phase, I knew, lurked recklessness and error. I pitched to my feet unsteadily. I had no particular goal in mind – just an impulse to get away from Maria as quickly as possible. The floor beneath my feet felt tacky. I lurched to a halt in the middle of the dancefloor. The girls on the stage were now windmilling their baubled breasts in unison, wearing identical expressions of simulated rapture. I scanned the perimeter of the club but there seemed to be no exit.

Sean Sweeney rocked up out of the bordello gloom, one eye bleared shut, a stripper on each arm. '—,' he said, using my old school nickname (with which I will not deface these pages), 'have you met the girls? This one's *Oriana*, yeah, and I swear to God I'm not fucking with you, this other one's name is *Floriana*, am I right, ladies?'

The girls were six inches taller than Sweeney in their hypodermic heels. They did not smile. Sweeney sucked a Marlboro down to the filter and daubed it vaguely in the direction of a heaped ashtray. 'Why don't you get one of these?' he yelled, gesturing.

In a bucket chair nearby Mark Foley was being subjected to the strenuous attentions of a lap-dancing blonde girl.

I was swaying on my feet. My plan was collapsing around me. There would be no contracts. There would be no payout. I had to get home: to Clio, to my stupid parents in their stupid, safe house.

'Think,' I said, my jaw working. 'Think I go back to hotel.'

Sweeney threw his truck-driver's arms around me and shouted something that I eventually deciphered as, '*Show! They're going to put on a show!*'

Pushing Sweeney away, I stumbled through the murk, and now, I'm afraid, my memory becomes a thing of shreds and patches: I do remember accosting James Mullens and demanding to know when we were going to sign the contracts. 'Tomorrow, tomorrow,' Mullens said, 'take it easy.' I seem to have tripped and fallen, and I found myself lying dead weight on top of a naked girl, and I scrambled to my feet and tried to apologise, and I remember the sound of glass breaking, and I also seem to remember – though this can't possibly be right, can it? – standing next to Ratko, who grinned lasciviously as he extinguished a cigarette against the skin of his own damp palm. I also remember Bobby Hayes high-fiving me and saying, 'You see Yasmina there, yeah? Just got a hummer off her in the champagne room, it was fucking amazing, and you know what the best thing was? It cost like *twenty quid!*'

The club had filled up with strangers, swarthy middle-aged men in Hawaiian shirts who stood around ostentatiously grappling with their own genitals as the dancing girls hunkered and swung, and the music screened out everything, like white noise. By the time I finally located the exit and made it outside, I saw that there was no one else around, and our limo sat there, dormant, its mirrored glass reflecting curved bands of nightclub neon, and the streets were wet with recent rain and dead black and darkly gleaming.

Dublin

A week after the Echo REIT launch, my second paycheque arrived – ahead of schedule, and described by Mullens as 'an advance'. I had not yet managed to spend all of my first paycheque (though I had made, I thought, a pretty good effort, picking and choosing among the pouches and wraps available from within the recesses of Barry Hynes's multi-pocketed camouflage coat). Coupled with the two halves of my signing bonus, these sums added up to an amount that made me feel, whenever I checked my bank balance online, as if I had been transferred to the financial equivalent of a room with padded walls and circular furniture: no matter where I fell, I would not be hurt. Perhaps this feeling – that nothing can really hurt you any longer – explains why rich people act like they're out of their minds the whole time. Having lots of money is like being one of those kids who are born without nerve endings and, feeling no pain, hurl themselves recklessly against the world, relying on other people to tell them when they're damaged.

The plan was to cast off the splints of the past (family, writing, Clio, drugs) in a single pristine jump, and thereafter to live as if I needed nothing. Fed by money, my aspirations became increasingly grandiose. Passing through the quotidian world on my way to and from the Echo REIT offices every day, I conducted snarling internal diagnoses of the state of the West: look at all those trapped people, gazing into the black screens of smartphones built by suicidal Chinese engineers, treading streets above noisome sewers jammed with fatbergs, dwarfed by buildings owned by tax-evading multinationals who have poisoned the oceans with microplastics ... I was going to scam my way out of it all. This was my solution to the problem of living in a hypercapitalist culture. I wasn't going to go around money. I was going to go through it.

While I brooded like a miser about my present and future successes, Clio was brooding about her failures. At the beginning of August she had appeared in an original play written by one of her actor friends. Set in a rural kitchen, this play consisted of three monologues by women who had all been sexually abused by their fathers. The sole review it received, in the *Irish Independent*, contained the phrases 'tonally wayward', 'tasteless', and 'stiff, unconvincing performances'. I had to waste a whole pilled-up night, on the periphery of a house party, talking Clio out of abandoning her dream. 'Artists get bad reviews,' I remember saying. 'It's the price you pay for trying to make something real.' Privately I had regarded the sexual-abuse play as maudlin to the point of somnolence (i.e. I had fallen asleep during the second act). But I sensed that a Clio who had given up on trying to become an actor would be a Clio who needed moral support of a depth and range that I was, under current conditions, quite unable to supply. There was also the fact that I entirely lacked the courage to break up with her – I knew that any such breakup would exact a pro-hibitively high emotional price – and the even more pertinent fact that I had nowhere else to live besides her apartment.

It was the latter that spurred me, a week or two after my first paycheque arrived, to lease a penthouse at The Brokerage. This was a luxury development built on a plot of land in the south inner city that had, at one point, been the most expensive tract of real estate in Europe – or so I was informed by Sean Sweeney, who already lived at The Brokerage and who had been lobbying me to rent the empty penthouse next to his since our first drunken morning as co-employees of Echo REIT.

I didn't need much convincing. Aside from being rented solely in Clio's name, the apartment we shared had long since become a go-to session gaff, and was now a slum of stains, roaches, dust bunnies and crumpled cans. The wooden surface of the coffee table was permanently grooved with traces of white powder. And then there was the headquarters of Atlas-Merritt, which occupied a brutalist slab of office space three hundred yards up the street. I could see it from our bedroom window. It unnerved me to be so close to the epicentre of my father's disgrace.

What finally persuaded me to call the letting agency for The Brokerage was a tour of Sweeney's apartment there. It was a cubic hectare of black marble and curvilinear chrome, like my mother's idea of a fancy bathroom. Sweeney had invited me over for pre-dinner cocktails (we were supposed to schmooze the lads from Healy-Dunlop later that evening). He showed me his haute couture flatware, his Nordic-fusion couches. He also showed me the view from his glass-walled terrace. We looked down on the workday city, at the nodes of snarled traffic, the rooftop satellite dishes pointed skywards like cupped ears. We were above it all, or it was all beneath us.

'Place next door is going for ten grand a month,' Sweeney said. 'It's a fucking bargain, man.'

I would need a short-term lease, I thought. I didn't plan to stay past the beginning of October.

'I can't believe you keep doing this huge life shit without *telling* me,' Clio said, when I brought her to see my new penthouse and told her that I had already put down a security deposit. Presented with the four-poster bed and the room-sized closets, she had said nothing. She was also mute on the subject of the bathroom jacuzzi and the directional lighting set into the ceiling above. It wasn't until we were back in the living room that she told me where I had gone wrong.

That I had gone wrong at all came as a genuine surprise to me. 'I thought you needed a nice surprise,' I said. 'You've been so down lately.'

'Oh, and this is going to help,' Clio said. 'I tell you I'm

219

worried you're turning into an asshole and your response to that is to act like even *more* of an asshole.'

I could scarcely believe it. Here I was once again, clawing my way through the intricate matrix of loneliness, boredom, calculation, fright, frustration, ethical one-upmanship and need that constituted our every argument: all because *I had rented a new place to live!*

'How is this acting like an asshole?' I said. 'I've found us an incredible place to live.'

'No, you've found *yourself* an incredible place to live.'

'Well, you don't have to move in with me,' I said. 'You can stay in your old place. A few nights here, a few nights there. I can cover the rent for both places.'

'Do you even hear what you're saying? You're saying, "I don't want to live with you anymore." Look at you. You're about three seconds away from telling me you need some space.'

Semi-involuntarily, I produced an encompassing wave: at the skylit ceilings, the airy gaps between partition walls. Here was nothing if not space.

'Space for *us*!' I said, preparing an elaborate riff on how we might flourish together if we had room to pursue our separate passions, here in the brave new upland of The Brokerage.

But Clio had already changed the terms of the argument. 'You're not yourself anymore,' she said, shaking her head with a mixture of wisdom and sorrow. 'Hanging out with those guys isn't good for you.'

We were, at least, in agreement on something: hanging out with The Lads *wasn't* good for me. But I had my reasons for acting like an asshole. From watching my father – and from close observation of James Mullens, Sean Sweeney, *et al.* – I had concluded that *acting like an asshole* was a foundational pillar of the international businessman's lifestyle. The success of my plan *depended* on acting like an asshole. But of course I couldn't explain this to Clio without revealing that my plan involved abandoning her entirely when the money came through.

I decided to change the terms of the argument myself. 'Do you like it, at least?'

Clio stuck out her lower lip. 'What does that matter?'

'You do like it,' I said. 'Look at that couch. I want to fuck you on that couch.'

'I can't believe you did this without telling me,' Clio said again.

'I want to fuck you in the walk-in wardrobe. I want to fuck you in the kitchen. I want to fuck you out on the balcony so the people in that building over there can see us.'

I took her hand and led her to the window. Across the surface of the canal a solitary swan was gliding, the bird and its reflection like two halves of a broken heart, or like a question mark on top of a Spanish question mark – delete as preferred.

Clio looked around doubtfully. 'It's kind of cold. The decor, I mean.'

'We'll warm it up,' I said.

I moved in the next day. It wasn't a major operation: I owned barely enough to fill a single roll-aboard suitcase. Clio and I celebrated by drinking a €300 bottle of Moët and attempting to have sex in the walk-in wardrobe. But we had also snorted €200 worth of coke, and my hard-on withered as quickly as it had arrived, and Clio complained that she was tired, and we settled for spooning chastely in the folds of the curtained bed until the coke wore off and we twitched ourselves to sleep. *So far, so good*, I reassured myself, as my heart hammered away in my chest. *So far, so good.*

Sexually speaking, this was the beginning of a rough patch that may or may not have been responsible for Clio's actions later on, when she – no, wait a second. Let's try to keep things in chronological order, for the sake of my sanity. The problem, at least initially, was me: I was taking too many drugs, in too many unpredictable combinations, and it was hell on my ability to perform. Clio did her best – dressing up in stockings and garters and so forth – but generally we settled, at the end of the evening, for a cuddle and a vaguely worded promise to step down our drug intake until our sex life returned to normal. If I felt like a cad when I made these promises (I had, after all, no intention of stepping down my drug intake until I had fled the country for a life of solitude and purity in the wilderness). I reassured myself with the thought that Clio, too, was lying: she hoovered up coke and pills just as greedily as I did, and wasted no time inviting her actor friends back to The Brokerage for a party that rolled over from Friday evening to Monday morning. Ah, Clio's friends. Aside from Barry Hynes, who sold me the bulk of my drugs, I paid hardly any attention

222

to them, reasoning, sensibly I think, that to do so would constitute a truly epic waste of effort. Clio's friends were actors. They wore experimental hats and dabbled in bisexuality. They dwelt perpetually in that sub-realm of cultural endeavour where what you are asked to admire is not the thing achieved but the effort expended in trying to achieve it.

The other problem with our sex life was Clio's career, whose downward trajectory was on the verge of marooning her in a state of permanent self-loathing.

'I'm not getting cast,' she said, hugging a cushion on my new modular couch. 'I'm just not. I don't know what I have to do. I work *so* hard. Do you have any idea how depressing it is to spend *all* of your energy on something and to just continually *fail*?'

I didn't, really. But I was damned if I was going to say that out loud. 'The periods of failure are what make the periods of success feel even better,' I suggested.

'But there *are* no periods of success,' Clio said. 'I stay up all night getting ready for auditions. I'm putting my whole self out there, you know? I don't even get *callbacks*.'

'Maybe you should try getting a good night's sleep,' I said.

This was the wrong tack. 'You don't give a shit,' Clio said. 'You've never failed at anything. And do you know why? Because you've never *tried* at anything.'

'I'm trying at something right now,' I said.

'Oh, your *business deal*,' Clio said. She expressed an artist's contempt for the money world, the business world. I applauded this, privately. It was one of the very few things that we had in common, besides drugs. 'Like you're working *so hard* on that. You're just going along with whatever they tell you to do. You don't even go into *work* half the time.'

'I'm buying myself time to write,' I said, with a high-minded sniff. I mumbled something about the necessity of making compromises. But Clio had already moved on. Pivoting on the couch, she opened her laptop and waggled the mouse-pointer over the greyscale tessellations of an Excel spreadsheet. It was a list of auditions: dates, names of plays, names of companies. Beside each one was a large red X. 'That's twenty-four auditions in a row,' she said.

'Maybe you shouldn't be staring at a list of your failures,' I said.

'Why not?' Clio said. 'That's what I am. A failure.'

Hardly surprising, then, Dr F, if our sex life took a turn for the moribund. Sex was, by this stage, what we had in place of genuine emotional rapport. It was what we used to restore each other's wavering self-confidence: *Hey, look! I still want to fuck you! You must be awesome!* Without it, we risked acknowledging the truth: that we were using each other to fulfil obscure emotional needs that we were otherwise unable to confront or understand. We still tried, for a while: I would grab Clio's ass when she got out of the shower, or she would desultorily massage my crotch as we watched nature documentaries on my new 110-inch Ultra HD TV. But very little ever came of these overtures.

Insofar as I had a sex life at all, by that point, it entailed lying on my four-poster bed in The Brokerage with my dick in my hand, trolling Nikki's social media pages for sexy snaps. There weren't many. Nikki was an infrequent poster (sample effusion: *Please consider donating to ALONE this Xmas, they do such amazing work for older adults this time of year!!*). She was not the sort of girl who posted glam shots or duck-billed selfies (*Here I am in the bathroom at a party! Envy my life, that I may envy it, too!*). Her sparse photo stream consisted mostly of snaps of Nikki running marathons, or trekking alone around European capitals with a rucksack on her back. But buried deep beneath the Photos tab was a folder labelled 'MAJORCA '16!!' Here I found a picture of Nikki in a pink bikini, standing waist-deep in clear water. She was looking over her shoulder unselfconsciously. The holiday sky above her was the zero blue of pack ice. I revisited this photo on an hourly basis, trying to ignore the fact that it had surely been taken by James Mullens, who knew, as I did not, what Nikki looked like when she took the bikini off. It seemed, this photo, to have something to do with my new life – the one that would begin when I had received my lump-sum payoff and decamped to foreign shores. I began to imagine that Nikki might somehow become a part of this life, though I could not imagine a scenario in which she broke up with Mullens voluntarily, or even a scenario in which I revealed my deepest self to her and she did not recoil in horror and disgust. But let me be clear – let me speak with the clarity of hindsight. I knew next to nothing about Nikki. Who she was. What she did with her time. I wanted her in the same way that I wanted to leave Dublin and hide away in simple splendour at the ends of the earth: because I thought that this was the way to save my soul.

Starved for facts about Nikki, I mulled over what I did know. Her attitude to Mullens puzzled me. She seemed to view his business-bullshit act with a wary scepticism that was very different from the sort of uncomplicated cheerleading that the girlfriends of The Lads usually engaged in. *He had you all fooled*, Nikki had said of Mullens, at the Shelbourne launch. What did that mean? Was it possible that Nikki's relationship with Mullens wasn't quite as secure – wasn't, as Mullens himself might say, quite as copper-fastened – as it looked? Might I, with a little tact and the proper leverage, find a way to break them up?

As it happened, this is precisely what I was thinking on the afternoon that Clio called, in tears, to tell me that her streak of bad luck had come to an end. She had been cast in the Fringe Festival's most exciting play. Her career was taking off at last.

'That's incredible,' I said. 'Congratulations.' I was lolling in the four-poster bed, scrolling through Nikki's Instagram account and tugging away at my uncooperative member.

'Baz was cast, too,' Clio said. 'We're going to be working together!'

Tremendous, I thought. *My girlfriend and my drug dealer, working side by side!*

There was no doubt about it: this would save me an awful lot of time.

*

I had been living in The Brokerage for almost two weeks when I exited the lobby to find my father waiting for me on the other side of the street. He was leaning against the door of his ancient BMW – the one with the grey-brown apron of dust on the bonnet and the cracked rear indicator light. This was the car that my father had driven throughout my childhood: the family-holiday car, the lifts-to-school car, the ambassadorial emblem of his early successes in banking. Now it had a collapsed look, and sat low to the ground in a way that made me think of the word *craven*. My father stood with his arms tightly folded. We looked at each other through the flicker of passing traffic. Over the last few days he had been leaving me abrupt voicemails: 'Ah, Ben, ah, hmm. Give me a ring if you get a chance. Nothing major. Just … Okay. Bye.' These I deleted. I had also been spotting the usual headlines, in shops, on social media: REVEALED: [REDACTED]'S DESPERATE PHONE CALLS TO 'GOLDEN CIRCLE'. Now my father raised his hand in a slow wave and grinned, as if to say, *Indulge me*.

'Let's go for a drive,' he said, when I had made my way across the street.

The interior of the car smelled of old leather and motor oil. 'They took the Landcruiser,' my father said, his eyes on the road. 'This one could probably do with a tune-up. It was sitting in the garage for what – five years? But they make a reliable car.'

I said nothing.

'We might go out to the Yacht Club,' my father said. 'Have a spot of lunch.'

But when we reached Dun Laoghaire he parked on a concrete bluff overlooking the pier and sat behind the wheel, unmoving. Across the bay the brown brunt of Howth Head was visible through an Alka-Seltzer mist.

'You're getting on okay?' my father said, and coughed. He was wearing some sort of dowdy anorak or windcheater that made him look like one of those dumpy losers who spend their spare time watching planes from the Old Airport Road. This, I thought, was the man once described, in newspapers, as 'the best networker of his generation'.

'Tickety-boo,' I said, choosing – deliberately – one of my father's favourite pre-war Britishisms.

My father clicked the headlights on and off. 'This deal you're involved with,' he said. 'What is it, exactly?'

'That's privileged information, Dad,' I said.

'Some property thing, I gather,' my father said. I had forgotten that he still knew people: bankers, solicitors, journalists. He still read the business pages.

'If you know what it is,' I said, 'why are you asking me about it?'

'I'm just asking,' he said, in a tone of despair.

He was silent. I fiddled with the cartilaginous fabric of my seatbelt.

'You've probably been reading the papers,' my father said.

'Not really,' I said. 'How's it all going?'

My father took off his sunglasses and peered out at the harbour, which bristled with the masts of sailboats. 'We have

the best men in our corner,' he said. 'But there's a momen-
tum . . .' He paused. 'You probably heard. They've moved the
start date for the trial.'

'Nope,' I said.

My father gave me a sidelong glance. 'The twenty-
first,' he said.

'Of September?' I said. I was rather enjoying myself.

'September,' my father said. 'Initially, you know, we'd
thought the best thing would be for your mother to be out of
the country. Along with yourself, if that's what you wanted.
But you didn't want it, so . . .'

'I assumed,' I said, 'that Mum would have moved to
Connecticut by now.'

My father watched a seagull claw its way across a low
stone wall. 'We've taken some advice. Seemingly from an
optics standpoint it plays better to have some family members
in attendance. From the point of view of the cameras. And
even the judge, you know. It makes a difference.'

I began to divine the purpose of my father's visit. 'Does
it?' I said.

'You're angry,' my father said.

'No, I'm not.'

The mist was congealing into rain. Beyond the pier, the tide
was chopping out its fat white lines of surf.

'You've every right,' my father said.

'I'm not angry,' I said. Then, for reasons I didn't fully
understand, I added: 'I know what I'm doing.'

'Do you remember coming down here when you were

small?' my father said. 'For Teddy's ice cream. We'd walk out to the end of the pier and try not to get blown away.'

This, I thought, was a low blow. 'No,' I said, 'I don't remember.'

'You were very small,' my father said. The rain was threading the windscreen with its transparent needlepoint. 'I don't ask you for much. But I'm going to ask you for this. I'd like you to be there. Just for the first day of the trial. So at least it looks like we're presenting a united front.'

I had my *coup de grâce* prepared. 'I'll be in Belgrade. We're meeting our partners. The nineteenth to the twenty-sixth.'

Coldly, I watched my father absorb this new intelligence. He seemed to find it satisfactory, in some obscure way. 'Belgrade,' he said, chewing his lip. 'You're all going?'

'This is the heart of the deal,' I said. 'I'm a Development Consultant. We go over there, we do the hard sell.'

My father seemed to have reached a decision. He nodded, once. 'You can postpone,' he said. 'I mean, you personally.'

'Can I?' I said dryly.

'Look, I know how this works,' my father said. 'The other lads can hold down the fort. You can delay for a matter of two days.'

'It hinges,' I said. 'It hinges on that week. I'm sorry. There's nothing I can do.'

'I did what you're doing,' my father said, 'all my life. When I was your age I thought it was all about the hard sell. You stay in the dodgy hotel and you get up at five in the morning so you can have breakfast with the point man.

Get the signature. Get the promise. Let me tell you. That's the bullshit approach. What you do is, you show up late. You tell them you can't stay long, you're too busy. You don't give a shit whether they sign or not. You let them know that their time means zero to you. Less than zero. You let them know their time is shit. They're shit and their time is shit.'

This was startling. Never in two decades of listening to my father talk about work had I heard him speak in anything but emollient clichés. Plainly, his desperation was getting the better of him. I said nothing. I was waiting for him to continue. But he simply rolled down the car window and let the rain sprinkle the arm of his windcheater.

After a moment I said: 'The tickets are booked.'

'An hour in the morning,' my father said. 'Maybe less.'

'It's out of my hands,' I said.

I looked out of my own window. Farther along the pier was a building site. A quartet of fat concrete footers had been cultivated from the mire of a shallow trench. Behind this, a freshly completed slab of black glass rose, like the screen of a locked phone. Everywhere building and tearing down. This was Ireland.

My father turned the key in the ignition. The panel lights came on. 'Anger is a funny thing,' he said. 'You can see through it, like ice. Without noticing how it distorts what you see.' Another mood swing: now he was Confucius, delivering gnomic epigrams. Distantly, I wondered if he would cry. I decided I wanted him to. A man, I thought, shouldn't attain the age of twenty-seven without seeing his father cry over something that isn't the Heineken Cup.

'Sorry,' I said.

'Your mother isn't exactly keen on doing a twirl for the cameras either, you know,' my father said.

'My hands are tied.'

'Look,' my father said. 'You have money now. Do you know why I spent my whole life chasing money? Because money means freedom. It means you have the ability to do what you want.'

I resisted the temptation to point out that my father's pursuit of freedom now seemed likely to imprison him altogether: a cheap shot, I felt.

'You can reschedule your flight,' my father said. 'Make an appearance. I'm asking you to do this for me. It's an hour. You don't have to say anything or do anything. Call it a favour, if you want.'

I folded my arms and stared out of the window: at the grey world, flecked with rain. 'What the fuck else would I call it?' I said.

'I'm begging,' my father said. He met my eyes. His face seemed to be developing new pouches and creases, even as I looked at it. His hair was limp and grey. 'I'm begging,' he said again.

I did not speak. It had finally occurred to me to wonder precisely how and when my father had learned that I was living at The Brokerage.

*

Under Dr Felix's ministrations, I have been trying half-heartedly to pinpoint it, the exact moment at which we stopped being a relatively normal three-person family and started being something else. And I wonder if it's possible to isolate a single instant from the long continuous humid churn of having-a-family, of being-in-a-family, and to say definitively, *This was when it happened, this was the start of our undoing.* Did we falter, at a given moment? Did we change? Perhaps it wasn't one mistake but many. Or perhaps there were no mistakes but simply drift, one tiny stupid step after another. And I remember – I don't know why – how my father used to take me swimming, when I was eight or nine years old, in the noisy public pool a short drive from our house. He taught me to spit in my goggles and rinse them in the chlorinated water. Held me afloat, my chest on his palm, and showed me how to kick – 'How the Olympians do it,' he said. Then he would swim energetic lengths himself, rising from the water and ducking back in, more determined than skilful, but unmistakably determined, ploughing ahead like a cannonball. The powerful arms. The hair-matted torso. Sons want their fathers to be strong. Finished, he stood upright in the shallow end, wiping his nose with stiff fingers. His sinuses were bad. The chlorine aggravated them. Eventually he had to give up swimming altogether.

Driving home from the pool one evening, he said, 'I'm sorry you never had a brother. It takes you out of yourself, having a brother.'

'Do I need to be taken out of myself?' I asked.

233

'You're fine as you are,' my father said, and smiled.

But I knew what he meant, or thought I did. I was used to interpreting my father's oblique remarks. What he meant was that there were only three of us, my father, my mother and me, and that this was potentially a fragile arrangement.

'Your Uncle Frank taught me how to swim,' my father said. 'Up in Lough Dan. We probably weren't supposed to be in there. When I think of it now. He'd show me the breaststroke and then he'd jump off a high rock. I thought he was going to die, every time. We must take you up there some weekend.'

Swimming reminded my father of his own brother. That was the connection. And I notice only now that my own swimming lessons stopped after my father's brother died – that my father was no longer willing, or able, to take me swimming, after that.

And I wonder if that means something. If I missed it at the time. If I've been missing things my whole life long, when everything I needed to make sense of the world was actually right in front of me, plain as day.

After our summit at Dun Laoghaire my father drove me home and, tutting at the weather, offered me the use of his black PING golf umbrella.

'I'm fine,' I said.

'It's a short hop anyway,' my father said.

I got out. The dense rain thrummed on the roof of the Beamer. 'I'll check with the lads,' I said over the din. 'I can't promise anything.'

'I trust you,' my father said. He hesitated. 'You might pay a visit to your mother, if you get a chance.'

'I'll have to check my calendar.' I slammed the door.

From a sheltered spot across the street – right next to the revolving doors of The Brokerage – a man in a brown trenchcoat was staring straight at me, through silver diagonals of rain.

Serbia

'PULL!'

'You don't need to say pull, you fucking goober. It's already up there. It's fucking hovering.'

'I know it's fucking hovering. I was telling you to pull me off. Here.'

There was a jaw-tightening crack as Sweeney fired his shotgun. Very close range. Blue smoke dissipating swiftly. I took my fingers out of my ears.

'Missed,' Sweeney said, and spat. 'Hold her steady, for fuck's sake.'

More nonsense with The Lads. We had assembled on the castellated promontory of an eighteenth-century Baroque fortress for a drone shoot: not just The Lads, but the Serbs as well. It was the second day of my trip and we were no longer in Belgrade. The town beneath us was called Novi Sad, and *Novi Sad* seemed like a reasonably accurate description of how you felt when you visited Novi Sad. The urban centre, which we towered above, was defined by the jagged spire of a yellow-brick cathedral. Around it radiated a cluster of buildings that looked like disused fallout shelters. The notched wall of the fortress overlooked also the slowly pouring Danube, which churned and foamed greenly, like a torrent of bile.

Above us, in the clear September air, three remote-controlled machines wavered and whined, holding aloft their blurred propellers like flimsy parasols. These we were supposed to shoot. On arrival The Lads had been issued with double-barrelled shotguns, with which they had immediately posed for selfies. A middle-aged man with a Bismarck moustache and a peasant's cloth cap – our tour guide – had doled out instructions in a lugubrious monotone. 'Both eyes open. No squinting. Weight on front foot. Back foot no weight.'

Off to one side, in the shadow of a campanile, Vuk sat at a small table, sipping from a demitasse. Behind him Nicolae and Ratko stood at attention, like sentries. Earlier that morning I had resisted the urge to google *Free Serbia Progress Construction* or *Voivode Holdings* (which was, according to James Mullens, the name of the holding company through which Vuk funded most of his development projects – 'Totally standard practice. Sure we're doing it ourselves,' Mullens had said, in his most soothing voice). I both did and did not want to know who our Serbian business partners were – what they might be hiding, what they might have done in the past. By now, the lineaments of my secret plan had become articles of faith (fragile, fragile), and I was reluctant to expose them to the harsh and destabilising light of provable facts. If our

Serbian partners were not on the level, what did that imply about Mullens's deal? What did it say about my future of well-funded solitude and peace? The less I knew, my reasoning went, the less I had to think about. And the less I had to think about, the happier I would be.

On the other hand, it was becoming increasingly difficult to ignore the fact that Vuk and his gang had not yet signed the contracts and tended, whenever signing the contracts was mentioned, to wave their hands and talk about delays with lawyers, builders, permits. To a cynical eye, it might – I thought – look very much like they were giving us the run-around. Exhibit A: after breakfast in the hotel (served in a blighted dining room and consisting of a small glass of prune juice and an omelette with no ingredients – that is, a fried egg folded in half), Nicolae and Ratko had herded us into the limo for the two-hour ride to Novi Sad, where, they said, we were to participate in certain 'activities of fun'. James Mullens, slumped across from me in the limo's spacious innards, ignored my pointed glare. His face was ashen. His eyes were concealed behind the iridescent band of his wraparound shades.

Nicolae gestured at the passing countryside as we drove. 'Is like Ireland,' he said.

It was not like Ireland. I clocked bleak rows of doomed-looking houses, black-grained quilts of ruptured tarmac. Every field seemed to have been inexpertly bandaged with its own white stripe of dirty mist. There were hardly any people.

To no one in particular I said, 'I presume we're signing the contracts after lunch, then.'

Ratko grinned, baring gingivitic gums. There was a general silence.

James Mullens appeared to be asleep.

Now – four hours later – it was almost lunchtime. The Lads were still firing their shotguns, but their energy was visibly declining. The sky was the colour of a fat grey pearl. As I watched, James Mullens detached himself from the gang and swiped at the smeared screen of his phone. Who was he texting? Nikki? I strolled over. 'Feels like we're wrapping up here,' I said.

He gave an irked shrug and did not look up.

'Last night was intense,' I said.

'Big time.' He shook his head, as if to apologise for the inadequacy of this response.

I let a silence fall. A drone zipped by, humming like a telephone wire. There was the firework snap of a shotgun blast.

'Have you spoken to Vuk?' I said. I was trying to sound hard-bitten, worldly. Was I succeeding?

Mullens massaged the bridge of his nose with two large square fingers. 'The situation is fluid,' he said. 'Seems to be fluid.'

'I'd like to know,' I said, 'exactly when we're signing. We've been here for forty-eight hours and frankly, I feel like we're wasting time. They're just driving us around the country and distracting us with this bullshit. I thought this was supposed to be a business deal. I thought, hey, we go in here, we let them know that their time means shit to us. They're shit and their time is shit.'

Over at his little table Vuk continued to observe proceedings with judicial impartiality.

Mullens pocketed his phone. 'Listen, man,' he said. 'I know you don't have much experience with the whole development side of things. But this is how it works, okay? We get wined and dined for a few days and then we sign the contracts as if it's just this whole embarrassing afterthought. So try and chill, yeah? It's happening.' He pressed a palm to his forehead. 'I'd really like to get in an hour at the gym. Lot of toxins circulating after last night. You probably feel the same.'

I had popped four Oxycontin in the limo. I was feeling fine. Briefly I considered offering one of my remaining Oxys to Mullens. But then I would have had fewer for myself, so I thought not.

'We should ask Vuk about timelines, at least,' I said.

'"We"?' Mullens said.

The sound of a shotgun blast – apparently inches from where we stood – made us both flinch. I looked over the parapet and down at the Danube: at the unhurried waters into which a wrecked drone had just been dispatched.

'GO ON, YOU CUNT,' Bobby Hayes yelled, his voice rebounding against the fortress walls.

Mullens said, 'We know about timelines. You're just too fucked to notice what's going on. The next thing is a tour of the site.'

He strode off in the direction of the limo, leaving me to mutter *Fuck you* to his departing back.

*

The truly bad news was that Maria had also joined us for the drone shoot. For a while she had ignored me. She sat at Vuk's table and watched The Lads in an unmoving silence that managed to convey, without the use of either word or gesture, a bottomless contempt for everything they did. Then she had disappeared, popping off on an unexplained errand. Now she had returned, wearing a pair of love-heart sunglasses. Her lower jaw was mysteriously swollen. She was walking towards me. I looked around. Aside from the Danube below, there was no escape.

'Fucking dentist,' she said, standing beside me and folding her arms. I did not invite clarification. 'I have gangrene of my gums,' she explained. 'Already yesterday, two teeth fall out – here.' She pulled back her cheek with an index finger and pointed to two missing molars. 'I haven't eat for two days. No coffee, no beer. Just Coke. I go to dentist this morning, he say I have two more teeth ready to come out.'

'You had cocktails last night,' I pointed out.

'This is alcohol,' Maria said. 'This does not count. And you. You disappear. I look around and you disappear like little leprechaun.'

'I, uh ... I wasn't feeling too hot,' I said.

'Last night you disappear,' Maria said. 'I think you are gay. You are gay leprechaun.'

Recoiling from this, I wondered if frank hostility was simply the way people flirted in Serbia – if Maria was, in being so unbelievably crass and unpleasant, simply obeying the dictates of her native culture. It was a charitable assumption, so I tried to make it. I also contemplated telling her that yes, I was in fact gay, and that I had a burly boyfriend at home who pumped iron and worked in graphic design. Then I could simply camp up my vocabulary by about 20 per cent for the remainder of the trip. Would that put her off? Would anything?

She was peering at me over the heart-shaped sunglasses. 'You not shoot,' she said.

This was true: offered a shotgun, I had refused and stoically endured the jeers of The Lads. It wasn't that I was a pacifist. It was that I was so hungover I was afraid I would drop the gun and shoot myself.

'I'm a lover, not a fighter,' I said, and cringed, thinking: *Do not use the word* lover *around this girl.*

'I shoot first gun when I am four years old,' Maria said. 'Semi-automatic. Boom, I take out rats. Is nothing.'

'That seems unsafe,' I said.

On the other side of the terrace, The Lads seemed to be handing their shotguns to the tour guide. They were high-fiving. Vuk had risen from his tin table and was beckoning with a spidery hand.

'Yes,' Maria said. 'Is lunchtime. I join you.' She smiled a smile full of dark red gaps.

I took a deep breath and reflected, not for the first time, that a deep breath without a heavy dose of nicotine in it has only limited calmative powers.

'Oh,' I said. 'That's super.'

*

Crushed up beside me in the limo was Mark Foley. 'I'm trying to remember the last time I saw a poor person IRL,' he murmured.

I checked to see if Vuk had overheard. But he had closed his eyes and was nodding, as if in silent prayer.

'Did you read the IMF report on this place?' Mark went on. 'It said foreign direct investment in Serbia has been increasing year on year since oh-six. But look at the state of it. You sort of have to wonder where the funds are going.'

The town rolled by, with its dingy parks of tousled lindens, its vagrant population of headscarved old crones toting string bags a-bulge with mutant tubers. The women were all dressed in black, like Sicilian widows.

Sean Sweeney was massaging his left shoulder with a spadelike hand. 'We know where the fucking funds are going,' he said. 'They're going to us.'

Something warm touched my leg. I looked down. Maria, sitting opposite, had shucked off one trainer and was pressing her bare foot to my calf. Her toenails had been painted a little-girl shade of pink.

'They fucking better be,' I said.

During my mandatory sessions with Dr F I have been availing myself of the therapeutic monologue – an undervalued art form, I feel. His prompts set me going like a tired old watch.

'Your uncle,' he said this morning. 'Your father sold his farm when he died.'

'That was how we got rich,' I said. 'Or richer. My dad was already pulling down six figures at that point.'

Dr Felix said, 'Pulling down six figures.'

You could hear the air quotes. These were meant to shame me out of my conceit. It worked. 'That was how we paid for the Great Remodelling,' I said, fighting off a blush.

'And that's all it meant,' Dr Felix said. 'More money. A nicer house.'

'My parents didn't make a big deal out of it,' I said.

Dr Felix said nothing. I know the drill by now. Into these gaps I am supposed to pour fresh batches of confessional slurry.

'I was eleven,' I said. 'You don't really take these things on board when you're eleven. My father just seemed sort of gruff for a while. Two or three weeks, maybe. But he was never exactly florid with his emotions. I always wondered if that was why he was disappointed in me. Because I was kind of emotional.' I invited a response. But Dr Felix said nothing. 'The day after the funeral,' I continued, 'it was like he was hoarse. He kept clearing his throat. He went into his study for a while. I think my mother set me up with the Nintendo. Then he came out and we just had dinner as normal. So it was kind of nothing, for me.'

'You skipped the funeral,' Dr Felix said.

'I don't remember it.'

'Yes, you do.'

'Are you going to hypnotise me? Draw out my repressed memories?'

'The funeral,' Dr Felix said.

Yes: the funeral. The ponderous Mass, the trip to the grave-yard. Afterwards, the wake, in a country hotel near Avoca. Cousins, uncles, aunts, family members, all with similar faces, like different editions of the same book. Also cattle dealers, middle-echelon Dublin bankers. My father's work-ing life had not yet climbed out of steerage. At later family gatherings there would be ministers, backbenchers, CEOs. Now there were raucous farmers singing 'Living Next Door to Alice'. I hid in a corner with my glass of fizzy orange.

'There you are,' my father said. He put a hand on the top of my head and then withdrew it, as if surprised by his own gesture. 'Are you getting on okay?'

My mother had coached me that morning. So I did not say, 'I'm bored.'

'Let me tell you something,' my father said. His eyelids grew heavy when he was drunk. 'The world is hard. And the only way to beat it is to be hard yourself. Do you know what I mean?'

I nodded.

'Your mother used to tell me I was soft,' he said. 'And I took her at her word. But it doesn't serve you well, being soft. It doesn't serve you well. So don't let her tell you the same thing, is what I'm saying.'

'Okay,' I said.

Unable to make sense of this, I did what children do: I can-celled it, deleted it from my memory. And it comes back to me only now, in the midst of this great process of data retrieval conducted by Dr Felix, this restoration of my life to its wonky factory settings, to tell me that my father did change. That he was one thing and became another, and that the hinge was grief, or death. I do not want this knowledge, but from knowing, as Adam and Eve might tell us, there is generally no easy way back.

'But she did tell you you were soft,' Dr Felix said.

'What?'

I had evidently been speaking aloud. And not realised it. How alarming.

'Your mother did tell you you were soft,' Dr Felix said again. 'If not in so many words, certainly by gestures. By attitudes. This is often how parents say what they really mean. And you took her at her word. So to speak.'

'If you say so,' I said.

'Buying you presents when you failed,' Dr Felix said. 'Excusing your non-participation in school sport. Telling you to become a writer.'

'Aren't parents supposed to be kind?'

'Up to a point,' Dr Felix said. 'After that, parents are supposed to prepare you to live in the world. The message from your mother was, you're sensitive. You're special. You fail your exams, you get a boxed set of Proust. What's the message there?'

'I always thought the message was that spending money could make you feel better.'

'What does it do to you, when you're rewarded for failing? What does it do to your soul?'

'You tell me,' I said.

Dr Felix's sneer was polite. But it was still a sneer.

Dublin

Now that I lived at The Brokerage – and now that Clio had been cast in her Big Play – things, I freely admit, began to get out of hand. My typical day, around this time, began at noon, when I would come around in my penthouse bedroom and jump-start my system with a highly focused wank. Now almost fully awake, I would slouch into the kitchen and mix myself a Bloody Mary, minus the celery, the Tabasco sauce and the tomato juice, and drink it, gagging. Then a double dose of Oxycontin would see off my headache, and it was time for a shower in the slate-walled wet room, a procedure I dispatched in a brisk half-hour of coughing, vomiting and sobbing. By now – all going well – it was two in the afternoon and time to check in at work. Here, in my charcoal-grey office, I put my feet up on the desk and activated a chrome-plated coffee machine that steamily expressed high-quality macchiatos at the touch of a button. Around 3.30 p.m. it was my habit to clock off for the day and cab it to the Morrison or the Merrion or the Marker for a mimosa or a margarita or a manhattan (not to mention the night's first rails, chopped and mustered and snorted in the marbled echoic hush of a high-end gents'). By now – getting on towards six – it was time to catch up with Clio, now that her rehearsals had wrapped up for the day. This meant a cab to Grogan's on South William Street, where Clio and the cast had gathered, and where I could buy a weekend's worth of yokes from Barry Hynes and a round or two of cocktails for the actors. Usually one or two or three of The Lads had tagged along, and there they stood, bantering with Clio and her mates as if they had known each other all their lives. Here – waiting until it was time to drop – I would sometimes fall into a meditative silence and study the people around me fondly, strengthened by the knowledge that very soon I would be leaving them all behind.

But for the time being, there was business to attend to. Around nine we gobbled our pills and plunged into a night-club, where the textures of our shared experience gradually underwent a numinous change: our conversations became fluent and driven and at last dissolved entirely in the grinding darkness of the dancefloor, and after the club it was back to my place, back to my brand-new penthouse, where friends and strangers basked, perspiring, on my rented couches. And my eyes were scrolling upwards in their sockets and my thoughts kept doubling back on themselves, like snakes with broken backs. And sometimes, in the last few hours before dawn, when I was wide awake and everybody else was too, and we were grinding up the last of our pills and snorting them, and we were smoking joints to bring us down, and we were no longer capable of finding anything funny, I would begin to suspect that all the drugs I was taking were really doing the opposite of what they were supposed to do. Drugs, I thought, were supposed to expand your consciousness – they were supposed to plug you in to the larger harmonies. But what drugs actually seemed to be doing was narrowing my consciousness down to a point so fine that its lineaments could scarcely any longer be discerned. All drugs left you with, it began to seem, was this one single moment – this one, here before you, now, so evanescent, so beautifully filled with the useless data of what your friends were doing or saying, which really meant filled with nothing much at all, and now here came this moment, equally empty, equally full, and now this moment, and now this, and this, and all the others, until all you had was the present moment, in which nothing could possibly happen that had not already happened, nothing could possibly happen that was not already happening as you mourned it, here, now, until all the moments added up and toppled down upon you and all your friends went home and the session was at an end and you were alone, in a bed you didn't recognise, with a girl you weren't sure you really liked. And: 'You okay, babes?' Clio whispered, in the darkness of the penthouse bedroom, in the silence just before the dawn.

'No,' I said. 'Not really.'

'I'm here,' Clio said, snuggling closer. 'I'm here.'

'I know,' I said, but I was no longer talking to Clio. 'I know.'

Serbia

After lunch – another terrible meal in another terrible restaurant, with Ratko and Nicolae watching us with smiles of weird approval as we ate – the limo ferried us northwards, into the countryside that bordered Novi Sad. Mullens had assured me that we would soon be visiting the site of the Echo Lake development. But our actual destination was a monastery in the middle of nowhere. By now, even Bobby Hayes was beginning to grumble about the delay. 'A fucking monastery,' he said, as we followed Vuk and Ratko across a rolling lawn. 'With what, like, fucking monks and shit?'

Nicolae was striding close behind. 'You take little tour while site is prepared,' he said in his buzzsaw voice. 'Monastery is good for soul.'

'When you say prepared,' Mark Foley said reedily, 'what exactly do you mean?'

Nicolae smiled. The eyepatch shifted, disclosing a crimped half-inch of salmon-coloured scar tissue. Mark looked down at his feet.

The monastery reared up before us, spired and brownly barbed, like a cactus made of earwax. Aleks, the translator, fell into step beside me. He had joined us at lunch.

'Four centuries old,' he said, nodding towards the monastery.

'Mm,' I said. I was attending to a series of gastric cramps and twinges.

'May I ask,' Aleks said. 'You are a reader of poetry?'

'I used to be,' I said, surprising myself with my own frankness.

Aleks fished around in the olive-drab canvas knapsack that was slung across his lanky torso. 'I bring you gift.' He handed me a small paperbound volume with Cyrillic letters on the cover. 'My first book,' he said, blushing. 'Is not best work. I have new book, much better. But this is not in print of yet.'

On the book's verso cover was a black-and-white photograph of Aleks, sitting at a desk, surrounded by leatherbound volumes. It reminded me of my favourite spot in the university library, next to the long shelves containing a hundred years of the US *Congressional Record*.

'This is a real book,' I said.

'You keep,' Aleks said. 'I have copies.'

'Thank you,' I said. For some reason I bowed, like a Japanese diplomat. 'You know I can't read it.'

Aleks shook his head and said, 'There is language obstacle. But books . . .' He paused. 'My English is not so good. I try to think of name for object of belief, like small religious.'

'Totem,' I said.

'Totem,' Aleks said. 'Book is totem. So language is not so much important.'

Aleks's book was digest-sized, small enough to fit in my pocket. 'What's the title?' I said.

'Is historical reference,' Aleks said. 'In English I think *Attack of the Barbarians*.'

'*The Barbarian Invasion*,' I suggested.

We were smiling at each other, like friends.

'Ants,' Bobby Hayes said, scuffing with a heel at the monastery path. 'Wish I had a magnifying glass. Look at the size of these bastards.'

Sean Sweeney hunkered down. 'Those are some fucking *huge* ants.'

'Your foot,' Aleks said.

'Did you ever do that when you were a kid?' Bobby Hayes said. 'Burn ants with a magnifying glass.'

'Your foot,' Aleks said again. He tugged at my sleeve. I looked down at the toe of my Converse trainer, where an ant the size of a chocolate bar had climbed. 'Do not move,' Aleks said. Gently he pushed the ant back onto the path's hot tarmac with the toe of his combat boot. 'Your shoes are not strong,' he observed. 'Black ants will bite straight through. You experience much pain. You spend much money on shoes that are not strong. Army boots are better.'

'Here,' Bobby Hayes said, addressing Aleks. 'Were you in the army, or what?'

'In Serbia is compulsory military service,' Aleks said. 'But I refuse. I am conscientious objector.'

'So did you, like, go to jail?' Bobby Hayes said.

'I work with children,' Aleks said. 'Special needs.'

Bobby looked disappointed.

Sweeney was squashing ants beneath the soles of his wing-tips. 'So you have to either join the army or do community service?' he said, sneering. 'Fuck that. If they asked me to do that I'd tell them to fuck off. I'd be, like, send me to jail, you cunts.'

'Is law,' Aleks said.

'Is fucking stupid law,' Sweeney said.

In the porch of the monastery church Ratko held a finger to his lips and pointed to the crucifix that hung above the doors.

Sweeney giggled. 'Right, yeah,' he said. 'Jesus's gaff, lads. No messin'.'

'No messin',' Bobby Hayes said.

As we entered the church Aleks blessed himself and knelt for an instant at the burbling fountain of holy water.

'Are you, like, religious?' Bobby Hayes whispered.

'I am raised in Orthodox Church,' Aleks said.

'That's, like, Greek, yeah?' said Bobby Hayes.

'It's Russian, you spa,' Sean Sweeney said, cuffing Hayeser on the elbow.

'Is Serbian Orthodox Church,' Aleks said, but Hayeser and Sweeney had already disappeared into the church's main hall, their shoulders tense with silent mirth.

Inside, Mark Foley was sitting in what appeared to be the church's only pew. Behind him was a shelf crowded with icons – chunks of wood painted with pietas or Stations of the Cross, the little scenes framed with rows of cheap paste gems. I sat down and said, 'You've done this before. Is it normal? Them delaying like this?'

'Sure,' he said. 'It's fucking Texas Hold 'Em. Have we got the money? Have they got the site?'

'But we don't have the money,' I said. 'Their government has the money. Or our buyers have the money. Whichever it is.'

Mark pressed his bony knuckles into the orbits of his eyes. 'Christ, I'm hungover. Of course we have the money. Or we have enough to make them think there's more on the way. This is how it works. You spend a few days getting pissed with each other and at the end of it you're business partners.'

'So this is normal,' I said again. In the shadow-laden transept, I could discern the pale shapes of Nicolae and Vuk. They were laughing quietly and nodding their heads. Closer to the altar, Aleks stood with his head bowed, murmuring.

'He's really praying,' Mark Foley said. 'Here. Is that a bat?'

Mark Foley. In school he had been a gamer and a comics geek. His bedroom was full of mint-condition action figures and special issues preserved in mylar sheaths. In the living room of his parents' house in Booterstown one afternoon he had shown me his collection of *X-Men* comics and played some scenes from a Korean martial arts film. 'It's obviously heavily indebted to the side-scrolling beat-'em-up,' he said, pausing the DVD at a crucial moment. In his grown-up incarnation he was a money nerd, Echo REIT's Chief Financial Officer. For a while, back in school, Mark's nerdishness had led me to believe that he was one of our year's few intelligent men. When I heard he had gone to Trinity to study business, I wrote him off entirely. And now? I was, of course, getting ready to write him off again – as soon as I was rich enough to leave The Lads behind for ever. We might have been friends,

Mark and I, if we hadn't been, in our separate ways, such self-deluding dickheads.

'They want to get out,' Aleks said. He pointed towards the rafters, where two bats were flitting together in a binary panic. I knew how they felt. Up at the altar, Maria was whispering something in Vuk's ear and looking in my direction. Directly above them was a large stone angel, its eyes averted in horror or shame.

'Vuk doesn't seem to be the praying type,' I said.

'His name,' Aleks said. 'It means *wolf.*'

'So I hear,' I said. 'What does Aleks mean?'

'It means strong man, defender,' Aleks said. He made a demurring face. 'This is irony, for me.'

'My name doesn't mean anything,' I said dreamily. The Oxycontin was starting to take effect. 'Who is she, anyway?' I said, indicating Maria. 'Vuk's nephew.'

Aleks pursed his lips judiciously. 'When Maria is very small, her father is killed in war with Bosnia. It is peaceful between Serbia and Bosnia at present time. Before ten years, not so much peace, and also much tensions. War break out, for which many people blame Serbia. Because Serbia is largest nation in Yugoslavia, there are Serbs who think it should be in charge.'

'This is why you have no bridges,' I said.

'You know of this,' Aleks said. 'And you know also perhaps that ongoingly many people who feel Serbia should be in charge remain.'

'Her father was killed,' I said. 'How old was she?'

'She is eight years old when this happen,' Aleks said. 'She is adopted by Vuk who makes her his daughter by legal process. For Vuk, Maria's father is great friend, great hero. Is great national martyr.' Something about Aleks's tone suggested that he did not 100 per cent support this analysis. 'When I am young,' he continued, 'I protest government that goes to war. Tear gas? I have been full of tear gas. You know what is like, to be afraid of police?'

'Not as such,' I said.

'When you have nothing and they have guns and batons,' Aleks said. 'I carry my friend away in a coat. His head is covered with much blood.'

'You were very brave,' I said.

'No, no,' Aleks said. 'I am not brave. But we had to protest. State was doing terrible things in our name. Now terrible things happen no more. But people who made up state still are in Serbia.' He directed his gaze to the two figures at the altar. Vuk smiled back at us, and waved a long-fingered hand.

'Shit one,' I said. Up above, the bats were squeaking faintly.

'Your name,' Aleks said. 'Benjamin. It does have meaning. It means child of father's right hand.'

'Now that *is* irony,' I said.

It was almost six o'clock. We trudged back to the limousine in silence. As I walked I examined Aleks's book of poems. If books are totems, Dr F, what are they totems of? Perhaps of a world in which a hidden order supervenes and everything eventually makes sense. Our limo driver – until now an invisible presence – was leaning against the car, aggressively chewing tobacco. He wore a brown cloth cap and a suit of deteriorating dark-blue wool. With a sudden shock I recognised him: it was Boris, the taxi driver who had driven me to the Hotel Karlovsky. 'Boris!' I said. 'Hey, Boris! Have you been driving us around this whole time?' But Boris looked past me and said nothing.

Even then, at that late stage of things, I was confident that my plan would work – that everything was going through okay. But the problem with confidence, Dr F, is that it's bullshit. Wouldn't you say? Confidence is a confidence trick. Confidence is a confidence man, and we are all his dupes.

Dublin

One week before my father's trial was scheduled to begin – and five days before I was due to board a plane to Belgrade – I left the Harcourt Street offices of Echo REIT and walked towards Café en Seine on Dawson Street. I was on my way to meet Barry Hynes, who was going to sell me some Oxycontin. 'Jesus, man,' Barry had said, when I called him to place the order. 'You're putting my kids through college.' Is it a bad sign, when your drug dealer thinks you're buying too many drugs? As I passed the café that now occupied the former Anglo Irish Bank building on Stephen's Green, my attention snagged on a familiar shape. Sitting at a table by the window was Nikki. She was concentrating on the screen of her laptop, pausing now and then to check something in the pages of what looked like an academic journal. I went inside and ordered a cappuccino.

'Sit,' Nikki said, when I had feigned surprise at finding us both in the same café. 'I'm working on a conference paper and I'm seeking fresh avenues of procrastination. I'm at that stage where it's ten minutes over time so I'm trying to take stuff out while still indicating that I've *thought* about the stuff I've taken out and not just ignored it. You used to be an academic, right? You know what I mean.'

She was wearing jeans and a grey hoodie with the Trinity College Dublin logo printed across the chest. There were dark smudges under her eyes and her hair had been tied into a perfunctory ponytail.

Trying to imagine myself into the skin of a kind and solicitous person, and thereby to summon the sort of warm and empathetic tone of voice that invited disclosures of an intimate nature, I said, 'Everything okay?'

'I don't sleep,' Nikki said. 'Or, no. I do sleep. I just do most of my sleeping between three and six in the morning.'

'You're worried about something,' I said.

'I'm worried about everything,' Nikki said.

'Your social anxiety,' I said.

'Well,' Nikki said, looking away. 'You know what that's like.'

'I wouldn't characterise my problem as social anxiety,' I

said, surprising myself with my own honesty. 'It's more like hatred. Social hatred. Hatred of the world.'

The mood of our chat seemed to have skidded off in its own unpleasant direction. What was it about Nikki that compelled you – compelled me, anyway – to say what you actually thought? It made her impossible to flirt with because you ended up – I ended up, anyway – using words like *hatred* when the word I really wanted to use was *love*.

She scratched her nose thoughtfully. 'With social anxiety, the problem is supposed to be you. As in, you can't deal with normal situations that everybody else is fine with. But you're saying it's the world that's the problem.'

'The world is at least fifty per cent of the problem,' I said.

'Then everything's hopeless,' Nikki said, smiling sweetly. 'Wouldn't you say?'

I had no response to this, except for the unutterable *Hopeless for everyone else, maybe, but not for me*. My eye was drawn to a paperback book on the table. I picked it up. It was a literary novel by a young woman who lived in Brooklyn. The jacket copy described it as a work of 'blackly funny autofiction'.

'Have you read it?' Nikki said. 'I can't decide if it's pure hipster narcissism or if she's really on to something.'

I tried to remember the last time I had read anything longer than a WhatsApp message. 'You must lend it to me,' I said. 'Unless James wants to read it first.'

Nikki regarded me steadily. 'What was your PhD on, if you don't mind me asking?'

'It was, uh . . .' I said. 'It was on James Joyce.'

'Early Joyce or later Joyce?'

'. . . Early,' I said.

Nikki wrinkled her nose. 'Because who wants to read *Finnegans Wake*, right?'

'Aren't you a radiologist?' I said. 'How do you have time to read all this fiction?'

'I'm a researcher,' Nikki said. 'So I spend all day in work reading this.' She held up the academic journal. 'When I get home I want to read stuff for fun.' She sipped from her over-sized mug, clasping it in both hands. 'So the deal seems to be going okay,' she said.

'Tickety-boo,' I said, and cursed myself for sounding like my father.

'It's certainly taking up a lot of James's time,' Nikki said.

'He's a busy man,' I said.

'Are you spending a lot of time with him?'

'Not really,' I said. 'I mean, it's not like we all go into the office every day. I hardly see any of The Lads except on weekends.'

It had, in fact, occurred to me lately to wonder exactly how James Mullens whiled away the hours of his working week. I presumed that he was taking meetings, making phone calls, sending emails. But I had never actually *seen* him do any of these things. His office at Echo REIT was always empty. On the other hand, my office at Echo REIT was usually empty, too. This, I reflected, is what it means to have a good job: you don't ever actually have to do it.

'Really,' Nikki said. She looked down and seemed to

perform a brief internal reboot. When she looked up, she said, 'It must be strange, switching careers like that.'

I shrugged. Our conversation was not unfolding as I had imagined it would. I tried to get it back on track, using as a compass the vague impression that Nikki wanted to talk about James Mullens, and the even vaguer hope that I might, through the use of some as-yet-undiscovered rhetorical strategy, be able to persuade her of his general unsuitability as a boyfriend. 'We're off to Belgrade next week,' I said. 'You'll probably miss James when he's gone.'

'I'll be at this conference,' she said, levelling a finger at her laptop screen. 'I just mean, you must have had a lot of catching up to do. Learning a whole new language.'

'It's bullshit language,' I said, feeling suddenly uncomfortable. 'All that business stuff.'

'That's what a lot of business people say,' Nikki said. 'Like they speak the language, but they want you to know they know it's bullshit. If you get me.'

'Yeah,' I said. For some reason my forehead had broken out in a chill sweat. 'I mean ... It's not as if I'm planning to stay in this job for ever.'

'No?' Nikki said.

'No,' I said. 'I have a longer-term plan here. I'm just passing through.'

Nikki smiled. 'You'll be a lot richer when you're done,' she said. 'How much is it again?'

'High seven figures,' I said. Her smile had hit me like a snort of Ritalin. I smiled back. 'I shouldn't be saying this to you. But I'll be out of here by Christmas. Before Christmas, in fact.'

'Just passing through,' Nikki said, and looked away. She was no longer smiling. 'I really hope it works out.'

'It will,' I said. I too had abruptly stopped smiling. The meaning of Nikki's question about how much time I was spending with Mullens had just caught up with me. She didn't know what he was doing with his work week, either. We were, both of us, in the dark.

But I had bigger problems. In an attempt to defuse yet another argument with Clio (this one was about my refusal to sit in on rehearsals for her Big Play), I had agreed, at last, to meet her parents, something that, by deploying various strategies of evasion, feigned illness and outright mendacity, I had now avoided doing for almost eleven months. It wasn't that I didn't *care* about meeting Clio's parents, on that much I insist. It was that I viewed the prospect of an amicable lunch with two middle-aged hospital consultants in their ramshackle house in Terenure much as a man in a wheelchair must view the prospect of climbing Everest. Nevertheless, when Clio ousted me from the four-poster bed at noon on the appointed day, I managed to rise, lurching, to the occasion. So committed was I to making a good impression – or, perhaps, such was my guilt about lying to Clio – that I didn't even prime myself with any drugs.

The house was a bourgeois-bohemian mess. Three, or possibly four, bicycles lay entangled in the hallway. On the telephone seat by the coat rack was a shallow earthenware dish full of bulldog clips, and beside this, another identical dish full of elastic bands. The living-room couch was piled with books (*Postcapitalism*, *Admissions: A Life in Brain Surgery*) and medical journals (*The Lancet*, *Annals of Internal Medicine*). Potted ferns thrived in the uterine heat.

Clio's father was in the kitchen. He was literally wearing a plastic apron that said DAD AT WORK. He was also, equally literally, whisking something in a copper pan. 'Hope you're not a veggie,' he said, as he smiled and shook my hand. 'This one was a veggie when she was a teenager.' He nodded at Clio. 'We went without meat for three years. Couldn't wait for her to move out.'

'Shut *up*, Dad,' Clio said. She was sitting on the kitchen counter, chewing on a breadstick. Her father squeezed her knee with one bearish hand. She rolled her eyes.

'The famous Ben.' This was Clio's mother, who had appeared without warning and who now involved me in an embrace that went on much too long to be described as merely a hug. She was literally wearing a paint-smeared white smock. She was also, equally literally, holding an ancient piebald cat under her arm.

'Oh, hey, Snow Pea,' Clio said.

'Uh,' I said. 'Hey.'

'Oh my God,' Clio said. 'Snow Pea is the cat, you goon.'

We all had a good laugh about this.

'He's been to the vet, hasn't he?' Clio's mother said, rubbing the cat's nose with her own.

'He's eighteen this year,' Clio's father said. 'He has arthritis. But he still gets around. Don't you, Snow Pea?'

'Yes, you do,' Clio said. She was also now nose-to-nose with the cat.

'I'm sorry,' someone said. After a moment, I realised that the person who had said these words was me.

My armpits had abruptly developed a maddening itch.

Clio and her parents were looking at me expectantly. 'For what?' Clio's mother said. She reached out to touch my hand. 'Is everything all right?'

'Sorry,' I said again. I shrugged. I could think of nothing else to say. I had no idea why, as I watched Clio and her mother rub noses with their cat, I had suddenly felt compelled to apologise. I had no idea to whom I might be apologising, or what I might be apologising for.

Clio's mother handed me the cat. For a moment I held it – I pressed its warm fur to my face.

'Who's a good puss,' I said. 'Who's a good puss cat.'

'You never told me you liked cats,' Clio said. She pointed a raised eyebrow in her mother's direction. 'See? I told you he was nice.'

It won't surprise you, Dr F, to hear that it took me less than twenty-four hours to squander the goodwill that had accrued to me at that surprisingly restful lunch. We were watching TV in my penthouse the following evening when Clio said, 'My phone's charging in the other room. Can I have yours for a sec?' Unthinkingly – i.e., in the same way I do everything – I handed it over. Clio opened my Facebook app to find herself confronted with the photograph of Nikki in her pink bikini. Far too exhausting to write out in full the back-and-forth of yet another dismal contretemps ('Who is she? You were talking to her in the Shelbourne! OH MY GOD ARE YOU FUCKING HER!', et cetera). Enough to say that my mumbled explanations ('I must have clicked into it by accident') were so half-assed that Clio eventually put on her coat and left without saying anything in reply. When she had gone I punched the lintel of the kitchen door, gouging deep grooves in the skin of my knuckles, and poured some medicinal rum into a pint glass.

The rollercoaster was clicking its way to the top of the track. Soon it would peak, hover, and—

... *ticktickticktickticktickticktickticktick* ...

Two days later, The Lads brought their dads down to Wicklow for a golf weekend at Druids Glen. We were almost ready. Everything was set. The contracts for the Serbian deal had been drafted. Our plane tickets were booked. There was nothing more to do – except, it appeared, play golf. I viewed the whole weekend as a time-killing exercise (not to mention a significant intrusion on my carefully laid plans to take a lot of drugs) and tried to get out of it altogether. But Mullens was insistent.

'We need to be sharp for this trip,' he said. 'That's why you get a bit of R and R beforehand. So you can hit the ground running.'

It seemed to me that a weekend of the kind of R & R that Mullens was proposing would tend to leave us the opposite of sharp – it would leave us blunted, hampered, dulled. But I said nothing, and went along. *Nearly there*, was my weekend mantra. *Nearly there.*

We were supposed to play eighteen holes of golf and then booze our way through a four-course meal in the hotel restaurant. But in practice everyone started drinking at lunchtime, and Tynan brought a sports bag full of craft beers out onto the course, and by the time we had reached the ninth tee Sean Sweeney's father was regularly disappearing into the woods to urinate, yodelling apologies over his shoulder and explaining about his swollen prostate as he defiled another hundred-year-old oak or sapling birch. Over dinner there were speeches. The Lads embraced their dads. Tears were shed. It was at this point that I decamped to the bathroom to sober myself up with some coke. It was a cheap batch – like snorting dental anaesthetic. But it did the trick. It always does.

Numb-faced, I tried to find my way back to the residents' bar. Stricken with paranoia, I coasted to a stop in the middle of an anonymous corridor. Here presences lurked behind each door of eggshell blue. Doors, doors. Why did there have to be so many closed *doors*? At its farthest end the corridor terminated in gloom. But I seemed to discern there a bipedal shadow, lurking. I felt the air with my hands and idiotically smiled. My phone was buzzing in my pocket. It was Clio.

'HI, BABES,' she said when I answered. Behind her, I could hear the din of a nightclub dancefloor.

Clio and I had reconciled that morning. I had couriered two dozen white roses to her old apartment, along with a note, the craven contents of which I do not particularly feel, just now, like sharing.

'What's, eh,' I whispered, 'what's up?'

'I'M WITH LIKE RACHEL AND KIMBERLEY AND THEM,' Clio said. 'AND BAZ.' The line cut out and then returned. '—ORRY,' Clio was saying.

'What?' I said. 'BAZ WANTS TO—' Another interruption. My nerves jangled. Then I heard Baz Hynes's voice, also crackling in and out. 'HEY, MAN,' he said. '—IG DEAL SO DON'T WORR—'

'WHAT?' I said.

'—APPENED BEFORE WE—'

'Oh, fuck this,' I said, and pressed END.

Once more I peered into the darkness at the end of the corridor. The man-shaped shadow had receded, or perhaps there had been no man-shaped shadow in the first place. I took an experimental step backwards. The coke had expanded the limits of my sensorium, until I became tinglingly aware of the edges of the carpet where they softly met the walls, of the texture of the surface of each pine-laminate doorway, cool and faintly ridged, like old leather. That was a normal feeling, right? That was more or less part of the general run of human experience?

My phone rang again. 'I'm outside now,' Clio said, over

the airy sound of traffic. 'Did you hear what Baz was saying there?'

'It kept cutting out,' I said. 'What's up?'

'It's nothing,' Clio said. 'Just Baz talking shite.'

'Okay,' I said.

'Listen,' Clio said, 'I just thought you should know, your mother came by.'

'My what?' I said.

'Your mother,' Clio said. 'She called by the apartment this morning at like eleven o'clock. I hadn't even had a shower. And she was being *super* weird.'

'What the fuck did she want?' I said. The coke – it must have been the coke – was prompting my heart to new feats of alacrity.

'She was being all, like, pretend-polite?' Clio said. 'I don't mean to be a bitch or whatever but she was *kind* of horrible to me?'

'That's her,' I said.

'She wants you to come see her or something,' Clio said.

'Okay,' I said. Through the phone I could hear the rumble and fuss of cars passing on a damp street. 'I miss you,' I said.

'I miss you too,' Clio said. 'See you tomorrow for snuggles?'

'I'd like that,' I said. The call dropped.

Pocketing my phone, I spotted a furtive movement, down at the far end of the corridor. Hallucinations, surely. Although, on the other hand . . .

From the gloom, a man in a brown trenchcoat emerged and began to walk towards me.

'You cunt,' I said involuntarily. 'Who the fuck are you, anyway?'

He was squarely middle-aged. The face was that of a man whom you could easily picture sloping out of the bookie's at noon on a weekday, on his way to the pub for a hair of the dog. The expression was a leer of private amusement. As he passed, he gave me a wink. In his wake an eddy of disturbed air travelled. I felt it in the fibres of my nerves.

The corridor was suddenly very cold and my teeth were beginning to chatter.

As I groped my way back to the bar I told myself in stern tones that the man in the brown trenchcoat was unquestionably nothing more than an extremely vivid and detailed hallucination, and that I definitely wasn't being followed everywhere I went, and that there was nothing sinister going on beyond the various machinations that Mullens had already explained to me, and that very soon my plan was going to rescue me from my car-crash life, and that the freezing sensation in my heart was just the coke, just the coke, just the coke.

The next day I cabbed it to my parents' house to find out what my mother wanted. My original intention, of course, had been to ignore her summons. But my curiosity got the better of me. The vibe in the house was approximately that of Hitler's bunker circa April 1945. The curtains were drawn and the walls were bare. Through the open door of my father's study a landslide of banker's boxes spilled, shedding documents, notepads, folders, newspapers. My father himself was not in evidence. The hallway smelled of mildew and of something else, a vague sepsis. The kitchen looked uninhabited, like a showroom – or like the ghostly kitchen at the Naas Road warehouse rave. On the counter, a laptop displayed a website: HARTFORD REALTY – LUXURY HOMES IN CONNECTICUT, VERMONT & MAINE. Beside it, a golf magazine invited its readers to 'Kill Your Slice and Pure Your Irons'.

Halfway down the garden my mother was refilling the wire seed containers that hung from her bright-blue wooden birdhouse. This was part of her daily routine. Birds were her acknowledged hobby. She kept an encyclopaedia of Irish species on her bedside table and a pair of sniper-grade binoculars by the Belfast sink. Every morning she put fresh orange peel around the flowerbeds to ward off the neighbours' cats. The seed containers attracted chaffinches, goldfinches, pied wagtails. My mother cleaned the wire cages twice a week, wearing disposable rubber gloves to protect her from avian flu. Look at that, Dr F: I suppose I can't avoid acknowledging at this point that my mother did, in fact, have a life outside drinking. She had birds. She had even taught me the names of birds when I was a kid. I'd forgotten that, till now. She also taught me to dislike magpies – ill-mannered birds, she always said. Thieves and jeerers. For her, the rules of politeness applied even to members of the animal kingdom. That was my mother. She could forgive anything except bad manners.

On the patio table – I had now stepped outside – reposed a half-empty bottle of Chardonnay and a tray of empty wine glasses. After a moment my presence seemed to cause some quantum fluctuation in the air: my mother became aware of me and pivoted, shading her eyes with a palm.

'Since you're here,' she called, 'you might as well pour me a fresh glass.'

Through the greened-in branches of maples and birches above her head the sunlight was finely tangled.

I poured a glass for myself, while I was at it.

Thinking about the birds, I am reminded, by a lateral move of memory, of something else – of several something elses, in fact. My mother's mother – my grandmother – died when I was eight, in the middle of a January freeze. Just before the final vigil (my grandmother had been moved to a hospice ward, but had not yet faded into her final unconsciousness), a sparrow flew into our kitchen. My father waved it gently back outside with a newspaper. 'That's a death in the family,' my mother said. 'A sparrow in the house. It means someone's going to die.' ('Sparrows are supposed to carry the souls of the dead to the underworld,' Dr Felix said, when I told him this. 'The technical term is *psychopomp*.' 'That's so helpful for my therapy,' I said. 'Thank you.')

My mother organised the entire funeral with a gin and tonic in her hand. She even tried to bring a tumbler of Grey Goose into the church (I seem to recall my father removing it from her grip as we climbed the steps and passing it, ice clinking, to one of his trusted retainers). Of course, the funeral and the afterparty were superb occasions – beautifully stage-managed and decorated. My mother was a gifted project manager. Over cocktails at lunch she would dope out a guest list and seating plan for her latest charity ball. Sipping a negroni at dinner, she would balance the household chequebook. 'Your mother,' my father once told me, 'is a four-star general in a dress.' In the funeral car, on the way to the graveside, she told me not to cry, if I could help it. 'We have to put a brave face on the occasion,' she said (and has my memory added that fresh G & T in her black-gloved hand?). 'It's a question of taste.'

In the graveyard we stood around in sub-zero conditions, stamping our feet. The coffin, in situ on a mechanical hoist, seemed to have displaced its own weight in black earth. Frost glinted from the banked soil like mica. We were tended by a quartet of men in long black coats and stovepipe hats. In the mortality business. As who is not? One of them had a large bulbous growth on his nose – a wen. In the cold this growth was the same port-wine colour as his flushed face. The coffin was lowered. For form's sake – was it? – I took my mother's hand. She leaned down and whispered, 'You'd think he'd get that thing removed from his face. As if people wanted to look at *that*, at a funeral. So ugly.'

'For a minute I thought you were your father,' my mother said. She was sitting in one of two cane chairs that seemed to be the only furniture left in the conservatory. I stayed on my feet. I didn't want to create the impression that I was planning to stick around.

'Where is he, anyway?' I said.

'Barrister,' my mother said. 'I'm surprised to hear you ask, actually. For a while I kept expecting you to show an interest in what was happening to your family. But you seemed determined to run away. So I stopped expecting.'

'Is this why you showed up at my apartment?' I said. 'To bully me?'

'I can't *make* you feel empathy for your father,' my mother said. 'I've watched you run away from reality since you were a little boy. I don't know why I thought this would be any different.'

'I'm going to go,' I said.

'Let me ask you something,' my mother said. 'A direct question. Do you think your father is guilty?'

I said nothing.

'Because,' my mother said, 'you're acting as if you do. You're doing everything in your power to disassociate yourself from us. Ignoring us for months on end. Running around, pretending to be a businessman. Making a fool of yourself, from what I've heard. So tell me. Do you think he's guilty?'

'I don't care,' I said, and as I said it, I realised it was true. 'It doesn't matter whether he's guilty or not. That's not the point. The point is, I don't care.'

'It doesn't matter,' my mother said, and smiled. 'It doesn't matter to you. I shouldn't need to remind you that it bloody well matters to me. It bloody well matters to your father.'

'You're not going to be fucking cellmates,' I said. 'The happiest married couple in the joint.'

My mother was silent. Beyond the open French doors a family of sparrows was making a racket in the branches of a whitethorn bush.

'I've got to go,' I said.

'I'm trying to repair this family,' my mother said. 'Before it's wrecked beyond all hope. And it isn't this trial that's going to wreck it.' Her eyes were clear. 'Your father is innocent,' she said. 'And he can prove it. He won't be going to prison. You won't be able to pretend he's just disappeared. When this trial is over, you'll have a choice. You can either have a relationship with your father, or you can live with the knowledge that you weren't able. And I can tell you that when he's found innocent, you're going to feel *appalling* that you didn't support him when it mattered.'

'Fine,' I said, in a burst of anger. 'I'll go to the fucking trial. The first day. But that's it, okay? After that I'm gone.'

'You can do what you want,' my mother said. 'We're not going anywhere.'

In the cab on the way home I called James Mullens and told him I would need a later flight to Belgrade. He didn't seem to think it was a problem.

Serbia

We were heading north, into open country. The limo – with Boris at the wheel – bore us past more spurned-looking shacks, more boarded-up factories. Then the buildings

273

dwindled and a palisade of trees rushed past. With a wink of pearlescent light the sun disappeared behind a mountain. Maria, asleep in the jump seat, was pressing her bare left foot against my inner thigh. James Mullens was still staring at his phone with a sour expression on his face. We had still not signed the contracts.

I looked at Maria's sleeping face. I had been unforgivably rude to her. She had, it turned out, solid reasons for being so abrasive and dour all the time. On the other hand, she was clearly also a horrible person, independently of any trauma that she may have experienced in her past. What to do? After some thought, I decided to continue being unforgivably rude to her, while simultaneously acknowledging to myself that she had had a very difficult life and therefore deserved at least a modicum of compassion. I sighed. It was no picnic, pretending to be an international property developer.

The limo jolted to a stop. I was thrown forward against my tensed seatbelt. Maria's foot jabbed me squarely in the balls.

'We eat,' Vuk croaked from where he sat hunched in the seat behind the driver's partition.

Beyond the tinted windows dusk had settled.

'Is bayou,' Aleks said, as we neared a slumped shack perched on the edge of a mass of dark water. 'Town is famous for fish caught. Exporting to all of Serbia.'

Rounding a bend in the shore, we beheld a small agglomeration of lights, clustered around the stub of a dock. Three black, mastless boats sat unmoving in the weedy shallows.

Half a mile downstream, a chimneyed refinery spurted clouds of sooty effluent into the twilight's upper reaches. The water looked protozoic. I searched the vicinity for Boris the driver, but he seemed to have disappeared.

Nicolae muttered something to Aleks, who said, 'We are here to meeting official from State Department of Economy. Also to have dinner of locally caught fish.'

I looked out across the bayou – at the swamp trees with their bone-white bark, the creepers with their wilting hippie haircuts.

'Regularly my family eat fish from this town,' Aleks said.

'Nothing wrong with that,' I said.

Up ahead, in the wan porch light of yet another fucked shack, Maria was waiting, tapping her foot impatiently as I made my way across a field of muddy grass.

The fucked shack turned out to be a restaurant. In the foyer, Vuk introduced us to a man dressed in a three-cornered hat, red pantaloons, a white frilly shirt, and laced-up leather boots with pointed toes. 'National costume of Serbia,' Aleks murmured in my ear, by way of explanation. Sweeney openly guffawed, cupping his mouth with a gym-calloused hand. Aleks shook his head in disapproval. 'Is official from State Department of Economy,' he said. 'Also Mayor of town.'

As we watched, the Mayor performed a Cossack-ish dance, folding his arms and kicking, while his retinue – a group of gnomelike men in gingham suits – clapped along. I wondered, briefly, if I was hallucinating again. It was, I concluded, time to take more drugs. On my way to the bathroom, I was intercepted by Maria, who said, without otherwise greeting me, 'You miss girlfriend.'

We were in a narrow hallway panelled with cheap imitation pine. From a shelf, the glazed eyes of a shot fox gleamed, reminding me, uncannily, of my mother.

'You what now?' I said.

'You have girlfriend,' Maria said. 'This you tell me. You are away from her, so you are missing her.'

'I suppose,' I said.

'Is traditional for woman in Serbia to remain in the home and serve,' Maria said. 'Your Irish girlfriend, she is also traditional.'

'In a sense,' I said.

'She not work,' Maria said.

'I can honestly say she's never worked a day in her life,' I said.

'You know what this means, to serve?' Maria said. Was that a wink or was it just a facial tic?

'If you'll excuse me,' I said, 'I really need to—'

'To serve in every way,' she said. She was definitely winking.

I bolted for the gents'.

Dinner was served at a banqueting table in the shack's main room. The Mayor in his three-cornered hat and frilly shirt presided eagerly. In the middle of the table, on a tarnished silver platter, sat what appeared to be a fossilised swordfish. It was three feet long and grey-skinned, with lustreless protrusive eyes. Beside it was a bowl of small, spined creatures that resembled crayfish. They lay in packed ice, budging each other up, in a frozen hurry. There was no other food in view. Shots of *rakija* did the rounds. The Lads had perked up: Paul Tynan was telling the Mayor all about how he had successfully sued his gym after an accident involving a loose screw in the hack-squat machine. My own mood had stabilised somewhere in the upper ionosphere. My nasal cavities burned sweetly from the coke and I was happily tending to two cigarettes at once. I was also on a mission. I was going to have a private word with Vuk, just as soon as the opportunity presented itself. It was time to get those contracts signed. In the meantime, I was still perforce engaged in faintly hostile badinage with Maria, who had made a point of choosing the chair beside mine.

'Boyfriend of before,' she was saying, 'was not compatibility in bedroom. He is man who does not dominate. I am looking for man who will take sex when he wants. Not submissive man who will wait for woman.'

'This ex of yours,' I said. 'He sounds all right, actually.'

'Was not all right,' Maria said. She flicked her hair over her shoulder with a stiff palm. 'With him I waste two years of life. I am expecting to have two children by age of twenty-five.'

'Christ,' I said, 'how old are you now?'

'This is rude,' Maria said. 'You do not ask woman her age.' She helped herself to a slice of pre-Cambrian fish. 'In Ireland woman is more like man. Maybe they are used to being treated with rudeness. Women in Ireland are feminists.

277

I know this type of woman. They act like men, not like women.'

'Excuse me,' I said.

Vuk had risen from his seat and seemed to be heading for the door.

I cornered him in the panelled hallway. 'Man of Black Pool City,' he said, regarding me curiously. 'I watch you with Mačka. You two find together much of which to talk. To bring young people together. This I am glad to see. Maria I raise like daughter. And to you I have feeling as of son.'

'I was wondering—' I began.

'From little girl I raise Maria,' Vuk said. 'And in present time I hope for her to find a strong man of business which to be happy.'

I decided to ignore this. 'I wondered if we could have a quick chat,' I said, 'about getting these contracts signed.'

The wheedling eyebrows twitched like whiskers. 'Now is time for social togetherness,' Vuk said. 'Later, I think, is time for business.'

'I just need to know when,' I said.

I must have sounded desperate, because Vuk's expression softened. 'When you are young,' he said, 'you are impatient. And for you in particular is this true, I think. I see young man when you first come in Belgrade. And I think, this is impatient young man. This is young man who has lost something and who is looking around everywhere for it. I have seen war. I have seen men of your youth who have lost many things.

278

To look for what you have lost in the right way, I discover, this is secret.'

'Secret to what?' I said.

'To living,' Vuk said. He stepped past me into the gents' and let the door swing shut behind him.

I found, as I lit a cigarette, that my hands were shaking.

'Here,' Sean Sweeney said, an hour or so later, 'you're not actually going to ride that mingbag, are you?' We were on the porch. Behind us, the restaurant was thronged. The muddy field apparently served as a car park and now overflowed with Soviet autos: with Yugas and Zeks, GAZs and ZiLs. For reasons I could not discern, Nicolae and Ratko were prowling among the ranks of cars. They had taken off their jackets, revealing T-shirted torsos packed with gorilla muscle. Now they seemed to be trying to get a car to start – they were nudging it forward with their shoulders.

'What are they doing?' I said. I had just performed an inventory of my pharmacopeia. My stocks were dwindling. I had not helped matters by doling out a few grams of coke to The Lads after dinner. The coke had made me generous. It had also made me greedy. Once again I was tasked with reconciling two incompatible urges. My phone had zero signal. I was very far from home, or home was very far from me. I found myself wanting to call Clio. I wanted to ask her if everything was going to be okay. But when you lie to someone, you create a credibility problem: you no longer believe them, either.

Nicolae and Ratko were drawing closer to where we stood. Beyond the car park's pool of urine-coloured halogen light, I could see only a fluid immensity of country darkness.

'Your bird, though,' Sweeney said, drawing on his cigarette. He smoked the way a hard-bitten army drill sergeant might smoke: his fingers pinched, his eyes narrowed, the whole operation charged with subliminal contempt.

'Clio,' I said distractedly.

'Yeah, Clio. She's a fucking stunner. I'd eat the dress off her just to get a go of her gash, you know what I'm saying?'

'Yeah,' I said. 'Cheers, man.'

From the door of the shack Paul Tynan and Bobby Hayes now bullishly emerged. 'All I had was fucking bread,' Hayeser was saying. 'Did you see the state of that fish? It was like fucking jelly.'

Who were they – The Lads? In a sense they were ordinary people. Civilians. Optimists. They had simple goals. They believed that winning a game of rugby was something that could be construed as a destiny. They believed that if you went to the gym on the reg and developed your muscles and ate steak and protein powder for breakfast, you would be able to win a fight with another man if another man ever tried to start a fight with you. They believed in immutable rules of deportment and dress. They believed in holding doors open for women and they believed that eventually everyone should settle down and have a family, because that was just what you did. They believed that 99 per cent of problems could be solved by the simple expedient of being privileged enough never to have encountered them. They had scared the hell out of me in school and they scared the hell out of me now. I wanted them to like me. And I wanted never to see any of them ever again.

'You are coming to see,' said a jagged-sounding voice. It was Nicolae. With his one good eye he was staring at us from the edge of the car park. Beside him, Ratko rocked on his heels and rubbed his hands enthusiastically, like a man looking forward to a good meal. 'You are in time to come and see,' Nicolae called, gesturing backwards, into the darkness.

At once I had a vision of the four of us – me, Sweeney, Bobby Hayes and Tynan – digging our own graves in a mist-cloaked forest, while Nicolae and Ratko urged us on with submachine guns.

'See what?' Sweeney said. The coke was making him sniff.

'We put on entertainment,' Nicolae said. 'Come, come.'

Bobby Hayes was already vaulting down the porch steps, saying, 'This should be good.'

With maximum reluctance, I trailed The Lads as they followed Nicolae and Ratko through the maze of cars. The humid night air entered my lungs like a rubber glove. We arrived at a stationary car: a square-shouldered yellow hatchback, parked near the muddy field's main entrance.

'We show you how we entertain in Serbia,' Ratko said. 'You see.'

He pointed downwards. Creased beneath the stout rubber

of the car's front tyre was a blue-grey banknote. Nicolae and Ratko had evidently tucked this under the tyre and pushed the car until the note was trapped beneath it.

'Five thousand dinar,' Nicolae said. 'Now we go back.'

Obediently, we followed them back to the porch. From the shadows in which we stood, we had a clear view of the boxy yellow hatchback.

'What are we waiting for?' I said.

More locals were arriving: tubercular young men in army fatigues, girls in jeans and chunky neon trainers. They passed the yellow car on their way to the shack.

'Five thousand dinar,' Paul Tynan said, jabbing at his phone. 'That's, like, what – forty quid?'

'Is lot of money in Serbia,' Nicolae said. He and Ratko, as they lounged against the porch rail, had about them a sly expectant air, as if they were waiting for the punchline of some subtle practical joke. And yet their faces were impassive, lumpen, void of affect, like the faces – I thought – of professional soldiers. Who the fuck were these guys, anyway? What was Securitate? Was it like Interpol? And what was the deal with Romania? Wasn't it basically a democracy? My phone had no signal. I couldn't check these things, even if I'd wanted to.

'I don't get it,' Bobby Hayes said.

Then it happened. A couple appeared at the entrance to the car park. The man was middle-aged, paunchy, wearing an ancient suit with a flared collar. His bald crown gleamed in the halogen light. The woman was young, with a blonde tower of ringleted hair and jutting boobs. They passed the yellow car. The man seemed to exclaim. The woman, still walking, turned and stopped. The man's upper body at once disappeared from view.

Beside us, on the porch, Nicolae and Ratko watched without moving. I looked at Sweeney, and then at Tynan and Bobby Hayes – at their eager, uncertain faces.

The man with the flared collar stood up again and seemed to consider. He looked around – his face, too, had an eager expression. The woman seemed to wave him on – *Hurry up, hurry up!* She stood with her arms folded, and looked towards the shack. Time seemed to have distended itself. *We put on entertainment.* The middle-aged man now braced the trunk of the yellow car with his shoulder and heaved. The car did not move. He tried again, his feet pedalling slickly in the mud. The car rocked on its springs.

Nicolae and Ratko had dropped from the porch and were moving swiftly among the parked cars, taking an indirect route, homing in on the yellow hatchback.

'*Come* on,' Bobby Hayes hissed.

The three Lads followed. I stayed where I was.

Now the man in the flared suit was thumping his shoulder against the car like someone trying to break down a door. Nicolae and Ratko were twenty feet away. When Nicolae called out, his voice was like a gunshot – I was physiologically reminded, I found, of that morning's drone shoot in Novi Sad. *Crack! Boom!* The anger in his voice was incredible – it was like the snarl of a chained-up dog.

The man in the flared suit instantly straightened and quailed – it was a single movement, and again I thought of a dog, cringing beneath a raised newspaper. Nicolae was screaming in Serbian, pointing at the car in simulated outrage. Beside him, Ratko was pulling on a pair of black leather gloves. A few feet away, The Lads, smiling, hovered uneasily.

The man in the flared suit held up his hands and spoke. Nicolae stepped towards him, and now it became possible to observe how very much larger Nicolae was than the man in the flared suit, how uneven was the contest that was being proposed. The woman with her tower of blonde ringlets was also speaking, not calmly, and gesturing in the direction of the shack. Nicolae shook his head and screamed again.

Ratko, who was still fiddling in an actorly way with the cuffs of his leather gloves, took an accidental-seeming step towards the blonde woman. As the man in the flared suit was pointing in self-exculpation towards the wheel of the yellow car, Ratko raised a gloved fist and thumped the blonde woman's face with it. She immediately fell to the ground.

The three Lads, taken by surprise, flinched as one. It took a moment or two for the smiles to disappear from their faces so that, when the man in the flared suit, no longer frightened, lunged towards Ratko with a sneer of hatred on his face, and Nicolae chopped his throat with a flattened palm, The Lads were still smiling. And they were still smiling, an instant later, when the man dropped to his knees in the mud and gasped, clutching his throat as if he were about to drown.

Dublin

Early this morning Dr Felix steered me to the deserted day room and subjected me to a game of Scrabble, which he claimed would be 'good for [my] cognition'. My fellow inmates were out in the garden, tottering their way through a sequence of ersatz Tai Chi moves: Salute the Sun, Fall Over, Vomit, Weep. I moved my lettered tiles with a sodden heart, producing what Dr F described as 'examples of negative vocabulary' (*death, bored, grim, trick, cry*). Dr Felix himself frankly cheated, introducing a second and then a third set of tiles in order to manipulate his moves. He produced 'OPTIMISM' on the first move, and 'PESSIMISM' on the second.

'Our texts for the day,' he said, in the unctuous tones of a Protestant minister opening his Book of Common Prayer. 'Has it ever occurred to you that your performative pessimism is just the mirror image of your father's performative optimism?'

'I love that you've given my life so much thought,' I said.

'Answer the question, please.'

On the board, I constructed the word 'UGH'. 'If you mean that I thought my father was deluded, then sure. Why not?'

'But you didn't think you were deluded. In your pessimism, I mean.' Dr Felix's latest move had produced the word 'ERROR'.

Triumphantly I placed the word 'SYSTEM' in front of the word 'ERROR'. 'I'd say I was confirmed in my pessimism. More than confirmed.'

'Genuine pessimists don't take drugs,' Dr Felix said.

'That's a fucking ridiculous thing to say,' I said. 'Genuine pessimists are the people *most* likely to take drugs.'

'No,' Dr Felix said. 'The person who takes drugs because the world is a terrible place is an optimist. He's someone who can't accept that the world is terrible. He thinks there must be a better way.'

I would have liked to make the word 'SOPHISTRY' but I lacked the relevant tiles. 'So you're telling me I'm actually an optimist.'

'I'm telling you both attitudes are wrong. Besides, you were never a pessimist. You were something else.'

Dr Felix had contrived to play the word 'PARANOID'.

My next move was ready to go. I felt briefly euphoric – was my cognition, whatever that means, actually improving because of this ridiculous game? I placed five tiles on the board.

'I was wondering when you'd bring up that word,' I said. 'But I wouldn't call myself paranoid. I'd say I was dealing with something else.'

The fives tiles spelled 'LIARS'.

Dr Felix nodded in a preoccupied way. He was shifting tiles around on his little plastic rack. 'You're thirty points behind,' he said. 'I'm trying to give you something to think about here. Which is that attitudes distort reality. Optimism, pessimism, paranoia. They're prejudices, in the truest sense of the word. They mean we only see what we expect to see. Try looking at what's really there. Then exert the faculty of judgement. Not the other way around.'

'And what,' I said, 'is really there?'

Dr Felix frowned and turned his plastic rack to face me. He had spelled out the word 'PENIS'.

The opening night of Clio's play was scheduled for 20 September, which was also, in one of those instances of nightmarish synchronicity that lead you to suspect that we are all already in hell and that the secret purpose of all life is to suffer, the night before the first day of my father's trial. I had, of course, hoped to avoid attending either event (and I had invested a good deal of emotional energy in reassuring Clio that I would be attending her play on the evening of my return from Belgrade – literally, if possible, the very second I stepped off the plane). But now that I was going to be flying out two days after the rest of the Echo REIT gang, I had no choice but to show up for the premiere. 'They reserved a seat for you in the front row,' she said, hopping out of bed and scrabbling around for her clothes. We were in my penthouse. Our sex life had lately improved to the point where I could sustain an erection long enough for Clio to grind herself to orgasm as she lay beneath me. This I had achieved by scaling back my intake of coke during business hours: a sacrifice, but worth it, I thought.

'I can't wait,' I said.

As Clio got dressed, I contemplated the number and variety of admiring faces I would be called upon to make as I watched the play, and reached for the bottle of single malt on the bedside locker.

There was a message on my phone. It was from my father. JUST A REMINDER, it said, 9.30A.M TOMORROW CNTRL CRIMINAL COURT. FORMAL DRESS BUT NOT BLACK TIE HAHA.

Not long now, I told myself. *Not long now!*

Clio's play was being staged in a theatre in Temple Bar that was either still under construction or had been intentionally designed, for obscure aesthetic reasons, to resemble a building site. Taking my seat, I peered at the programme. Under RUNNING TIME, it said 2 HOURS 30 MINS. This was a blow. But I soon rallied. I had, after all, smuggled in a glass of bulk-bought wine. I had also inhaled 90 per cent of the contents of a bag of speed that I had purchased several hours ago from a Scottish gentleman whom I had met in the bathroom of the Westbury Hotel. Having nothing else to do, I had spent the afternoon on the piss, and the speed was my insurance policy: it would counteract the booze and keep me awake for the duration of the play.

The lights went down. Clio appeared, dressed in rags. Affecting a north Dublin accent, she spoke some kind of overture.

'Two steps,' she said, 'from Aleppo to a boat on a raging sea, they're swept into a worldwide web of stress, their lives a mess, they're bloodied, dispossessed, alone, drone-bombed . . .'

Her recitation was accompanied by a sequence of stylised gestures: jazz hands, wide eyes, step back, pivot, kick, wave. It was like watching someone dance the Charleston in slow motion.

'... hurt millions crossing borders, men with guns shouting orders, why won't you meet my eyes? – surprise! We're all the same, no blame, this is why we're blessed, in this land of redress we seek our rest, so lend a helping hand, let us stand *together* – make a prophecy that we will *change* our policy ...'

I peered once again at my programme. Under RUNNING TIME, it still said 2 HOURS 30 MINS. I was not as prepared as I had hoped to be. The speed was ramifying dendritically throughout my central nervous system. My teeth were stuck together as if by toffee. My left thigh was developing a tremor. No, wait! The tremor was my phone! The wavering screen – I was having some trouble focusing my eyes – displayed a message from my mother. DON'T BE LATE, it said.

'Fuck off,' I said aloud, causing several of my fellow theatregoers to turn their heads in my direction. Unselfconsciously, I sipped my wine. What I hated about plays, I thought, as I watched Clio dance some sort of expressionistic tarantella – no, what I hated about *actors* – was the way they went at emotions from the outside in: as if evoking feelings in other people were entirely a matter of gestures and shouting. Time passed. The play evolved into a sequence of stilted tableaux in which inscrutably angry characters bore down on one another endlessly. I was finding the action difficult to follow, but I couldn't be sure if this was because I was witnessing a masterpiece of the post-linear avant garde or because I was wrecked on cheap speed. A stooped figure in a burka straightened and became

Barry Hynes, who was pretending to be (was it?) the UK Home Secretary. Baz delivered a heavily end-rhymed monologue to his own clenched fist. The lighting shifted: now a spotlight, now a wash. It was a bit like being in a terrible nightclub.

Now Baz Hynes, adopting a culturally appropriative Compton-gangsta voice, was delivering the peroration: 'They had to *leave* their heartland, so let us be a *smart* land, an open-hearted, take-*part* land, let's hold up those welcome signs combined with *warm* hands, man, be strong and *kind*, man, we need to be a port in a *storm*, man, and when that storm has *passed* our *pasts* will be what unite us, light us, deliver us from plight as we bring ourselves online *together*, man, in a long line, fight as one kind ...'

An aeon more of this. Then the lights went out. Limply, I contributed to the applause. The actors did their bend-at-the-waist bit. Clio's face, I observed, was congested with emotion. Beside her, holding her hand, Baz Hynes was beaming. The house lights rose. Sitting diagonally opposite me, on the other side of the stage, not applauding, was the Man in the Brown Trenchcoat.

Serbia

Bobby Hayes was staring at a cheaply printed pamphlet. '*Festival* of the *National Cake*,' he said, at top volume. 'They have a fucking *national cake* ... And they have a fucking *festival* for it!'

Sean Sweeney peered glumly down at his glass of wine. 'I think I've sessioned myself sober,' he said.

The good news was that we were no longer in the middle of nowhere. The bad news was that we were back in Novi Sad, after what turned out to have been a completely pointless 300-mile round trip. It was the evening of my third day in Serbia. We were attending a reception in the tennis-court-sized atrium of Novi Sad's town hall. The municipal budget had not, it seemed, been sufficiently flexible to cope with three decades of regional regime change. 'Was originally built as headquarters of Communist Party in Novi Sad,' Aleks had remarked, as we passed beneath a framed portrait of Mikhail Gorbachev.

We had spent the day in the limo, travelling south. We had not signed any documents. Nor had we seen even a single square yard of real estate. Over breakfast, Vuk had mumbled something about the solicitor's office being located 'in business district of Novi Sad'. But we had been in Novi Sad for hours, and all we had done was eat another dubious meal (consisting, so far as I could make out, of fried cubes of lard: 'Is national delicacy,' Aleks had said, on cue. But The Lads no longer appeared to find this funny).

Of Maria there was no sign. Nicolae and Ratko, on the other hand, were still very much with us. They had accompanied us to dinner and they had accompanied us to the wine reception, and now they stood on either side of a gigantic potted fern, eating prawn cocktails from little plastic goblets. I had been avoiding them all day. I had, I supposed, been hoping that Ratko and Nicolae were ugly and frightening but essentially harmless to humans, like basking sharks. But now – following the incident in the bayou car park – it was clear that they were ugly and frightening and incredibly dangerous, like great whites. After the man in the flare-collared suit had fallen to his knees, grasping at his throat, Nicolae had lifted a steel-toed boot and gently prodded him in the small of his back. The man tipped forward, landing face-first in the mud. From where I stood on the porch, I could hear the blonde woman. She was weeping softly, as if in resignation. Ratko removed his gloves and leaned his shoulder against the boot of the yellow hatchback. The car slid forward. Nicolae bent and extracted the 5,000-dinar note from underneath the tyre. He held it above the prone man's body. It fluttered downwards, like an autumn leaf. 'He will need,' Nicolae said, 'for to clean. Suit now very muddy.' He turned to Sweeney and Bobby Hayes. Everyone was smiling. Bobby looked around quickly, and then chipped at the ground with his right foot, spattering mud across the trousers of the fallen man's suit. Now there was general laughter, a round of high-fives. As I watched, Sweeney raised his gym-pumped arms above his head in silent triumph. The halogen light above the car park's entrance flickered once and then went out.

On the other side of the town hall atrium, at the bottom of two converging marble staircases, a small podium and a set of bleachers had been erected. Behind these hung four huge lengths of red fabric, each emblazoned with a faded hammer and sickle. 'There is to be show,' Aleks said when I cornered him at the buffet table.

'Listen to me,' I said in an urgent whisper. 'How did you get this job? This translator gig?'

'I am in right place, right time,' Aleks said. 'I am hustler.'

'Did they contact you? Did you know who they were?' I said. I was clutching my wine glass so tightly that I felt it creak.

'You must have of this cake before you leave,' Aleks said. 'Is very delicious.'

'Back in the monastery—' I began. But before I could continue, I felt someone grab my elbow. It was James Mullens.

'You're shouting,' he said. He was murmuring in my ear. I could smell his aftershave: very nice, I thought.

'No, I'm not,' I said. 'I'm whispering. And if you don't mind, I'm having a private conversation here with Aleks.' My glass swooped outwards of its own accord, splashing the marble steps with wine.

'Outside,' Mullens said.

On our way to the door we passed Boris, our limo driver. 'Boris!' I said. 'Hey, Boris! Remember me?' But Boris ignored me and continued to eat cocktail sausages morosely, as if in penance.

From the town hall steps we could see the Petrovaradin Fortress, which loomed like a giant black molar, awaiting extraction by some god-sized dentist. Suavely, James

Mullens took the empty wine glass from my hand and placed it on the ledge of a nearby pillar. He watched as I struggled to light a cigarette. My stomach roiled and heaved. I kept remembering the sound that Ratko's gloved fist had made, connecting with the blonde woman's face. 'We have to get out of here,' I said. 'This isn't working. These guys are crooks.'

'Take a deep breath,' Mullens said. 'You're hitting the Daz pretty hard.'

'It isn't the Daz,' I said. 'You weren't there. They beat the shit out of these two people. They're fucking criminals.'

Mullens put his hand on my shoulder. Unwillingly, I noticed how firm his grip was and how steady and reassuring it felt. 'The bodyguards?' he said. 'They're bruisers, all right. I'd say they've done some skeevy shit in their time.'

'Why does a builder need bodyguards?' I said. 'We're not asking these questions. We should be asking the right questions.'

'This is the Wild West,' Mullens said. 'Or the Wild East. I'd have bodyguards if I lived here.'

'That's fucking bullshit and you know it,' I said. 'Who *are* these fuckers?'

Mullens seemed briefly assailed by some scruple. 'Okay,' he said after a moment. 'I'll level with you. But this goes no further, okay?' He looked back towards the town hall atrium, as if listening to the multiplied sounds of awkward chit-chat. 'Vuk's had his issues with the, ah, the authorities here. Some tax stuff, as far as I can gather. He was running a business that went tits-up. This was back in oh-eight, right? The credit crunch was fucking everyone. He ended up owing the revenue, whatever, a few million quid. And that's before you get to his creditors, who are seriously dodgy.'

'Dodgier than him?' I said.

'Dodgy,' Mullens said firmly. 'Like, mafia shit. This is very much on the DL, yeah? He can't sell his assets, and they've no equivalent of NAMA here, so Vuk had to bankrupt himself cleaning up the mess. But he's connected, right? Government contacts. So he sets up Voivode Holdings. He sets up Free Serbia Progress Construction. He hires a couple of body-guards in case the gangsters come knocking. This is him basically getting back on his feet. Now I'm seeing this as a very good thing for us. D'you know why?'

'... Why?' I said.

'Because he needs this way more than we do,' Mullens said. 'I never said these guys were decent human beings. I said they were desperate. That's why we're here. They're so desperate they're not going to look at things too closely. And that means we can manipulate them.'

'If he's desperate,' I said, 'then why isn't he rushing to sign the contracts?'

Mullens smiled. 'Why did you tear up my business card when I gave it to you the first time? People have their self-respect.'

'How much longer,' I said, 'is their self-respect going to keep us here?'

'Just hang on,' Mullens said. He put his hand on my shoulder again. 'You're doing great. I know you've had a rough year, with your ... your dad, and all that.'

Our eyes met for an instant, before we both looked away in confusion or shame.

The crowd in the atrium broke into applause. On the bleachers, a group of people was arranging itself in tiers. 'Is choir,' Aleks said, appearing at my shoulder. And indeed it was a choir, composed mostly of young girls, dressed in blue-grey pinafores. But the girls were ...

'Is choir of children with developmental challenge,' Aleks said. 'Much work is done for these children in Novi Sad.'

The girls were elbowing one another and smiling at the crowd. More applause. The children began to sing, their voices joined together precisely. The atrium filled up with a high, sweet sound.

Aleks was nodding in recognition. 'Is famous song of folk,' he whispered. 'About war against invasion of Turks in 1603.'

I found myself watching a fair-haired girl at the front of the choir. Her pinafore was shabby but neatly ironed. She sang with her eyes closed and her hands folded, as if entirely to herself. She must have been eleven or twelve years old. Small for her age.

The song lasted for five minutes. When it was over, Aleks silently passed me a Kleenex.

'Is very moving,' he said. 'You must have ancestry of Serbs in your veins.'

Dublin

The first night of Clio's play having degenerated – via a quick visit to Clio's flat to pick up booze and drugs – into an all-night party at The Brokerage, it was a radically below-par Ben who returned to consciousness the next morning in a single spastic jolt, like someone clawing their way out of a nightmare. Looking at my phone, I remembered, with horror, that I was due at the Central Criminal Court at half past nine for the family perp walk. Leaping into action, I poured myself a quadruple Scotch and chased it, retching, with three Diazepam, after which, on the whole, I still felt like shit. There was, I told myself, a slim but definite chance that the booze and the benzos I had just consumed and the MDMA and the coke I had taken the previous evening would at some point succeed in cancelling each other out, resulting in a kind of temporary homeostasis that would enable me to get through at least the early hours of the day. This, at any rate, was what I was counting on, and as I showered and dressed, I did begin to feel marginally better – if I wasn't absolutely spiffing, neither was I about to collapse in a welter of nauseated tears. This would have to do.

In the living room, the play's cast and crew had blacked out, fully clothed, on my modular couches. In the middle of the floor, on the deep-pile rug, Clio and Barry Hynes lay spooning. They also appeared to be holding hands. But there was no time to think about that now. It had taken me twenty minutes to shower (I kept zoning out in the steam

297

and forgetting to wash) and ten minutes to position my trousers at such an angle that it was possible to get into them and I was on the verge of running late. In the lift – with miraculous foresight I had thought to bring a hip flask – I bolted down another shot or two of Scotch. *So far, so good!*

Nodding quickly at what I took to be the doorman, I zoomed through the lobby and hailed a cab. As we swung through the weekday morning traffic I nursed my comedown lockjaw and listened vaguely to the murmur of grown-up voices on the radio news. Amid the headline hubbub I heard my father's name – my surname.

'Can you turn that off?' I said, waving a hundred at the driver, who seemed, I thought, pretty resentful for a man who had just made a 400 per cent profit on his fare.

I sat back and in a moment of appalling clarity I thought: *Doorman?* The Brokerage did not have a doorman. Tenants gained access using a security card. So who had that been, standing in the lobby at twenty to nine in the morning, wearing a ratty brown trenchcoat? *Oh, bad! Very bad!*

The cab had stalled in traffic on the south quays. The driver was now playing an R&B track, which lent our silence the louche, precoital air of that five-minute period at the beginning of a porno movie when the actors still have all their clothes on. It was 9.22 a.m. My phone came alive in my hands, causing my heart rate to double on the spot. The caller ID showed my mother's name.

'Where are you?' she said, as soon as I answered.

'And good morning to you, too,' I said.

'Are you in a cab?'

'I'm on Aston Quay,' I said. 'I'll be there in five minutes.' The driver fiddled pointedly with the holy-hummingbird gewgaw that hung from his rear-view mirror. 'Ten minutes max,' I amended.

'Don't pull up to the steps of the court in a taxi,' my mother said.

'What the fuck else do you want me to do?' I said.

'We all need to arrive in the same car,' my mother said. 'Meet us outside the Ashling Hotel on Parkgate Street. We've hired a town car.'

'You've hired a *town car*?' I said. 'I thought we were trying to *avoid* looking like we had two hundred million quid squirrelled away in the Cayman Islands.'

'Tell your driver to hurry up,' my mother said.

The line went dead.

The cab nosed forward incrementally. Across the river, on the roof of the old Woollen Mills, a man in welder's gear was tending a bouquet of orange sparks. The sparks foamed upwards and fell carelessly into nothing. More building, more tearing down. The city could not be permitted to remain as it was. And why was that? Because of money. Money changed hands and buildings rose and fell. It was like living in earthquake country.

Having shouldered our way through a phalanx of reporters on the steps, and pushed and heaved our way through the scrum at security (passing, en route, a gold-chained skanger who yelled, 'Yeh fuckin' crook, yeh!' at my father in his three-piece suit), we entered the great louvred pudding-bowl that housed the Criminal Courts of Justice and at length ascended in a glass-walled lift to Court 19. There were five of us: my father, my father's pompously gowned barristers (let's call them Tim and Tom), my mother and myself.

'Good impression,' Tom said.

'Handled it well,' Tim said.

'Keep your chin up, now,' Tom said.

'Final hurdle,' Tim said.

My father stood with his hands in his pockets, looking down at the crowd. Beside him – and resolutely facing the door of the lift – my mother stood. Her face was concealed behind a pair of large smoked glasses. She looked as if she were about to bestow her blessing on the latest issue of *Vogue*.

'Animals,' she said, addressing no one in particular.

'You can't please all of the people all of the time,' my father said. 'Though I must say, I know a few young women who've tried.'

Tim and Tom laughed an Old Barbarian laugh.

So far, no one had thanked me for being present for the perp walk, or indeed acknowledged my presence in any way. This was, in its way, a relief: I wasn't sure I was capable of engaging in anything like an extended conversation, or even of ginning up a tolerable facsimile of sobriety.

'That's the worst of it,' my father said. But out on the

landing we confronted yet another swarm of reporters brandishing notepads and microphones. The miner's headlamp of a camera swung my way. I attempted to duck, but my father, his head aloft, seemed to have cleared a path Mosaically through the rabble, and suddenly we were in the courtroom itself and some sort of equerry or retainer was closing the gigantic double doors against the press of press.

'We've seats reserved for you,' my father said, and led us confidently to the front row, as if he were showing us round his new home, which in a sense, I suppose, he was.

My mother perched impressively on the pew. She had not taken off her frosted glasses and would not, if I remember correctly, take them off for the remainder of the morning.

We sat behind the barristers' tables. There were vastly more documents on the prosecution's table than there were on the defence's. 'I'll be sitting there,' my father said, indicating a snug notch in the walnut panelling. This, I understood, was the dock. 'And the jury, of course,' he said, pointing at a wainscoted enclosure to our right.

'How long will this take?' I said.

'Oh, this is mostly just a formality,' my father said. 'Get the ball rolling. I'll be entering my plea, and so forth.'

Behind us, the public seats were filling up. Among the reporters, there seemed also to be a large contingent of middle-aged men who wore anoraks and clutched plastic shopping-bags, and who stared up at the bench with baleful looks on their faces. Finally it struck me: these must be the outraged former clients of Atlas-Merritt, the very men whose pension schemes and investment profits my father stood accused of misappropriating.

'Stop fidgeting,' my mother whispered in my ear. 'Just sit there and look straight ahead.'

'I'm not the one on trial here,' I said.

After a millennium or two of procedural non-time all rose and the trial began. The presiding judge as he took his seat grinned encouragingly at everyone like a priest welcoming a confirmation class. During the opening remarks – from Tim and Tom and from the prosecution – my father sat in the dock, smiling vaguely. I tried to follow my mother's advice, and gazed alternately at the burgundy carpet and at the dormant flatscreen TVs that reflected the courtroom like dull black mirrors.

Eventually the jury shuffled in and the judge in his supervisory drone delivered an instructive spiel. While this was going on, my father took a tube of Polo mints from his inside suit pocket. He unwrapped the dusty silver paper, set three individual mints on the little desk space in front of him, tucked the spare foil over the rest of the tube and slotted it back into his pocket. Then he put the first Polo mint in his mouth and began to suck on it meditatively. Perhaps, I thought, his long-overdue collapse had finally arrived and he had undergone a total psychotic break, right there in his walnut-panelled naughty corner.

The reporters in the seats behind me began to murmur and twitch. We seemed to have arrived at a crux. Tim (or was it

Tom?) was rising to speak. In the dock, my father had moved on to his second Polo mint.

'With the court's permission,' said Tim or Tom, 'my client has requested me to enter the following points into the record at this time.' He brandished a sheaf of stapled pages. (I'll do my best to recreate this bit from memory, if I can manage to do it without falling asleep. The problem, of course, is that I was falling asleep when it actually happened, as the pills, the Diazepam, and the Scotch battled for control of my central nervous system.) 'As follows. One. With due acknowledge-ment of the highly conscientious and dedicated work of the members of An Garda Siochana in the investigation of this case ...' There followed a torrent of legal verbiage, which at length resolved, once more, into sense. 'From the very beginning, my client was established as a patsy or mark in the prosecution of a case that depended on "evidence" of a highly circumstantial nature, to wit: the allegation that my client was present at a meeting at an address in Oslo – excuse me, your Honour, I don't have the precise address to hand.' Some papers were shuffled. 'Yes, that's right, at 34 Jens Bjelkes gate, Oslo, on the following dates ...'

In the dock, my father was rolling his third Polo mint around his mouth.

'*On* which date my client can establish beyond all doubt that he was playing golf at the K Club ...'

'Sit *still*,' my mother whispered, leaning towards me.

'I *am* sitting still,' I said.

'Point *four*,' Tim or Tom was saying. 'Despite strenuous

efforts, the Criminal Assets Bureau have proved themselves unable to locate a considerable percentage of the sums of money allegedly misdirected by my client. The grounds of the prosecution's case resting almost entirely on a coincidence in the amount of sums deposited in accounts bearing my client's name, we will be establishing beyond all doubt that those sums related to investments in a pension fund made on my client's behalf by the firm of Croker, Manning, and originated in savings undertaken legally by my client over the course of several decades . . .'

I suppressed a yawn. The trial was precisely as boring and obnoxious as I had feared it would be. I wondered if, having smiled for the cameras, I was now permitted to leave. But then I noticed that my father was no longer chewing. He was sitting up.

Tim or Tom had turned to the last page in his sheaf of documents.

'Point *five*,' he said, and paused for effect. 'My client is prepared to enter into evidence the name of the individual who was, in actual fact, responsible for the misappropriation of sums totalling six hundred million euro during the period concerned.'

Hesitation. Uproar. Shouts from the men with plastic bags. Reporters, mobiles in hand, scrambled for the exit. The judge tapped his microphone and said, 'Quiet, please.'

'Just to reiterate, your Honour,' Tim or Tom said, raising his voice. 'My client is prepared to go into evidence with the name—'

Beside me, my mother remained completely still. 'Look straight ahead,' she said. 'Don't say anything.'

My father's hands were clasped between his knees. He was looking at the jury box and smiling broadly, as if he had just spotted an old friend on the other side of the street.

As soon as the jury was excused, I bolted for the door. The lift seemed not to respond to my frantic jabbing at the call button. Two men in suits were waiting with me. 'Did you hear [REDACTED]'s going into evidence?' one of them said. 'Should be good,' said the other, smirking. Bailing on the lift, I jogged down three flights of stairs until I was standing outside in the crisp autumn sunshine. Here the trees were dumping their melancholy garbage of used leaves, as they did, annually, like punctual householders. 'Pure grandstanding,' I heard someone say. Queasily I lit a smoke, and queasily inhaled. *Your father is innocent*, my mother had said. *And he can prove it*. What did this mean? It meant that it was more urgent than ever that the Belgrade deal go through – so that I could avoid inhabiting, for the rest of my life, a world in which my parents had been proved right. Behind me someone said, 'Bit of a twist in the tale, eh?' I turned to see the Man in the Brown Trenchcoat. He was standing three feet behind me, smoking a cigarette of his own. At once I set off down the steps and waved hysterically at a passing cab. 'Airport,' I said, gasping, as I flopped in the back seat. The Man in the Brown Trenchcoat watched me go with a small sad smile on his face, as if we had known each other for years and this was the last time we would see each other – as if there would be no more chances, after this.

And now it is drawing near, the worst thing, and there is nothing I can do to stop it. There was nothing I could do then and there is nothing I can do now. I'm sorry I'm sorry I'm sorry I'm sorry I'm sorry.

Serbia

'There are no wolves in Serbia, right?' I said to Aleks over breakfast.

It was, for me, Day Four. We were sitting on the terrace of another cheap hotel: the Hotel Globo. Overnight we had travelled north, into a country of forests and mountains.

'Wolves?' Aleks said, chewing his breakfast goulash. 'Yes are wolves. Especially here, in north of country. And small bears, too.'

'Small bears,' I said. 'Great.'

From the balcony of my room at dawn I had watched an animal lope through a low white mist, heading for the hotel's desolate, unpeopled playground. Whatever it was, this animal, it was humpbacked and quadrupedal, and bristled with coarse dark fur. It might – I thought optimistically – have been an Alsatian.

Four hours later, the mist still floated in the hotel grounds. Above its gauzy tideline, slopes of dense black forest loomed.

A hundred yards from the Hotel Globo's front door stood the precast concrete stem of a gargantuan TV tower – an onion-bulbed Soviet relict, two hundred metres high, festooned with satellite dishes and radio receivers. It was, according to Aleks, 'famous landmark. Key to network of communications. Damaged by NATO in airstrikes.'

'What the fuck *wasn't* damaged by NATO in airstrikes?' Sean Sweeney asked, in a tone of genuine bafflement. 'And wasn't that, like, twenty years ago? Why haven't you *repaired* this shit?'

According to my fitfully operative phone our current location was called Iriski Venac. The limo had deposited us here after midnight. The Hotel Globo looked, and felt, like an abandoned ski resort. Its insides were coated with pale-brown carpet and the whole place reeked of bleach. Behind the front desk was an antediluvian telephone exchange, all valves and paired cords.

'No sesh,' Sean Sweeney said, noting that the bar was closed.

Bobby Hayes yawned and stretched. 'Fine with me,' he said. 'I'm crashing. Hayeser out.'

My room was on the ground floor. It contained a child-sized trundle bed and a television that had long since burned its own anamorphic shadow into the painted wall behind. In the bathroom, above the rusted nozzle of the showerhead, a bouquet of exposed electrical wire hung from a gash in the ceiling.

Having no choice – a gumbo or bouillabaisse of drugs was still sloshing its way through my system – I stayed awake until dawn, smoking on the balcony, trying not to look at the spaceship bulk of the TV tower as it hummed and bristled in the unfamiliar night.

'I cannot wait to get the fuck out of this fucking shithole country,' Bobby Hayes said when we convened in the lobby at 9 a.m. 'There's fucking electrical wire in my shower. Can you believe that? I had to wash my knackers in the sink.'

'Today's the day,' James Mullens said. 'We see the site this afternoon. We're fifteen miles away. That's literally all we have to do. Then we're gone.'

'That better be true,' I said.

'Do you want to know what the best thing about this resort spa place we're building is?' Sweeney said, and waited.

'What's that?' Mullens said wearily.

'We'll never have to stay in it,' Sweeney said.

It was breakfast time. Nicolae and Ratko were beckoning for us to join them in the dining room. But The Lads said no. Instead they hiked across the hotel's sallow, unkempt lawn to the base of the TV tower, where they stood with their hands in their pockets, looking up.

Offered a choice of dining companions (on the one hand, Nicolae and Ratko, and on the other, Aleks), I chose Aleks. We sat on chairs of faded red velvet and looked out through the windows at the mist. Except for the four of us, the dining room was empty. A solitary fly circled our bread basket in an elliptical orbit. I ignored my plate of oily goulash and drank cup after cup of coffee.

Aleks held up a small plastic coffee spoon. 'In Montenegro,' he said, 'such a spoon is called *the seed of the shovel*. Is bad luck to carry because if it grow, you have to work.' He made a digging motion.

'Hah,' I said.

'You are sick,' Aleks said, evidently noting my tensed shoulders, my trembling hands.

'I'm not feeling tip-top,' I acknowledged.

'You take medicine perhaps,' Aleks said.

'Medicine is the problem,' I said. 'Hey. Tell me something. Why is there electrical wiring in all the showers?'

Aleks's face was expressive of polite disagreement. 'Is renovated hotel,' he said.

'No,' I said. 'It isn't. There were cameras in the showers, weren't there?'

Aleks looked away. 'Is place of diplomatic meetings in time of Yugoslav government,' he said. 'Is possible security services use hotel for spying.'

'Is possible,' I said.

Aleks fiddled with his plastic spoon. I had embarrassed him.

'I'm going to get your book translated,' I said, backtracking. 'When I get home. Hire a translation service so I can read it.'

'This is good,' Aleks said. He broke the plastic spoon in two.

Nicolae and Ratko rose from their seats in muscular unison. Vuk had entered the dining room. The collar of his long black coat obscured the lower half of his face like the robe of a conspiring cardinal. 'Sit, sit,' he said. Nicolae and Ratko did not sit. Vuk stopped at our table.

'You sleep well,' he said, addressing me. It sounded like an order. 'Air of country is beneficial. Your fellows, they have eaten?'

'They're outside,' I said. But when I looked out at the base of the TV tower, The Lads were nowhere to be seen.

'I wish to inform,' Vuk said, and paused. Then, looking at Aleks, he spoke for several minutes in Serbian. Aleks lowered his head and avoided Vuk's gaze. I became aware once again of Vuk's peculiar negative charisma.

'Vuk informs of scheduling change,' Aleks said at last. 'There has been issue with contracts. This is the wrong word, contracts. Men of work contract.'

'Contractors,' I said.

'Contractors,' Aleks said. 'Dispute over pay. Please be assured—' Vuk spoke again. 'Be assured,' Aleks said, 'of minority of matter. But will entail short delay in visit of site. Originally of today, but visit will reschedule for tomorrow.'

Vuk's face assumed a tragic cast. 'I much regret,' he said. 'This you inform your fellows. Very kind.'

I began to experience a stabbing pain in my side – in what may have been my pancreas, or my duodenum, or my islets of Langerhans. Vuk appeared to be waiting for my response.

'I'll, eh, I'll pass on the message,' I said.

'Enjoy day of hotel,' Vuk said as, followed by Nicolae and Ratko, he headed for the exit. As he passed the doors of the terrace he added a few syllables of Serbian.

'He mentions swimming pool,' Aleks said with an expression of distaste. 'Also room of steam.'

Outside, beyond a stretch of damp, uneven ground, I picked out The Lads in their Louis Copeland suits. They were skulking among the fixtures of the ruined playground (the hingeless see-saw, the unsprung rocking horse, the tetanus-infested slide). Paul Tynan was doing chin-ups from the bar of a splintered swing set.

'Fantastic,' I said, and torched a smoke. As soon as I inhaled, the pain in my side grew worse by an order of magnitude.

Paul Tynan. Have I done him yet? Let's leave it at this: once, standing outside a nightclub, Tynan was approached by a homeless man carrying a disposable Starbucks cup full of coins. 'Any spare change, lads?' the homeless man said. 'That's a cup full of spare change,' Paul Tynan said. The homeless man grimaced. 'Smart cunt, are you?' he said. 'Yeah,' Tynan said. 'That's why I'm not homeless.'

It was Tynan who hailed me, as The Lads blustered back into the lobby. 'Are we doing this?' he said, raising his arms in a Nixonian V-for-Victory salute. 'Actually—' I began. This was met at once with a vigorous quorum of disparagement. 'Fucking amateurs,' Tynan said.

Mark Foley was poking his phone's glass screen with slender fingers. 'They know we're flying out tomorrow, right?' he said. 'I mean, we can reschedule the flights but we're talking a six-hour layover at Frankfurt—'

James Mullens was crisply dismissive. 'Listen,' he said. 'Game faces, all right? Game faces. It is what it is. We chill out here tonight. Tomorrow we take a nice little drive. We give the site the nod. And we get the fuck out of here. Yeah?'

Mutters of agreement. 'I will literally kiss the ground at Dublin airport,' Bobby Hayes said, rubbing the back of his head aggressively.

Through the grubby glass panes of the hotel's revolving door, I saw a taxi lurch to a halt in the gravelled drive. After a few seconds, the taxi's rear door opened, and Maria climbed out.

I headed at once for my room. But the corridors of the Hotel Globo seemed to have shuffled themselves into a novel order – everywhere I went, I saw the same dull stretch of brown carpet and smelled the same boiled-cabbage smell – and very soon I was lost. Frantically I turned corners, checked room numbers. At one particularly nasty moment I found myself back in the lobby, where Maria stood at the reception desk, shouting at the Igor. I reversed course and at length managed to pinpoint the number I was looking for.

A man was standing outside my door. My heart at once seemed to immerse itself in freezing bilge-water. *No*, I thought. *Not here. He can't have followed me all the way here.* But it wasn't the Man in the Brown Trenchcoat. It was – of all people – Boris, our driver. He wore a dowdy anorak and had a stalked or hungry look – the look of a cat trespassing in a junkyard. I was almost glad to see him.

312

'*Dober dan,*' he said, as I approached. 'I give.' He thrust a grubby envelope in my direction. 'You leave,' he said. 'Hotel Karlovsky. I keep.'

The envelope contained my passport. The pain in my side appeared to have opened up a new franchise behind my ribs. I flipped through the pages of the passport, checking out my own harried mugshot on the stiff first page.

'Why do you have this?' I said.

Boris produced a meagre smile. 'You will need,' he said. 'Fly home.' He flapped his arms and stood on his toes, like a child impersonating a bird. What did it mean, that he had my passport? What did it mean that I had left the fucking thing behind and forgotten it, three days ago, in Belgrade? I didn't know what it meant. I didn't know what any of it meant.

'I forgot this,' I said, processing aloud.

'Is safe,' Boris said.

'Yeah, but,' I said, 'if you hadn't been our driver . . .'

For an instant, the world seemed to tremble on the brink of legibility – as if reality were a sentence in a foreign language that I had just typed into Google Translate, and all I had to do was press ENTER.

Boris put his hand on my shoulder and said, 'Home soon. Is nice hotel.' Then he shuffled off, fiddling with his pouch of chewing tobacco as he went.

I locked myself in my room and did the only thing I could think of: I broke into my pharmacopeia, popped three Xanax, and lapsed into a brief coma. (Imagine, please, a description of my lengthy and elaborate nightmares: the severed limbs, the mauled right eyes, the endless deferrals at airport security.) Four hours later, I was roused by a knock at the door. *Consciousness*, I thought, an instant after waking: *Always consciousness. What a pain in the tits.*

'Is Aleks,' a voice said. 'You are still sick?'

'Go away,' I said through the pillow.

'You come for walk,' Aleks said. 'Is something I show.'

I groaned.

'Is matter of importance,' Aleks said. 'Also walk will improve feeling.'

'Nothing will improve feeling,' I said.

Passing through the lobby, I observed that the hotel now appeared to be open for business: where formerly there had been no one, now two or three members of the local lumpen-commentariat sat chewing their bridgework at the bar. It was two o'clock in the afternoon. At any moment, I felt, I was going to die. But Aleks was right: the walk outside was improving my feeling, very slightly. Following Aleks's lead, I crossed the gravel drive and cleared the playground. The mist was thinning out under the dehumidifying action of a feeble sun. From the ground the odour of damp vegetation now freely rose. Pine cones lay like pale turds in the shallow grass. Perhaps because of the appalling condition of my lungs – I was, as usual, smoking a cigarette or two – Aleks quickly outpaced me. He stopped and jotted something in a small black notebook. He really was a poet, I thought. It was as if the sight of Aleks standing there in silhouette against the forest's fringe of military green, scribbling with his little golf pencil, served as a more profound confirmation of this fact than even the cheaply bound paperback book that was sitting on the nightstand in my room.

'Are you writing a poem?' I gasped, catching up.

'I make note,' Aleks said, pocketing the notebook and resuming his long-limbed stride.

'What are we looking for, anyway?' I said. Above us, the TV tower was materialising through the mist like the advance guard of an alien invasion. We crossed into thicker, darker grass. It occurred to me to wonder if Aleks was leading me into the forest for nefarious purposes: for a murder, a mugging, a kiss. 'Hey,' I called, just to be sure, 'do you have a girlfriend?'

'Yes, I have girlfriend,' Aleks said. 'Of four years.'

'Is she a poet, too?' I said.

'She is journalist,' Aleks said. 'Expose corruption. Very noble.'

We climbed a banked ridge and paused to look back at the hotel. Through the windows of the terrace restaurant a figure could be seen, reclining in a grubby wicker chair and holding up a newspaper like someone's dad on his day off. It was Nicolae, I sensed, or Ratko. One or the other.

Aleks was looking down at something that lay half concealed in the long grass.

'What is it?' I said.

Among the weeds lay a long, cracked cylinder of some grey ceramic substance. The larger shards had been spray-painted with red Cyrillic letters.

'Is shell of NATO rocket,' Aleks said. 'From bombing of TV tower in 1999. Attempt was made to cut off communications with north of Serbia. This rocket miss, and land here.'

'What does the graffiti say?' I said.

'Is obscenity,' Aleks said. 'Anti-NATO.'

He turned to face the woods. The highest branches of the nearest pines seemed to sublime into wisps of smoke at their topmost points. I nudged the rocket casing with the toe of a trainer. '1999,' I said, aware that I was not getting the point.

Aleks was assembling a rollie with swift, parsimonious gestures. 'Was very bad time,' he said. 'After breakup of Yugoslavia, was much hatred of other religions, other ethnicities. Hatred of Muslims, especially. Now, in West, is popular to hate Muslims. But in Serbia we were ahead of the ball. This is correct expression?'

'More or less,' I said. 'Wait. There are Muslims here?'

'Yes are Muslims,' Aleks said. 'In all nations of former Yugoslavia are Muslims. Also Serbs living in Bosnia, Bosnians living in Serbia, Serbs living in Croatia, Albanians living in Kosovo. Many complex relations. During Communist period ethnicity is not so much important, because in Communist society all are equal. Yes? But when Communism go away, much tension.' He finessed his rollie with a rapid lick. 'Much hatred, waiting for many years beneath surface.'

'So there was a war,' I said.

'Yes was war,' Aleks said. 'Milosevic responsible for causing many old hatreds to rise, for making Serbs crazy with
need for land and power. Serbia begin invading other countries, expelling non-native Serbs. Killing them. Putting them
in work camps. Also rape camps. They make rape of women
and children into weapon of war. There were also massacres.
You know of Srebrenica.'

I said nothing.

'Was shooting of eight thousand people,' Aleks said. 'Men
and boys. Deposit of bodies in mass graves. Serbian army of
the time claims is normal combat operations. But this is lie
to conceal their crimes and to protect their persons. Now it
is many years and there have been not many prosecutions.
Are many men in Serbia who take part personally in rapes,
in murders, in burying of bodies. They are doctors, judges.
Normal men with families. After war, they go back to this.
No one wants to send such men to jail.'

'How old were you,' I said, 'when . . . ?'

'I am in early teenage years,' Aleks said. 'So personally
I am safe. But I experience much guilt, ever after. I say to
myself, Aleks, you do nothing. You do not even protest until
much later.'

'It wasn't your fault,' I said. 'You were just a kid.'

'Is phenomenon of collective guilt,' Aleks said. 'You are
in a country when it acts a certain way, is responsibility of
everyone. Do you not think?'

There were swarms of midges seething in the gloom
between the pines.

317

'Camps,' I said. 'Like—'

'Yes,' Aleks said. 'Your friends are not aware of this, I think. Are not familiar with recent past of Serbia.'

I shrugged. 'They did their research,' I said. 'They said your economy is on the up.'

Aleks compressed his lips. 'For rich people is on the up,' he said. 'For others, not so much change. Not so much change in economy, not so much change in thinking. Is not will for change. In this, is much as before. Was not will to stop war. Massacre of Srebrenica take place in 1995. Only in 1999 does NATO begin campaign of bombing. This is intended to stop massacres.'

'Did it work?' I said.

'Some say yes,' Aleks said. 'Some say no.'

'But the war is over,' I said.

The large head wagged slowly. 'Now is much peaceful in Serbia,' Aleks said, 'as I say before. But men who committed crimes still here. Many of the worst, still here. Many of those men who kill thousands, who rape women, who wish to exterminate Bosnian Muslim seed from face of the earth.' He had turned around and was looking back in the direction of the hotel. The white roof was just visible on the other side of the ridge. 'They go back to jobs,' Aleks said. 'Have lives of normality. But inside, they are not changed. Are still same men as before.' For a moment he said nothing and when he spoke again, he appeared to have forgotten I was there. 'And everybody knows where they are,' he said. He put his rollie to his lips but did not light it. 'Everybody knows,' he said again, his voice barely audible above the sudden rising breeze.

Despite painstaking reconstructive efforts, I seem to have lost the next six hours to the Memory Void. Circumstantial evidence suggests that I passed out on my trundle bed, having ordered a pint of Scotch from room service and ransacked my dwindling stock of downers. I was woken by the pain in my side, which had now opened multiple outlets and was doing business as far north as my oesophagus and as far south as my balls. When I came to, I scrabbled around until I located my passport, which I seemed to have stuffed into the waistband of my boxer shorts. Through the uncurtained window I could see a harvest moon, its surface as white as a laboratory mouse. The stars were also near, shedding their curiously adulterated light. The heat was equatorial. My lungs itched. I pawed at my phone until it told me the time: 12.07 a.m. There were also eight missed calls from my father and a text message from Clio that said I'M SORRY. By Clio's usual standards, of course, this counted as crisply informative. The bad news was that my pharmacopeia was now seriously depleted. During my blackout I had apparently smoked two of my three remaining pinners and swallowed one of my two remaining Valium and two of my eight remaining Xanax. At some point I had also used the backside of my phone to mash up a pill – judging, at least, by the caked yellow powder that now stickily adhered to the black glass. What a combination! No wonder I felt like death.

More pressingly, I was now down to one Valium, six Xanax, one pinner and a twist of coke, barely enough to get me through an average workday, even under normal conditions. How the fuck had I let this happen? I was going to have to *drink* my way through the next twenty-four hours. It was a scandal. But this, too, presented a difficulty. My pint of Scotch was empty and my hip flask had been drained. It was after midnight. Room service in the Hotel Globo terminated at nine. My options, I concluded, were twofold. Fold one: I could sacrifice a Xanax or three in a (probably doomed) attempt to put myself under once again. Fold two: I could scour the hotel until I found some booze. My phone, of course, had no reception – I couldn't even call Sweeney to ask if he had a bottle going spare. But I could certainly bang on the door of his room.

He was three doors down, in 108. I knocked. No answer. *'Sean!'* I hissed, and knocked again. Silence. Silence also from room 110 (Bobby Hayes) and room 112 (Paul Tynan). What was going on? Were they all unconscious? Had I missed an impromptu sesh?

I set off for the lobby. But something seemed to have gone wrong. The numbers on the doors now said 207, 209, et cetera. How had that happened? I pressed on: more brown-carpeted corridors, more identical doors. The air seemed to be full of a just-departed ringing sound, as of struck crystal. Turning a corner, I found myself on the landing of a stairwell, next to an open window. I checked my phone and saw a bar of signal. I thumbed Sweeney's number and heard a female voice: *The person you are trying to reach is unavailable at the moment, or may have their mobile powered off. Please—* I tried James Mullens and the same thing happened. I tried Tynan, Hayeser, Foley. The bar of signal vanished, as capriciously as it had arrived.

The struck-crystal hum gave way to the bandsaw whine of anxiety. Following a Cyrillic sign, I ventured left. Now the numbers on the doors were going up: 223, 225. I retraced my steps. I found some stairs and went down them. Through sheer chance, I had arrived in the lobby. Behind the front desk a bespectacled Igor sat, reading a magazine.

'Excuse me,' I said, with a wheeze of relief. 'You couldn't serve me something from the bar, could you?'

The Igor looked up. *'Izvinite?'* he said.

'Bar,' I said, making a gesture (one hand waving at the other) that could have meant absolutely anything at all.

'Is closed,' the Igor said. Then he stopped moving. His face assumed an empty expression, as when you switch off the ignition of a car and all the needles on the dashboard drop to zero.

'What about the restaurant?' I said. 'I'd take a bottle of wine from the kitchen.'

The Igor said nothing.

I decided to find the restaurant kitchen myself and plunged back into the maze, confronting at every turn another enfilade of closed doors, another stretch of dull brown carpet. At random, I opened a door, and found myself looking at a rack of headless, child-sized naked bodies. At each throat was an open red wound surrounded by white flesh. A draught of chilled air passed my face. I relaxed. It was a walk-in freezer. The bodies were pigs. They lay with their hooves extended, their trotters glazed with frost. I was making progress. If I could find a freezer, I could find a kitchen.

But the next six doors I tried were locked. Gradually the humidity intensified. I seemed to smell chlorine, or cleaning products, or some noxious combination of the two. Pushing through a pair of glass doors, I found myself in the leisure centre. Vuk, I recalled, had said something about a swimming pool. *Also room of steam*, Aleks had contributed. Perhaps there would be a vending machine – one of those sophisticated European vending machines that sold miniature bottles of wine.

Visually frisking the dormant gym and the empty locker rooms, I tiptoed through to the pool itself. The sound of lapping water seemed feverishly loud. There was someone in the pool – a girl in a black bikini, doing a slow backstroke. It was Maria. Panicking, I did a quick feasibility study: could I make it to the door without her noticing? I could not. She had noticed. She was splashing her way to the pool's brink.

'You have found me,' she said. 'You get my note and you come.'

'Note?' I said. I was backing away, towards the lifeguard's chair.

'I leave note under door of your room,' Maria said. 'I propose late-night swim. And now you are here.'

'I was just looking for something to drink,' I said.

322

'We have drink,' Maria said. 'I have *rakija* in my room. But first we swim.'

I was paralysed. On the one hand, I didn't want to give Maria the impression that I actually wanted to sleep with her. On the other hand, she had booze, which I could perhaps pilfer, if I played along for a bit.

I said, 'I don't have any togs.'

'Togs is not required,' Maria said. 'I remove swimsuit, since you are embarrassed leprechaun. Then we are both naked.'

I was keen to forestall this eventuality. 'How about,' I said, 'how about we have a drink first? Pop back to your room? Then we can swim.'

As I spoke, an idea was congealing, down there in the drug-addled murk of my mind. Maria was Vuk's adopted daughter, according to Aleks – rescued after her father, his great friend, had been killed. Presumably Vuk would listen to Maria's advice. If I went back to her room, it was possible, though perhaps unlikely, that I could cajole her into having a word with him about the contracts – persuade her to help us get things moving. James Mullens would be proud of me. More to the point, the minute the contracts were signed, I would be free: rich enough to escape Serbia and The Lads and Vuk and Maria and Nicolae and Ratko and the semi-fraudulent Echo Lake development and never look back. The risk, of course, was that Maria would try to fuck me. It was not a negligible risk. But I felt reasonably sure that I could deflect her advances, no matter how insistent they became.

And then, a microsecond later, I was struck by another

thought. When Maria had first arrived in the steakhouse, four days ago, Aleks had referred to her as Vuk's niece. Which was she? Why had Aleks changed his story?

Maria had climbed out of the pool and now stood dripping on the tiles. Helplessly, I observed that her nipples, beneath the black fabric of her bikini top, were erect. 'You hand me robe,' she said, cocking a hip.

Draped across the lifeguard's chair was a white dressing gown. I tried to hand it to her without actually moving from where I stood.

As we navigated the imbroglio of brown corridors that led back to her room, she linked her arm through mine, as if we were already a couple.

Before I had a chance to broach the subject of the contracts – or, even more crucially, to assess her room and determine the location of her bottle of *rakija* – Maria had closed the door and shrugged off her robe. At once her tongue was in my mouth and she was tugging at the belt of my slacks. As gently as I could – which was not, on reflection, all that gently – I pushed her away. Undaunted, she moved in for another kiss. No matter where I looked, I seemed to find my gaze drawn to her breasts in their translucent fabric cups. She pressed her open mouth against my stoically averted lower jaw. Her palms were flat against the wall on either side of my head and her wet, slippery body was jammed up against mine.

'You find me because you know,' Maria said. 'Is last chance. Tomorrow you leave. This is last chance to fuck.'

'Maybe we should have a drink first,' I said.

'You not shave,' Maria said, nuzzling my five-o'clock shadow. 'This I like.' Her fingers were insinuating themselves between the buttons of my shirt.

'Or we could talk about the contracts,' I said.

'You want to talk business instead of fuck,' Maria said.

'Not necessarily *instead of*,' I said. 'But, you know ... in *parallel with*.'

'Shhhh,' Maria said. She took a step backwards and placed a hand on the crotch of her bikini bottoms. With a curled finger she tugged aside the wedge of wet fabric. 'You see,' she said. 'Hairless.' Then, with an abbreviated curtsey, she stepped out of the bottoms.

What, I wondered, was the right move here? Should I just run? Might that not, somehow, screw the whole deal? What would James Mullens do, under these (rather difficult imaginatively to transpose) circumstances? Maria was slinking towards me once again. She placed a hand on my groin. In the same moment, we both became aware of the fact that I had an erection. Plainly my errant libido – bewildered at having been dragooned so peremptorily into service – had chosen to follow the path of least resistance. Encouraged, Maria dropped to her knees and yanked down my slacks. For a few moments I watched the head of my cock appear and disappear as she moved her mouth around it. Her method was to suck for a few seconds at a time, stop, and, during these intervals, to look up at me and smile. With dismay, I found that this technique just made me harder.

'I'm never going to come if you keep stopping like that,' I heard myself say.

'You want to fuck me,' Maria said.

'. . . Sure,' I said.

'You want to fuck this hairless pussy.' Maria stood and walked to the bed – which was, I noted with relief, not a flimsy wheeled cot but a king-sized behemoth – and undid the strings of her bikini top. 'I go on top,' she ordered, and stood with folded arms while I undressed and reclined on the tautened topsheet. Almost as soon as my cock was inside her she began to emit a sharp rhythmic wail that coalesced, at length, into speech.

'Yes. Yes. You fuck so good. Oh, you fuck so good, my big Irish leprechaun.'

'Oh, come *on*,' I said.

Maria, mistaking my despair for encouragement, bucked harder. She rode me with porn-like professionalism, grabbing her small, conical breasts and shrieking at maximum volume. On the pillows and sheets was a chill fuzz of damp. Maria's wet hair – smelling of chlorine – hung in coils against my face. The loose headboard rocked and banged. 'You smack my ass,' Maria cried. Dutifully, I whacked her flank with an open palm. 'Yes, yes,' she said. 'You make me come. YOU MAKE ME COME.'

She froze, and shuddered silently for five seconds, ten. 'Now you come,' she said, and began to grind her hips again, frowning down at me and resting her hands on my chest.

Please let me come, I thought, *oh God, please let me come soon!* I shut my eyes tight and imagined, half successfully, that the pussy that was wetly smothering the length of my cock at that precise moment was, in fact, Nikki's pussy, and that the soft skin I could feel beneath my hands was, in fact, Nikki's soft skin, et cetera et cetera. *You are fucking Nikki!* I told myself sternly. *You are fucking Nikki right now!* Eventually, by this method – and after an eternity of heaving and straining – I came, grasping Maria's hips and emptying myself into her with a desperate grunt. Maria immediately stopped moving.

'You like,' she said. She disengaged and snuggled up beside me, scratching the fuzz on my chest with a black-painted nail. 'Of course, you must not tell anyone about this,' she said.

'I wouldn't dream of it,' I said as I laboured to control my breathing.

'I am full of your come,' she said complacently.

My *post coitum triste* at once gave way to a fear that shelved beneath me like the gradient of an ocean trench. I had not worn a condom.

'You're, eh, you're on the pill, right?' I said, sitting up.

Maria's lip curled. 'I am not whore,' she said.

'So in terms of contraception . . .' I said.

'Pah,' Maria said.

'You're fucking with me,' I said.

'I fuck you,' Maria said. 'But I don't fuck with you.' She rolled over happily and lit a cigarette. 'I get morning-after pill,' she said through a cloud of smoke. 'No freak-out. All is good.'

I thought about where we were: the lonely hotel, the

uninhabited mountains. I said, 'Where the fuck are you going to get the morning-after pill around here? We're in Dracula's fucking castle.'

How would my life unfold, I wondered, if I ended up as Maria's baby-daddy? There was nothing else for it: I would have to fake my own death. Even eight or nine million euro would not be enough to insulate me from a catastrophe of that magnitude.

Maria stubbed out her cigarette on the polished wood of the headboard. 'I get next week,' she said. 'In Belgrade.'

'No,' I said. 'You have to get it tomorrow. That's how it works.'

'You are worried that I will have little rug-muncher kids with you,' Maria said. 'I not want your rug-munchers. I tell you before, I want man who will marry me. And this you are not.'

I was, for some reason, offended. 'You've been trying to fuck me all week,' I said.

'You are good to fuck,' Maria said. 'But you are not man I would marry. I will marry man who knows what he wants in life. And this is not you.'

I was already putting on my boxers.

'Who the fuck asked you anyway?' I said.

Dublin

The taxi I had hailed outside the Central Criminal Court was halfway up the Swords Road before I realised that my flight wouldn't take off until the following morning. Collecting myself, I told the driver to turn around. The Brokerage penthouse was deserted. Clio's phone, when I tried it, went straight to voicemail. In the bedroom a white shirt – not mine – lay on the floor, one stricken cuff pressed to its heart. On Clio's dressing table a battalion of cosmetic arcana had been knocked flat, spilling beige powder all over the floor. In the living room, on the coffee table, was a Kilimanjaro of unsnorted cocaine. This I decanted into a series of clingfilm wraps. Then I lay down on the four-poster bed. The sheets, I noticed, had developed a potent vinegary aroma, probably because I had been soaking them with drug-sweat every night for a month. But there was no point in trying to remedy this now. I unhinged my laptop and went online. Under the news tab on my homepage I glimpsed a headline: [REDACTED] PROMISES TO NAME 'RESPONSIBLE INDIVIDUAL'. I clicked my way to a couple of my favourite porn videos. But the images seemed, mysteriously, to have been drained of their power to arouse – they might as well have been videos of deserts or gardens or, I don't know, bowls of fruit. I seem to have fallen asleep. An unknown period of time later – my phone battery had died, but the city outside blared with evening rush-hour traffic – I stumbled out onto the terrace and looked down: at the tinfoil ducts and piping of the nearby buildings, at the jagged black gumline of the horizon. The sunset was framed like a blueprint by the T-squares of construction cranes. The buildings seemed to absorb the twilight and turn darker as I watched. For a moment I imagined that I could reach out with a confident hand and turn the city on its axis – that I could tilt the world until all the junk and poison was dislodged and what remained, when I set things right again, was entirely pure, and rational, and safe, and free.

I arrived at Departures with three hours to spare. Clio had left a voicemail on my phone at some point that morning. 'I can't believe you didn't call me last night,' she said. 'There's this huge thing going on in your life and you're freezing me out of it. It's like, I really *want* to care about you, Ben. I really *want* to. But if you can't even be bothered to *call* me on one of the most important days of your life, then—' At this point the message cut out. I did not call Clio back.

From the multicoloured pill residue that adhered to my coffee table, I had scraped together the constituent elements of a small bump. This had carried me through check-in and past security and along the duty-free concourse in a state of tranquillised elation. Now the glow imparted by my post-sesh chemistry set of particulate Class A substances was fading. The colours of the world brightened and then dimmed, leaking light.

Booze was the cure. In a bar near the gate I ordered two mojitos and sat at a damp wooden table. For a while I watched the galvanised ticker tapes of the 24-hour news channels – the international ones, thank Christ, which were unlikely to report anything about my father. I tried, unsuccessfully, to read the opening pages of a paperback about wealth management that I had purchased in the airport bookshop. *Rich-Think!*, this paperback was called, or *Imagine Wealth!* I was looking for some clues about how to think rich, how to manage my impending wealth. But the book seemed to be written entirely in graphs and pie charts. I went back to staring at the news. This is what I was still doing, an hour or so later, when someone said, 'There you are. I'm glad I found you. I was going to call you if I couldn't find you here.'

It was Nikki. She was wearing a hiker's rucksack and carrying a folded copy of *The Economist*. Slung across her shoulder was a large grey plastic tube.

I forced myself to sit upright in my chair. 'What are you doing here?'

'I'm going to Innsbruck,' she said. 'For a conference, remember? Hey, what are you reading?'

Forced to improvise, I inhumed *Rich-Think!* beneath the pages of a nearby newspaper. 'Someone must have left it behind,' I said.

'Do you mind if I sit?' She shrugged off the rucksack. 'You always end up buying weird things to read in the airport. Like, I panic-bought this.' She waved *The Economist*. 'And now I know all about, like, China's plan to reduce carbon emissions by 2050.'

'Gotta reduce carbon,' I said. My mouth was exceedingly dry. I tried to take a discreet sip from my latest mojito, but I missed the straw and spilled crushed ice in my lap. I brushed it away. Nikki smiled sympathetically.

'We don't actually know each other that well,' she said. 'So it feels a bit weird, just coming up to you like this.'

But we DO know each other well! I wanted to say. Instead I said, 'I'm always happy to see you,' which was, I thought, actually a pretty nice thing to say, when you thought about it.

'Sometimes it's easier to talk to a stranger if you're worried about something,' Nikki said. 'Not that you're a stranger. I mean, someone you don't know that well. You know what I mean.'

She raised her hands and dropped them helplessly.

Her obvious nervousness was making me less nervous – the gift that socially anxious people give to the rest of us.

'You're worried about something,' I said.

We were facing each other across the little wooden table. For a moment I found myself imagining what it might be like to live with Nikki. A three-bed apartment, with offices for both of us. Books everywhere. Coffee and croissants with the Sunday papers. A 5k in Phoenix Park. A healthy lunch. A passionate discussion about a novel we'd both read or an arthouse film we'd watched the night before. The knowledge that neither of us had anything to be ashamed of, or frightened of, or bitter about, as long as we were together.

'Are you okay?' Nikki asked.

'I'm fine,' I said.

'Okay,' Nikki said. She had rolled up her copy of *The Economist* and was gripping it tightly. 'I'm going to say something. And I hope you won't be offended or think I'm being weird or anything like that.'

'I could never be offended,' I said, my voice crackling strangely, 'by anything you said.'

'Okay,' Nikki said. 'Okay, good. So, tell me something. What is a REIT, exactly?'

'A real estate investment trust,' I said.

'Beyond that,' Nikki said. 'How do they work? Have you looked it up? Because I looked it up. I wanted to know what James was doing. He was out all the time and when I called his office nobody ever answered.'

'There's no secretary,' I said. 'Sorry. Administrative executive.'

Nikki was sucking on her lower lip and frowning, and something about the distracted way she looked down at her fingernails caused me to wonder, for the very first time, if it wasn't perhaps a tad unusual for a multimillion-euro property development company not to employ someone to answer the phone.

'Anyway,' Nikki said. 'I called a few academics I know and I asked them what a REIT was. And I found out that a REIT can't function unless it's floated on the stock market. That's the whole point of a REIT. They're not trusts at all. They're publicly traded.'

'Right,' I said, and smiled.

'So I asked James,' Nikki said, 'what about an IPO? Otherwise Echo REIT isn't a REIT, is it? It's just a limited company. And he ... Well.' She blew upwards, ruffling her fringe. 'We've been, I guess, disagreeing about other stuff. Maybe it was just an excuse.'

'Your excuse or his?' I said. This was promising. Nikki and Mullens were not getting along. If I could only apply the lever in the right place . . .

'We didn't have a fight,' Nikki said. 'James doesn't do fights. He charms you out of a fight and you forget what you were angry about.'

'I think James mentioned something about an IPO,' I said. 'I think it's scheduled for later this year.'

Was this true? The problem was that I had only ever half-attended to the reams of business guff that James Mullens had been spouting for the last five months. It might have been true: an IPO might have been just around the corner. It probably was true. Besides, what if it wasn't? The deal was going ahead. I was on my way to Belgrade right this minute. I had the Memorandum of Understanding in my pocket. And while we were on the subject, how come Nikki knew so much about the stock market and the difference between a trust and a limited company, whatever those terms actually meant? Wasn't she a radiologist?

Nikki was frowning again. 'I don't like this deal,' she said. 'I think there's something really wrong with it. I think James is calling his company a REIT when it isn't and I don't know why he'd do that.'

'He knows what he's doing,' I said.

'That's what I'm afraid of,' Nikki said. 'Who are these guys, anyway? The partners?'

'The Serbs?' I said. 'Developers. You know. Looking for some foreign direct investment.'

'Mm,' Nikki said. She looked away. 'I'm probably totally out of line saying this. You can tell me to fuck off if you want. I just think you should be really, really careful about what you sign and who you talk to. I have a weird feeling.' She shook her head and smiled. 'I'm probably being paranoid.'

'You and James,' I said. 'How long have you been together?'

'Nearly two years,' Nikki said.

'So you know him pretty well,' I said.

Nikki said nothing for a moment. 'I wouldn't say that,' she said. 'Sometimes I think I don't know him at all. But it's not that either. It's this. Sometimes I think there isn't anything there to know.'

This was what I wanted to hear. Nikki's relationship with James Mullens was walking around with a poisoned arrow in its back, and at any moment it was going to fall down dead. More promisingly still, Nikki had taken the time to sit down and share her worries with me. I had better, I thought, start getting in shape for those Sunday afternoon 5ks in the park.

'I'll miss my plane,' Nikki said. She shrugged into her rucksack and lifted the long grey tube.

'Hope your paper goes well,' I said.

'It's just a poster now,' Nikki said. 'I know it's sort of crazy to go all the way to Innsbruck just to present a poster. But I've never been. And, you know. I kind of wanted to get away for a while.'

'I know what you mean,' I said.

335

She walked off down the concourse, the poster tube swinging from her hands. Out on the runway, beyond the slanted glass, the men with the earmuffs and the luminous cones were waving at the planes – waving their slow, sad semaphore of goodbye.

Serbia

'I don't believe it. Like I *actually* don't believe it.'

'I don't fucking blame you.'

'That's just ... Fuck me.'

'This isn't possible. Like, what are the fucking odds.'

'... I told you,' James Mullens said, raising his arms above his head in triumph. 'Didn't I fucking tell you.'

We stood, the six of us – me, Paul Tynan, Bobby Hayes, Mark Foley, Sean Sweeney and James Mullens – in strong autumn sunshine, atop a ridge of sculpted earth. We could hear the creak of earthmoving equipment. We could see the cataract-grey of construction plastic, strapped over foundation trenches, rippling in the breeze. We could smell the dour odour of freshly upturned soil. And all around us, men in high-vis jackets and hard hats were confidently striding, holding clipboards, shovels, bags of blue cement.

'Like, this is an actual building site,' Sean Sweeney said.

Bobby Hayes said, 'There's an actual lake.'

This was true. The site was on the shore of a body of crystalline water, perhaps three miles across. In the distance, a low horizon of saw-toothed peaks charted its blunt NASDAQ of booms and busts.

'It's beautiful,' I said, meaning the site, the lake, the weather, the world. I was exploring the contours of a vast relief, purer in its way than any drug I had ever taken. Just that morning I had repeatedly retched in terror at the thought that Maria was pregnant with my child, but now none of that mattered: we were at the site and everything – the whole gamble – was paying off. Additionally reassuring was the fact that Vuk, Nicolae and Ratko were now chatting soberly to the project foreman, a rotund Slav in a string vest who was using a pencil to point at various documents on a clipboard. If you ignored the scar tissue around Nicolae's missing eye – he was not wearing his patch – it looked very much like the sort of conference you might see on any building site, anywhere in the world.

'Echo Lake,' Mark Foley said, gesturing at the water.

'Is not name of lake,' Aleks said. He was peeping out from the fur-lined hood of an army-surplus jacket and rolling yet another cigarette. 'We are on border with Bosnia and Herzegovina. Name of lake is in Bosnian language.'

'Not anymore, pal,' Paul Tynan said.

As we arrived at the site I had looked around for Maria. She had not appeared at breakfast and – it seemed – she had not joined us for our tour of the site. With luck, I would make it all the way to Tesla, later that day, without having to speak to her again.

Vuk was gesturing for us to join him outside the prefab

337

office. We descended from our promontory ridge and stood around, our feet making chewing-gum noises as we squelched them about in the mud. Bolted to the prefab hut was a sign that said FREE SERBIA PROGRESS CONSTRUCTION in slanted sea-green letters. As the foreman mumbled, Aleks translated in a flat voice. 'When project is complete, will be big day for Serbian–Ireland collaboration, and beginning of great age of cooperation between two countries.' General applause. 'Koala,' Sean Sweeney said. 'Tell him koala, there, Aleks.' The foreman disappeared into the prefab and emerged a moment later carrying an enormous bunch of flowers: carnations, of a dozen different colours. Ceremonially, he handed these to Sweeney, who sniffed them and posed for pictures, smiling like a debutante.

Vuk raised his hands like a priest at the close of Mass. 'At start of great enterprise,' he said, 'flowers must be exchanged.'

'Almost makes you feel bad,' Mark Foley said in my ear, 'that we're taking them for a ride.'

'I'm taking you all for a ride,' I said, too low for him to hear.

Aleks had retreated to the leeside of a man-sized section of concrete pipe, where he struggled to light his cigarette against the breeze. 'What's the matter with you?' I asked. He offered a shrug – a variant of what I had come to recognise as the Serbian national gesture: a defeated lift of the shoulders that seemed to say, *Yes, the present situation is awful/ridiculous/ embarrassing/historically tragic, but what can you do? What can any of us do, in this vale of tears?* Since our conversation in the woods outside the Hotel Globo, Aleks had been largely silent and had refused to meet my gaze, as if, by failing to grasp the point of what he had told me, I had insulted him, or disappointed him in some obscure way.

'You don't want to be here,' I said, and hesitated. 'If I've upset you somehow—'

'History is here,' Aleks said. 'And also the forgetting of history. This is the tragedy of Europe in twenty-first century. That we do not recall and want only to build. Make money.'

'Did something happen here?' I said. 'Is this, like, a heritage site, or something?'

But Aleks shook his head and turned away.

The foreman gave us a tour of the site. We tramped past trenches and through fields where circular tufts of coarse marsh grass sprouted, like the crowns of vegetable kings. I was, I realised, unconsciously massaging a spot above my left hip, where a dull pain still thrived. I resolved to think about seeing a doctor as soon as I got back to Dublin. In the meantime, there was business to conduct. I fell into step beside James Mullens and tapped him on the shoulder. 'So,' I said. 'All that's left is to sign the contracts.'

'We signed the contracts,' he said. 'Last night. Vuk's solicitor finally came through and had them couriered up from Novi Sad. We looked for you. But you didn't answer when we knocked on your door and your phone kept going to voicemail.'

The wind was driving morbid clouds across the sky above the lake. Our suit jackets flapped behind us as we negotiated a pathway of wooden planks. 'I must have passed out,' I said. 'That's it, then. We get paid.'

'Yep.' Mullens looked out across the lake – at the hills that rose in steps like the seats of an amphitheatre.

'Straight away,' I said, 'or—'

'I never said straight away,' Mullens said. 'You're looking at a couple of weeks, maybe longer. These things take time.'

'How much time?' I said.

'Relax,' Mullens said. He seemed irritated. 'It'll happen when it happens.'

'I'd like a clear timeline,' I said.

'I can't give you a clear timeline,' Mullens said.

'But a couple of weeks,' I said.

A couple of weeks was okay. That would give me time to choose a destination, book a one-way flight, and investigate my real estate options. But even as I was picturing my future library – with its stout leather armchairs and its angled skylight – an unpleasant thought obtruded. Mullens had just said, or at any rate implied, that he had tried to call me last night. But when my phone had finally relocated a carrier this morning, there had been no missed calls. And when, precisely, had he knocked on the door of my room? Presumably during the hour or so I had spent looking for booze and fucking Maria. Was that merely a coincidence? Surely it was. Nobody could have known that I would, at the appointed hour, lurch off down the hotel corridors, looking for a drink to put me to sleep. Although – and here the pain in my side recrudesced with a new and quite compelling urgency – there was the question of Maria's note: an invitation scribbled on a slip of scratch paper and left under the door of my room. She had wanted me to join her, and at a very specific time: half past one in the morning. It was only an accident that I had, in fact, run into her in the swimming pool at more or less precisely that moment. If the contracts had indeed been signed (and I had, I was forced to recognise, only Mullens's word for this), why might Vuk, or The Lads, or whoever, not want me to be on hand?

Mullens had stopped and was watching a powerboat turn waspish circles in the middle of the lake.

'I was wondering,' I said, 'about the IPO.'

'The what?' Mullens said.

'You know, the flotation,' I said. 'I thought you mentioned it. It's what you do with a REIT, isn't it?'

'Oh,' Mullens said. 'Right. Yeah. I'm still looking at how to time it out. Basically this ...' He indicated the site, which stretched before us like an archaeological dig. '... puts us in a much stronger position when we do go public. But you don't need to worry about any of that stuff yet.'

'Because I ran into Nikki at the airport,' I said. 'And she mentioned that a REIT can't really function unless it's publicly traded.'

Mullens's look was gratifyingly sharp. 'This deal is confidential,' he said. 'I told you that. We don't tell our girlfriends, we don't tell our families, we don't tell our fucking therapists.'

'I didn't tell her anything,' I said. Plainly I had struck a nerve. 'She just expressed some concerns.'

'Ah, yeah,' Mullens said. 'She's a great one for the old concerns.' His mood abruptly shifted. The muscles of his face relaxed and he shook his head as if he had just remembered something. 'Sorry, man. I knew you wouldn't say anything. Just, you know. Birds.'

'Yeah,' I said. I seemed to have missed something. The wind was growing stronger. I was about to speak when we heard a shout from one of the construction workers at the far edge of the site.

We had caught up with the rest of The Lads, who were standing around a pile of bricks making noises of counterfeit interest as the potbellied foreman explained the theory of sewage in his fitfully accurate English. Sean Sweeney was the first to turn – he held up a hand to shield his eyes from the waning sunlight and said, 'Trouble at mill, lads.'

Another shout carried on the breeze, and the other construction workers seemed to be downing tools and leaving their stations, heading in the direction from which the shout had come.

'What's up?' I said.

More shouts. Now the construction workers were taking off their hard hats and running.

I looked around for Vuk, but he seemed to have disappeared.

Aleks, too, was no longer present. From the promontory ridge above the site an anoraked figure – it was, I saw, with a strange catch or quiver in my throat, Boris the driver – stood gazing down at us.

'Some sort of problem with the foundations,' Mullens theorised.

But it had become clear that whatever was happening required the attentions of every man on site. The foreman himself was jogging across a stretch of plastic sheeting with an expression of pained urgency on his face.

I hugged my jacket to my chest and said, 'I'm going to see.'

'Leave it,' Mullens said.

But I was already running.

The construction workers had gathered in a knot around a freshly dug trench. The storm had almost reached us. The air seemed needlingly full of the rain that was about to fall. I pushed through the crowd's outer layers and found myself standing on the lip of the trench, looking down.

Two burly men in coveralls were kneeling in the dirt, pushing it aside with large gloved hands. The foreman said something in Serbian that might have been *Get back, get back*. Beneath the gloved hands the packed earth turned over and loosely fell. And now we could see part of what was there, and the workmen, who had been whispering among themselves, fell silent.

Sweeney was standing beside me. 'What the fuck is that?' he said. 'Is that, like, cabling, or . . . ?'

The two kneeling men no longer moved. No one spoke. The air was wet. Against the forest darkness, the rain stood out like silver webbing.

Paul Tynan said, 'What did they do, dig up a caveman?'

I remembered some of the things that Aleks had said. *Normal combat operations. Lives of normality. We are near border with Bosnia. Many men of Serbia who take part personally in rapes, in murders, in burying of bodies. Inside they are not changed. Are still same men as before.*

History is here, he had said.

'That's an animal,' Bobby Hayes said. 'That's definitely an animal. It's too small to be a human being.'

I turned away and began to walk towards the limo. The Lads stayed where they were, looking down at the crooked little skeletons in the wet black earth.

3

No Big Deal

We step through the doorway, and the door closes behind us. But the door is made of glass, and so we can turn and see, with the utmost clarity, what it is that we've left behind. And for a moment, it looks as if we can still go back.

My group session this morning was chaired by Dr Felix. Through the windows of the day room I could see the orange sun squashed against a bank of dead grey cloud like a peach in a stainless-steel sink. It was a low-serotonin sky, a mood-disorder sky. Dr Felix smiled at us – at the junkies assembled for our daily chat, with our tales of woe, our terrible need to confess. Freshly tanned, cross-legged on his vinyl-foam mattress, in white linen trousers and a white shirt, Dr Felix looked like an American consultant on a yoga retreat. Normally our group sessions are run by a former social worker named Angela, who gets us to make horses out of plasticine. This, the general feeling goes, is the sort of therapy you can get behind.

We sat around, lotus-legged, our ankles going numb.

Finally, Dr Felix said, 'Why did you take drugs?'

The question seemed to be directed at everyone – or at no one in particular.

'Because we're addicts,' someone said.

'No,' Dr Felix said. 'I'm not looking for the medicalised answer. I'm looking for the truth.'

Nobody knew what to make of this.

I spoke up: 'All you've given us is the medicalised answer.'

'Then I've let you down,' Dr Felix said.

My fellow addicts mumbled restively. This is not what we were formerly told. To my left a fiftyish man – he was, I recalled, a retired bus driver who had destroyed his marriage using nothing more potent than over-the-counter pain medication – raised a querulous finger and said, 'Sorry, I don't understand.'

Dr Felix smiled his fourth-stage-of-enlightenment smile. 'Let me rephrase,' he said. 'What's the world like, without drugs? Tell me.'

'Tough,' said someone.

'Difficult,' said someone else.

'Intolerable,' I contributed.

'No,' Dr Felix said. 'Without drugs, the world is there. With drugs, it isn't. What would you call someone who was afraid to look at the world?'

I almost said, *Wise*. But Dr Felix wasn't really asking.

'A coward,' he said. 'Which is what you are. All of you. Cowards.' He turned his smile on me. 'You especially,' he said. 'You're the biggest coward of all.'

'Ah, here,' the bus driver said. His eyebrows had crawled halfway up his affronted forehead. 'That's abuse, that is. I thought this was supposed to be a safe space.'

Dr Felix was looking directly at me. I did not move.

'This isn't a safe space,' he said. 'This is the world.'

At Tesla, the WiFi prospered unpredictably, but as the cabin was pressurised for takeoff I was nonetheless able to scan a page of search results for *Securitate. Socialist Republic of Romania*, I read. *Nicolae Ceauşescu. Harassment and physical attacks. Police terror. Torturing and killing political opponents.* For *Vuk Mladic* or *Free Serbia Progress Construction*, Google returned nothing. But a search for *Voivode Holdings* produced the information that *voivode* was an Old Slavic word for *warlord*. The WiFi dried up before I got around to typing *Real Estate Investment Trust*. It was probably just as well.

Beyond the circular windows the airport was arc-lit, like a TV set. To my lasting relief, The Lads were sitting a couple of rows behind me, meaning that I was not obliged to talk to them or to look at their handsome, impassive faces. When I did glance back, I saw that James Mullens was watching a film. He wore a pair of earbuds that made him look like a doctor listening to a stethoscope. Paul Tynan and Bobby Hayes were mixing drinks from miniature plastic bottles. Mark Foley and Sean Sweeney were asleep, their mouths identically ajar. Around us people were tucking themselves into stiff blue airline blankets. The man in the seat beside me was reading a book: one of those masculinity-bolstering thrillers in which every sentence gets its own paragraph. Perhaps, I thought, our plane would crash, taking all my problems with it. Whenever I closed my eyes – something I now planned to avoid doing for the rest of my life – I saw the black earth of the building site, the small pellets of greyish white in a familiar fantail pattern: radius, ulna, carpals, meta-carpals. All of them very small – too small, as Bobby Hayes had said, to be the bones of an adult human being. *History is here*, Aleks had said. Oh yes. History was there. And we had dug it up – we had caused the Echo Lake development to take place. Me. The Lads. James Mullens. It was our responsibility. We had trespassed on old earth, old hatreds, knowing noth-ing. I remembered some words from my former – and now implacably remote – life: *I had not thought death had undone so many*. But they were just words. They availed me nothing.

To distract myself – insofar as such a thing was possible – I took out Aleks's book of poetry. It was the slimmest of slim volumes, perhaps twenty or thirty pages. What did Aleks write about? His troubled conscience? The history of his ter-rible, tragic country, with its fields full of human bones? Or perhaps they were love poems, to his journalist girlfriend, who exposed corruption and was noble. I studied each line, unable to decipher a word. On the flyleaf at the back I dis-covered a handwritten note: a string of digits, and a message: 'Call if needed'. He had given me his phone number. Why?

The plane took off. Behind me, James Mullens had fallen asleep, his face illuminated by the movie still playing on his seatback screen.

We had departed the site in a rancorous silence. Of the Serbian contingent – Vuk, Nicolae, Ratko, Boris and Aleks – only Boris remained. To this day I have no idea where the others disappeared to. The workmen also had mostly abandoned the site. Standing above the trench, they had blessed themselves. Then they began to file off towards the makeshift car park on the bluff.

Boris waited patiently while we settled ourselves in the limo. Soon we were driving through the dank Serbian countryside – past the farmhouses with their puffing chimneys, the lopsided roadside *rakija* stalls. The silence persisted. I looked at The Lads, who looked out at the passing trees. Sean Sweeney folded and refolded his arms like a dad outside a maternity ward. Mark Foley picked at the skin around his fingernails. Paul Tynan jiggled first one knee, then the other. Bobby Hayes slowly banged the back of his head against the soft fabric of his headrest. And then – an hour or more had passed, and we were approaching the outskirts of Novi Sad – Mullens took out his phone and made a show of thumbing the email app. An incoming message arrived with a *bong!*

'We've sold our first apartment off plans,' he said. 'Two more prospective buyers lined up. I'd say we'll have them in the bag by the end of the week.'

There was a pause.

'Good buzz,' Sean Sweeney said.

Baggage claim. Dublin Airport. Our Samsonites circled in the torpid dawn like obedient beasts of burden. As James Mullens hauled his bag to the floor I grabbed his upper arm – that tree-trunk of gym-built muscle – and said, 'It's not happening, is it?'

He blinked. 'What's not happening?'

'The fucking deal,' I said. 'The payout. It's not happening. You saw what I saw. It's a fucking mass grave.'

'I didn't see that,' Mullens said. He jabbed an index finger at my chest. 'I didn't see that at all. I saw some bones. Could be anything. Probably fucking Neolithic. This shit happens all the time. You start digging, you turn up some bones, construction is delayed while you let some archaeologists or whoever take a look at it, blah blah blah.'

I was still squeezing his bicep. Irritably, he shook me off. 'Why don't you go home and get some sleep and we'll catch up on Monday. Yeah?'

'Those two guys,' I said. 'Nicolae and Ratko. They beat the shit out of two people right in front of us. They're fucking animals.'

'Do you know what I have?' Mullens said, turning to face me. 'I have signed contracts. Let me explain to you what that means. It means that the construction is a pile of bullshit. It means that whatever happens over there from now on is nothing to do with me, or you, or with *anyone* on

352

this side of the deal.' He made a sound that was a snort, or a gasp, or some hybrid of the two. 'I can't believe you don't get it. I can't believe you don't get that it *doesn't fucking matter* if that resort gets built or if they all just sit over there with their dicks up their arses for the next twenty years. Because I have *signed contracts.*' He tensed his shoulders. 'The deal is done. That's how it works. And if you want to keep your job, I'd suggest that you figure that out at some point and stop wrecking my fucking head with shit that doesn't matter.'

Abashed, I took a step backwards. I had known James Mullens for almost two decades. This was the first time I had ever seen him lose his temper. I felt strangely flushed, as if I were coming up on a snack-sized dab of MDMA.

Mullens took a deep breath. 'I'm tired,' he said. 'Just tell me this. The payout is coming. We're talking weeks. *Maybe* days. Are you still in?'

This was it. He was offering me a chance to turn my back on the Serbian deal and everything it represented: Vuk, Nicolae, Ratko, Maria, The Lads, Echo Lake, Aleks, the crooked little skeletons – most of all these last.

I imagined what would happen if I said no. No more job at Echo REIT. No more penthouse at The Brokerage. No more money to buy drugs. No more chances to seduce Nikki (or at least to convince Nikki that I might make a worthwhile prospect, someday soon). I imagined returning to my father and telling him that my top-secret business venture had failed and that if he still had any contacts in

America, perhaps he might . . . ? I imagined living a life in which my greatest achievement consisted of writing forty pages of an unpublishable novel and sixteen pages of an incoherent PhD thesis. I imagined interviewing once again at BlueVista Marketing Solutions, or at one of its myriad clones, and spending parched years clicking and dialling in my swivel chair while some equivalent of Richie Gibbons told me not to be such a miserable cunt. I imagined all of this as James Mullens rubbed his eyes and sighed, and as the airport crowd seemed to move around us at synaptic speed, all those ordinary people managing their ordinary lives.

I did the worst thing.

'Yeah,' I said. 'I'm still in.'

A childhood memory, unearthed today in group (although I kept it to myself). My father used to take me to the Wellington Monument in Phoenix Park on winter evenings. I was very little. The huge grey obelisk with its sloping steps. Our breath making little megaphones of smoke in the cold air. We climbed to the plinth and my father told me to press my tummy against the stone and look up. The monument's square tip stayed still, became the centre of your vision. The clouds moved past it. You felt what it was to be standing on a planet, moving through space. The stars glittering above the clouds. It made me dizzy and my father steadied me with a strong hand, laughing. *I'm sorry you never had a brother,* my father told me, when I was older.

It takes you out of yourself, having a brother. But in his case, ultimately, it was *not* having a brother that took him out of himself, wasn't it? Pancreatic cancer. *That's a bad death.* And my father had seen it, close up. He no longer had a brother. And this fact seemed to have shoved him out into the world. Away from our family. Away from me. He began to call home at dinnertime from various locations. The family farm, where he was talking to the surveyor. The solicitor's office, where the deal was going through. Was he in work, or was he on private business? There may have been no particular distinction, in his mind or in ours. The maid (now we had a *maid*) served dinner to my mother and me, and my father radioed in his apologies from wherever he was. A greenfield site in Kinnegad. The Horseshoe Bar of the Shelbourne Hotel. The clubhouse at Mount Juliet. 'Keep my plate warm,' he said, and returned after midnight, and was gone again before I got up for school. *The world is hard. And the only way to beat it is to be hard yourself.* He had never said anything like this to me before. It was a new message. It may have surprised even him. It may have been born during the months he spent watching Frank die, or it may have been latent within him always, waiting for the moment of ripeness. It was a new message but it became his only message. It became the message he was driven to broadcast on all frequencies as he moved through the world, getting older, getting richer, becoming steadily more opaque. Driven, yes. Perhaps death is a driving force. You see it, and you turn the other way, and you run. Isn't it funny? When I think of our house during the years of my adolescence, I see myself, and I see my mother. I see myself doing my homework at the kitchen table and I see my mother sipping wine and watching TV, or paging through her appointments book. But my father is somewhere out of frame. He is elsewhere, in his world of pinstriped moneymen. And it wasn't like that, when I was little. When my father was still soft and we were still together, as a family.

Why do I know these things now? Why did I not know them then?

Everything happens too late.

Will I be permitted to burn these pages, I wonder, when I'm done? Let no one ever see them. Let no one ever look into my heart and see nothing but open sores.

'It's too simple,' I told Dr Felix (this was – when? Yesterday?).

'What's on your mind?' he said.

Our session had just begun. The Doc was sipping his 9 a.m. cappuccino. No coffee for me. I hardly sleep as it is.

'My father did change,' I said. 'Yes. Okay. After his brother died. He went out and made himself rich. And we never saw him.'

'Uh huh,' Dr Felix said. 'And you're angry at him for changing. For abandoning you.'

He picked up a miniature watering can and sprinkled a few droplets on the leaves of his bonsai tree: a new addition to the office bookshelves.

I thrashed about restlessly in the ergonomic hot seat.

'But he didn't abandon me,' I said. 'He gave me all this money. He tried to tell me how to have a career. He never left me alone, for fuck's sake. So it's too simple. Like there's this obvious logical progression from my uncle dying to my father changing his personality to us getting rich to me ending up in rehab. That isn't how life works. Life's not that simple.'

'Life's absolutely that simple,' Dr Felix said again. 'He abandoned you. He was your father and then he wasn't. And you didn't know why it happened. You're only beginning to understand it now. And you're still rationalising and repressing.'

'Bullshit.'

'You want your problem in a nutshell? Buried anger. You protect yourself from it by telling yourself you're smarter than everybody else. When you couldn't do that anymore, your psychological stability collapsed. Then you took a lot of drugs so you could avoid thinking about it. But you're hurt and angry and you blame your parents. Boom. We're done.'

Vehemently I shook my head. 'That's the pop psychology answer.'

'It's the real psychology answer,' Dr Felix said. 'I don't know what more you want, aside from a free pass to continue being obtuse.' He pantomimed exasperation. 'Nobody's that fucking complicated, Ben. Least of all you. But you know what they say.'

He paused. I rolled my eyes and dutifully said, 'What do they say?'

357

Dr Felix waved the little watering can. 'You can lead a horticulture,' he said, 'but you can't make her think.'

Of the pharmacopeia with which I had arrived in Belgrade five days previously, only one pinner and a single Oxycontin now remained. My immediate priority was clear: I needed to buy more drugs. It was too early to call Barry Hynes. He was never awake before noon. Loitering by the taxi rank outside Arrivals, I sent a text to a number that I had stored in my phone under EMERGENCY CONTACTS. It was the number of Barry's wholesaler, whose name, Barry had told me, was Mick. 'He's twenty-four-seven, man,' Baz had croaked, as I copied Mick's number into my phone at the tail-end of a session. 'Buzz him whenever.' This I now did. LOOKING TO BUY, my text said. FRIEND OF BAZ'S. Five minutes later the reply came in: OCONNEL BRIDGE 1 HOUR. NO SMALL SHIT. The system worked!

My nerves tingling, I cabbed it to the city centre. Here I withdrew €500 from an ATM and stationed myself in the middle of O'Connell Bridge just as the morning traffic reached its peak. To the south, the skyline presented nothing but the silhouettes of construction cranes. The city was a Ship of Theseus, constantly replacing its worn-out parts. Or, no: strike that. Beneath the text of its infrastructure, the city was a white page, *tabula rasa*. Every building was a blinking cursor, there and gone from one second to the next. Warily I leered at every chav in a tracksuit who slouched past, smoking: was this Mick? An hour went by. Then another. Oh, rue the dead time, the afternoons squandered, the mornings pissed away on street corners, in car parks, under dripping railway bridges, waiting for someone to come along and sell you drugs.

For a while I watched two young male Mormon missionaries accosting people on Bachelor's Walk. They wore suits and neat 1950s haircuts and their lapels bore matching pins of the American flag. Everyone waved them away but they kept smiling and trying again. They seemed happy, as if they knew that the long equation of the world would eventually add up and tell them what they needed to know. I thought of Aleks, praying at the altar of the monastery church. The world challenged you to find it meaningful, and gave you various options to choose from: art, business, faith, family, drugs. There were probably less idiotic choices than religion. But perhaps it made no difference, in the end.

I was halfway through my fourteenth cigarette when a blank-faced young man in jeans and a hoodie drifted into position beside me.

'Mick?' I said.

'Story,' he said.

'I got your number off Baz,' I said. 'Listen, man, I really appreciate this.'

My heart fluttered. Whenever I meet a new drug dealer, I tend for some reason to act like a teenage girl at her debutante ball.

'Sound, man, sound,' Mick said. Beneath his sidling eyes, his jaw seemed loose or faultily hinged, as if, some time ago, the lower half of his face had simply given up on the rest of him in disappointment or disgust. His eyes moved in rapid calculation. 'What are ye lookin' for?'

'Whatever's going,' I said. 'Yokes. Coke. Definitely downers.'

'You're lookin' for pills, I can get you pills,' Mick said.

'You're holding right now?' I said.

'Nah, man,' Mick said. 'Back in my car.'

This presented me with a quandary: it was never a good idea to go to a second location.

'I know what you're thinkin',' Mick said. 'You're thinkin', this fucker's gonna bring me back to his car and fuckin' stove me head in with a crowbar and rob me wallet.'

'That is pretty much exactly what I was thinking, yeah,' I said.

'Listen, man,' Mick said. 'I don't make money that way. All right? I sell a bit of white, a bit of weed, a few pills. I just don't like doin' it out in the open, you know? Me car's in the Brown Thomas underground car park.'

I did some hasty rationalising. After all, I thought, a drug dealer who operated out of the BT underground car park couldn't be all bad. There was also the not wholly unpleasant realisation that if Mick decided to murder me, I would no longer have to worry about Maria or Maria's baby or Clio or my father or the crooked little skeletons or any of it anymore.

'Cool,' I said.

Cowled in his hoodie, Mick led me to the car park, where he opened the boot of his '07 Micra and took out a plastic bag that bulged with multicoloured pills. Briefly, we haggled, by which I mean Mick told me how much everything cost, and I paid him. Total haul: ten yokes, three grams of coke, thirty Xanax and a bumper pack of Adderall.

'D'you know what I have as well?' Mick said. He dangled a baggie of white powder. 'AMT. This is industrial-grade shit. It's even illegal in *Russia*.'

'What does it do?' I said.

'It's like yokes without the euphoria,' Mick said. 'A bit speedy, a few visuals. Top you up at the end of a sesh.'

'That sounds terrible,' I said.

'Doing a special,' Mick said. 'Two grams for a tenner.'

His eyes offered a vile encouragement. I bought two grams. Our business was now completed. Mick reached into the boot and held up a crowbar. 'Gimme the fuckin' drugs back, you upper-class cunt,' he said.

I whimpered in fright.

'On'y messin' with yeh,' Mick said, putting the crowbar away and shaking his head fondly. 'Can you imagine?'

Earlier this afternoon, I knocked on the door of Dr Felix's office. I don't know why I did it. We weren't scheduled for a chat. I found him pruning his bonsai tree. He grunted at me and did not turn around. Whenever I step into Dr Felix's inner sanctum I have the uncomfortable bisected feeling that I am at once utterly safe and in terrible danger, though whence this danger might derive, I have no idea.

'I see you're bullying me in public now,' I said, taking the hot seat.

'You enjoyed it,' Dr Felix said. 'Being singled out.'

'Did I?' I said.

Dr Felix sat behind his desk and snipped his secateurs in the air. 'Yes,' he said. 'You did.'

'You called me a coward,' I said.

'You are a coward,' Dr Felix said.

'If this is some new therapeutic strategy—' I said.

'You're a coward,' Dr Felix interrupted, 'because you won't look at your real feelings. Only at the surface. You're afraid that if you look at your real feelings, they'll destroy you. But it's the not looking that's destroying you.'

'So that's your message,' I said. 'Trust my feelings. Ralph Waldo Emerson by way of Obi Wan Kenobi.'

'Let the mask drop,' Dr Felix said. 'Let it drop for one moment. That's all it will take. Then you won't be a coward anymore.'

I opened my mouth to speak, and no words came out.

And now, as I sit on the floor of my cell, scribbling in this notebook, I discover that one of the nurses has slipped a note under my door. On the folded sheet, in Dr Felix's neat script, are two quotations, with attributions in parentheses. *If you bring forth what is within you,* the first one said, *what you bring forth will save you. If you do not bring forth what is within you, what you do not bring forth will destroy you (Gospel of Thomas).* And: *The inner world is full of phantoms and false lights (Nietzsche).* The inner world, indeed.

*

From the Brown Thomas car park I took another cab back to The Brokerage. By now the pain in my side – which had been getting steadily worse since it had first announced itself on our last night in the Hotel Globo – was now quite impressively bad and required, unless I missed my guess, serious medical attention. Taped to the U-bend of the kitchen sink was my secret stash of codeine: six 30mg Solpadol tablets, plus a sleeve of some 12mg over-the-counter soluble discs. Cogitating for a moment – and palpating my side with worried fingers – I decided on a belt-and-braces approach, and used a glass of the soluble discs to knock back three of the 30mg tablets. In the bedroom, Clio lay face down on the four-poster bed, wearing knickers and a T-shirt.

'Ohmygod you're *home*,' she said, blinking through her fringe and making a smacking sound with her mouth.

I climbed out of my sweat-wrinkled suit.

Clio sat up. 'I need to talk to you,' she said.

'No, you don't,' I said. I was already asleep.

I awoke five or six hours later to find Clio fiddling with an earring as she stood over the bed. 'We're going up in two hours,' she said. 'It's our last night.' Rolling over, I discovered that she had left a Turin-Shroud imprint of herself on the sheets. As occasionally happened, she had gone to sleep wearing a fresh coat of fake tan. I performed a quick self-diagnostic and concluded that I would continue to feel 'good' (i.e. I would not start vomiting in pain and confusion) for precisely as long as I stayed beneath the bedclothes and didn't move.

'The play's still on?' I said. My voice was muffled by the max-tog duvet. 'But I was gone for so *long.*'

'You were gone for five days,' Clio said. 'How was it?'

I almost said: *It was a nightmare.* But this would have invited the sort of follow-up questions that I had neither the ability nor the desire to answer.

'It was good,' I said.

'Obviously,' Clio said. 'You stink of booze.'

'But I haven't had any booze,' I said.

'Well, you stink of something.' Clio was moving around the bedroom. 'Do you know how I know how long you were gone?'

'Because I told you?'

'Because you didn't answer a single text I sent you for the entire five days.'

'. . . No signal,' I said.

'They were WhatsApps,' Clio said. 'I could see the two blue ticks. I know you read them.'

'You've no idea how busy we were,' I said.

'I don't exactly appreciate being ghosted by someone who's been my boyfriend for this long,' Clio said. 'It's the sort of thing that tends to make me think, *This person isn't actually my boyfriend.*'

'But I love you,' I said. This would, I suppose, have been the moment to emerge from my duvet fortress, offering hugs and desperate entreaties. But I couldn't do it. The physical stakes were too high.

'I think we should talk,' Clio said. 'I think we should have a serious conversation about where we are. But I don't have time.' I heard the high-pitched snort of a jacket zipper being angrily closed. 'I'll see you later.'

'Wait,' I said.

'You were shivering a lot in your sleep,' Clio said. Her voice had moved away. 'Maybe you should go to the doctor.'

She had left the bedroom. I sat up. The pain in my side had receded. On the other hand, my lungs felt like two leather gloves full of hot sauce. Perhaps unwisely, I lit a smoke. Two or three minutes into the coughing jag that followed, Clio exited the penthouse, closing the door behind her with what was almost certainly meant to be an ominous finality.

In the bathroom I hacked up what felt like several litres of yellow phlegm and enjoyed a brief restorative snooze on the tiles. Wrapping myself in a fluffy bathrobe, I stepped out onto the terrace. The summer evening sky was slowly mixing its chill shades of cobalt and cornflower and charcoal and gunmetal blue. In an effort to reassure myself, I checked my online bank balance: the third – and first officially sched-uled – instalment of my Echo REIT salary was due to arrive in my account that very day. But although it was now 7 p.m., there was no sign of it. Dismissing this – thinking brightly, *There's always more money!* – I searched among the living-room flotsam until I located a half-empty bottle of Courvoisier. I have, it appears, consigned the following hour or two to the Memory Void, because the next thing I remember, I am dialling 999 and a female voice is saying, 'Emergency services.'

'Hello,' I said, quite suavely, I thought. 'Good evening. How are you?'

It was a woman's voice. She sounded impatient. 'This is the emergency services, sir. Are you calling to report an emergency?'

'Absolutely I am,' I said. 'A really big emergency.'

'I didn't hear that, sir. You'll have to speak more clearly.'

'I'm calling to report a mass grave,' I said. 'There are bodies. Buried. In a mass grave.'

'Sir, are you calling to report the discovery of human remains?'

'Yes,' I said. 'Human remains. That's it, exactly.'

'Okay, so you'll need to provide us with a location for the remains you've discovered.'

'They're not *here*,' I said scornfully. 'They're over *there*. In Serbia. Near the border with Bosnia. I don't know the exact spot. But there's a big construction site so you can't miss it.'

'Have you drink taken, sir?'

'I'm not *drunk*,' I said. 'Well, no. I am drunk. But I have to report . . . I have to report this to the proper authorities.'

'We take prank calls very seriously, sir.'

'It isn't a prank,' I said. But at this point, the conversation seems to have come to an end and the next thing I know . . .

. . . it is 4 a.m. and the penthouse is full of people and it seems clear that the cast of the Big Play has come back here for the afterparty, and I am briskly insufflating the powdered guts of a Blue Ghostie and telling Baz Hynes about what a complete shithole Serbia is, and Clio and her friends are dancing dreamily to some slow-grind ambient track, and somehow the fact that I ignored a week's worth of Clio's texts while I was in Serbia has become irrelevant, and I am chewing gum and smoking cigarette after cigarette, and I am telling someone I have never met before how amazing it's been, getting to know him over these last few months, and I am in the bathroom, staunching a nosebleed with a twist of toilet paper, and everyone is in the kitchen, holding hands, and Clio is holding my hand and saying, 'I really have to tell you something,' and she tells me what it is, and the knowledge drops from my brain at once, and it is 7 a.m. and the floor is climbing upwards intently, and I am leaning against it for balance, and just before I pass out I realise that I know, without knowing exactly how I know, that this is the Final Session, that there will be no more sessions after this, and that everything is about to change . . .

The doorbell rang. I opened my eyes. I was lying on the floor in the vestibule. My eyeballs were fluttering in their sockets. The pain in my side had become the pain in my everything. The doorbell. The doorbell was ringing. I argued my body into sitting up. There was someone at the door. I levered myself upright using an occasional table.

'You're up,' my mother said when I opened the door. She strode past me into the living room.

*

I was still high. My body was a busy social network of pain: the headache had friended the jaw ache, the jaw ache had friended the neck ache, the neck-ache had friended the shoulder ache ... In the living room I blinked and perspired while my mother surveyed the party wreckage: the unconscious actors, the puddles of spilled bong water, the caterpillars of loose-leaf tobacco crawling across the coffee table. When I closed my eyes, I saw a chorus line of crooked little skeletons, dancing the can-can at twenty-four frames per second. My mother pulled the curtains and opened the sliding door. The sunlight felt like an explosion.

'You don't reply,' she said, 'when we text you. You don't answer your phone when we call.'

'I've been out of the country,' I said. My voice sounded like a chainsaw. 'Do you ... Do you want some coffee? I was thinking of having some coffee.'

'That would be lovely,' my mother said.

Ransacking the kitchen, I failed to locate coffee beans, a coffee grinder, a coffee percolator, instant coffee, a cafetiere, a kettle, or a cup. 'We're out of coffee,' I informed my mother, returning to the living room.

'I'm not staying long,' she said. 'I'm here to offer you some help.'

'Help?' I said. 'Help with what?'

'Look at the way you're living,' my mother said.

'What's wrong with the way I'm living?' I said. On the coffee table in front of me was Aleks's book of poetry, now smeared with pill dust. Beside it was a pack of menthol cigarettes. I lit one and suppressed the urge to vomit. 'I'm tickety-boo.'

'You look sick,' my mother said.

'Well I feel fantastic,' I said.

'Your father's worried about you,' my mother said. 'I'm worried about you. You're not yourself.'

'And who,' I asked haughtily, 'is myself? I don't know if you noticed, but I wasn't exactly setting the world on fire before, was I?'

'You were never this unhappy,' my mother said.

'I'm not unhappy now,' I said. I groped for a nearby bottle of water and sipped from it. The water tasted bilious, like flat champagne.

My mother turned away and folded her arms. 'I don't know what we did,' she said, 'to make you so bitter. You never had to worry about anything. You had the whole world in front of you.'

'Still do,' I croaked.

'We talk about you, you know,' my mother said. 'Your father and me. We talk about you all the time.'

'That must be why I constantly feel like people are walking over my grave.'

'I wonder about your generation,' my mother said. 'About what happened to you. Why you all seem to think that nobody ever had feelings before you did. Why you all think there's some particular way life is supposed to be, if only your parents had been nicer to you. And do you know what I think? I think it's our fault. We overcorrected. We told you all you were special because nobody told us we were special. We wanted so badly for you to have the things we didn't have that we didn't know when to stop.'

'That's a truly fascinating bit of sociological analysis, Mum,' I said. 'But I'm not feeling great and I'd really, really like to have a shower. If you don't mind.'

My mother looked out across the city. 'I was thinking,' she said, 'about how my mother did the laundry when I was small. We had no washing machine, no tumble dryer. She set up a tub on two chairs and boiled kettle after kettle. Then she scrubbed every shirt and towel on a washboard. By hand. Passed everything through an iron mangle – grinding the big handle. Then she hung everything up to dry – in the garden if it was a dry day. In winter everything was hung near the fire.'

'Mum,' I said. 'What's your point?'

For a moment my mother said nothing. 'I've made some enquiries,' she said. 'There's a place called St Augustine. In Killiney. Very highly regarded. They offer a residential programme for ... for people in your situation.'

'Mum,' I said, 'I have no idea what you're talking about.'

'I told you I wanted to repair this family. It breaks my heart that I even have to say this. But if this is what it takes ...' My mother was facing me now. My mind had gone blank, as if it had been unexpectedly exposed to a powerful flashbulb. 'It's a detox programme, Ben. For addicts. Which is, as far as I can see, what you are.'

I laughed. 'Oh, yeah,' I said. 'That's me, all right.'

'You can't see what's right in front of your face,' my mother said. 'And you're so *cold*. You haven't asked me how your father is. You haven't even asked me how *I* am.'

'Oh, right,' I said. 'The trial. How's that going?'

'We're going to win,' my mother said.

'Goodie,' I said.

There was another silence. My mother's face was taut. 'I've talked to the people at St Augustine and there's a place for you there. Right now. I can drive you myself. You have time to pack some clothes and toiletries.'

'No can do,' I said. 'There's a business deal I'm keeping an eye on. And while we're at it, can I just point out the irony of the fact that it's *you*, of all people, who's standing there trying to get me to go to rehab. What did you have for breakfast this morning? Vodka and lime?'

'They warned me that you'd say no,' my mother said. 'And that you'd say hurtful things. They said it isn't you. It's whatever shit you're taking.'

'I need to get to work,' I said.

'Ben,' my mother said. 'I'm giving you an option here. You can escape what's coming down the tracks. You can walk away from it all, right now.'

'Don't worry about it,' I said. 'That's already taken care of. I'm out of here. I'm already gone.'

'I'm saying,' my mother said, 'that this is your last chance. I want you to listen to me. You can still get out of it.'

I flopped into an armchair. 'Give my best to the old man when you see him,' I said.

'You don't understand anything,' my mother said. 'Do you?'

'Your parents,' Dr Felix said. Once again I had gone to see him out of office hours. I can't imagine why. In my hand was the slip of paper on which he had written those enigmatic quotations.

'Still harping on parents,' I said.

'Do you think I don't recognise the Shakespeare stuff, or what?' Dr Felix said. 'Put away the clever quotes for a second and look at what's in front of you.'

I held up the slip of paper. 'I thought you were in favour of clever quotes.'

Dr Felix swivelled slowly in his counsellor's chair. 'Do you know the Gospel of Thomas?'

I rolled my eyes. 'I must have been sick that day.'

'It's apocryphal,' Dr Felix said. 'I'm assuming you know what apocryphal means.'

'So it's Insult My Intelligence Week, is that it?'

'Here's your assessment of yourself,' Dr Felix said. 'You're smarter than everyone else and you're stupider than everyone else. I'd call that a contradiction, wouldn't you?'

'Two things can be true at the same time,' I said.

'Neither of those things are true,' Dr Felix said.

'One of them is,' I said, perhaps a tad huffily.

'No,' Dr Felix said. 'You're not smarter than everyone else and you're not stupider than everyone else. Both of those propositions are false. And either way, you're giving yourself too much credit. You're not looking in the right direction.'

'So in what fucking direction should I be looking?'

'At your parents.'

'Still harping on parents,' I said, in what was unmistakably a snarl.

'We're getting somewhere,' Dr Felix said.

Consider, Dr F: What goes around comes around. Bad people are unhappy. All bullies are cowards. It evens out in the end. Useful fictions all. The next morning, I reported to the Echo REIT offices to find out what was happening with my salary – and to hassle James Mullens about the payout. It had become a matter of the gravest urgency that I leave the country and embark on my renovated life in the pure air of some sylvan bolthole. My rent was late. My mother was trying to send me to rehab. My father's trial was due to conclude at any moment. In the charcoal-grey pod of the conference room The Lads were throwing around a miniature rugby ball made out of spongy foam. I cornered James Mullens in the doorway.

'It's no big deal,' he said when I asked him about my salary. 'Temporary cash-flow issue. We're all in the same boat. We had to pay the lads at Sliney and Nihill before the end of the month. Tell you what. Give me your IBAN there and I'll transfer it directly. Call it an advance.'

'And the payout,' I said. 'You haven't said anything. No emails, nothing. Is there some problem with the deal?'

I refrained – though only just – from using the words *mass grave*, or *war criminals*, or *Securitate*.

'That's what we're about to find out,' Mullens said. He invited me to take a seat at the long table, where The Lads were now shuffling documents and typing on laptop keyboards. It was like watching a troupe of Chippendales playing businessmen in a movie.

James Mullens tapped his Mont Blanc pen for order. 'So we've had a bit of back and forth with the guys in Belgrade about the, ah, the issue that arose with the site ...' He looked down at the table. 'But we're going to check in with Vuk now and I think he's got some good news for us.'

He nodded at Mark Foley, who began to operate the matte-black console that formed the table's centrepiece. The room filled up with the sound of a ringing phone.

'Game faces, lads,' Mullens said, and rested his chin on his hands.

'*Da*,' said a distant voice.

'Mr Mladic,' James Mullens said. 'What's the story?'

'*Dober dan*, Meester Moollens.' The voice was unmistakably Vuk's. It was a shock to hear him speak. Unconsciously I had assumed that he was now in jail, and I would never have to think about him again. But no: he was still a free man. And he was still our business partner, in whatever sense that term still applied, cheerily making conference calls from one time zone to the next. 'I trust that all is well in city of Black Pool.'

'Just to be aware,' Mullens said, 'We have Ben [REDACTED]

374

sitting in with us today.' He smiled – not at me, but in my general direction.

The line fizzed and crackled and seemed to drop. 'This I understand,' Vuk said. He cleared his throat with a dry rattle. 'I bring news of development. I am to say we have resolved difficulties with archaeological discovery of site. I speak to many experts of archaeology. I speak also to ministers of government who are taking involvement in progress of hotel.' More crackles, more fizz. James Mullens looked at the ceiling. 'Is good,' Vuk said at last. 'Is go-ahead for proceeding with construction.'

Bobby Hayes made two fists and shook them, mouthing the words, *Get in!* 'That's good news,' Mullens said, waving at him to shut up. 'So you had the researchers in or whatever.'

'Is no need of research,' Vuk said. 'Building of development will proceed as schedule.'

Mullens sat back and folded his arms. He was looking at me. 'And the transactions and everything,' he said. 'They went through okay?'

'We conclude our business,' Vuk said.

The line went dead.

The Lads whooped and applauded. 'That's fucking whopper,' Sean Sweeney said. My own contribution was drowned out by the noises of celebration. 'He said *archaeological discovery*,' I said. 'That's what he said, right?' A smile of foolish relief was establishing itself on my face. In spite of everything – in spite of my clear memory of the whiteness, and therefore the presumably inarguable modernity, of the bones that I had glimpsed in the black earth of the building site, in spite of my equally clear memory of how the blonde woman had fallen, when Ratko had punched her with his black-gloved fist, in spite of everything that Aleks had said (*History is here*) – I told myself that finally, there was nothing to worry about, my concerns had been absurd, there was simply no way that a man like James Mullens would go into business with people he knew to be monsters – that a world in which such a thing could happen would be a world that was ultimately beyond my power to shape or to understand, and that we did not, after all, live in such a world. My new life beckoned, with its solitude, its peace, its total financial security.

'So that's it,' I said. 'We get paid.'

Bobby Hayes grabbed my shoulder. 'We get *paid*, yo,'

'Seventy-two hours,' James Mullens said. He was smiling at me as if to say, *I told you so, you idiot*. I remembered what Nikki had said about him in the airport: *Sometimes I think there isn't anything there to know*. But this, surely, was wrong. Mullens's charm was like armour. He wore it to protect himself. But that just meant that he felt himself to be a thing worth protecting. He was – I thought, imagining how he might look from Nikki's perspective – the sort of person with whom you could very easily fall in love.

Mullens stood. 'Don't overdo the celebrations tonight,' he said. 'We've dinner with the investors tomorrow.'

*

'I saw nothing,' I said. Dr Felix was silent. It was early evening. I had circled back to his office. 'I understood nothing.'

'You knew it wasn't an archaeological discovery,' Dr Felix said. 'So you understood that.'

'I don't even know who they were,' I said. 'Those people in the ground. Were they Serbs, or Bosnians, or Croatians, or whatever? Were they Muslims or Christians? I don't know how they died. I still know nothing.'

'The likelihood,' Dr Felix said, 'given what we now know about Vuk Mladic and his cronies, is that they were the victims of a massacre perpetrated by Serbian nationalist forces during the wars of the late 1990s.'

'You see them at night,' I said. 'You don't know who they are but you see them at night when you close your eyes. When you've been through . . .'

Dr Felix said nothing for a long moment. 'At the going down of the sun,' he said at last, 'we will remember them.' He paused. 'You're using the second person singular a lot.'

'And what does that mean?' I said.

'That you're still the star of the show,' Dr. Felix said. 'That you're still thinking primarily about yourself.'

I was pacing the length of his office. Six, seven, eight paces from the bookshelf to the window. Eight, nine, ten paces from the window to the bookshelf. On the latter, standing upright between two cast-iron bookends, were various therapeutic volumes: *The Addictive Personality, Understanding the Borderline Mother, The Disordered Mind, Overcoming Anxiety, Why Can't Johnny Just Quit?* 'You asked me to write it all down,' I said. 'My life story. Who else would I be think-ing about?'

'I think you're looking for a way out of thinking about yourself,' Dr Felix said. 'You're starting to think about those people whose bones you saw. You're starting to wonder who they were.'

'That doesn't exactly feel like a breakthrough.'

'Breakthroughs are bullshit,' Dr Felix said. 'I told you. Self-knowledge is an arduous process. And it often involves looking outside the self, at the world that helped to produce that self. At the family, in the first instance.'

'My self,' I said, pacing with measured steps and refusing to swallow this particular dangled hook, 'is someone who pretended he hadn't seen a mass grave in order to get rich.'

'There's no shame in turning away from the unspeakable,' Dr Felix said. 'At least not at first. It would be shameful if you were still pretending that what you'd seen was an archaeo-logical discovery.'

'That I pretended at all,' I said. 'That's enough.'

'The question is *why* you pretended,' Dr Felix said. He leaned back and put his feet on the corner of his desk. 'This facility is named after St Augustine of Hippo. Have you read *The Confessions*?'

'You're going to tell me about the pears,' I said. St Augustine's theft of the pears is commemorated in a Giotto-like mural that adorns the wall of the clinic's entrance hallway, which means that it is the first thing you see when you wash up here, in the throes of withdrawal.

'Augustine tells us that he didn't really want or need the pears,' Dr Felix said. 'That they were, in actual fact, inedible. So why did he steal them?'

'He wanted to get rich?' I said.

'He says he stole them,' Dr Felix said, 'because of a perceived good. He wanted his friends to like him. He wanted to experience a sense of fellowship. It was a perceived good that led him into error.'

'So all this happened because I wanted The Lads to like me,' I said.

Dr Felix shook his head. 'You were led into error by a perceived good. In your case, it was the desire to escape from your parents. Consciously or not, you believed that escaping your parents was the most important thing you could do. But you were wrong about that. It wasn't the most important thing.'

I had stopped in the middle of the carpet. 'So what was the most important thing?'

'Simply looking,' Dr Felix said, 'at what was really there.'

You see them at night. I see them at night. Not in dreams but as a kind of memory: the families rousted in darkness from their warm homes, the men with guns, the arc lights, the trucks or trains. The father holds his son and sings the same lullaby that used to put the son to sleep when the son was a baby, but now the song is just a song of death. They are already living in the white city of the dead. I don't even know who they were. But I saw them, father and son, in the earth where they were buried. I saw them, and I did nothing – until it was all too late.

From Dr Felix, this afternoon, a genuine surprise. 'You have a visitor,' he said, appearing in the doorway of my cell.

A hot rash of shame trickled all the way from my head to my feet. It was succeeded by a hot rash of anger. *How dare they?*

'I thought visitors weren't allowed,' I said.

'It's discretionary,' Dr Felix said. 'Normally I'd say no. But this particular visitor might be useful.' He pursed his lips. 'Up to you, of course.'

Up to me. I followed Dr Felix along the disinfectant-odorous corridors to a hitherto unknown wing of St Augustine – a small suite of visitors' rooms, each one over-looking a miniature apple orchard that slopes down towards the main Killiney road. Waiting in a room furnished with the traditional therapeutic bucket chairs and Kleenex boxes was Nikki.

'Hi,' she said, and waved her hands awkwardly.

Dr Felix left us to it.

I was wearing my rehab pyjamas and my rehab robe. I was also hollow-eyed, unshaven, gaunt. In the last two weeks I have lost just under a stone. You could, I suppose, observe that my general aura nowadays is one of purifica-tion, asceticism, saintliness. Or you could just say that I look like shit.

Nikki wore jeans and a T-shirt and a big pair of hipster

specs. Compared to me, she looked like an emissary from some utopian planet of perfect human specimens.

'It's you,' I said stupidly.

She smiled, and blushed. Her physical presence had a strange effect on me. Seeing her was like seeing the final figure on some sort of hideously conclusive bank statement: mathematical proof of how completely I have fucked my life.

'If you want me to go, I'll go,' Nikki said. 'I really don't want to ...'

'No,' I said. 'Stay.'

We sat in the bucket chairs. I found myself nodding silently like some sort of Eastern sage.

'So,' Nikki said. 'How are ... How are you?'

'I've been better,' I said. 'You?'

Her expression was pained. 'I tried to call you. But someone else answered your phone.'

'Dr Felix,' I said.

A moment of vertigo: imagining Nikki talking to Dr F. How did *that* go?

'He told me to come in,' Nikki said. 'He seems nice.'

'He's an asshole,' I said.

Nikki said nothing. As the shock of her visit wore off, I began to feel something else. Like the weight of an inverse moral gravity. Hitting rock bottom, it turns out, confers a kind of authority. The rotten kind, I suppose.

'It's, uh,' I said, 'it's nice to see you. Thank you for coming.'

'I wanted to see you,' she said. 'After what happened.'

She had come all this way. I aimed at generosity. 'You tried to tell me,' I said. 'But I didn't listen. I'm sorry.'

'I didn't know anything,' Nikki said. 'Not really.'

I shrugged.

'When I heard about what James did,' Nikki said, and stopped. 'You must hate him.'

I shook my head. 'He did what he did because he is who he is. You met his father. You know what kind of men they are. I'd say you broke up with him just in time.'

'He's very plausible,' Nikki said. 'Men can do that. They can be very plausible.'

'What about me?' I said. 'Was I plausible?'

She took off her glasses. There were two dark oval smudges on the bridge of her nose, which she rubbed self-consciously.

'You seemed sad,' Nikki said.

I nodded. 'What about now?'

'Less sad now.'

'You should see me in the middle of the night.'

The sunlight through the windows was apple-green. I looked at Nikki. My shame had evaporated. Where had it gone?

'When someone tricks you,' Nikki said, 'you should really blame them. But you don't, do you? You blame yourself. Because how could I have been such a fool?'

'You're better off without him,' I said.

In the past, I would have meant this flirtatiously. *Dump him! Get with me!* But now I found that I simply meant it.

'You, too,' Nikki said.

'Our mutual ex,' I said.

She smiled. 'How are you really? Can I ask?'

I pondered for a moment. 'I'm not finished yet,' I said.

Another smile.

'Good,' Nikki said. 'Me neither.'

Of course you're not finished, I thought. Because you move through the world with a special power, the power to banish shame. Which is the power people have when they know who they are. When they know who you are.

After she had gone, I felt a peculiar agitation: as if I had just realised that I was late for a crucial appointment, and the buses weren't running, and I had no other way to get where I needed to go.

When James Mullens said 'dinner with the investors', he meant, of course, dinner with The Dads of The Lads. This was scheduled to take place in a brand-new restaurant in Ranelagh that offered, according to its website, 'deconstructed versions of old favourites', i.e. burgers and salads that you assembled yourself from their constituent parts. The idea of sitting through a meal in the company of other human beings filled me with a nameless terror. The pain in my side – it felt like the kind of stitch you might get after running on a full stomach, if what you had eaten was poison – was now inhibiting my physical progress to the point where I wondered if I should simply give up and buy a cane. When I coughed, I dredged up lumps of mucus that had the unmistakable savoury taste of infection. From my own interiority – as from the bearer of unwelcome tidings – I steadfastly averted my gaze. Nonetheless I was determined to attend. My Echo REIT salary had not yet materialised in my bank account and I had the strangest feeling that if I didn't keep a close eye on James Mullens's activities during this crucial period, he would somehow elude me, or simply vanish, like smoke in a high wind. Undergirded by steel beams of Adderall (I had, you will recall, bought twenty pills from Barry's wholesaler Mick), I took my place at the long table. I was sitting opposite Bobby Hayes's father, the gravel merchant. In his right hand, as if defensively, he gripped a butter knife. 'Overdid it, did we?' he barked, apparently addressing me.

'Under the weather,' I managed. 'Not feeling the best.'

Mr Hayes (I never did learn his first name) produced a sly little grin that showed you he thought of himself as shrewd.

Beside him was Martin Mullens, as usual *soigné* and self-contained – and freshly returned, according to his son, from Oslo, where he had talked up the Echo Lake development deal with some interested Scandi investors.

'I've been meaning to say,' Martin Mullens said, as he scrutinised me above the rims of his reading glasses, 'do send your father my best, when you see him.'

I gripped my glass of wine with a tightly knuckled hand and said nothing. I had hoped to find myself sitting beside Mullens *fils*, so that I could complain about the non-arrival of my salary. But he was sitting at the head of the table, twirling a silver fork and repeatedly checking his phone.

'Really,' Martin Mullens continued, 'I think it's disgraceful, the treatment he's received.'

'Hear, hear,' someone chimed in – it might, perhaps, have been Mark Foley's father, with his houndstooth sports coat and his features of clerical cut.

'It's barbaric,' Martin Mullens continued. 'Seeing the carpers and complainers come out of the woodwork. People who never contributed anything to public life beyond a negative attitude. When I think of the opposition he faced, trying to drag this country kicking and screaming into the twenty-first century.'

I seemed, not for the first time that year, to be encountering a hermeneutic difficulty – a problem of interpretation. 'It's been a stressful time,' I said, endeavouring to muster a neutral tone.

Our starters had arrived: Dublin Bay mussels and, in a transparent gravy jug, a lumpy white sauce. At once Bobby Hayes's father attacked a mussel with his butter knife, lifting his elbows as he winkled out the little yellow clitoris of meat. Discreetly, I pushed my plate away. Martin Mullens was ignoring his own plate and studying me.

'We had a bit of an issue,' I heard myself say, 'with the site.'

'Oh,' Martin Mullens said. His expression did not change. At the head of the table, James Mullens raised his head and set down his phone.

'The workmen dug up some human remains,' I said.

'So I hear,' Martin Mullens said. He dabbed at his face with his napkin. He had the lips, I noticed, of a reformed smoker:

the yellowish cast, the tributary creases. 'Prehistoric, I gather,' he said, his gaze unwavering.

'They didn't look prehistoric,' I said.

'Well, how would you judge?' Martin Mullens said. 'You'd need an expert eye for that sort of thing.'

'Oh, I think you can tell,' I said. 'You don't need to be an expert to recognise human bones. They make a pretty recognisable shape.'

What was I doing? Was I *trying* to queer the deal? Martin Mullens took off his reading glasses and lowered his chin, as if to say, *This is hardly appropriate dinner conversation.*

Acting under a compulsion that I didn't fully understand, I pressed my point. 'A hand, for instance. You'd recognise a human hand, if you dug it up.'

And then Martin Mullens did something so strange that, for a long time afterwards, I wasn't 100 per cent sure that I'd actually seen it. He raised his right hand and, spreading his fingers, tugged on each one with his left thumb and forefinger.

'This little piggy went to market,' he said. 'And this little piggy stayed at home. This little piggy had roast beef. And this little piggy had none. And *this* little piggy went *wheee-wheee-wheee-wheee.* All the way home.'

Around us, after a moment, general conversation resumed.

Somehow – my will bolstered by another Adderall or three – I made it through dinner. As soon as I decently could, I hobbled outside for a smoke. Under the awning, among the pruned greenery, I found James Mullens. He was holding his phone but not looking at it. He was also smoking. This was new. Seeing me, he waved a dismissive hand. But I stood my ground. Above us the awning dripped with recently fallen rain.

'I hope this dinner is on expenses,' I said, 'because I still haven't been paid.'

'What's wrong with you?' Mullens said. 'You look like fucking Frankenstein's monster. You're in there babbling all sorts of shit. If you can't manage to keep yourself together, you should just stay home.'

'Don't get pissy with *me*,' I said. 'You're the one who's not keeping it together. All you're doing is staring at your phone. Everyone else might be too stupid to notice but I'm not. You're worried Vuk and those lads aren't going to fall for it. You're worried the money's not going to come through.'

'Ha,' Mullens said. His cigarette crackled in the rain-damp air. 'Nothing gets past you.'

'Then tell me what the fuck's wrong,' I said.

'I broke up with Nikki,' Mullens said.

'Oh,' I said.

We looked out at the street. A hundred yards away I picked out Sean Sweeney and Bobby Hayes, using an ATM. From Mullens's tone I inferred that it was Nikki who had initiated the breakup. Presumably she was looking for a better boyfriend. Presumably she was looking for me.

'I'm sorry,' I said.

Mullens looked briefly nihilistic. 'You win some, you lose some.'

'Did she, uh,' I said. 'Did she give you a reason?'

Mullens shook his head. 'It was mutual, man, all right?'

'Of course,' I said.

Down the street, Hayeser and Sweeney had concluded their business with the ATM and were now strolling back towards the restaurant, shoving one another like kids with a secret, and looking speculatively at the queue of costly cars parked by the kerb. Above them, like the promise of a better world, was the dusk-tinged, luminous, expectant evening.

'Women are weird,' Mullens said. 'They're all, like, you should be completely honest with me. But when you actually tell them the truth, they lose their fucking minds.'

'Yeah,' I said.

Bobby Hayes and Sean Sweeney were no longer walking towards us. They had stopped beside a black BMW roadster, and Sweeney was whispering in Hayeser's ear. Hayeser was clutching something in his hand, something that looked like a piece of paper. Sweeney pointed to the parking ticket propped up behind the roadster's windscreen. Then he pointed to his watch – the gold Rolex that he had inherited from his paternal grandfather and of which he was volubly proud – as if to say, *Time's almost up*. Bobby Hayes scanned the street and looked down at the piece of paper in his hand.

'Anyway,' Mullens said. 'Don't mention it to the other lads, yeah? Not tonight, anyway.'

Bobby Hayes wasn't holding a piece of paper, I now saw. He was holding a banknote. A purple and white banknote, which would make it a €500 bill.

Mullens dropped his cigarette and turned to go. 'State of those cunts,' he said, nodding towards Hayeser and Sweeney.

'You should tell them to stop,' I said.

But Mullens merely frowned and, opening the door of the restaurant, stepped inside.

Twenty yards away, Bobby Hayes was now kneeling beside the roadster's front tyre, and Sean Sweeney had braced himself against the rear fender. I felt dizzy. Someone had turned up the gravity and the earth was pulling me downwards with all its buried magnetic force. Sweeney, red-faced as he nudged the car forward like a hooker in a scrum, was smiling, his white teeth bared. I ditched my smoke and began to walk away, towards home, towards The Brokerage, and soon I was running, through the rising wind and the failing light, and the leaves on the trees were turning blue and then grey, and then a darker grey, and then they turned altogether black against the deeper black of the evening sky.

'You ran away,' Dr Felix said. We had left his office and now we were walking in the clinic grounds. We passed a stand of silver birches. The birches stood, loosely jacketed in their onionskin bark. It was evening here, too. I tightened the belt of my therapeutic robe. If anyone had spied us from the windows of the main building it might have looked as if Dr Felix was taking a stroll with his own sad ghost. 'There's a pattern here,' Dr F continued. 'You ran away from your father's arrest. You ran away from Clio, in a sense, by refusing to have sex with her. Or by refusing to take her seriously as a human being. You ran away from your job in the call centre. You ran away from your father's trial. You ran away from the strip club in Belgrade. You ran away from what you discovered at the building site.'

'Okay,' I said. 'Enough.'

'And of course, in the largest sense,' Dr Felix said, 'you ran away from the world by taking drugs all the time.'

'I thought you were supposed to run away from dangerous things,' I said. 'Basic survival instinct.'

'Cowardice,' Dr Felix said.

'But some of that stuff was just bigger than me,' I said. 'It was a mass grave, for Christ's sake. That's a . . . that's a world-historical tragedy. Those people actually died, whoever they were. Doesn't that put all my bullshit in, I don't know, in perspective?'

'First we look at the self,' Dr Felix said. 'Then we address the world. If you do it the other way around, the self gets lost.'

For a while we kicked and crashed our way through a dross of fallen leaves in silence. Dr Felix walked with his hands in his pockets. His physical presence – have I admitted this before? – gives me a strange sense of security. Sometimes I have to stop myself from reaching out to take his hand.

'I wonder,' he said, 'at what point you realised that your plan didn't actually exist. That it was just our old friend the Geographical Solution in a new dress. Move abroad

somewhere and get clean. You never chose a specific destination, did you? For your new life?' I said nothing. 'You never
asked how much money, exactly, you were supposed to get
from the deal. You never even looked into how Mr Mullens's
scam was supposed to work. Do you see the pattern?'

We were rounding the ornamental fountain, with its head-
piece of urinating cherubs. I did not speak.

'There was a plan,' Dr Felix said. 'It just wasn't yours.'

And now things began to happen very quickly, as if some
crucial joist or tendon had at last been cut and there was no
longer anything left to impede my fall. When I got home,
The Brokerage penthouse was empty. I crawled into bed
and dialled Clio's number. 'I left you a voicemail,' she said.
'We're doing two extra nights. We got this amazing review
in the *Irish Times* and this, like, refugee charity got in touch
to sponsor us. I know we need to have a conversation. But I
think it's better for us to wait. Okay?' There was more in this
vein. When next I tuned in to my own activities, I was in the
kitchen, using a mortar and pestle set (and where had *that*
come from?) to grind up a mixture of Xanax and Solpadol,
and the pain in my side had returned, and then I appear to
have toddled into the bathroom to take a piss. I stood over
the bowl, waiting for the contents of my bladder to seep past
the permanently pill-pinched valves or vesicles of my urinary
tract, and in the mirror I saw the hulking shape of a man in a
brown trenchcoat standing in the wet-room stall, and when
my urine finally began to flow, it was the colour of cranberry

juice, which was not, I thought, at all a good sign. Another ellipsis follows, and I am in the four-poster bed, thrashing my way through a sequence of slasher-movie dreams, calling out for my father, and then ...

My phone rang. 'Hello,' said a cheerful male voice. 'Am I speaking to Mr Benjamin [REDACTED]?'

I opened my eyes to fading daylight. The air of my bedroom looked hazy, as if someone had been smoking in it for weeks. I lurched upright and dropped my phone. When I once again succeeded in pressing it to my ear, the voice was still speaking. '... Brian from Allied Hibernian Bank. How are you today?'

'Oh, shit,' I said. 'Look, if this is about me bouncing my rent, I'll have it by tomorrow. There was, eh, there was a temporary cash-flow issue.'

But Brian from Allied Hibernian Bank needed to confirm a few details for security purposes. As he wittered on I retrieved a crooked Marlboro from one of Clio's half-dozen handbags. Every inhalation caused the pain in my side to grow in scope and depth. 'Yeah, yeah,' I said, waving a hand like one of the barristers at my father's trial. Half-attending to Brian's questions, I gibbered on about a delay with my salary and Mullens's promise of a direct transfer.

I was (I think) aware, at a subliminal level, that Allied Hibernian was not, in fact, my bank, and that there was no obvious reason for them to call me. To the extent that I gave this mystery any actual thought, I assumed that

Allied Hibernian was my landlord's bank. Which still didn't explain why they seemed to have my personal details on file.

'So, following on from that,' Brian from Allied Hibernian said, 'would I be able to confirm that you are Benjamin [REDACTED], the sole trader responsible for the assets and liabilities of Echo Holdings LLC?'

'Yes,' I said. 'Wait. I mean no. No, I *work* for Echo *REIT*.'

'So just to confirm,' Brian from Allied Hibernian said, 'that on the twenty-seventh of July this year you were the sole signatory of a short-term loan facility document with ourselves for the purposes of developing property overseas?'

'Oh, this is a work thing,' I said. 'You don't want me. You want James Mullens.'

'And it's yourself who's the director of Echo Holdings,' Brian from Allied Hibernian said.

'What? No. No no no. Mullens is the director. I can give you his number.' I scrabbled among the nightstand detritus for a pen and paper.

'As I'm sure you're aware,' Brian from Allied Hibernian droned on, 'if there *are* other named directors of the company, there's a regulatory requirement that—'

'Hang on,' I said. 'Why am I giving you Mullens's number? You fucking *have* his number. Whatever it is, just call him, okay?'

Brian was undaunted. 'The reason for my call, Mr [REDACTED], is that we've received a communication from your solicitors to the effect that the overseas development deal has fallen through. And as you obviously know, in the event of noncompliance by either party, the bridging loan is scheduled for full repayment within seventy-two hours of notification.'

'Aha,' I said. 'Ha ha. I get it. You're taking the piss. Sweeney told you to do this, didn't he?'

Brian remained doggedly upbeat. 'I'm sure you're aware, Mr [REDACTED], of the communication dated this morning, originating with Sliney and Nihill, corporate solicitors, informing ourselves and other interested parties of a halt to on-site construction at a location near Iriski Venac in Serbia, pending further investigation into certain legal matters . . .'

I was now pacing the devastated kitchen, looking for another smoke. For some reason, I was bristling with injured *amour-propre*. I thought: *Fuck this guy.* I rustled up a tone of plummy hauteur. 'Firstly,' I said, pointing a debater's finger at the ceiling, *'firstly,* I'm not even a hundred per cent sure you've got the right guy here. Secondly, assuming you do have the right guy – and can I just say that your intel on this is all over the shop – assuming you do have the right man, I can tell you that *A,* the deal hasn't fucking fallen through, and, and fucking *B,* we talked to the investment partners yesterday, and they said everything was fine.' I had found a Marlboro Light. Having misplaced my lighter, I bent to the gas stove and lit the hob.

Brian's tone became noticeably less warm. 'Nonetheless,' he said, 'in the light of the communication from Sliney this morning, we're compelled to act in full compliance with the terms of the loan facility letter, and as the sole signatory of said letter it falls to you to provide us with restitution of the borrowed funds.'

'Restitution?' I said. 'What the fuck are you talking about?'

'Under the clawback provision of the loan facility letter,' Brian said, 'which I think if you look at the letter you'll find in paragraph thirteen, subsection four point oh—'

'I never *signed* a fucking loan facility letter,' I said. 'So obviously I don't *have* it in *front* of me.'

'This is just a courtesy call, Mr [REDACTED],' Brian said. 'To make you aware that you have seventy-two hours to provide the funds in full. But given your behaviour I feel I have to advise you that if restitution of the funds is not forthcoming, we will be forced to pursue legal action.'

'I don't know where to start with this,' I said. 'I'm an employee of Echo REIT. That's R-E-I-T, as in real estate investment trust. I'm not the company director. I'm not the signatory of the loan facility letter and I don't know where you'd get the idea that I am. *I have no idea what you're talking about.*'

With a sudden chill shock of fear, I remembered what Nikki had said in the airport. Something about a REIT only working if it was publicly traded. Something about being very careful what I signed.

'You signed a personal guarantee,' Brian said. All bonhomie had now been drained from his tone. 'This would have been made clear to you when you met with our business advisor.'

'But I *didn't* meet with your business advisor,' I said. 'I want to see this fucking loan facility letter you're banging on about.'

Brian was now brusque. 'You took out a bridging loan of five hundred and thirty-five thousand euro,' he said. 'The deal didn't go through. Now it's a simple matter of returning the unspent funds. If you'd like to meet with me personally, I'd be happy to arrange that.'

'I don't want to fucking meet with you personally,' I said, 'because I never borrowed five hundred and thirty-five fucking thousand—'

I stopped. Something seemed to have happened to the kitchen – to the air, the objects, the furniture. Behind my back – on the sly – everything seemed to have been replaced with a blasphemous mockery of itself. That cup, with its grey rime of ash. The refrigerator, with its grey coating of artificial steel. These things had been pasted up, like wallpaper, to hide the truth, and now the wallpaper was curling at the edges and the truth was peeping through. It was as if the visible world had at last shirked all pretence and confessed that it had been, all along, merely the flimsiest – the least convincing – of masks.

'I want to see the letter,' I said, swallowing the taste of bile. 'I want to see every document you say I signed.'

'As I say,' Brian from Allied Hibernian said, 'I'd be happy to arrange a meeting—'

'Everything,' I said. 'The contracts. The stuff from the Department of Foreign Affairs. Everything.'

'I wouldn't have access to those particular documents,' Brian from Allied Hibernian said. 'You'd have to speak to your solicitors.'

'You bet your fucking tits I will,' I said, and hung up.

Immediately I called James Mullens. 'The number you have dialled,' said a reproving, schoolmarmish voice, 'is not in service.'

I called Sean Sweeney. 'The number you have dialled is not—'

I called Bobby Hayes. 'The number you have dialled—'

I called Mark Foley. 'The number you—'

I called Paul Tynan. 'The number—'

I struggled into a pair of trainers and strode out into the corridor, where I banged for fifteen fruitless minutes on the door of Sweeney's penthouse. At length the door of a neighbouring apartment opened and a middle-aged man in a dressing gown popped his head out to say, 'He's not there. Stop banging on the fucking door.'

Dismissing this with a raised middle finger, I dialled James Mullens once again. 'The number you have dialled is not in service,' said the electronic schoolmarm.

Opening my laptop – and Xing out of seven tabs of previously loaded porn – I typed *Echo REIT* into the search box. *Did you mean Echo Realty?* the search engine asked politely. I clicked on *Echo Realty*. It was an American firm. There was also *Echo Investment*. But they were headquartered in Warsaw. I typed *Echo REIT Dublin James Mullens*. This produced a page of results about Mullens's career with Standish, Curran, and nothing else.

Puffing furiously on another Marlboro, I tried various iterations of *Echo Holdings LLC*. In the history of the internet the phrase had been used only once, in some small print tucked away on the website of the Companies Registration Office. What did all this mean? It meant that Echo REIT did not exist and had never existed. I had been working for a ghost company.

In a moment of inspiration I found Nikki's work email address on a careers site and tapped out a desperate message: *Was James scamming everyone??? Please you have to tell me!* But as soon as I clicked SEND I received an Out of Office reply: *I will be out of the country for the next few weeks with sporadic access to emails. If your message is important …*

I called Nikki's number. 'The person you are trying to reach,' said the voice, 'is not accessible at the moment.' At last – I was now panicking – I called Clio and got her voice-mail. 'I'm in rehearsals right now,' this went, 'so leave a message and I'll call you back!' I tried to calm myself with a deep breath. There seemed to be some sort of burr or barrier obstructing the entrance to my windpipe. The walls of the penthouse looked glaucous, dream-lit. *All fake*, I thought. *Rehearsals. Clio's play.* I was running for the lift.

'They took out a loan in your name and used it to pay for everything,' Dr Felix said. We had completed our circuit of the grounds. Night had fallen. 'Your salary. Renting the offices. Renting apartments for themselves. The flights to Belgrade. The hotel rooms. Probably the launch at the Shelbourne. There was never going to be a payout. You were depending on imaginary money.'

'Not just the money,' I said. 'It was all imaginary. My whole life. I was wrong about everything.'

'Good,' Dr Felix said. 'Excellent. When you've already gotten everything wrong, you can start to get things right. You can start to grow.'

'When you've already gotten everything wrong,' I said, 'there's nowhere left to grow.'

'I was addicted to heroin for five years,' Dr Felix said. 'I was supposed to be studying medicine at UCD. I dropped out. I lived in squats with people I only cared about because they were addicted to heroin, too. I came from a middle-class family. But I didn't seem to want the life that my parents were offering me. At the time I would have told you that they were hypocrites. They had no idea what reality looked like. But there I was. Shooting up to avoid reality.'

I said nothing. This was the first time that Dr Felix had ever told me anything about himself. Worse: I had never asked.

'How did I get out of my trap, you obviously want to ask,' Dr Felix said. 'My mother died. After that, I was free to think about what kind of person she'd been. And therefore, to some extent, what kind of person I was. It wasn't exactly what I'd call a fun experience. But it led me out of myself. It led me back to college. Eventually it led me to a doctoral degree in clinical psychology, with a specialism in addictive behaviours. First we gain self-knowledge. Then we address the world.'

'So,' I said, 'you're saying, kill my mother.'

'Glib,' Dr Felix said. 'Glib, glib, glib.'

'Why do you want me to get better, anyway?' I said.

'I just told you,' Dr Felix said.

'I must have missed that,' I said.

Dr Felix exhaled a long, fatalistic sigh. 'You said you felt as if the world was wearing a mask,' he said.

'It was,' I said.

'And then the mask came off.'

'The horror, the horror,' I said, dryly.

'That was what you saw beneath the mask?' Dr Felix said. 'The heart of darkness?'

'The world is poison,' I said.

'No,' Dr Felix said. 'The world is just the world. Some parts are poison. Many parts are not. Of course, you're wrong about all this, anyway.' He knelt to retrieve a stone from the gravel path and hurled it into the darkness. 'It wasn't the world that was wearing a mask. It was you.'

Arriving at the theatre in Temple Bar ten minutes before showtime, I muscled past the ticket-takers and spent several minutes panicking my way around the maze of backstage corridors until I at last located Clio. She was sitting on an upturned plastic bucket beneath the cinched folds of a tall black curtain and moving her lips in a sequence of warm-up exercises: *Unique New York, Unique New York.* She looked, to my startled eyes, like a complete stranger. It was borne in upon me that we had not exactly been acting like a couple in recent weeks. I blamed myself. I had been a terrible boyfriend – selfish and preoccupied. As I threw my arms around her I felt, perhaps somewhere in the region of my heart (but who could tell?), a burst of mingled affection and pity and regret. For quite a long time, I realised, I had wanted Clio to go away and stop complicating my life. But this was foolish. What I should have been looking for was Clio's help – the sort of help that she had given me all those months ago, when, jobless and penniless, I had been forced to move out of my parents' house and needed desperately for someone to take me in hand. My beloved Clio: she had saved me before. She would save me again. Full disclosure: I had taken an Adderall in the cab, to pep myself up in this time of crisis.

'I think something's gone badly wrong,' I said.

'Oh,' Clio said. 'You're here.' She was looking at me with a peculiar intensity, as if she expected me to puzzle something out.

'Give me your phone,' I said. 'I think there's something wrong with mine.'

Wordlessly, Clio surrendered her phone. I thumbed James Mullens's number into the keypad. *The number you have dialled is not—*

'*Fuck*,' I said with maximum vehemence.

'Ben,' Clio said. 'We're going up in five minutes and you're kind of stressing me out.'

'I don't know what to do,' I said. I pressed a palm to my

forehead and massaged the sweat I found there into the hair of my crown. I was uncomfortably aware of a pressure building in the tendons of my neck. 'I'm on the hook,' I said. 'I'm on the fucking hook.'

'You have to stop shouting,' Clio said. 'You're freaking people out.'

'*I'm* freaked out,' I said. '*I'm* freaked out. I can't get in touch with anyone. Nobody's answering the fucking phone. Their phones aren't even in *service*!'

'Oh,' Clio said. 'This is a work thing.'

'No, it's not a fucking work thing!' I said. 'The bank called me two hours ago to say I owe them half a million euro! And it's fucking *Mullens* who owes them half a million euro! This isn't a work thing! This is my *life*!'

Clio now wore an expression of distant pity. 'I don't know how shouting at me is going to fix it,' she said.

Taking the hint, I endeavoured to moderate my tone. 'I just need you to be my girlfriend here,' I said. 'I need you to sit down with me and help me figure this out. We need to go to Sliney and Nihill and get some of the documents I signed, then I can show them to Allied Hibernian and we can get this cleared up. And we need to go to James Mullens's house' (saying this I realised at once that I had no idea where James Mullens actually lived but neither I nor the speed that I had recently taken were going to let such a paltry detail get in my way) 'and punch the cunt in his smarmy fucking face.'

'I'm sorry this isn't working out for you,' Clio said. 'But I have to go on stage. The reviewer from the *Independent* is here.'

'I know you've got your play,' I said irritably. 'I don't mean right this second. I mean when the show is over or whatever.'

On Clio's face was a look that I have, since I first woke up in St Augustine and was forced to spend time in the company of mental-health professionals of various stripes, learned to recognise. It is a look that combines pity and understanding – a look, above all, that tells you that you are no longer fooling anyone. Seeing this look, I realised that it was the first thing I had seen – really *seen* – Clio do in a long time. I had used her when I was at my worst and then I had been too afraid to dump her, and she knew this – she had probably known it all along.

'Whatever you've got yourself into,' she said, 'I can't help you with it. It's not my job anymore.'

'But I need you,' I said. One last roll of the dice. 'You're my girlfriend.'

'But I'm not your girlfriend,' Clio said.

'What?' I said. The lights above us flickered. 'What did you say?'

'I tried to talk to you about this,' Clio said. 'Don't you remember? I told you at the party the other night. I said I think you need, like, proper psychiatric help, and I just can't be with someone who basically just refuses to address their mental health and treats me like shit because of it. I deserve better than that.'

'My *mental health*?' I said.

'You're a drug addict, Ben,' Clio said. 'You're a drug addict and you act like you hate me.'

'*I'm* an addict? You're the one who introduced me to drugs in the first place! We spent the first six months of our relationship fucked out of our game!'

Clio's face was now expressionless. 'We were together for almost a year,' she said. 'What happens to people once a year, Ben?'

I was lost. 'What the fuck are you *talking* about?'

'People have birthdays. Once a year. I thought you were going to surprise me. But you never even asked *when my birthday was.*'

'Okay,' I said. 'Okay. Okay. Let's say I do have a small drug problem.' (When in doubt, meet your accuser halfway.) 'Let's say I'm self-medicating. But you have to listen to me. I have a *plan.* I'm going to make a lot of money from this Serbian deal. Like, high seven figures. And I want you to come with me. I'm moving away and I want you to come with me. I'll make it up to you. We can do *two* birthday parties next year.'

'It's too late,' Clio said. Her shrug was eloquently simple. 'We're over.'

I placed a palm on either side of my head in what psychiatrists call a gesture of self-comfort. 'This doesn't make any sense,' I said.

'We talked about this,' Clio said. 'Remember? I'm seeing David now.'

'Fuck off,' I said. 'Wait. Hang on. Who the fuck is David?'

'The director,' Clio said. 'I told you. We had this overpowering attraction and we fought it for ages and ages but eventually we just had to go with our hearts.'

'What the fuck are you talking about?' I said. The speed was sticking my teeth together. 'You're still living in my fucking apartment.'

'We *talked* about this,' Clio said. 'I'm staying there until David gets his new place sorted. You were okay with it. I said we weren't good for each other anymore and you agreed with me.'

I laughed and continued laughing. Oh yes, here it was, the bad news, and it was just so goddamn *funny*. 'You were fucking this guy all along!' I said, through my snorts and hoots.

'Only for the last few weeks,' Clio said. 'I thought you knew.'

'I knew *nothing*,' I said. My laughter had reached a hysterical zenith. 'I thought you were fucking *Baz*.'

'Me and Baz had a thing,' Clio said. 'But that didn't mean anything. It's totally over.'

'Oh,' I said, still laughing. 'Well *that's* a fucking relief. Fucking *David*.'

My laughter began to abrade my lungs. I propped myself on my knees and massaged my sternum with the heel of my hand.

'Oh my God,' Clio said. 'I can't believe I had to break up with you twice.'

It was showtime. The lights in the corridor went out.

More Memory Machine shenanigans. A conversation with Clio – this would have been a week or two before I flew to Belgrade, a week or two before I jetted off to make my rendezvous with disaster in the White City. We were in my apartment at The Brokerage. I was complaining about my parents while Clio ordered dinner on her phone. I had just that afternoon scanned a brief interview that my father had given to a reporter from the *Irish Examiner*. He had, as far as I could tell, spoken almost entirely in cretinous orotundities. He had made a big production out of refusing to comment on the charges or the trial. 'If he didn't *do* it,' I said, 'then why doesn't he just fucking *say* so? Why does he have to be so fucking obtuse about everything?'

Clio swiped and thumbed. 'You tell me,' she said.

'What does that mean?'

'Nothing,' Clio said.

'No,' I said. 'Go on.'

A half-smile. 'It's not like you're not like him, you know. You can be obtuse when you feel like it.'

'No I can't,' I said, folding my arms.

'Like, strategically obtuse. Anyway, I think you're like him. You look like him. You have the same front teeth and the same eyebrows. Plus you both think you're keeping yourselves hidden from everyone. But you're not, really.'

'How would you know,' I said, 'about what I keep hidden?'

I had tried to sound playful. But I had ended up sounding cruel.

'Will I get prawn crackers?' Clio said after a moment.

At this point, Dr F, you might perhaps have expected me to swing into action – to call the cops, or Interpol, or to set about tracking down James Mullens, determined to get to the bottom of things and to extricate myself from my burden of debt. Instead – clinging to the old life, which had served me so poorly for so long – I went out and got wrecked. Bribing my way into a series of decreasingly classy bars and nightclubs, I made a sizable dent in the stock of drugs I had purchased from Baz's friend Mick. I also spent most of the money that remained in my bank account. At three o'clock in the morning I paid a flying visit to the emergency room of St Vincent's Hospital, where I told a kindly subcontinental nurse that I no longer believed in observable reality and was forced to argue my way out of a psychiatric referral. At five o'clock in the morning I chased two young men along George's Street, shouting that they had solved the problem of meaning and that I wanted to learn their secret. I had mistaken them for the Mormon missionaries I had seen while waiting to buy drugs from Mick a couple of days before. Finally, at 9 a.m., I found myself in an early house on the north quays, drinking alongside the night-shift workers in their overalls and suits. Here, recollected at last to my purpose, I formulated a plan. The Dublin headquarters of Sliney & Nihill, corporate solicitors, was located in the docklands. I would storm down there and demand to see some documents: contracts, plans, loan facility letters. So many of the papers I had signed had borne the curlicued logo of S&L. Once I could examine these papers properly, we could begin to get this bullshit straightened out.

Outside, I hailed a cab and gave the driver a largely coherent account of where I wanted to go. As we zoomed though the light-sluiced streets I shook the contents of my pharmacopeia onto my lap. Here, too, matters had reached a point of crisis. Aside from a dozen or so Xanax, all I had left was the bag of mysterious white powder that I had purchased from Mick in the Brown Thomas underground car park. What had he called it? AMT? Reasoning that I needed something to perk me up (and to counteract all the beer and whiskey that I had forlornly consumed in the early house), I measured out a pinkie's worth and snorted it.

'What the fuck are you doing?' my taxi driver said, goggling at me in the rear-view mirror.

'Waking myself up,' I said. Still studying the mirror, I watched myself make an assortment of interesting faces as the drug began to tingle and burn its way along my mucous membranes.

'Don't let the Guards see you doing that,' the driver said. His moustache twitched.

'My girlfriend dumped me,' I said, huffing and sniffing. 'And my friends are all crooks.'

'I'm sorry to hear that,' the driver said. 'But I hope you don't mind me saying, you're not doing yourself any favours with that shit.'

We had arrived outside a cuboid building of louchely tinted glass.

'I know what I'm doing,' I said, tossing a €50 note into the passenger seat.

Back into the Memory Machine, as my subconscious rises, or sinks, to the occasion: I am fifteen, and it is the morning of my first Junior Cert exam, and it is raining, and my father has taken the morning off work to drive me to school.

The car sloshed through the rain. My father hummed gently to himself, his left hand occasionally creeping towards the radio – in deference to my need for a few last minutes of revision, he had listened only to the half-hour business head-lines on *Morning Ireland*, and then turned it off.

'Put it on if you want,' I said after a while.

'No, no, you need to concentrate.' He drummed on the steering wheel. 'I don't really remember my Junior Cert, I have to say. I remember my college exams, all right.'

'Dad, if you tell me the nun story again, I swear to God.'

'You know the nun story,' my father said. 'Of course you do.'

The nun story was that my father, in his first year at uni-versity, had made a point of befriending two fellow students who happened to be nuns. 'They had the best notes,' he said. 'I didn't even need to go to lectures. I just borrowed their notes. And you could have great chats with the nuns. Great chats.' This story would certainly have appeared on any album entitled *My Father's Anecdotes: The Greatest Hits*.

We were driving up the gently sloping driveway of Old Barbarian High, between the massed beeches, past the out-buildings with their seepage of greying ivy.

'I started out from nothing,' my father said. 'That's the point. No advantages. I came into Atlas knowing fuck-all. I had the idea that if you did a good job, you made your way up the ladder. But I got stuck. There I was, just trundling along.

409

For years I looked at the big lads, wondering what they were doing. Wondering what they knew that I didn't. And it took me years to realise it.'

I said nothing.

'I thought it was the job,' my father said. 'But it wasn't the job those lads were interested in. It was the money. They went for the money first, and the job was something they worried about later.'

The car coasted to a halt at the school's front doors.

'Break a leg,' my father said.

After the exam I stood with the rest of my Junior Cert class in the shelter of the portico, waiting for him to pick me up. I looked out across the empty rugby pitch at the beech trees. The massed leaves swarmed together in the summer rain, shifting and recombining like germs under a microscope. *No advantages*, my father had said. He seemed to have forgotten that he had been a student here. Lined up along the driveway, like a painting of a traffic jam done exclusively in shades of corporate grey, were the cars of the waiting fathers: the Mercs, the Beamers, the Landcruisers, the Lexuses, the Jaguars, the Rovers, the Alfa Romeos.

The lobby of Sliney & Nihill's HQ was a crypt of polished black granite. Behind a battleship-sized desk – also made of polished black granite – a blonde woman sat, wearing a taupe business suit that seemed to be 90 per cent lapel. As I approached the desk I felt myself sober up at triple speed. The AMT, like so much else, had been a con: caffeine powder, probably, mixed with monosodium glutamate. Not to worry: I could still assume the air of unhurried privilege available to an Old Barbarian, class of '09. 'Uh, yes, hello,' I said. 'My name is Benjamin [REDACTED] and I client for a company of yours – I mean I company for a client of yours – I mean Echo REIT, is a company client of yours.'

'Excuse me?' said the blonde woman (nametag: JEN). She seemed to be reaching for something underneath the desk: perhaps a panic button.

Things were not unfolding as smoothly as I had hoped they might. The problem, of course, was that I had stayed up all night, drinking and doing drugs, and therefore looked and sounded like a man who had stayed up all night, drinking and doing drugs.

'I'm sorry,' I said. 'I'll try that again. I work for Echo REIT, we're a client of yours.' Jen's hand retracted. 'I'm wondering if I could speak to whomever is our officer in charge of our case, if you know what I mean.'

'What's the company, sir?' Jen said. She was one of those people who filtered her voice through her nose.

'Echo REIT,' I said, adding, helpfully, 'Real Estate Investment Trust.'

Jen touch-typed without breaking eye contact. 'And do you have an appointment?' she said.

'No,' I said, 'but it's in a bit of an emergency and I'd appreciate whoever to have a meeting. With me. ASAP.'

'Echo . . . ?' Jen said, peering now in befuddlement at her matched plasma screens.

'Echo REIT,' I said. 'Maybe search under James Mullens. He's our CEO.' I sniffed. A sweet gob of whatever I had just snorted travelled slickly through my sinuses and dripped down the back of my throat, causing my gorge to rise.

Jen shook her head. 'I'm sorry, sir. And would you have been in touch with one of our client managers?'

'No, it wasn't *me*,' I said. 'It was *Mullens*. He was talking to everyone.'

'You're very welcome to make an appointment to meet with one of our client managers,' Jen said, 'but you'd have to call them directly.'

'I'm not trying to set up a new *account*,' I said. 'I'm trying to tell you, we already *have* an account. I want to see some fucking *documents*.'

Jen turned as stiff as a mummy. 'I have to say, sir,' she said, 'I don't appreciate your tone.'

'Listen to me,' I said. 'I signed a whole bunch of papers that said "Sliney and Nihill" on the top and I want to see them. I want to see what I signed.'

'As I say, sir,' Jen said, with icy civility, 'we have no record of your company. You must have mistaken us for somebody else.'

'No,' I said, 'I haven't mistaken you. Sliney and Nihill. You processed the paper on the deal.'

Jen was reaching once more for the panic switch.

'All right,' I said. 'Tell me something. Do you know who Martin Mullens is?' Jen's hand paused. 'Martin Mullens,' I said, in a *fuck-you* tone, 'is a major shareholder in our company and I know *for a fact* that he's a client of yours. So I want you to get somebody down here *right now* with the papers for the deal. Okay?'

Jen's mouth curled up at the edges. 'If you'll take a seat, sir,' she said, 'I'll make a call.'

I stationed myself in a nearby chair and watched, squinting like a yokel, while Jen whispered into her phone. Up above, a closed-circuit TV camera fixed me with its nonpartisan gaze. At last, the doors of the lift trundled open and two men emerged. The first was young, bespectacled, in shirtsleeves. The other, middle-aged, wore an ill-fitting blue jacket fringed with the gold braids and tassels of a private security firm. I stood. The shirtsleeved man shook my hand and then posed with his fists on his hips, as if to say, *What's to be done about this, eh?*

'Echo REIT,' he said. 'I'll be honest. We've never heard of you.'

Behind him, the security guard stood with his hands cupped over his balls and an apologetic look on his face.

'But I signed the papers,' I said. 'I even talked to Brian. You know, from Allied Hibernian. He said you had everything on file. The loan facility letter. Serbia. Iriski Venac. We're building a golf resort.'

The shirtsleeved man shook his head. A small scrap of bloodstained toilet tissue adhered to the underside of his poorly shaven jaw. 'Are you sure it was ourselves you were dealing with?'

'Am I sure?' I said. Perhaps it was the presence of recorded birdsong in the Sliney & Nihill lobby, or perhaps it was the lush greenery of the corporate landscaping (each black granite pillar, I now perceived, was draped with money-coloured moss), but I was afflicted, at that moment, by a vision of my dream: the millionaire's cabin in the woods, the freedom from financial woes, the hours of tidy solitude. Within me, some pivotal piece of scaffolding tottered and fell.

'Those cunts,' I said, or possibly shouted, and I must have gone on shouting because the next thing I knew, I was being manhandled through the revolving door. 'I want to speak to your top man!' I yelled. 'I want to speak to Sliney! I want to speak to Nihill! I want to see some fucking *PAPER!*'

'Fuck off out of it,' the security guard said. 'Fucking junkie.'

Then, hesitating, he patted me on the back as if it had just occurred to him that I had been given some very bad news.

'If I were you,' Dr Felix said, 'I'd feel relieved.'

'*Relieved?*' I said. It was almost midnight. We were dawdling over plastic cups of peppermint tea in the day room. Barring Piotr – the po-faced Ukrainian orderly or nurse – everyone else had gone to bed.

Dr Felix shrugged. 'There was no deal. You never did have the chance to escape to another country and live out the rest of your life in denial. I'd call that pretty good luck, wouldn't you?'

I shook my head in disbelief. 'I had no girlfriend. No friends. No family that I could rely on. No money. No job. Nowhere to live. What's lucky about that?'

'In other words,' Dr Felix said, 'all the things that people

414

conventionally find meaning in had proven, for you, to be illusions. You were radically free. You *are* radically free.'

I made a dismissive noise. 'You've spent three weeks telling me I'm enslaved to illegal substances. Which is it? Am I a slave, or am I free?'

'I'm trying to get you to see *why* you enslaved yourself to drugs,' Dr Felix said. 'I've dragged you to the water. I'm waiting for you to drink.'

'You're going to need to push my head in,' I said.

'Your parents,' Dr Felix said.

'What about my fucking parents?' I said.

'When you get angry,' Dr Felix said, 'that tells us something. What do you think it tells us?'

Night pressed against the day-room windows. I tried, once again, to speak.

What was I? I was an upper-middle-class person in trouble. So I did what upper-middle-class people in trouble do: I called my dad. His phone rang out. It was a weekday morning. He was probably in court. Through the cranes and vacant lots of the docklands a keen wind blew. My wallet contained ten Xanax and the last of my cash reserves: a €100 bill. I walked for perhaps two miles (ditching the bag of AMT in a gutter along the way) before I found a taxi driver who was willing to break a hundred. Curling into a ball in the back seat, I gave him my parents' address. 'Nice houses out there,' he said. Entering my parents' neighbourhood, I saw the familiar trained myrtle bush above the door, the familiar motorised gates. Here my father had served tea to the people who were protesting his alleged crimes. 'Really nice houses,' the driver said. I paid my fare, which left me with total cash reserves of €67.23.

My key still worked – I had fretted, in the cab, that I would get there to find that all the locks had been changed – but the house was empty. Not just empty, abandoned. The rooms were bare of furniture and the walls were bare of pictures. I looked into my father's study and saw no desk, no shelves, no rowing machine. A single lidless bankers box lay on its side, containing nothing. In the cupboard under the stairs I found a collapsible golfing trolley and a bottle of berry-flavoured sports drink. My bedroom had been denuded of posters and books.

In the kitchen, the only item of family furniture that remained was my father's model clipper ship, which sat in the middle of the floor, pointed stoutly towards the conservatory windows. I sat on the terracotta tiles with my head in my hands. No help, I thought. No help from any direction. Night was closing in. The garden was already silting up with dusk. I could hear the screech and titter of birds. The world was a jeering mockery. See the wallpaper peeling? Or, no: it was I who was the mockery – the fool, the mug, the mark. I was an easy target. The easiest. My mind was full of junk and my body was full of poisons and my phone was full of photographs of people I didn't recognise. I thought about the crooked little skeletons and saw, as if for the very first time, the impersonal malice of the matter-of-fact: the broken world with its broken people. I felt like Adam, naming the animals. *And this is betrayal and this is cruelty and this is hatred and this is stupidity and this is loneliness and this is fear.* My life was a tasteless joke scribbled in the margins of a tragedy. I could have no purchase even on my own humiliation and disgust – how could I dare, in the face of the thing that I had seen, the thing from which I had averted my gaze with greed and fear in my heart?

I was now lying flat on the hard-tiled floor. A rectangular shape was jabbing me in the hip. It was Aleks's book of poetry. I had kept it with me, in the pocket of my coat. *Book is totem*, he had said. I turned to the handwritten message on the flyleaf: *Call if needed*, and a number.

'If needed,' I said aloud, and keyed in the digits. What did I expect? More defeat. More nothing.

'*Zdravo*,' said a male voice.

'Aleks?' I said.

'*Da*,' the voice said. 'This is Aleks.'

'Aleks,' I said. 'It's me. It's Ben.'

There was a scrabbling sound. '*Da*,' Aleks said again. 'Ben of Irish. Is very good to hear of you.'

'Aleks,' I said. 'I'm in trouble.'

'You are finding fraudulence of deal,' Aleks said.

The kitchen was now mostly dark. I could hear my own ragged breathing. 'You knew,' I said.

'*Da*,' Aleks said, 'this I was aware of.'

'Holy Christ,' I said. 'Why didn't you fucking *tell* me?'

'Is situation of extreme delicacy,' Aleks said. 'Is not for discussing over telephone. You have proof of fraudulence?'

417

'What?' I said. 'No, I don't have proof. I tried to get the contracts but there aren't any. They were all fake.'

From my pocket I took my copy of the Memorandum of Understanding – signed by Mullens, signed by me. I scrunched it up into a ball and threw it at the model clipper ship. It lodged in the rigging, like a miniature bird's nest.

'This is not problem,' Aleks said, after a moment. 'Is of most crucial importance that you come to Belgrade now. As soon as available.'

'I can't come to Belgrade,' I said. 'I'm broke. There wasn't any money. It was all a scam.'

More scrabbling. I heard voices in the background. 'We will pay for you to be on next flight to Belgrade,' Aleks said. 'This may involve your transferral at airport of Frankfurt.'

'Frankfurt,' I said. 'What the fuck are you talking about? How can you pay for flights? I thought you were a poet.'

'Is availability of funds,' Aleks said. 'Please not to worry.'

'Aleks,' I said, 'what's happening? How did you know about this?'

'We are getting information of flight,' Aleks said. 'Will have in one minutes. I must ask you please to come. To prevail upon kindness of friendship.'

'... I can't,' I said in a hoarse whimper. 'I'm afraid this is just another trick.'

'Time of tricks is over,' Aleks said. 'As matter of your legal safety, we recommend in strongest terms you travel here to us.'

'My legal safety,' I repeated.

'I must ask you, please,' Aleks said. 'Is not much time.

We are sending tickets. Please to give us your address of email.'

I said nothing. The line ticked patiently.

'Aleks,' I said at last. 'Who's "we"?'

The Memory Deluge continues. All out of order now. No time to give it shape. I was, I think, thirteen or so when my mother enlisted me, for the first and only time, as a factotum at one of her charity lunches. This one was being held in a function room of the old Montrose Hotel in Stillorgan, since gutted and turned into student accommodation, in obedience to the rule that every building in Dublin must be transformed by the abstract movements of money every twenty years or so. The charity lunches began shortly after my father sold the family farm and the influx of money began to lift all three of us upwards, like boats on a spring tide. They were my mother's hobby, or her job. From her command post at the dining-room table she booked venues, sent invitations, chose colour schemes. At breakfast, for several years running, I ate my cereal surrounded by stacks of violet-scented thank-you notes or menus written out in calligraphy. The Montrose event was typical. A catered lunch. A sommelier dispensing curated wines. A speech by a writer or a campaigner or a former president. My jobs were minor: check place cards, take coats. I was bored, of course. I passed the time by auditioning new attitudes internally. Look at these hypocrites, with their fur coats and their fake laughs! They knew nothing about real life! Already the literary man. I suffered through the speeches, the toasts. I hung around looking sullen while my mother talked to her friends. It was a Saturday afternoon. I wanted to be at home, watching TV. At four o'clock my mother was still standing in the middle of a group of women – the stragglers. I tried to catch her eye. Time to go, Mum! She had fallen silent and was staring into space. The muscles of her jaw were working. I realised that she was bored – that she was as bored as I was. I had an impulse to walk over and take her hand, to lead her to the car. Boys want to protect their mothers. It makes them feel like men. If I had been younger, I might have done it. But I was fourteen: young enough to feel the impulse, old enough to scorn it. When we did eventually make it to the car my mother turned the key in the ignition and sighed. 'I wish I still smoked,' she said. When we got home, the house was empty. My father was in work. He had begun to work on weekends. And in a sense, he never stopped. My mother was bored and my father was away. These were just the facts. Just the facts, just the facts, just the facts.

'I misread everything,' I said. 'Everything.'
   Dr Felix waited.
   'Because I didn't want to see,' I said.
   Dr Felix nodded.
   'Because it was too painful,' I said.
   Dr Felix waited.

My flight to Belgrade – there was, in the event, no need to connect through Frankfurt – was delayed by two hours. In the airport I popped a couple of Xanax and hung around a sequence of sports-themed bars, drinking and failing to get drunk. What else could I do? Here, in this departure lounge a week or so ago, I had run into Nikki, who had tried to warn me about Echo REIT – about the REIT that was not a REIT, about the contracts that were not contracts. The pain in my side had returned and was sending urgent signals to my crotch, my chest, my brain. My only luggage was Aleks's book. Beyond the rain-swept sloping windows, the sunset burned along the black horizon like a lit fuse. Foolishly, irrelevantly, uselessly, I thought: *Is there nothing on earth that's capable of keeping the promise of beauty?* Aleks, too, had tried to warn me. In the shadow of the TV tower at Iriski Venac, he had said it: *Inside they are not changed. Are still same men as before.* I had ignored him. I had ignored everything. I still had no idea what was happening, or who was responsible – though I swore to myself, gripping my wine glass tighter, that I would have my revenge on James Mullens, as soon as the opportunity arose. As I queued at the gate I caught a glimpse – did I? – of the tail-end of a brown trenchcoat, flapping out of sight behind the plastic bubble of a public payphone. I was running out of time.

My plane outraced the night and landed smoothly. No lightning, not this time. After the usual purgatorial interlude in passport control, and following a brief, unpleasant skirmish with the armed guards and their straining drug dogs, I passed through, into Arrivals. Waiting in the collection zone – holding up a sign that bore my name – was Boris, the driver.

In his war-torn Yuga Boris drove us deep into the concrete warren of downtown Belgrade. 'Where's Aleks?' I said as we bumped along. 'Is not safe for Aleks,' Boris said. I accepted this. I was accepting everything now. The black buildings of the white city smouldered under a bleached-clean sky. In the balconied squares, gangs of schoolgirls chewed on their uniform sleeves. Boris parked outside a tall, narrow house on a dead-end street and opened the Yuga's door for me with a bow.

'Is restaurant,' Boris said. 'We eat.'

I followed him down some rutted steps to a dimly illuminated basement. Through the tacky gloom I made out chequered tablecloths, candles dribbling in cheap tin cups. There were no other customers. Boris directed us to a table in the back.

'You're not a limo driver,' I said.

'I am *Bezbednosno-informativna agencija*,' Boris said. He was sitting opposite me. The grey skin, oxygen-deprived. The avuncular face with its demoralised moustache.

'Which means?' I prompted.

'Like American CIA,' Boris said. 'Agency of intelligence. Is good place for food.' He jutted his chin, indicating the restaurant. 'Also very good for coffee. Is serving best *espresso* in Belgrade.'

'You're a spy,' I said. 'And so is Aleks.'

'Aleks is not direct employee of *agencija*,' Boris said. 'Is more of helper. Is translating into English for good disguise.'

A middle-aged woman in a floral-print dress – she, too, had the grey skin and the demoralised moustache – clinked a silver pot and two demitasse cups onto the table.

'You were after Vuk,' I said.

Boris's nose twitched. 'Yes, for many years,' he said. 'Is perpetrator of war crimes. Leader of massacre during time of war.' He poured coffee into the cups. 'Is living for many years under false identity,' he said. 'We know of this identity but we do not have proof to link this man to crimes of war.'

'His name's not Vuk Mladic,' I said.

Boris shook his head. 'This is manufactured name,' he said. 'In reality he is man wanted by International Criminal Court since before many years. There is blood of many on his hands. When deal of business arrives with Irish, we are interested. We hear of involvement of Vuk Mladic and we think, opportunity has descended.' Boris lifted his cup and took a dainty sip. 'Is very good coffee,' he said. 'We offer Aleks as services for translation. To have man on inside. Aleksandr is patriot. He wishes to help in apprehension of such criminals who bring shame to Serbia.'

Is phenomenon of collective guilt, Aleks had said.

'What I want to know,' I said, 'is who set up this fucking deal? Was it James Mullens?'

'This we do not know,' Boris said. 'But is not relevant to our purposes.'

423

'It's fucking relevant to *my* purposes,' I said.

Boris offered the National Shrug. 'In movies, as they say, we follow money. We find origin of funds in Oslo. Before, *whoosh*. Gone like smoke.'

'Oslo,' I said. Someone had mentioned Oslo recently. Someone had been there, conducting business. 'Trade Exchange Holdings,' I said. I felt numb. My arms were tingling. 'Headquartered in Oslo.'

'This is name of company,' Boris said, nodding. 'Is what you call company of dummies. We send men to investigate. Is address but no office.'

I lit a cigarette. I thought: *Oslo Oslo Oslo.* Up from the Memory Void bubbled a salient fact. 'Martin Mullens,' I said, swallowing a mouthful of vomit. 'He was in Oslo last week.'

'Money passes from company of dummies in Oslo to accounts of Voivode Holdings,' Boris said. 'This also is company of dummies, owned by man of name Vuk Mladic. It is, what you say? Washed.'

'Laundered,' I said.

'Laundered,' Boris said. 'But this man, this Vuk Mladic. He is not interested in money. He is interested in disguising evidence of his crimes of war. He will build resort of golf on site of massacre, and bodies of the murdered will not be found. But he hires cheap men of work, who are also honest men of work. They find bones and know what they see. They are not to go along with his plan.'

'So the Mullens family wants to launder some money and Vuk – or whoever – wants to hide his mass grave,' I said.

424

'And they don't want a paper trail so they get me to sign everything. And they leave me on the hook. Those *cunts*. They probably transferred the funds when ... when we were in the horrible fucking hotel in Iriski Venac and Maria ...'

I nodded, once, in bleak comprehension. They had sent Maria to distract me while they conducted their secret business. And it had been a coincidence – it had been sheer moronic fucking happenstance – that I had run into her in the swimming pool at the exact appointed hour. By that stage, there had been no need to manipulate me. I had been perfectly capable of manipulating myself. Because – the inward avalanche continued – I was a junkie and a loser and a patsy and a joke. Who could I blame but myself?

'These things we are still investigating,' Boris said. 'Are still some aspects of fraudulent procedure unexplained. But construction of resort will not proceed. Was attempt by man of name Vuk Mladic to replace crew of construction. Beginning crew refuse to continue with building of resort. But now is state matter. Already examination of forensics is underway.'

'So where's Vuk?' I said. 'Where are Nicolae and Ratko?'

'These are not their names,' Boris said. 'Men of names Nicolae Surkov and Ratko Marković are in custody of police. Against them also we have been making evidence for many years. Are of much interest to International Criminal Court.' He drained his cup and made a small sound of appreciation: *Aaah!* 'Man of name Vuk Mladic,' he said, 'is in current location of rural hamlet in Republika Srpska, under surveillance of *Bezbednosno-informativna agencija*. Soon we will arrest.'

'What are you waiting for?' I said. I was outraged. 'Arrest the fucker. Give him the fucking electric chair.'

'We are following careful procedure,' Boris said. 'We do not want this man to get away. We are waiting on final assessment of evidence from state police. And we are waiting also for you.'

'Me?' I said. My cigarette fumed unattended in my hand.

'*Da,*' Boris said. 'You are eyewitness to discovery of murdered victims at site of construction. You are eyewitness also of fraudulent business of Dublin.'

'*I* can't help you,' I said. 'I don't know anything. I was just a fucking puppet.'

'Of this we are aware since before your arrival,' Boris said. 'We locate your name on signing of documents. We believe you have been chosen from beginning as expendable in transaction of deal. Job of Aleksandr is to discover purpose of your presence in Serbia. Also to establish contact and arrange your return when necessary. We are also establishing very soon that you have problem with abuse of drugs. This chooses you as suitable man of ignorance.'

'Man of ignorance,' I echoed flatly. 'So you want me to, what – testify?'

'We will need recording of statement for now,' Boris said. 'Perhaps in future we will arrange testimony in court of law.'

'You bet your fucking ass testimony in court of law,' I said. 'And I'll tell you what else I'm going to do. I'm going to go back to Dublin and report Martin Mullens and his cunt of a son to the fucking Guards. There's got to be a paper trail on that end, right? Something I can shove in their faces?' I stopped. Something new had occurred to me. 'The man in the brown trenchcoat,' I said. 'That was you guys, right?'

Boris was extricating a wad of chewing tobacco from a plastic pouch. He frowned. 'Of this I am not aware,' he said. 'Please explain.'

'You've been following me,' I said. 'In Dublin. I keep seeing a man in a brown trenchcoat. I thought I was hallucinating. But that was you, you fuckers.'

'We have not resources to extend to Dublin,' Boris said. He mashed a wad of tobacco into his left cheek and wiped his fingers inefficaciously on the lapels of his sports coat.

'Then who the fuck has been following me?' I said.

Boris chewed and shrugged.

'Great,' I said. 'That's just fucking great.'

The woman in the floral-print dress had returned, bearing plates of fruit-covered pastry. 'You eat,' Boris said. 'Is good.' He watched the woman's rear end as she walked away. 'Is mistress of many years,' he said, with a reminiscent twinkle. 'Maker of best cakes in Belgrade.'

'You had a plan,' Dr Felix said.

'Yes, I had a plan,' I said. 'I was going to go to the Echo REIT offices and get my work laptop. There were emails on there that mentioned Sliney and Nihill and all the rest of it. The designers, Healy-Dunlop. I was going to track down that

427

guy Alan, from Carrigan Stuart. He was Mullens's solicitor,
he was there when I signed the first load of papers. I was
going to talk to the police. Tell them whatever. Tell them to
get in touch with Serbian intelligence. I was going to sound
fucking mental but I didn't care. We had a launch in the
Shelbourne, for fuck's sake! It was in the fucking newspapers! I was going to call journalists and tell them it was all
a scam. That it was James Mullens and his father. They'd
cooked the whole thing up and I wasn't going to let them
get away with it.'

'You were still,' Dr Felix said, 'refusing to look.'

'You can't blame a man for trying,' I said.

'But none of that happened,' Dr Felix said.

'No,' I said. 'None of that happened.'

I mumbled my statement into Boris's 1980s-era Dictaphone –
The Lads, the Serbs, the crooked little skeletons. Then Boris
drove me back to Tesla. 'You make me think of joke,' he said,
as we parked in the taxi zone. 'In Serbia, we have animals
in our jokes. So. Bear and parrot are smoking a joint. The
bear asks the parrot, "So, parrot, do you feel anything yet?"
"Not yet," the parrot says. They are smoking more of joint.
"So, parrot," says the bear. "Do you feel anything now?"
The parrot says, "No. I feel nothing. Not my beak, not my
claws ..."'

'That's hilarious,' I said, and slammed the Yuga's door as
hard as I could.

*

428

The whole thing had been a set-up. Anyone less idiotic than I was might have seen it from the start. It began with a coincidence, or what I must assume to have been a coincidence: James Mullens ran into me in the bistro that day in June. He saw the state of my life. And it gave him an idea. He needed a mule to help him move the money. And there I was, just hanging around, like a huge oblivious gift waiting to be unwrapped. It had not been an accident that he had shown up at that rave on the Naas Road, pretending to be high. He had been following my movements. He tracked me down at BlueVista and he gave me the hard sell. Drowned me in money, knowing I would spend most of it on drugs. Knowing that I would be greedy and arrogant and blind. How had he found Vuk and Nicolae and Ratko? Did it matter? They were in on it, too. In fact, they had their own scam going. The scams interlocked, touching at various points: Oslo. Echo Lake. Me, of course. Because I could be trusted not to notice. I could be trusted not to see. This is the story of my life. I have been, I am, the more deceived. Strangely freeing, to write it down. But I'm not finished yet.

What was the point of Mullens's scam? Money, of course. *Money* being the answer to so many of our questions. Why don't you break up with your partner? Why do you spend eight hours a day in an ugly building, doing boring work? Why is that man sleeping on the street? Why were your parents so unhappy?

What exactly have you done with your life?

'I have something for you,' Dr Felix said. He produced a manila envelope stuffed with documents. Warily, I dumped them out on the day-room couch. Pamphlets, printed FAQ pages from websites, membership forms, job applications. Amnesty International. Irish Red Cross. Centre for Justice and Accountability.

'What's this?' I said.

'You owe a debt,' Dr Felix said. 'I know you understand what I'm saying. These are organisations that work with the survivors of war crimes. Not just in the former Yugoslavia. Everywhere. They work to remember the dead. They try to stop it happening again. Do you see what I'm saying?'

The arc lights. The men with their trains and trucks. The white city of the dead.

'Why would they want me?' I said. 'I'm nothing. I'm a fucking junkie. I've never achieved anything in my life. All I wanted to be was a writer and I fucked that up, just like I fucked up everything else.'

'This isn't "being a writer",' Dr Felix said. 'It isn't pretending to make something valuable while you sit around indulging your narcissism. This isn't the geographical solution. It's leaving the world a little bit better than you found it. Just the tiniest fragment better than it was.'

'I can't do this,' I said. 'I'm not qualified.'

'So make yourself qualified. Look beyond yourself.'

I shook my head.

'Not quite there yet, I see,' Dr Felix said. He sat back. 'All right. One more time.'

*

On the Serbian CIA's dime I flew back to Dublin. I spent the last of my cash on four rum-and-Cokes. I had scribbled Boris's contact details on the flyleaf of Aleks's book of poems. This I would give to the proper authorities in Ireland. Boris's imprimatur would, I felt, do a great deal to bolster my case. The plane heaved its way through the upper atmosphere. The clouds below were wrinkled, like a tidal flat. I was walking across them – trekking across an insubstantial desert where the sun never fails to shine. I must have fallen asleep. I must have dreamed. I was remembering a song that I had listened to as a child: *Underneath the lamplight, by the barrack gate/Darling, I remember the way you used to wait.* Who was the woman who used to sing that song? She sang it in a soft Irish voice. And I remembered: it was my mother and I must have been very small, because we were in my bedroom, and she was holding my hand as I fell asleep. We had loved each other once, all three of us, it had been very easy then. And the plane landed and I walked along the strip-lit enfilade of ads and out through baggage claim and passport check, and when I got to the other side of the customs channel the Man in the Brown Trenchcoat was waiting for me, as he had been waiting for me all along, here at the end of the line.

'Actually, I think we should call it a night,' Dr Felix said.

It was three o'clock in the morning. We were still in the day room. Between us on the Formica table was a Monopoly board with its coloured cards: Community Chest, Get Out of Jail Free. The fluorescent lights blinked and fizzed. Piotr the nurse had fallen asleep on one of the curved couches.

'Reconvene tomorrow,' Dr Felix said. 'It's your last day, anyway.'

'What do you mean, my last day?' I said.

'Your twenty-eight days are up,' Dr Felix said. 'Congratulations. No drugs for four weeks. You look bushy-tailed, if I may say so.'

'No drugs except these,' I said, rattling the plastic bottle that contained the fruits of Dr F's most recent prescription.

'Aspirin,' Dr Felix said. 'Good for your heart.'

'Oh, fuck you,' I said. I was on my feet.

'Fooled again,' Dr Felix said. 'Doesn't that piss you off?'

I threw the plastic bottle towards the windows. They crashed against the Venetian blinds. Piotr stirred in his sleep.

Dr Felix didn't blink. 'Go on,' he said.

'Go on with what?' I said in a dull voice. I could feel the muscles of my face assuming an ugly expression. I could feel my fingernails digging into the palms of my hands.

'Go on with your story,' Dr Felix said, 'so you can finish and leave. Get to the point so I can go to bed. I need to be up early to sign your discharge papers.' He held up an Amnesty International brochure. 'Take these with you. Or leave them here. I don't care anymore.'

'You're throwing me out?' I said. 'Where the fuck am I supposed to go?'

'You can go anywhere you want,' Dr Felix said. 'But you can't stay here.'

432

'And what about this?' I said. I held up this notebook – my true confessions. 'What was the point of this?'

'I'd burn it, if I were you,' Dr Felix said. 'It's the tomb of a delusion. Not worth reading. Exorcise it. Up in flames. I imagine it would be very cathartic.'

'You *were* reading it,' I said.

'I've never looked at it,' Dr Felix said. He studied his fingernails. 'Why the fuck would I? I told you. There's enough bullshit in my life already.'

'... You tricked me,' I said.

'Do you feel like an idiot?' Dr Felix said. 'You should. Do you feel like a coward? Oh, that too. Look at everything you've run away from. Look at everything you've done, just to protect yourself from the truth.'

'No one else was protecting me,' I said.

Dr Felix said nothing.

I found myself hiccupping – or trembling internally in some hiccup-like way.

'No one gave a shit about me,' I said. 'And now you don't give a shit about me either. So fuck you. You pretended to care but you never actually fucking did.'

Dr Felix tilted his head to one side. 'Who were you talking to, just there? Were you talking to me?'

I was mute. I shook my head.

'You came to find me,' Dr Felix said. 'You sought me out and you kept me awake until three o'clock in the morning, going over a story we both already know backwards. And you still won't see what's there. You still won't look.'

A riot of undisciplined feeling was about to erupt in my chest.

'I can't,' I said.

Dr Felix put his hand on my shoulder. My breath seemed to catch on the wound in my heart. Kindness. How can any of us bear it?

'I can't,' I said again.

'If you bring forth what is within you,' Dr Felix said, 'what you bring forth will save you.'

'What if what's within me,' I said, 'is bad? Is wrong?'

'It's all right to hate people,' Dr Felix said. 'Even the people you're supposed to love. Perhaps especially them. If they let you down. If they turn out to be incapable of giving you the love you need.'

I began to sob. 'I needed them,' I said. 'I needed them.'

'I know,' Dr Felix said. His arms were around me. Through my mind, the words of a song were drifting. *Darling I remember the way you used to wait.* Time passed. Then Dr Felix said, 'You should go to bed now.'

I wiped my eyes on the sleeves of my robe. 'What about tomorrow?' I said.

Dr Felix cocked his head. 'How about this,' he said. 'Tomorrow you can tell me what you want to do. You're free to go. You can go into town and buy drugs. Or, if you think there's more work to be done, we can talk about extending your stay for another while. I can look into getting someone from one of these places ...' He gestured towards the pile of NGO bumf. '... to come in and talk to you. At this point, it's not up to me. It's up to you.'

I thought about leaving St Augustine – about returning to the world, which is a mystery. I felt the first glimmer of an idea. It was an idea about how my life might go, if I tried to see it clearly. The idea was this: I could find Clio and atone. More than that. I could go back to Serbia – I could make my pilgrimage to the white city. And I could atone there, too.

'I'm not a coward anymore, am I?' I said.

Dr Felix paused. 'That's up to you, too,' he said, and left.

I was alone in the day room except for Piotr, who still snored softly on his curved couch. For the next twenty minutes I sat on the floor. And what kind of a spectacle did I make, I wonder – a grown man hugging his knees and weeping because he didn't have the family he needed?

I needed them. But of course I did. It was almost dawn. An autumn morning. When the year turns. Piotr was still conked out on the couch. From the plastic pocket clipped to a lanyard around his neck I extracted his staff card and swiped it at the black plastic sensor beside the day-room door. The air outside was cold and smelled faintly of rotting apples. My feet crunched on the gravel. I walked down towards the apple trees. My limbs were stiff. Also my shoulders. I have been sitting hunched over the telling of my tale for weeks. I kicked off my rehab slippers and felt the dewy grass underfoot like a soft wet carpet. From here I could see the locked gates of the clinic complex. Piotr's staff card would open this, too. But where would I go? I remembered various things.

For example: when I was a child I collected model cars. My mother called them 'Dinky cars'. Precise in my habits, I lined them up according to the pattern of the carpet in the living room. Each car with its matched square. I left them parked there safely overnight. My father would switch them around while I slept. Silently, the next morning, I would restore each car to its assigned place. It was a game. 'You're an amazing man,' my father would say, rubbing my back. And again: my father, taking me to the Wellington Monument, showing me how to make myself dizzy by looking up at the stars. I could see the stars now, as I stood on the grass of the clinic grounds in my dressing gown. No clouds. As if the top of the world had been taken off and there was no longer anything interposing itself between you and the universe entire. Clear sight of everything. Clarity can't be given. It has to be earned. This is what Dr Felix has been trying to tell me. Why he made me write it all down. What did I think I was writing? I thought I was telling a story about money, and drugs, and failure, and lies. But perhaps it's just a story about the end of a family. The grass was cold beneath my feet. The sun was rising. I could hear the waves impending at Killiney Beach. I had spent my childhood weekends on that beach. St Augustine is less than two miles from my family home. And how absolutely typical of me, I think, that I have never really managed to notice this until just now.

Here we are. Where we have always been. The Man in the Brown Trenchcoat drove me in his black Mercedes all the way to Ringsend, through streets of converted labourers' cottages (all those family homes, each one enclosing a humid, intricate world of drudgery and love), beneath the hanging cranes with their wrapped burdens of concrete and steel, past the autumn trees in their trashy-lipstick colours: magenta, flesh-tone, candy-pink.

The car came to a stop outside the greyhound track at Shelbourne Park.

'Just head on in there,' the man said. 'He'll find you.'

Obediently I climbed out of the car. The paths were scattered with leaves, like notes of many currencies. I cranked a turnstile and weaved my way aimlessly through the crowd. I climbed up into the stands. People clutched their betting slips, waiting for the next race to begin. The Tote officials tramped about in their burgundy waistcoats. In the middle of the track, in the centre of a tan oval of floodlit sand, men dressed in white coats like doctors tended to their quivering dogs. The dogs lifted their delicate paintbrush feet and wagged their downcast tails. Who was I looking for? I knew, of course. I found him leaning against a crowd-control barrier with a betting slip in his hand. *Darling I remember ...* He was wearing his courtroom suit. He turned at my approach and said, 'I have a confession to make.'

'I used to come here all the time when I first started at Atlas-Merritt,' my father said. 'Little bets, a pound each way on a dog with a lucky name. Nothing major. Nothing too risky. But you know what? I got bored.'

'How much was it, again?' I said. 'Six hundred million euro? That was it, right?'

My father made an embarrassed face. 'Actually, it's a wee bit more than that,' he said. 'At least according to Martin. They only knew about half of it. He lost a fair amount to CAB, of course – the few bob I was holding on to. We had to let that go. But the remainder was certainly worth going to a bit of trouble over. The good news is, you don't need to worry about that half a mil you signed for. It's taken care of. Your credit rating is intact. I made sure of that.'

He turned towards the barrier. The dogs were twitching in their traps.

'You knew what they were doing,' I said. 'You knew.'

'I had some idea,' my father said. 'Very important that I not know any real specifics. I was very high-profile, after the arrest. At this point I feel I have to offer an apology. We did have to take you for a bit of a ride. It was important that there be no paper trail leading to any of us.'

'Any of us,' I repeated. 'James Mullens. Martin Mullens. The Lads. The Dads. Everyone knew.'

'This is how it works. I thought you'd figure things out, if we threw you in at the deep end.'

'What?' I said. 'So this was all some lesson in how to get ahead in business?'

'We'd all had a shock,' my father said. 'Sometimes a shock is just the ticket. Martin came to me with a plan. I said to myself, *Here's a chance to throw Ben in the deep end. See if he swims.*'

I nodded. 'The world is hard.'

My father frowned. 'What's that?'

'You told me that once,' I said. 'You said the world was hard and the only way to beat it was to be hard yourself.'

My father looked thoughtful. 'I wouldn't put it that way now.'

'Those guys,' I said. 'Vuk. The Serbs.'

'I don't know where Martin dug those lads up,' my father said. 'If you'll pardon the expression. Obviously we knew what we were getting into, in terms of their background and so on. But we did have an inkling that their days were numbered, if you know what I mean. I felt comfortable that you were never in any real danger. Besides, I had Dolan keeping an eye on you.'

'Dolan?'

'He's a private investigator. Used to do a bit of work for me during the Atlas days.' My father jingled the change in his pockets and looked out over the track where a miniature tractor was smoothing the sand before the race. 'Reliable man.'

I felt that at any moment my legs might collapse beneath me. My vision was strangely occluded, as if by a cloud passing the sun.

My mother had said: *If he asks you to do anything, anything at all, just tell him you'll do it and then come to me.*

'Mum knew,' I said.

My father removed his sunglasses. His eyes looked baggy, tired. 'Actually we tried to keep your mother out of it as much as possible,' he said. 'Plausible deniability and all that. She's worried about you. She thought it would be the kindest thing to keep an eye on you, and step in when things got out of hand. But for obvious reasons, we had to wait until certain, ah, issues were resolved.' He produced an expression I had never seen him use before: a shit-eating grin. 'Do you know, that fucker Mullens tried to cut me loose. I had to threaten to name names in court to get him to stay in line.' He shook his head in sad amazement. 'Anyway. We're through it now. We can get on with our lives.'

'Our lives?' I said.

'We've bought a house in – where is it? Vermont. Your mother's over there now, getting it aired out. Safer to get out of the country for a while, I think. Gerry Mason can handle things on this end. You can join us there when you're ready. I'd say you've learned a lot this year. You can put that knowledge to work. Plenty of corporate connections in the States, if you're at all that way inclined.'

The last of the Xanax was draining from my limbs. The pain in my side was throbbing rhythmically. I could no longer see clearly out of my right eye. 'But you can't leave,' I said, shaking my head to clear my vision. 'You're on trial.'

My father squinted at me. 'You don't read the news,' he said. 'They declared a mistrial. It was what we expected. The evidence was flimsy from the get-go. The DPP says they're going to prepare another case. I say, good luck to them.'

I braced myself against the crowd-control barrier. 'How could you go along with this?' I said. 'How could you get into bed with those people? You have no idea what they are. You didn't see it. You didn't see the bones in the fucking earth.'

My father raised an eyebrow. 'As I understand it,' he said, 'they're about to get their just deserts. Needs must, Ben. You don't have to like the people you do business with.'

'They're murderers,' I said.

My father's mouth turned down at the edges. 'I'm sorry you had to deal with that,' he said. 'Truly I am. I would never have wanted to put you through that. You're my son. I love you.'

I was frozen – stuck to the spot. I looked at my father's face with terror, with awe. Against the bright sky, for a moment, his face was blackly shadowed – impossible to make out.

'I don't know who you are,' I said. 'I've never known.'

My father fiddled with his cufflinks. 'There is another matter,' he said, 'that we need to discuss. Rather delicate. Now I don't want this to come across as ... What do they call it? An intervention.'

Suddenly there was a rattle and a cheer. The dogs broke out of their traps and ran, their heads lolloping as they bounded after the artificial rabbit on its motorised track. My father watched them run, his head slowly turning.

'How could you?' I said flatly. 'How could you do this to me?'

The dogs pounded into the home stretch.

'Sometimes,' my father said again, 'a shock to the system is just the ticket. Your mother said she dropped in on that apartment of yours. She said you were living in squalor. We're very concerned about you.'

'You're *concerned*,' I said. 'About *me*.'

441

'We've been worried for a while,' my father said. 'You have a problem. And I made a promise to myself. I said, when this is all over, you're going to get Ben the help he needs. I've spoken to some people who know about this sort of thing, the best. You're booked in for a stint at St Augustine. Apparently they do phenomenal work there. Dolan's waiting with the car. He'll drop you off when we're finished here. Don't worry, it's all paid for.'

The race was over. The owners were collecting their dogs. I lit a cigarette. It was the last one in the pack. Over the PA system a voice said, 'Place your bets, please, ladies and gentlemen, place your bets.'

'You did all this,' I said, 'for money?'

My father shook his head emphatically. 'I don't think you ever really understood this,' he said. 'It isn't about the money. Money is simple. If money's what you want, you can always get it. A deal here, a deal there. But that sort of thing gets boring, after a while. Taking a chance. That's what it's all about.' He held up a betting ticket. 'Shoot for the Stars at six to one. I had a feeling.'

I studied him – the pouched eyes, the enigmatic smile. In that moment I conceived a hatred for him so non-negotiable that I have not, in composing this misbegotten account of my misbegotten life, been able to bring myself to write out the letters of his name, which are also the letters of my name. Because fathers give their names to their sons, along with many other complex gifts.

'I wasn't what you wanted,' I said.

My father smiled sadly. 'It's time to go,' he said.

The traps rattled open once again. The crowd raised a dull cheer. The dogs began to run, chasing the rabbit that was not a rabbit through the last of the day's disappearing light.

I have nothing left to add. Just an empty impulse to move the pen across the page. I lived the wrong life. Forgive me. Teach me to live a better one. It is morning. Any minute now, Dr Felix will arrive in the doorway of my room, and he will stand there with his arms folded and a particular look on his face, a look that I can scarcely bear to think about, a look that will tell me that this man has known me all my life, and he will ask me . . .

I looked up. 'Well?' he said.

Postscript

A message from my parents yesterday: a letter, with a cheque enclosed. The usual return address in Hartford, Vermont. They make no mention of the fresh criminal proceedings against my father, or of those lately initiated against Martin Mullens, who is still, according to news reports, sequestered in Brazil, a country that happens not to share an extradition treaty with Ireland. I tore up the letter, of course, and have no intention of replying. All the same, I felt moved to add a few words to this notebook. I'm not sure why. I haven't looked at it in several years. But I found it easily enough, in an office cupboard, the one underneath the bonsai tree that I inherited from this office's previous occupant, who transferred himself, by directorial fiat, to classier digs last year.

Somehow I've kept it with me, this notebook, through several years of ups and downs. Is that significant? The habit of self-interrogation dies hard. Sometimes you need to leave yourself alone.

The cheque (for €5,000) I signed over to St Augustine. We're a registered charity here, and therefore my father will be able to claim a tax write-off, which I'm sure will make him happy, if I ever tell him. I'm going to use the money to put a library in the day room.

The kids – I refuse to call them clients – get sick of board games. I get sick of board games. Let them read some books, while they're here with us.

I have, over the last couple of years, occasionally succumbed to curiosity and checked in on the careers of various people I knew during the part of my life covered by this notebook. Clio (who was really very nice about accepting my apology) now has a one-year-old daughter and works as some kind of arts administrator. Baz Hynes started a podcast on which, with his ex-DJ pals, he discusses action-movie soundtracks. Paul Tynan works for the Banking & Payments Federation of Ireland – you can hear him on Drivetime *now and then, commenting on government policy. Mark Foley moved to London and got a job with a tech startup that failed spectacularly within a year of its IPO. Bobby Hayes works for his older brother, up in the border counties, and posts a lot of pictures of rugby matches on social media. Sean Sweeney took what he describes to friends as 'an early retirement package' and married his college girlfriend, Hannah Bailey. Now he stays at home looking after their two sons.*

Aleks has just published a nonfiction book, written in collaboration with his girlfriend, about the crimes that took place at the site now called Echo Lake during the wars of the late 1990s. I am having it translated so that I can read it.

Maria, as far as I have been able to determine, works in the marketing department of the Basketball League of Serbia.

Nicolae and Ratko are serving sentences in Sremska Mitrovica prison for racketeering, assault, and sundry other minor charges.

Vuk Mladic died in his cell in The Hague while awaiting trial for crimes against humanity. According to the postmortem report, the cause was a fatal cardiac arrythmia.

I did go back. To Serbia, I mean. To Echo Lake. I travelled alone. In my luggage I brought books about the Balkan Wars. The site of our impossible hotel is now a state memorial: a plain marker and a ring of sentry-like flagpoles, bare of flags. It was late October. Trees in russet and rose-gold and ochre and amber and fading green. A sour wind from the lake. I offered my presence. For what it was worth.

Of James Mullens – the man who, as I have come to see it, saved me from myself without meaning to – I can find no trace.

He had you all fooled, *Nikki said to me once.*

I wonder how it goes with Mullens, wherever he is. I wonder what he thinks about. I wonder if he thinks at all, in the way that most of us understand that word.

As it happens, I saw Nikki the other day – she works in the Blackrock Clinic and sometimes we find ourselves on the same bus, going home. We chatted about nothing in particular: her upcoming wedding, a film we had both hated. Saying goodbye – this is my stop! – I felt that, like nothing else, running into Nikki serves to remind me that what happened to me is mine, that I should not want to forget it, that it has made me what I am today and that I should not be afraid to remember it, or to grieve over it. I tell the kids about it, of course, when I think they're ready. I tell them the whole story: my father, Clio, Mullens, Belgrade, the bodies in the earth. I see them listen, and I see them half-believe. And I can see them thinking what I used to think: What the fuck does this old guy know about my pain?

Pain is the crucible, I say. Pain is your friend.

I see myself in them, of course. But that's not the point. The point is to work and weep and argue together until it's the other way around: until they see themselves in me. Until they reach out automatically to take my hand, and stop themselves, because they're so afraid of what comes next.

That was the easy part, I tell them, when they're crying in my arms.

Now we can begin.

Note & Acknowledgements

The Serbia that appears in these pages probably shouldn't be mistaken for the actual country of that name. I don't know that I'd offer the same caveat for the Dublin sections. Thanks are due. I'll keep it short. Love and gratitude to: Joan, Andy, Claire, Henry, Frances and Malachi: the best family. Marianne Gunn O'Connor, for keeping the faith. Suzanne Baboneau, Alice Rodgers and everyone at Simon & Schuster. Simon Hess and everyone at Gill Hess. I'm enormously grateful to the Arts Council of Ireland, which supported the writing of this book in its early stages. Carlo Gébler and John Boyne, for friendship when it counted. Simon Ashe-Browne, Dave Fleming, Lara Hickey, Ronan Raftery, Andrew Nolan, Stephen Jones: for everything. Dr Frank Kenny and the staff at Hanover Medical. Adam Kelly and Ríona Nic Congáil. Derek Hand and everyone in the School of English, DCU. Antony Farrell, Ruth Hallinan and all at Lilliput. Deirdre Madden, Eoin McNamee, Sophia Ní Sheoin and everyone at the Oscar Wilde Centre. Sarah Bannan. Margaret Robson and Darryl Jones. My wonderful colleagues in the School of

English, TCD. Steve Gallagher, Sean O'Connell, Trina Hyland, Anthony Hyland: for help with research. Ron and Breda Callan. The members of Where's the Pony?: Donal Flynn, Neil Burkey, Dillon Elliott, Bridget Houricane, Maggie Armstrong, Roisin Agnew. Anyone I've missed: thank you, thank you, thank you.